Atlas of
The Second World War:
Europe and the Mediterranean

Thomas E. Griess
Series Editor

AVERY PUBLISHING GROUP INC.
Wayne, New Jersey

Copyright © 1985. All rights reserved.

ISBN 0-89529-305-6

Contents

UWEC McIntyre Library

NOV 2 0 1987

EAU CLAIRE, WI

Foreword

Cadets at the United States Military Academy have studied military campaigns and institutions for almost a century in the course entitled History of the Military Art. Not until 1938, however, was that study supported by carefully integrated narratives and geographical portrayals. That year, T. Dodson Stamps, Head of the Department of Military Art and Engineering, introduced an atlas specifically designed to support the study of the campaigns of the American Civil War. Shortly thereafter, additional atlases were devised to support the study of other wars.

During World War II, members of Stamps' department hurriedly prepared pamphlets on operations as they progressed. Eventually those pamphlets, revised and corrected, became the basis for a departmental text entitled *A Military History of World War II*, which first appeared in 1953 and was jointly edited by Stamps and Vincent J. Esposito. A number of serving officers in the department wrote that text and designed its accompanying atlas. In 1959, Esposito served as chief editor for *The West Point Atlas of American Wars*, which included coverage of the Second World War and made use of carefully revised maps from the 1953 departmental atlas. That last text served its purpose well in a time which required expanding coverage of military history. But as the course in the History of the Military Art, taught in the newly created Department of History since 1969, required modification to include new events and more than purely operational military history, the treatment of the Second World War has been compressed and accommodated to new themes. Such changes required the development of a new text.

This atlas, which has been designed to support that new text, *The Second World War: Europe and the Mediterranean*, depicts primarily strategic coverage of the major campaigns of the war. Both text and atlas are original works written by officers in the Department of History, who extensively researched primary and secondary sources in preparing the narrative and developed new geographical depictions of the campaigns. The undersigned served as editor for the finished products. We are indebted to those officers for their dedicated work on the text and atlas alike. The following individuals contributed to coverage of the war in Europe: John A. Hixson (Poland and Campaigns in Norway and the West), David R. Mets (The Battle of Britain), Bruce R. Pirnie (Campaigns in Finland and the Balkans and the Russo-German War), Clifton R. Franks (Campaigns in North Africa, Sicily, and Italy), Thomas R. Stone (Campaign in Western Europe), Thomas B. Buell (Battle of the Atlantic), and James F. Ransone, Jr. (Grand Alliance). John H. Bradley prepared all of the material covering the war in the Pacific and Jack W. Dice prepared the chapter and maps pertaining to operations in the China-Burma-India Theater.

We are also indebted to Mr. Edward J. Krasnoborski and his assistant, Mr. George Giddings, who drafted the maps in final form. Mr. Krasnoborski, an unusually gifted and imaginative cartographer, supervised the drafting effort and did the majority of the maps; his effort and skill is imprinted everywhere on the finished product.

Thomas E. Griess
Series Editor

1939	POLAND	NORWAY	WESTERN EUROPE	BALKANS	NORTH AFRICA	RUSSIA	EAST ASIA AND THE PACIFIC	ALLIED CONFERENCES
SEPT.	Invasion							
OCT.	Surrender							
NOV.								
DEC.								
1940 JAN.			Minor Operations					
FEB.								
MAR.								
APR.		Invasion						
MAY			German Invasion of France					
JUNE		Allied Evacuation						
			French Surrender					
JULY								
AUG.								
SEPT.			Battle of Britain		Graziani's Advance		Sino-Japanese War (1937-1945)	
OCT.								
NOV.								
DEC.								
1941 JAN.				Italian Invasion of Greece	Wavell's Offensive			
FEB.								ABC-1 (Washington)
MAR.								
APR.				German Invasion of Yugoslavia,	Rommel's First Offensive			
MAY				Greece and Crete				
JUNE					Wavell's Counteroffensive	Invasion, Bialystok, Minsk		
JULY						Smolensk		
AUG.						Uman and Gomel		
SEPT.						Kiev		
OCT.						Vyazma and Bryansk		
NOV.					Auchinleck's Offensive	Approach to Moscow		
DEC.						Russian Counterattacks	Pearl Harbor; Malaya; Philippines	

1942	NORTH AFRICA	SICILY AND ITALY	RUSSIA	EAST ASIA AND THE PACIFIC	ALLIED CONFERENCES
JAN.			Russian Counterattacks		ARCADIA (Washington)
FEB.				Singapore	
MAR.					
APR.	Rommel's Second Offensive			Fall of Bataan	
MAY			Kharkov	Corregidor — Allied Retreat from Burma	
JUNE			Sevastopol	Midway; Kiska	
JULY					
AUG.			Caucasus	Guadalcanal Landing; Kokoda	
SEPT.	Alam Halfa				
OCT.					
NOV.	El Alamein / Allied Invasion		Stalingrad		
DEC.	Race for Tunis			Buna-Gona	
1943 JAN.			Russian Leningrad Offensive		Casablanca
FEB.	Kasserine Pass		Russian Campaign in Ukraine	Japanese Evacuate Guadalcanal	
MAR.	Mareth				
APR.					
MAY	Bizerte; Tunis Surrender				TRIDENT (Washington)
JUNE					
JULY		Invasion of Sicily	Kursk; Orel	New Georgia	
AUG.				Salamaua	QUADRANT (Quebec)
SEPT.		Salerno	German Withdrawal	Lae	
OCT.		Naples; Volturno River			
NOV.		Winter Line Campaign		Bougainville / Tarawa — Stilwell's Burma Campaign	Cairo-Teheran
DEC.			Russian Winter Offensive	Arawe / Cape Gloucester	

1944	WESTERN EUROPE	ITALY	RUSSIA	EAST ASIA AND THE PACIFIC	ALLIED CONFERENCES
JAN.		Anzio Landing	Leningrad		
FEB.				Kwajalein — Stilwell's Burma Campaign	
MAR.		Attack on Cassino	Ukraine	Japanese Imphal-Kohima Offensive — Manus	
APR.			Crimea	Hollandia	
MAY					
JUNE	Normandy Landing	Rome Campaign		Biak	
JULY	Avranches		Latvia; Warsaw	Saipan — Guam	
AUG.	Southern France		Rumania		
SEPT.	Arnhem		Bulgaria	Palaus — Morotai	OCTAGON (Quebec)
OCT.	Aachen / Westwall	Attacks on the Gothic Line			
NOV.	Metz			Leyte — Slim's Burma Offensive	
DEC.			Budapest	Mindoro	
1945 JAN.	Ardennes		East Prussia; Poland	Landing on Luzon	
FEB.	Advance to the Rhine			Iwo Jima	Yalta
MAR.	Remagen			Manila / Shimbu Line	
APR.	Ruhr Encirclement / Advance to the Elbe	Allied Spring Offensive	Vienna / Berlin	Okinawa / Borneo / Mindanao and the Visayas	
MAY	German Surrender (8 May)	German Surrender (2 May)	German Surrender (8 May)		
JUNE					
JULY					Potsdam
AUG.				Japanese Surrender (14 August)	
SEPT.					

TABLE OF SYMBOLS

BASIC SYMBOLS

Battalion	II	Air Force unit	⊠
Regiment	III	Armor	▭
Brigade	X	Artillery	·
Division, air division	XX	Cavalry	◿
Corps	XXX	Infantry	⊠
Army, air force, fleet	XXXX	Mechanized	⊠
Army group	XXXXX	Naval troops, ground employment	⚓
Airborne	⌒	Special naval landing force	SNLF

● ——————————

EXAMPLES OF COMBINATIONS OF BASIC SYMBOLS

Small British infantry detachment	Br ⊠	2d Marine Division	XX ⊠ 2 Mar.
34th Regimental Combat Team	III ⊠ 34 RCT	French Second Corps less detachments	XXX FR II (−)
Combat Command C of 1st Armored Division	X C ▭ 1	Third Army	XXXX THIRD
82d Airborne Division	XX ⊠ 82	First Air Force	XXXX ⊠ FIRST
1st Motorized Division	XX ⊠ 1 Mtz	Bradley's 12th Army Group	XXXXX 12 BRADLEY

● ——————————

OTHER SYMBOLS

	Actual location	Prior location		
Troops on the march	➜	⇨	Troops in position under attack	⬇⬇
Troops in position	⌒	⌒	Route of march or flight	➤ ➤ ➤
Troops in bivouac or reserve	⬭	⬭	Boundary between units	—— XXX —— (Appropriate basic symbol)
	Occupied	Unoccupied		
Field works	ᐱᐱᐱᐱ	ᐱᐱᐱᐱ	Fort	⊟
Strong prepared positions	⊓⊔⊓⊔	⊓⊔⊓⊔	Fortified area	⬯
Airfield	◎	○	Fuel pipeline	o—o—o
Covering force, armor or foot	● ● ● ● ●		Minefield	o—o—o
			Airborne landing	⛂

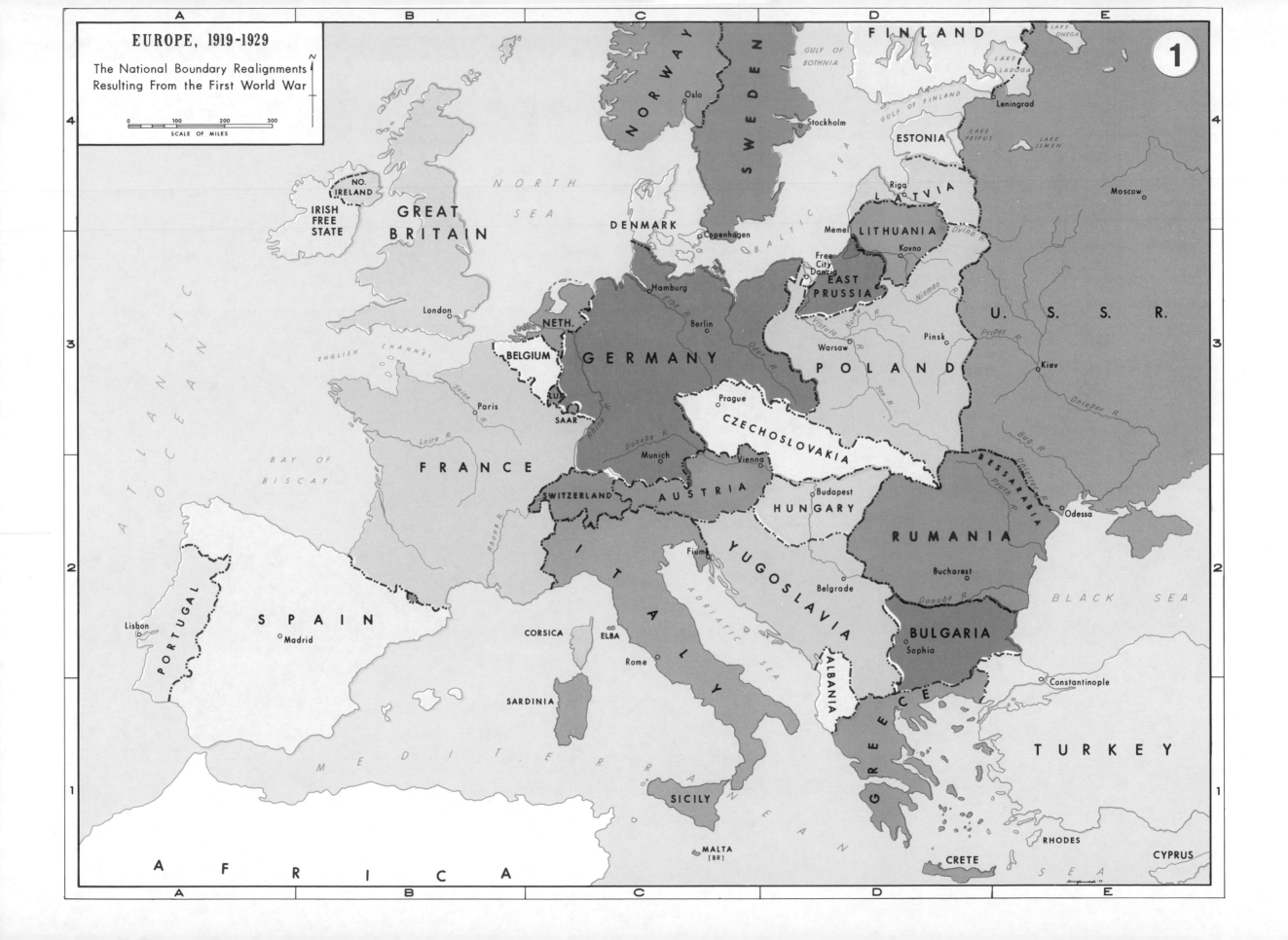

EUROPE, 1919-1929

The National Boundary Realignments
Resulting From the First World War

N

0   100   200   300
SCALE OF MILES

1

FINLAND

LAKE ONEGA

LAKE LADOGA

Leningrad

NORWAY

SWEDEN

GULF OF BOTHNIA

Oslo

Stockholm

ESTONIA

LAKE PEIPUS

LAKE ILMEN

Moscow

NO. IRELAND

IRISH FREE STATE

GREAT BRITAIN

NORTH SEA

DENMARK

Copenhagen

BALTIC SEA

Riga

LATVIA

GULF OF FINLAND

LITHUANIA

Memel

Dvina R.

Kovno

Free City Danzig

EAST PRUSSIA

Niemen R.

U. S. S. R.

Hamburg

ENGLISH CHANNEL

London

NETH.

BELGIUM

GERMANY

Berlin

Elbe R.

Warsaw

Vistula

Narev

Oder R.

POLAND

Pinsk

San R.

Bug R.

Pripet R.

Kiev

Dnieper R.

ATLANTIC OCEAN

Paris

Seine R.

LUX.

SAAR

Rhine R.

Prague

CZECHOSLOVAKIA

Munich

Danube R.

Vienna

Budapest

Don R.

BESSARABIA

Pruth R.

Dniester R.

Odessa

BAY OF BISCAY

FRANCE

Loire R.

SWITZERLAND

Rhone R.

AUSTRIA

HUNGARY

RUMANIA

Bucharest

PORTUGAL

Lisbon

SPAIN

Madrid

ITALY

Fiume

YUGOSLAVIA

Belgrade

Danube R.

BLACK SEA

Rome

CORSICA

ELBA

SARDINIA

ADRIATIC SEA

ALBANIA

BULGARIA

Sophia

GREECE

Constantinople

MEDITERRANEAN

SICILY

MALTA (BR)

TURKEY

CRETE

RHODES

CYPRUS

SEA

A F R I C A

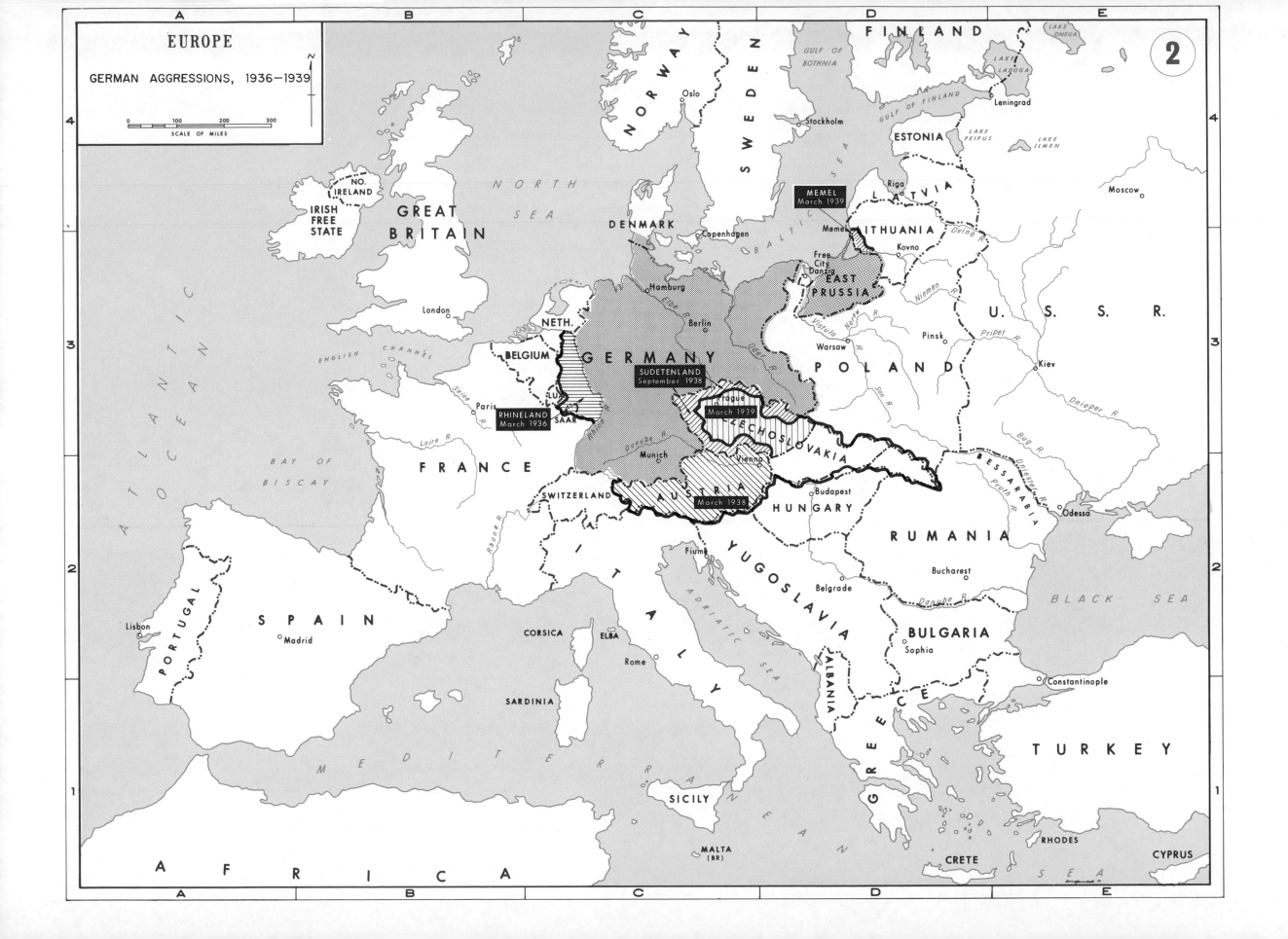

2

EUROPE

GERMAN AGGRESSIONS, 1936–1939

0   100   200   300
SCALE OF MILES

MEMEL
March 1939

SUDETENLAND
September 1938

RHINELAND
March 1936

Prague
March 1939

AUSTRIA
March 1938

NORWAY

SWEDEN

FINLAND

GULF OF BOTHNIA

LAKE ONEGA

LAKE LADOGA

Oslo

Stockholm

Leningrad

ESTONIA

LAKE PEIPUS

LAKE ILMEN

NORTH SEA

DENMARK

Copenhagen

BALTIC SEA

Riga

LATVIA

Dvina R.

Moscow

NO. IRELAND

IRISH FREE STATE

GREAT BRITAIN

London

LITHUANIA

Kovno

Memel

Free City Danzig

EAST PRUSSIA

Niemen R.

U. S. S. R.

NETH.

ENGLISH CHANNEL

BELGIUM

Hamburg

Berlin

GERMANY

Vistula

Narew R.

Pinsk

Pripet R.

POLAND

Warsaw

Bug R.

Kiev

Dnieper R.

ATLANTIC OCEAN

Seine R.

Paris

LUX.

SAAR

Rhine R.

Elbe R.

Oder R.

Prague

CZECHOSLOVAKIA

Danube R.

San R.

FRANCE

Loire R.

BAY OF BISCAY

Munich

Vienna

Dniester R.

BESSARABIA

SWITZERLAND

AUSTRIA

Budapest

HUNGARY

RUMANIA

Prut R.

Odessa

Rhone R.

ITALY

Fiume

YUGOSLAVIA

Belgrade

Danube R.

Bucharest

BLACK SEA

PORTUGAL

Lisbon

SPAIN

Madrid

CORSICA

ELBA

Rome

ADRIATIC SEA

ALBANIA

BULGARIA

Sophia

SARDINIA

MEDITERRANEAN

GREECE

TURKEY

SICILY

MALTA (BR)

CRETE

RHODES

CYPRUS

SEA

A F R I C A

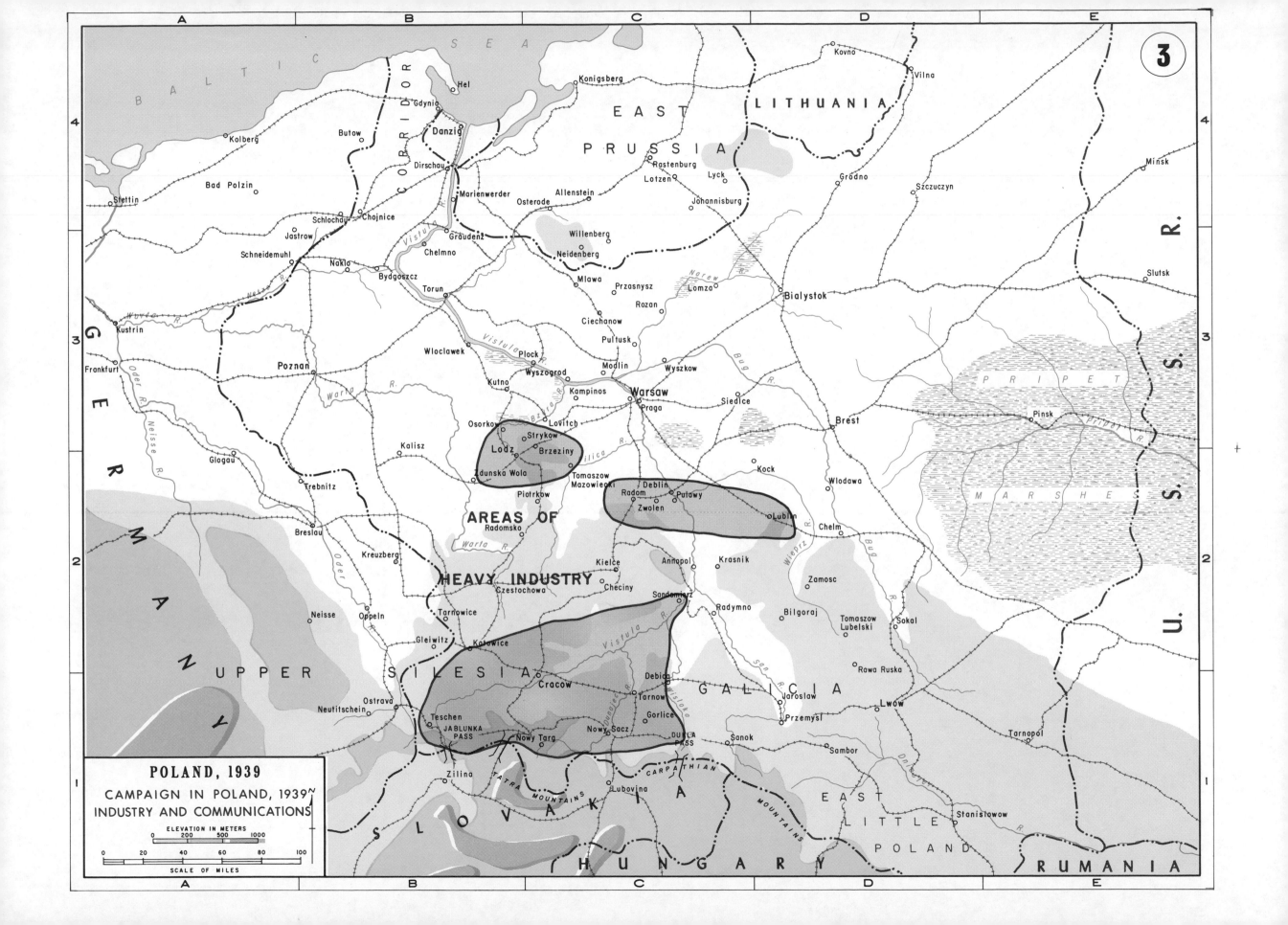

POLAND, 1939

CAMPAIGN IN POLAND, 1939
INDUSTRY AND COMMUNICATIONS

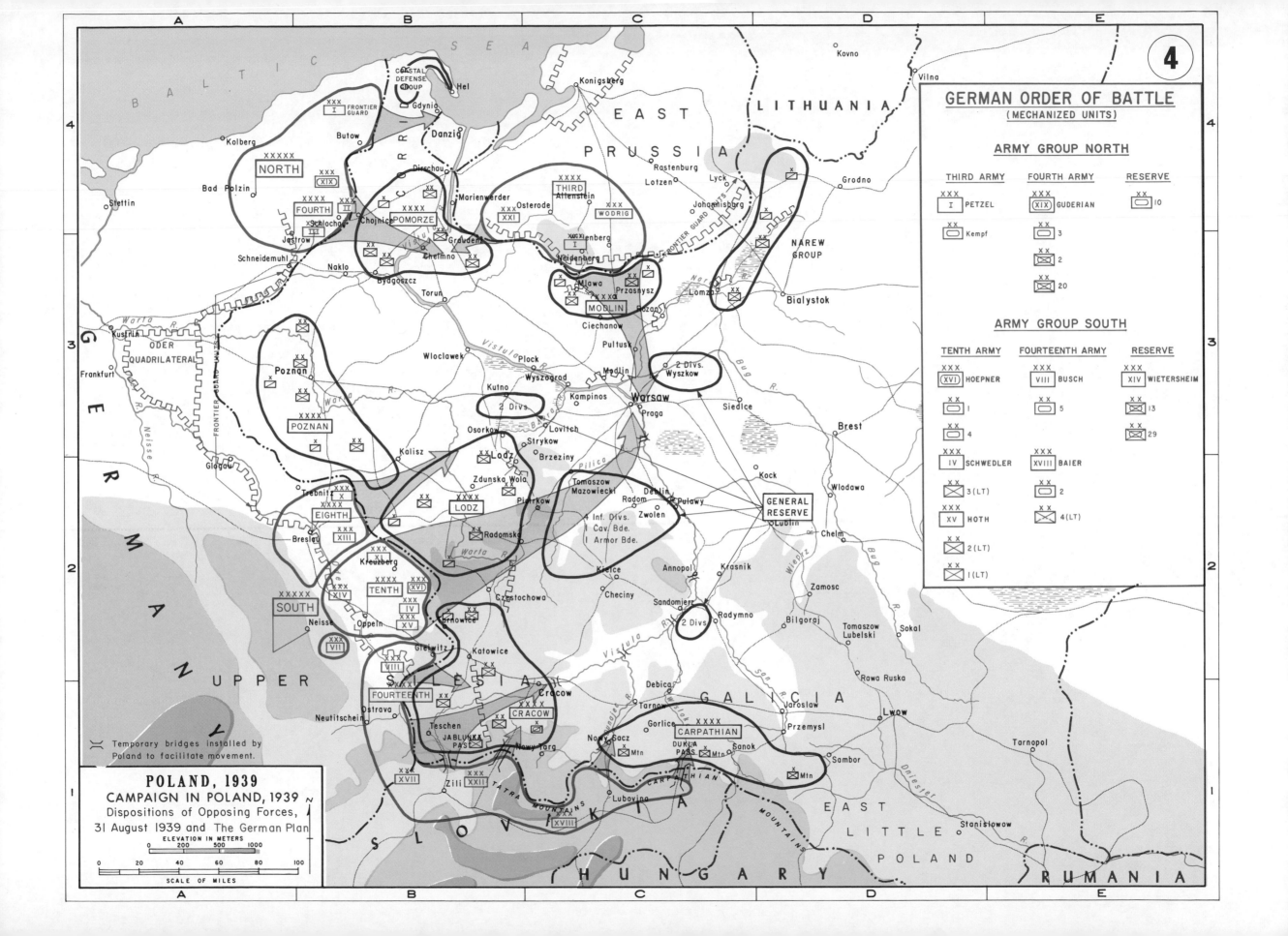

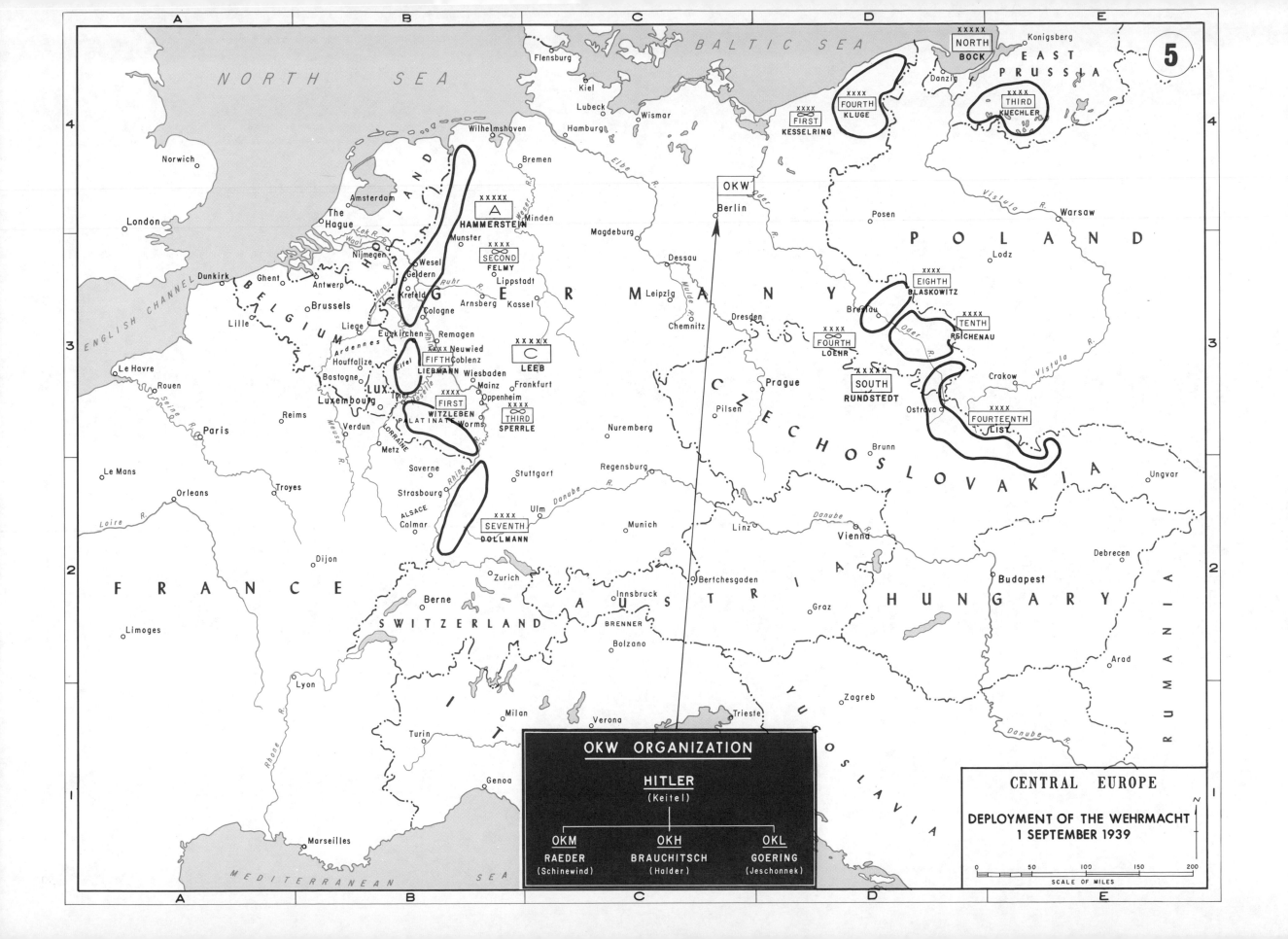

CENTRAL EUROPE

DEPLOYMENT OF THE WEHRMACHT
1 SEPTEMBER 1939

OKW ORGANIZATION

HITLER
(Keitel)

OKM — OKH — OKL
RAEDER — BRAUCHITSCH — GOERING
(Schinewind) — (Halder) — (Jeschonnek)

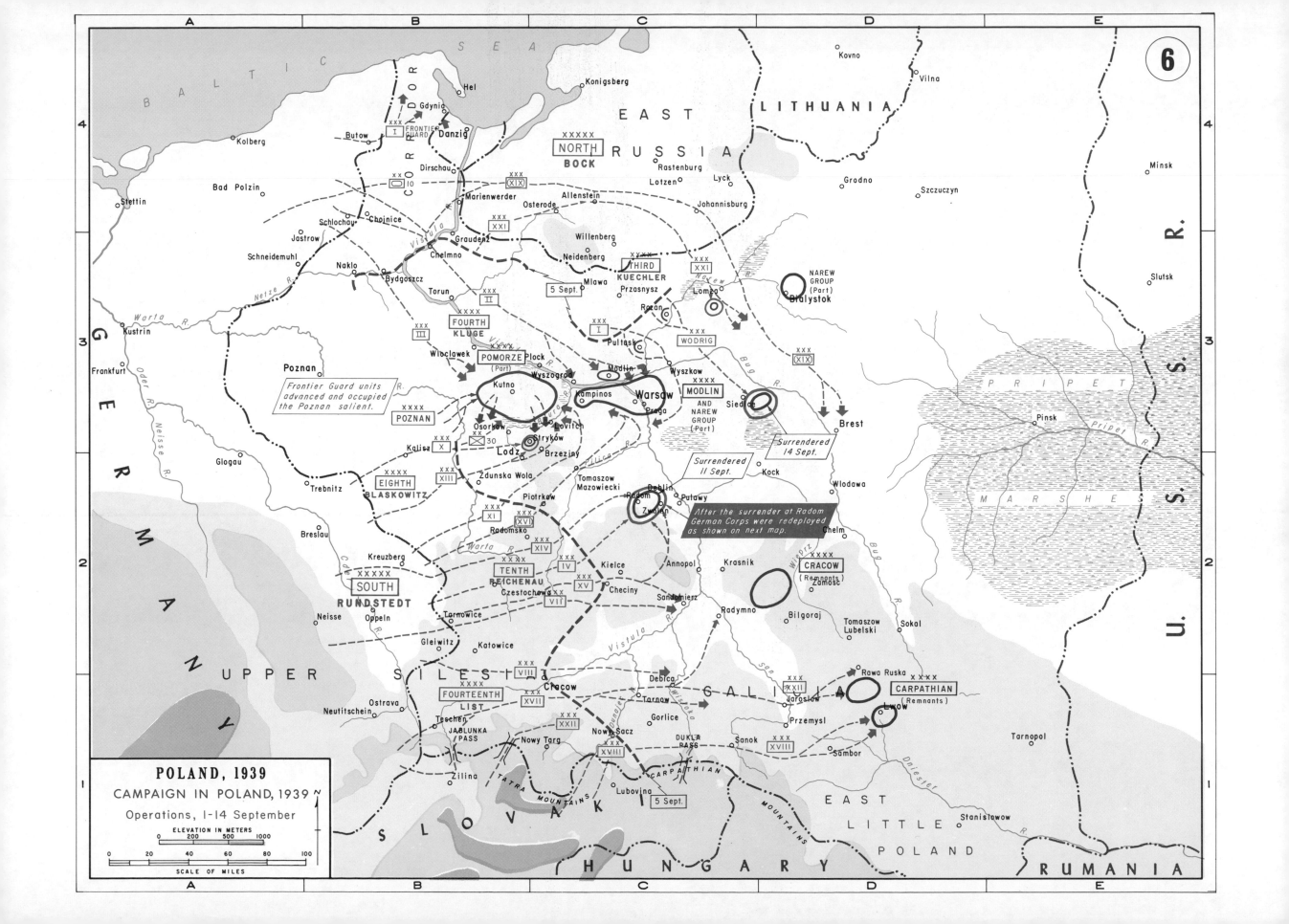

6

BALTIC SEA

CORRIDOR

LITHUANIA

EAST RUSSIA

Kovno

Vilna

Minsk

Szczuczyn

Slutsk

Konigsberg

Hel

Gdynia

Danzig

Butow

Kolberg

Bad Polzin

Stettin

I FRONTIER GUARD

XXX 10

Dirschau

Marienwerder

XXX XIX

Osterode

Allenstein

Johannisburg

Rastenburg

Lotzen

Lyck

Grodno

NORTH BOCK

Schlochau

Chojnice

XXX XXI

Jastrow

Schneidemuhl

Naklo

Bydgoszcz

Chelmno

Grandenz

Graudenz

Willenberg

Neidenberg

Mlawa

5 Sept.

THIRD KUECHLER

XXX XXI

Narew

NAREW GROUP (Part)

Bialystok

Frankfurt

Kustrin

Warta R.

Torun

II

FOURTH KLUGE

XXX III

Przasnysz

Rozan

I

WODRIG

XXX XIX

Bug R.

Oder R.

Netze R.

Wloclawek

Plock

POMORZE (Part)

Wyszogrod

Modlin

Wyszkow

MODLIN AND NAREW GROUP (Part)

Siedlce

Surrendered 14 Sept.

Brest

PRIPET

Pinsk

Pripet R.

Poznan

Frontier Guard units advanced and occupied the Poznan salient.

Kutno

Kampinos

Warsaw

Praga

POZNAN

Osorkow

Lovitch

Strykow

Brzeziny

Bzura R.

Lodz

Kalisz

XXX X

30

Zdunska Wola

Tomaszow Mazowiecki

Surrendered 11 Sept.

Radom

Zwolen

Deblin

Putawy

Kock

Wlodawa

Chelm

MARSHES

Glogau

Trebnitz

EIGHTH BLASKOWITZ

XXX XIII

Piotrkow

Pilica R.

After the surrender at Radom German Corps were redeployed as shown on next map.

Breslau

XXX XI

XXX XVI

Radomsko

XXX XIV

Kielce

Annopol

Krasnik

CRACOW (Remnants)

Zamosc

Bug R.

Kreuzberg

TENTH REICHENAU

IV

XXX XV

Checiny

Sandomierz

Radymno

Bilgoraj

Tomaszow Lubelski

Sokal

Neisse

Oppeln

VII

Czestochowa

Tarnowice

Gleiwitz

Katowice

UPPER SILESIA

VIII

GALICIA

Rawa Ruska

CARPATHIAN (Remnants)

Radymno

San R.

Wieprz R.

Warta R.

Ostrava

Neutitschein

Teschen

JABLUNKA PASS

FOURTEENTH LIST

XVII

XXII

Cracow

Debica

Tarnow

Gorlice

Nowy Sacz

Nowy Targ

XVIII

Dunajec R.

DUKLA PASS

Sanok

XVIII

Jaroslaw

Przemysl

Sambor

Lwow

Tarnopol

Dniester R.

Zilina

TATRA MOUNTAINS

Lubovina

CARPATHIAN

5 Sept.

MOUNTAINS

SLOVAKIA

HUNGARY

EAST LITTLE POLAND

Stanislawow

RUMANIA

U.S.S.R.

POLAND, 1939

CAMPAIGN IN POLAND, 1939

Operations, 1-14 September

ELEVATION IN METERS

0   200   500   1000

SCALE OF MILES

0   20   40   60   80   100

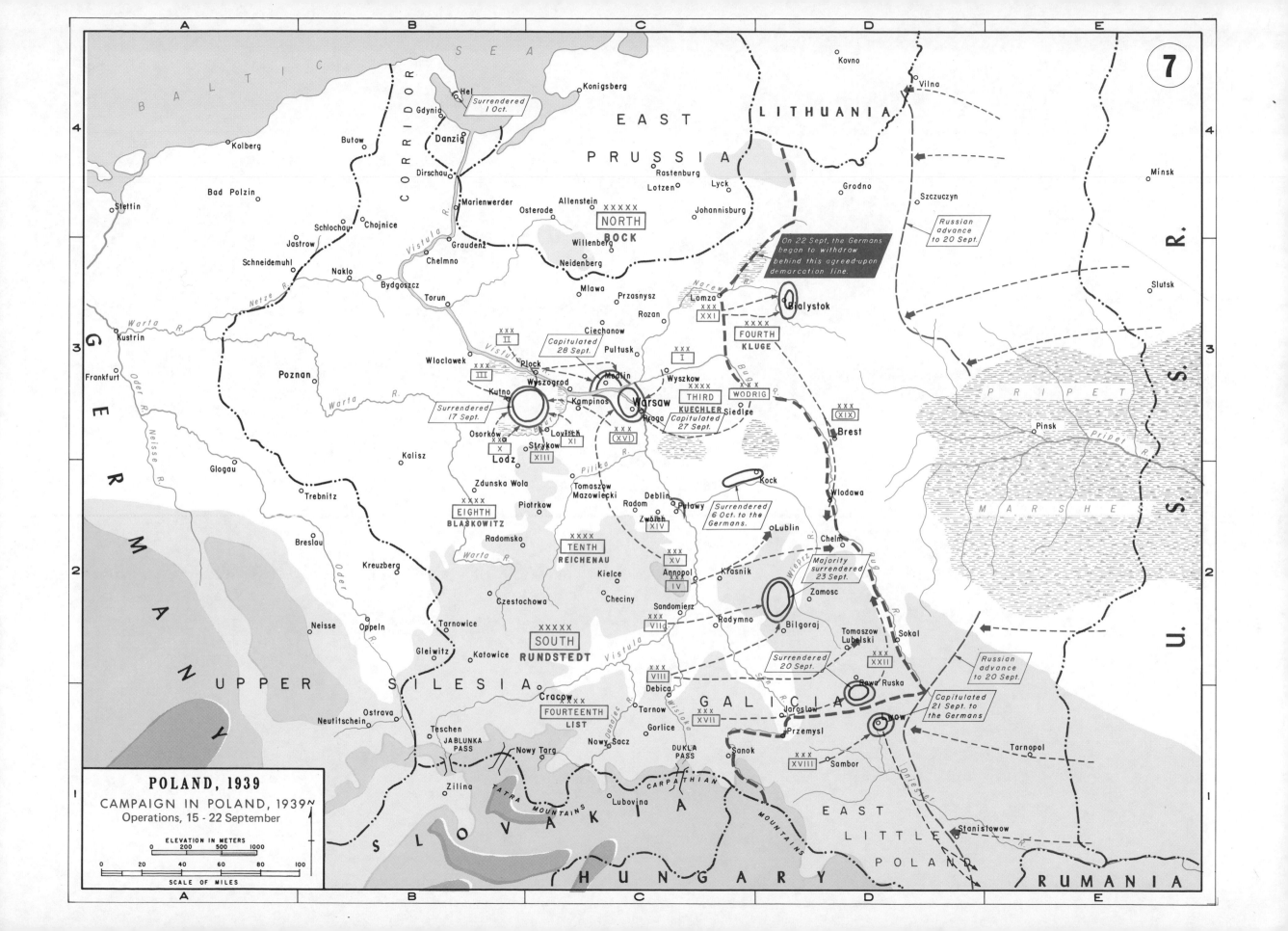

POLAND, 1939

CAMPAIGN IN POLAND, 1939

Operations, 15 - 22 September

ELEVATION IN METERS
200   500   1000

SCALE OF MILES
0   20   40   60   80   100

On 22 Sept. the Germans began to withdraw behind this agreed-upon demarcation line.

Russian advance to 20 Sept.

Russian advance to 20 Sept.

Surrendered 1 Oct.

Capitulated 28 Sept.

Surrendered 17 Sept.

Capitulated 27 Sept.

Surrendered 6 Oct. to the Germans.

Majority surrendered 23 Sept.

Surrendered 20 Sept.

Capitulated 21 Sept. to the Germans

NORTH
BOCK

FOURTH
KLUGE

THIRD
KUECHLER

WODRIG

EIGHTH
BLASKOWITZ

TENTH
REICHENAU

SOUTH
RUNDSTEDT

FOURTEENTH
LIST

XXXXX — NORTH BOCK

XXXX — FOURTH KLUGE
XXX — XXI
XXX — I
XXX — XIX
XXX — XXII

XXX — II
XXX — III
XXX — XI
XXX — XVI
XXX — X
XXX — XIII
XXX — XIV
XXX — XV
XXX — IV
XXX — VIIa
XXX — VIII
XXX — XVII
XXX — XVIII

BALTIC SEA

CORRIDOR

EAST PRUSSIA

LITHUANIA

R. S.

U. S. S. R.

GERMANY

UPPER SILESIA

SLOVAKIA

HUNGARY

RUMANIA

GALICIA

EAST LITTLE POLAND

PRIPET MARSHES

Kovno
Vilna
Minsk
Slutsk
Kolberg
Bad Polzin
Konigsberg
Stettin
Butow
Gdynia
Danzig
Hel
Rastenburg
Lotzen
Lyck
Grodno
Szczuczyn
Schlochau
Chojnice
Dirschau
Marienwerder
Osterode
Allenstein
Johannisburg
Jastrow
Schneidemuhl
Graudenz
Willenberg
Neidenberg
Naklo
Chelmno
Mlawa
Przasnysz
Bydgoszcz
Torun
Ciechanow
Rozan
Lomza
Bialystok
Kustrin
Wloclawek
Plock
Pultusk
Frankfurt
Poznan
Wyszogrod
Modlin
Wyszkow
Kutno
Warsaw
Siedlce
Brest
Kampinos
Praga
Pinsk
Glogau
Osorkow
Lowicz
Strykow
Lodz
Kalisz
Breslau
Zdunska Wola
Tomaszow Mazowiecki
Deblin
Pulawy
Kock
Wlodawa
Trebnitz
Piotrkow
Radom
Lublin
Chelm
Kreuzberg
Radomsko
Zwolen
Neisse
Oppeln
Kielce
Czestochowa
Checiny
Sandomierz
Krasnik
Zamosc
Gleiwitz
Tarnowice
Katowice
Annopol
Radymno
Bilgoraj
Tomaszow Lubelski
Sokal
Cracow
Debica
Tarnow
Lwow
Teschen
Jablunka Pass
Nowy Targ
Nowy Sacz
Gorlice
Jaroslaw
Rawa Ruska
Przemysl
Zilina
Dukla Pass
Sanok
Sambor
Tarnopol
Ostrava
Neutitschein
Lubovina
Stanislowow
Zilina

Tatra Mountains
Carpathian Mountains

Vistula R.
Netze R.
Warta R.
Oder R.
Neisse R.
Bug R.
Narew R.
Pilica R.
Wieprz R.
Dniester R.
San R.
Wisloka R.
Dunajec R.

7

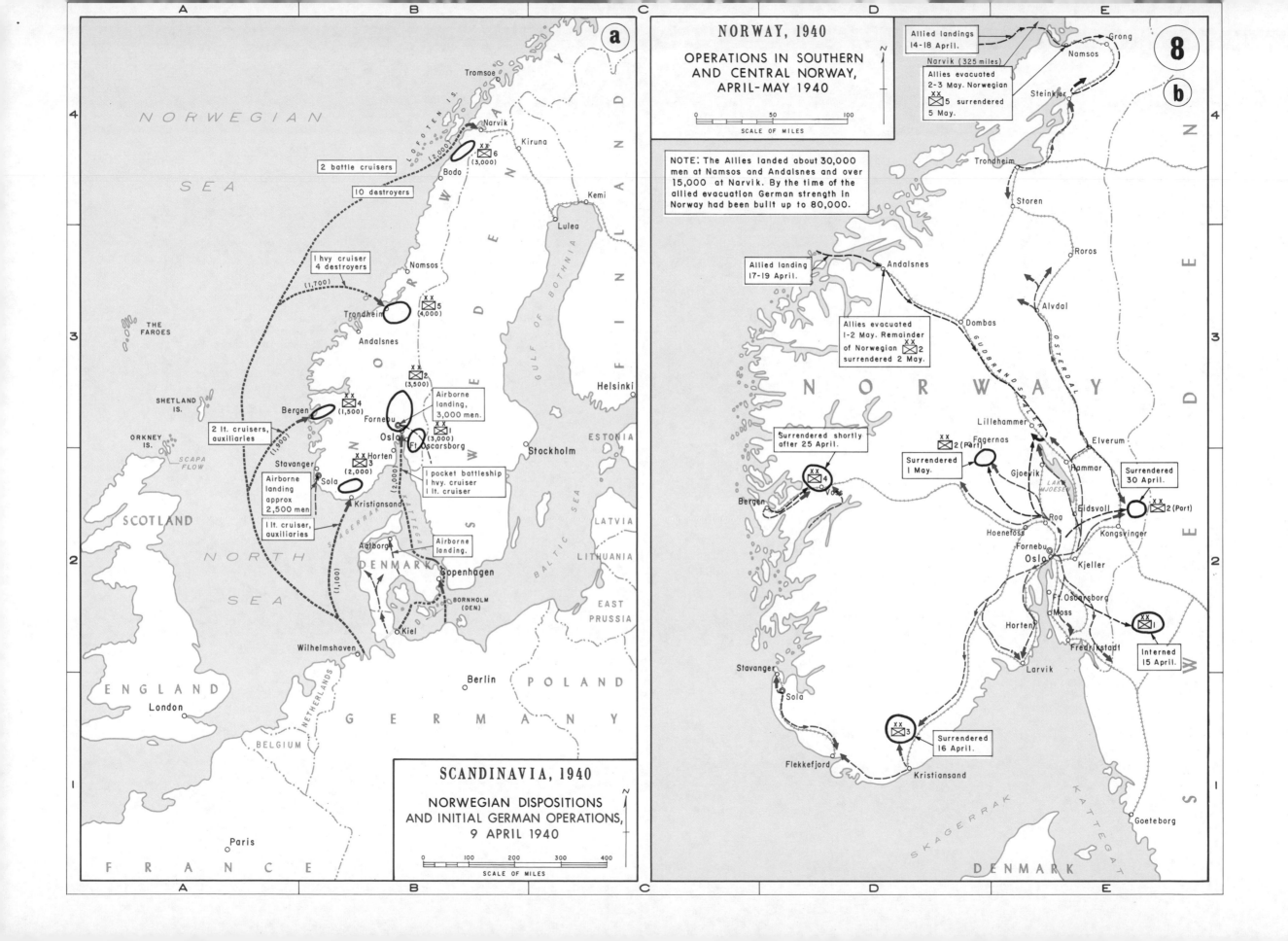

a

NORWEGIAN SEA

NORWAY

SWEDEN

FINLAND

THE FAROES

SHETLAND IS.

ORKNEY IS.

SCAPA FLOW

SCOTLAND

NORTH SEA

ENGLAND

London

Paris

FRANCE

Tromsoe

Narvik

Kiruna

Bodo

LOFOTEN IS. (2,000)

2 battle cruisers

10 destroyers

1 hvy cruiser 4 destroyers

(1,700)

Namsos

Trondheim

Andalsnes

(1,900)

Bergen

2 lt. cruisers, auxiliaries

Stavanger

Sola

Airborne landing approx 2,500 men

1 lt. cruiser, auxiliaries

(1,100)

Kiel

Wilhelmshaven

Kemi

Lulea

GULF OF BOTHNIA

Helsinki

Stockholm

ESTONIA

LATVIA

LITHUANIA

EAST PRUSSIA

BALTIC SEA

Berlin

POLAND

GERMANY

NETHERLANDS

BELGIUM

XX 6 (3,000)

XX 5 (4,000)

XX 2 (3,500)

XX 4 (1,500)

Fornebu

Oslo

XX 1 (3,000)

Ft Oscarsborg

Airborne landing, 3,000 men.

1 pocket battleship 1 hvy cruiser 1 lt. cruiser

Horten

XX 3 (2,000)

(2,000)

Kristiansands

SKAGERRAK

KATTEGAT

Aalborg

Airborne landing.

DENMARK

Copenhagen

BORNHOLM (DEN)

SCANDINAVIA, 1940

NORWEGIAN DISPOSITIONS AND INITIAL GERMAN OPERATIONS, 9 APRIL 1940

0 100 200 300 400
SCALE OF MILES

NORWAY, 1940

OPERATIONS IN SOUTHERN AND CENTRAL NORWAY, APRIL-MAY 1940

0 50 100
SCALE OF MILES

NOTE: The Allies landed about 30,000 men at Namsos and Andalsnes and over 15,000 at Narvik. By the time of the allied evacuation German strength in Norway had been built up to 80,000.

b

8

Allied landings 14-18 April.

Narvik (325 miles)

Grong

Namsos

Steinkjer

Allies evacuated 2-3 May. Norwegian XX 5 surrendered 5 May.

Trondheim

Storen

Roros

Allied landing 17-19 April.

Andalsnes

Dombas

Alvdal

OSTERDAL

GUDBRANDSDAL

Allies evacuated 1-2 May. Remainder of Norwegian XX 2 surrendered 2 May.

NORWAY

Lillehammer

Surrendered shortly after 25 April.

XX 4

Voss

Bergen

XX 2 (Part)

Fagernas

Surrendered 1 May.

Gjoevik

LAKE MJOESEN

Hamar

Elverum

Surrendered 30 April.

XX 2 (Part)

Eidsvoll

Kongsvinger

Hoenefoss

Roa

Fornebu

Oslo

Kjeller

Ft. Oscarsborg

Moss

XX 1

Interned 15 April.

Horten

Larvik

Fredrikstadt

Stavanger

Sola

XX 3

Surrendered 16 April.

Flekkefjord

Kristiansand

SKAGERRAK

KATTEGAT

Goeteborg

DENMARK

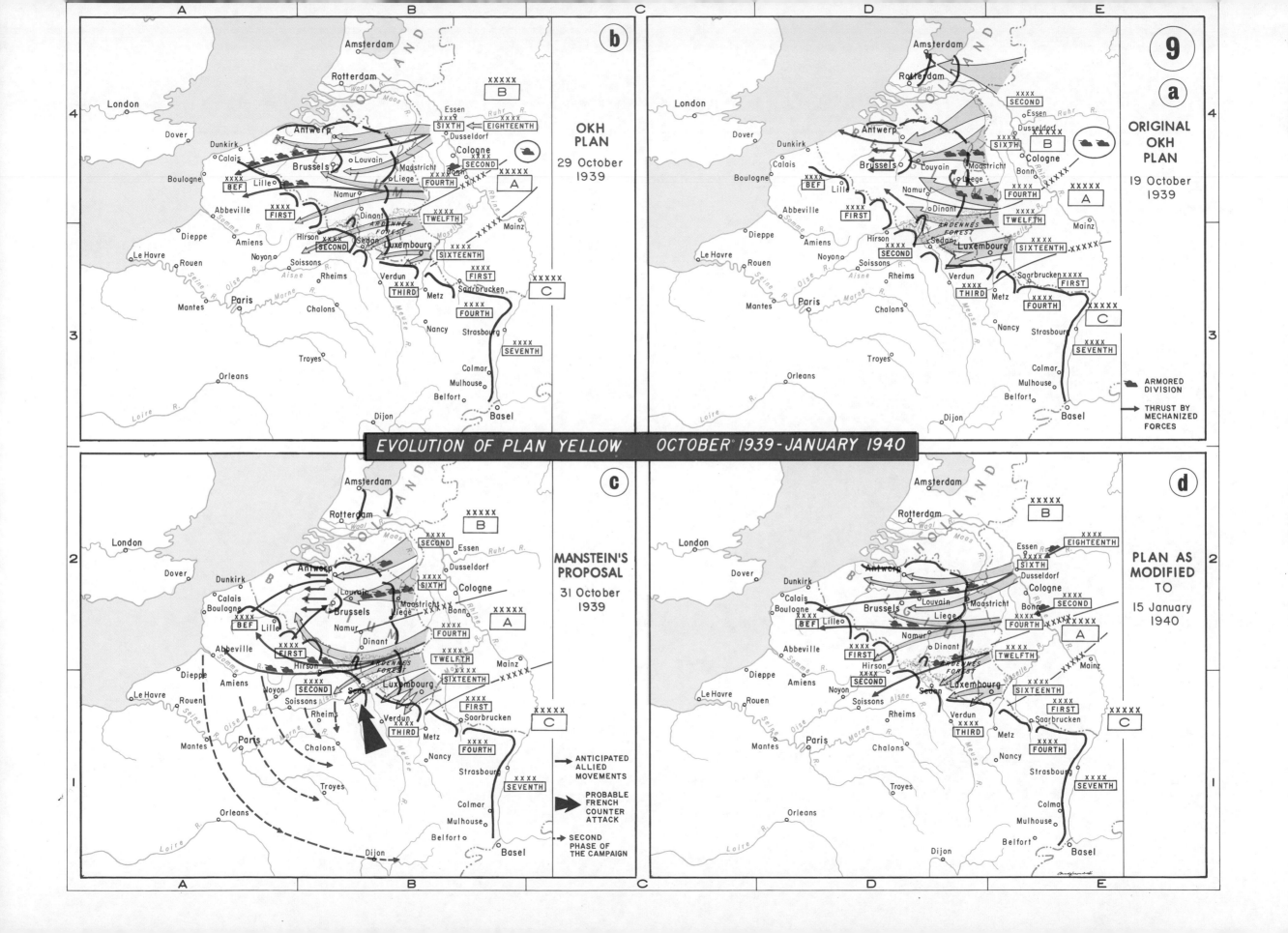

EVOLUTION OF PLAN YELLOW   OCTOBER 1939 - JANUARY 1940

b
OKH PLAN
29 October 1939

a
9
ORIGINAL OKH PLAN
19 October 1939

ARMORED DIVISION

THRUST BY MECHANIZED FORCES

c
MANSTEIN'S PROPOSAL
31 October 1939

ANTICIPATED ALLIED MOVEMENTS

PROBABLE FRENCH COUNTER ATTACK

SECOND PHASE OF THE CAMPAIGN

d
PLAN AS MODIFIED TO
15 January 1940

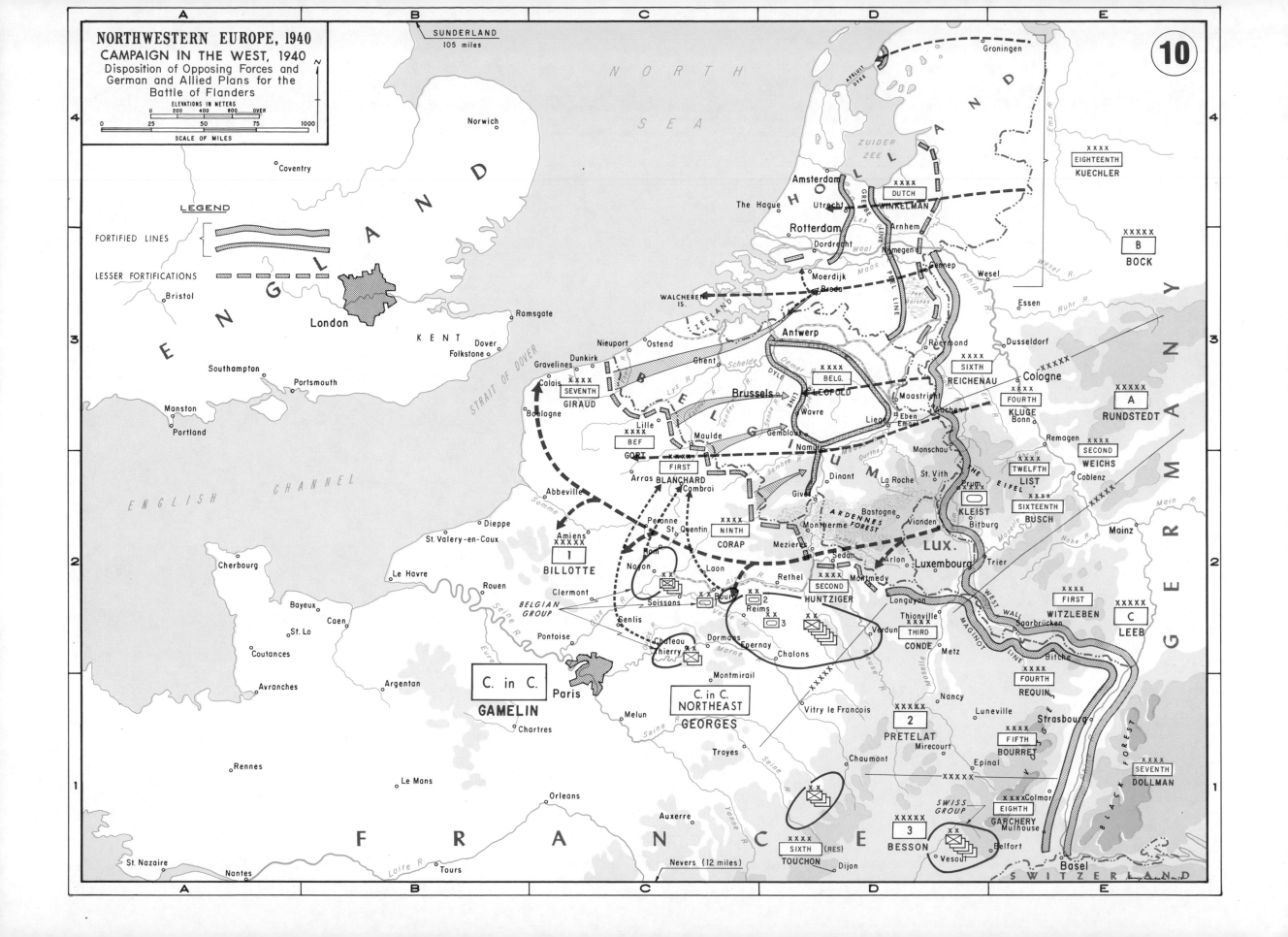

NORTHWESTERN EUROPE, 1940
CAMPAIGN IN THE WEST, 1940
Disposition of Opposing Forces and
German and Allied Plans for the
Battle of Flanders

ELEVATIONS IN METERS

| 0 | 200 | 400 | 800 | OVER |
| | | | | 1000 |

SCALE OF MILES

0   25   50   75

LEGEND

FORTIFIED LINES

LESSER FORTIFICATIONS

SUNDERLAND
105 miles

NORTH SEA

ENGLAND

Coventry
Norwich

London

KENT

Bristol

Southampton
Portsmouth
Manston
Portland

Ramsgate
Dover
Folkstone

STRAIT OF DOVER

ENGLISH CHANNEL

Cherbourg

Bayeux
Caen
St. Lo
Coutances
Avranches

Rennes

Le Mans

St. Nazaire
Nantes

Dieppe
St. Valery-en-Caux
Le Havre
Rouen

Argentan

Orleans

Tours

FRANCE

Clermont

Pontoise

Melun

Chartres

Auxerre

Loire R.

Nevers (12 miles)

HOLLAND

Groningen

Amsterdam
The Hague
Utrecht
Rotterdam
Dordrecht

ZUIDER ZEE

Arnhem
Nijmegen

Moerdijk
Breda

WALCHEREN
WALCHEREN IS.

ZEELAND

Nieuport
Ostend
Gravelines
Dunkirk
Calais
Boulogne

Antwerp
Ghent

Brussels

Lille
Maulde

Arras
Cambrai

Abbeville

Amiens

Peronne
St. Quentin

Ham
Noyon
Laon

Soissons

Genlis

Chateau
Thierry

Montmirail

Troyes

Vitry le Francois

Chaumont

SEVENTH
GIRAUD

BEF
GORT

FIRST
BLANCHARD

NINTH
CORAP

1
BILLOTTE

BELGIAN
GROUP

C. in C.
GAMELIN

Paris

C. in C.
NORTHEAST
GEORGES

Dormans
Epernay
Chalons

Reims

SIXTH (RES)
TOUCHON
Dijon

Winkelman
DUTCH
WINKELMAN

BELG.
LEOPOLD

Wavre
Gembloux
Namur

Dinant
Givet

Mezieres
Rethel

Bourg

SECOND
HUNTZIGER

Sedan

Arlon

THIRD
CONDE

2
PRETELAT

3
BESSON

EIGHTEENTH
KUECHLER

B
BOCK

SIXTH
REICHENAU

Cologne

FOURTH
KLUGE
Bonn

A
RUNDSTEDT

SECOND
WEICHS

TWELFTH
LIST

KLEIST

SIXTEENTH
BUSCH

LUX.
Luxembourg

FIRST
WITZLEBEN

C
LEEB

GERMANY

Essen
Dusseldorf
Roermond
Maastricht
Liege
Eben
Emael
Aachen

Monschau
La Roche
St. Vith
ARDENNES FOREST
Bastogne
Montherme
Vianden
Bitburg

Longuyon
Thionville
Verdun
Montmedy

Metz

Nancy
Luneville

Mirecourt
Epinal

Remagen
Coblenz
Mainz

Trier

Saarbrücken

WEST WALL
MAGINOT LINE

Strasbourg

FOURTH
REQUIN

FIFTH
BOURRET

SEVENTH
DOLLMAN

SWISS
GROUP

Colmar
GARCHERY
Mulhouse

EIGHTH
GARCHERY

Belfort
Vesoul

BLACK FOREST

Basel

SWITZERLAND

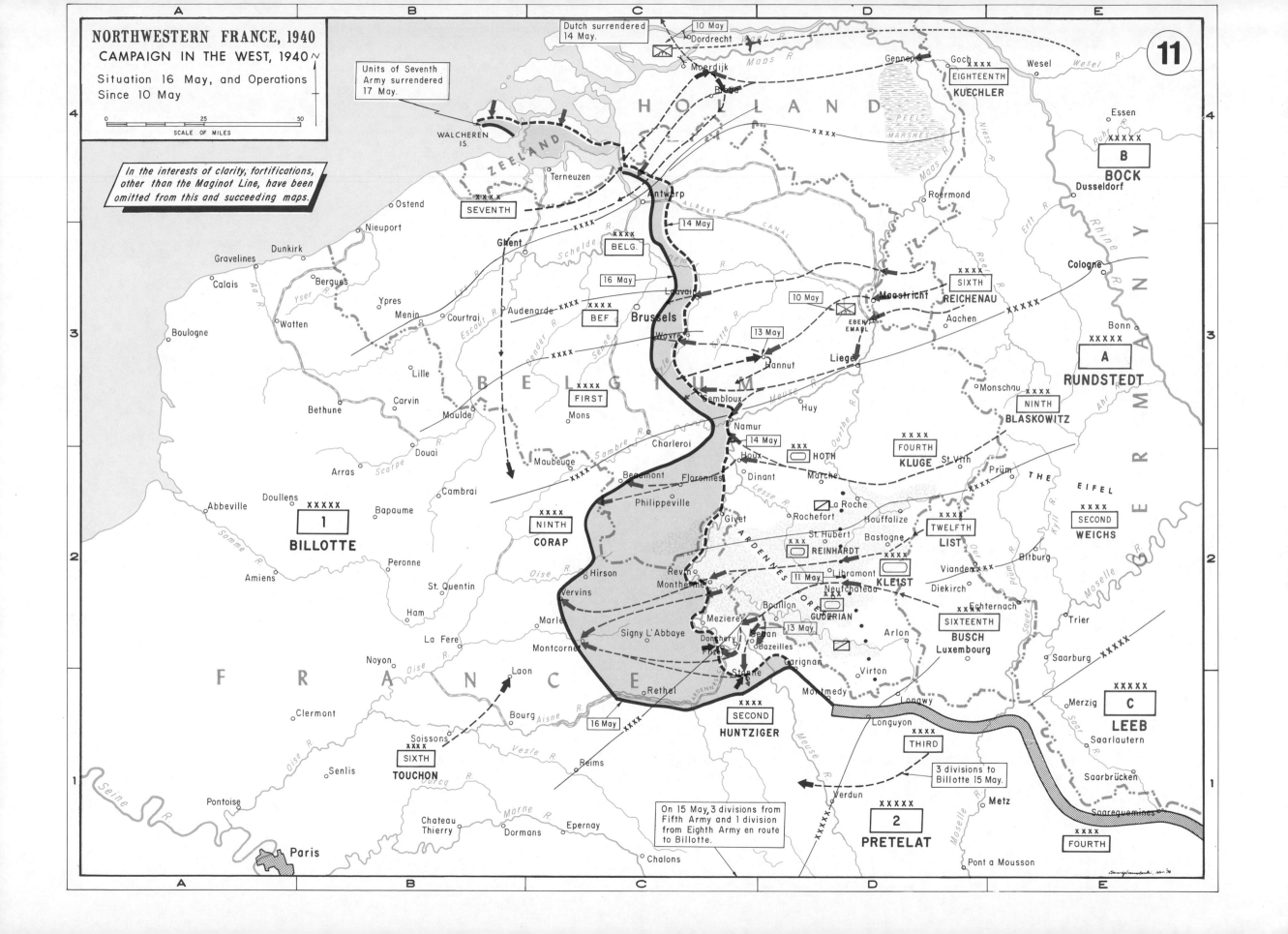

NORTHWESTERN FRANCE, 1940
CAMPAIGN IN THE WEST, 1940

Situation 16 May, and Operations
Since 10 May

SCALE OF MILES
0   25   50

In the interests of clarity, fortifications,
other than the Maginot Line, have been
omitted from this and succeeding maps.

Dutch surrendered
14 May.

Units of Seventh
Army surrendered
17 May.

10 May

HOLLAND

Gennep

Goch   XXXX   Wesel

EIGHTEENTH
KUECHLER

Dordrecht

Moerdijk

Breda

Essen

PEEL MARSHES

Maas R.

Niess R.

Roermond

XXXXX
B
BOCK

WALCHEREN IS.

ZEELAND

Terneuzen

XXXX   SEVENTH

Ostend

Nieuport

ALBERT CANAL

Antwerp

14 May

Maastricht

XXXX
SIXTH
REICHENAU

Cologne

Dusseldorf

Calais

Dunkirk

Gravelines

Bergues

Watten

Ypres

Menin

Ghent

Scheldt R.

Audenarde   XXXX

XXXX
BELG.

Lavai

16 May

10 May

EBEN EMAEL

Aachen

Bonn

XXXXX
A
RUNDSTEDT

Boulogne

Lille

Courtrai

Dender R.

XXXX
BEF

Brussels

Wavre

Dyle R.

13 May

Hannut

Liege

Monschau

XXXX
NINTH
BLASKOWITZ

Bethune

Carvin

Maulde

XXXX

Seine R.

XXXX
FIRST

Mons

Sambre R.

Gembloux

Huy

Meuse R.

Ourthe R.

XXXX
FOURTH
KLUGE

St Vith

Prüm

THE

Arras

Douai

Cambrai

Maubeuge

Charleroi

Namur

14 May

Houx

XXX
HOTH

Dinant

Marche

EIFEL

XXXX
SECOND
WEICHS

Abbeville

Doullens

Bapaume

XXXXX
1
BILLOTTE

Beaumont

Florennes

Philippeville

Givet

Rochefort

La Roche

Houffalize

XXXX
TWELFTH
LIST

GERMANY

Peronne

Amiens

St. Quentin

XXXX
NINTH
CORAP

Hirson

Revin

Montherme

St. Hubert

Bastogne

XXX
REINHARDT

Vianden   XXXX

Bitburg

Kyll R.

Ham

La Fere

Somme R.

Oise R.

Vervins

Marle

Signy L'Abbaye

Mezieres

Bouillon

Libramont

11 May

Neufchateau

XXXX
KLEIST

GUDERIAN

Diekirch

Moselle R.

Trier

Noyon

Laon

Montcornet

Sedan

Donchery

Bazeilles

13 May

Arlon

XXXX
SIXTEENTH
BUSCH

Echternach

Sauer R.

Clermont

Bourg

Aisne R.

Rethel

Stonne

Carignan

Virton

Luxembourg

Longwy

Saarburg   XXXXX

XXXX
SECOND
HUNTZIGER

Montmedy

XXXXX
C
LEEB

Merzig

Soissons

XXXX
SIXTH
TOUCHON

Senlis

Reims

Vesle R.

16 May   XXXX

Ourcq R.

3 divisions to
Billotte 15 May.

Longuyon

XXXX
THIRD

Verdun

XXXXX
2
PRETELAT

Metz

Moselle R.

Saarlautern

Saarbrücken

Pontoise

Chateau
Thierry

Dormans

Epernay

Marne R.

On 15 May, 3 divisions from
Fifth Army and 1 division
from Eighth Army en route
to Billotte.

XXXXX
FOURTH

Seine R.

Paris

Chalons

Pont a Mousson

Saareguemines

11

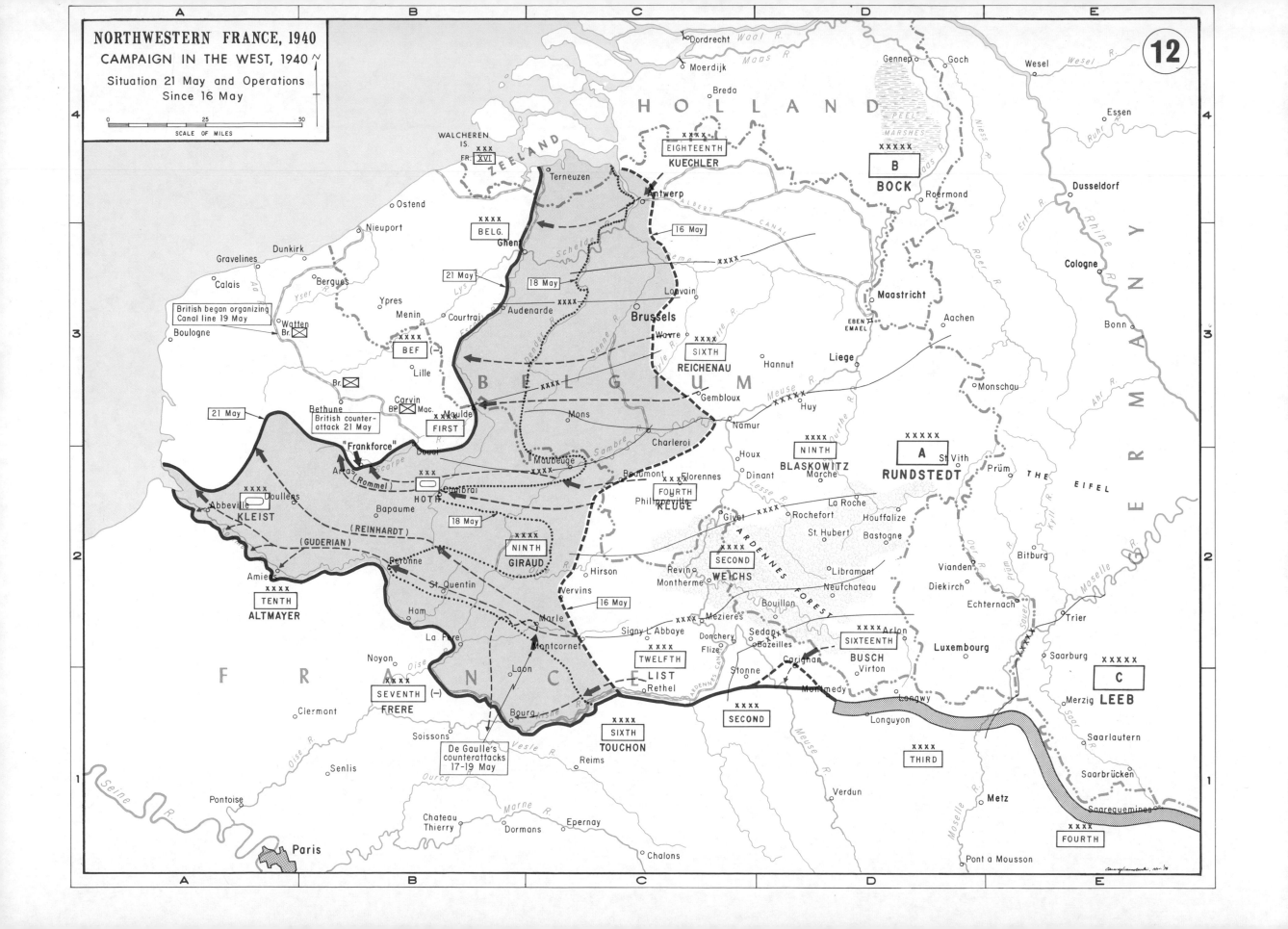

NORTHWESTERN FRANCE, 1940
CAMPAIGN IN THE WEST, 1940
Situation 21 May and Operations
Since 16 May

SCALE OF MILES
0   25   50

12

HOLLAND

Dordrecht   Waal R.
Gennep   Goch   Wesel   Wesel R.
Moerdijk   Maas R.
Breda   Roermond   Essen

EIGHTEENTH
KUECHLER
XXXXX
B
BOCK
Dusseldorf

WALCHEREN IS.
FR. XXX XVI
ZEELAND
Terneuzen   Antwerp   Maastricht   Aachen   Cologne

Ostend
Nieuport   XXXX
BELG.
Ghent   ALBERT CANAL
16 May   EBEN EMAEL   Bonn

Gravelines   Dunkirk
Calais   Bergues   21 May   18 May   Louvain   XXXX
Schelde R.   Liege   Monschau

Boulogne   Ypres   Menin   Courtrai   Audenarde   Brussels   SIXTH
REICHENAU   Hannut
British began organizing
Canal line 19 May   Watten   Wavre   XXXX
Br.   Lys R.   Senne R.   Hannut   GERMANY

XXXX   Lille   BELGIUM   Gembloux   Huy
BEF (-)   Dendre R.   XXXX   NINTH
Br.   Mons   Namur   BLASKOWITZ   St Vith   A
Bethune   Carvin   Maulde   XXXX   Charleroi   Dinant   Marche   RUNDSTEDT   Prüm
21 May   British counter-   Mac.   FIRST   Maubeuge   Houx   THE   EIFEL
attack 21 May   "Frankforce"   Douai   Beaumont   Florennes   Revin   FOURTH
Arras (Rommel)   Cambrai   XXXX   Philippeville   La Roche   KLUGE
21 May   HOTH   Rochefort   Houffalize
Doullens   XXXX   18 May   Bapaume   NINTH   Givet   ARDENNES   Bastogne
Abbeville   KLEIST   (REINHARDT)   GIRAUD   Hirson   SECOND   St Hubert   Vianden
(GUDERIAN)   Peronne   WEICHS   Libramont   Bitburg
Amiens   St Quentin   Revin   Neufchateau   Diekirch
XXXX   Ham   Vervins   Montherme   Echternach
TENTH   La Fere   Marle   Bouillon   Trier
ALTMAYER   Montcornet   Mezieres   FOREST
Noyon   Oise R.   Laon   Signy L'Abbaye   Doncherry   Sedan   Arlon   SIXTEENTH
16 May   Donchery   Flize   Bazeilles   BUSCH   Luxembourg
SEVENTH (-)   FRANCE   Bourg   TWELFTH   Carignan   Virton   Saarburg
FRERE   LIST   Stonne   Longwy   XXXXX
Clermont   Soissons   Rethel   Montmedy   Longuyon   C
De Gaulle's   SIXTH   SECOND   Merzig   LEEB
counterattacks   TOUCHON   Longuyon
17-19 May   Reims   Saarlautern
Senlis   THIRD
Pontoise   Verdun   Metz   Saarbrücken
Chateau   Epernay
Thierry   Dormans   Saareguemines
Paris   Chalons   Pont a Mousson   FOURTH

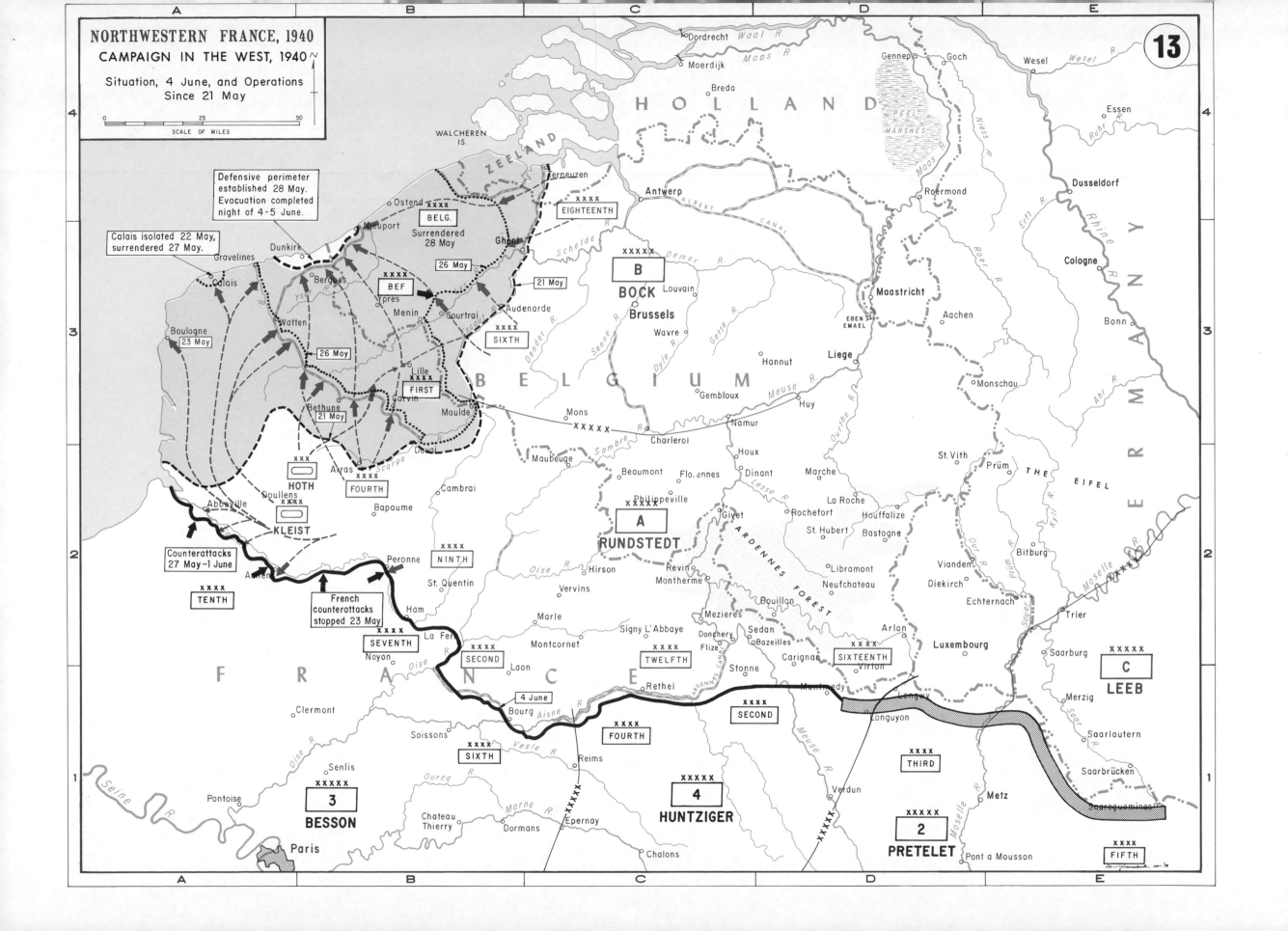

NORTHWESTERN FRANCE, 1940
CAMPAIGN IN THE WEST, 1940

Situation, 4 June, and Operations
Since 21 May

SCALE OF MILES
0   25   50

13

Defensive perimeter
established 28 May.
Evacuation completed
night of 4-5 June.

Calais isolated 22 May,
surrendered 27 May.

Counterattacks
27 May-1 June

French
counterattacks
stopped 23 May

HOLLAND

PEEL
MARSHES

Dordrecht   Waal R.
Moerdijk   Maas R.
Breda
Genney   Goch   Wesel   Wesel R.
Essen

WALCHEREN IS.
ZEELAND
Terneuzen
Ostend   Antwerp   Roermond   Dusseldorf
BELG.   EIGHTEENTH   ALBERT   CANAL
Surrendered   Ghent   Maastricht   Aachen   Cologne
28 May
26 May   B   EBEN   Bonn
21 May   BOCK   EMAEL
Mieuport   Louvain
Dunkirk   BEF   Brussels   Liege
Gravelines   Bergues   Ypres   Audenarde   Hannut   Monschau
Calais   Menin   Courtrai   SIXTH   Gembloux   Huy   THE   EIFEL
Boulogne   Watten   Lille   St. Vith   Prüm
23 May   Maulde   Mons   Namur   Marche   La Roche   Vianden   Bitburg
26 May   Carvin   Charleroi   Houx   Houffalize   Bastogne
Bethune   FIRST   Maubeuge   Flo.ennes   Dinant   Rochefort   Echternach   Trier
21 May   Doual   Beaumont   St. Hubert   Diekirch
HOTH   Arras   Philippeville   A   ARDENNES   Libramont   Arlon
Doullens   Cambrai   RUNDSTEDT   Givet   FOREST   Neufchateau   Luxembourg   Saarburg
FOURTH   Bapaume   Revin   Bouillon   C
KLEIST   Montherme   Mezieres   LEEB
Abbeville   Peronne   NINTH   Hirson   Sedan   Merzig
TENTH   Amiens   St. Quentin   Vervins   Signy L'Abbaye   Bazeilles   Virton   Saarlautern
Ham   Marle   Donchery   Carignan   SIXTEENTH   Longuy
SEVENTH   La Fer   Montcornet   Flize   Stonne   Longuyon   Saarbrücken
Noyon   SECOND   Laon   TWELFTH   Rethel   Montmedy   Longuyon
4 June   Bourg   Aisne   SECOND   C
Clermont   Soissons   Vesle R.   Reims   FOURTH   Verdun   Metz
SIXTH   THIRD
Senlis   Ourcq R.   Marne R.   Saarbrücken
3   4   Epernay   2
Pontoise   Chateau   Dormans   Chalons   PRETELET   Pont a Mousson
BESSON   Thierry   HUNTZIGER   FIFTH
Paris   Seine R.

HOLLAND   BELGIUM   FRANCE   GERMANY

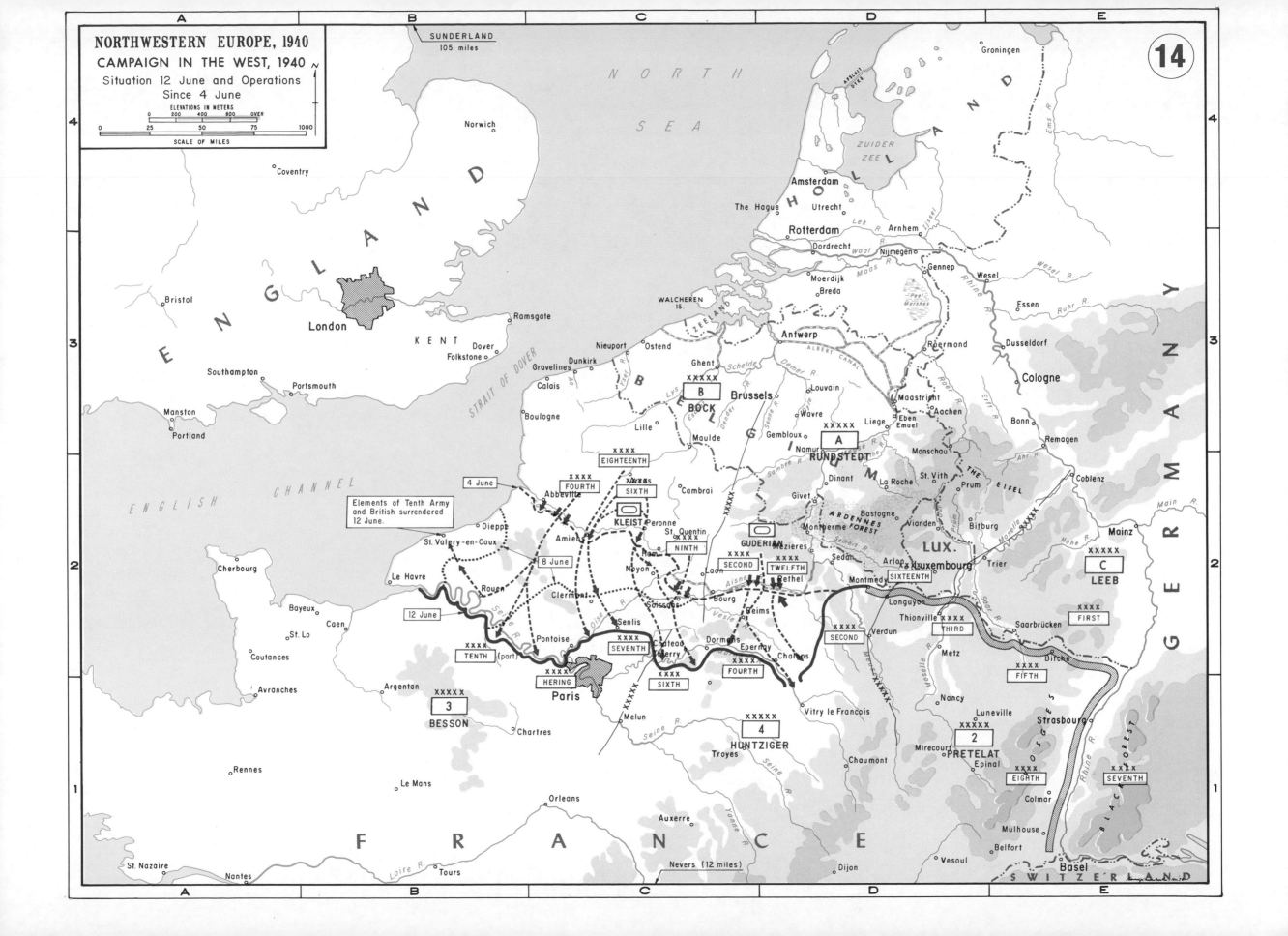

NORTHWESTERN EUROPE, 1940
CAMPAIGN IN THE WEST, 1940
Situation 12 June and Operations
Since 4 June

ELEVATIONS IN METERS
200 400 800 OVER
0   25   50   75   1000
SCALE OF MILES

14

Elements of Tenth Army
and British surrendered
12 June.

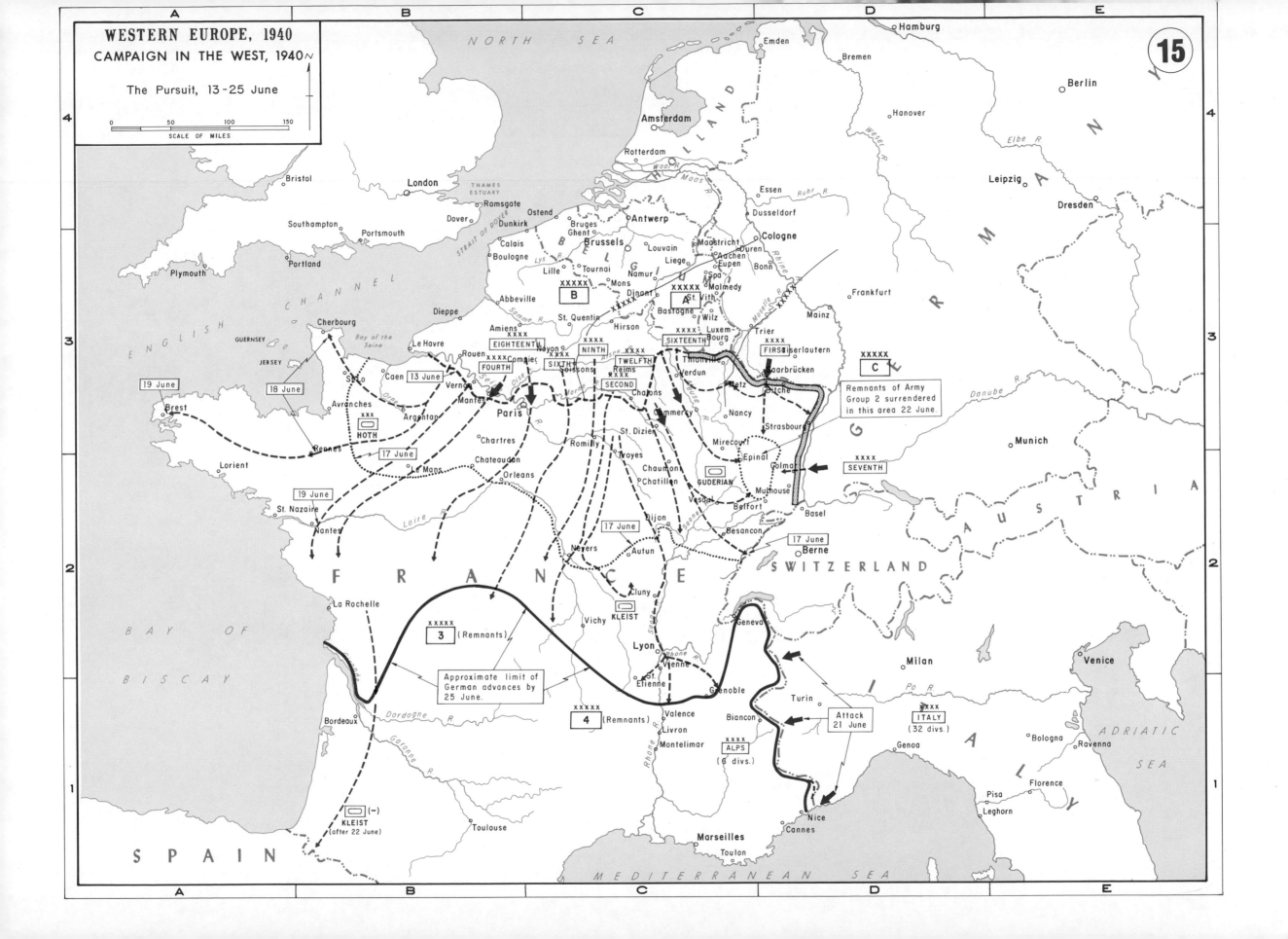

WESTERN EUROPE, 1940
CAMPAIGN IN THE WEST, 1940~

The Pursuit, 13-25 June

SCALE OF MILES
0   50   100   150

15

NORTH SEA

Hamburg
Emden
Bremen
Berlin
Hanover
Leipzig
Dresden

GERMANY

Amsterdam
HOLLAND
Rotterdam
Waal R.
Maas R.
Essen   Ruhr R.
Dusseldorf
Cologne
Weser R.
Elbe R.
Frankfurt
Mainz
Rhine R.
Danube R.
Munich

London
Thames Estuary
Bristol
Southampton
Portsmouth
Portland
Plymouth

ENGLISH CHANNEL
Ramsgate
Dover
Strait of Dover
Dunkirk
Ostend
Calais
Boulogne

Bruges
Ghent
Antwerp
Brussels
Louvain
Liege
Lys R.
Lille
Tournai
Mons
Namur
Dinant
Maastricht
Aachen
Duren
Eupen
Spa
Bonn
Malmedy

B
XXXXX

A
XXXXX
St. Vith
Bastogne
Wilz
Luxembourg
Trier
Moselle R.
Saar R.
Kaiserslautern
FIRST
XXXX

C
XXXXX

Remnants of Army
Group 2 surrendered
in this area 22 June.

GUERNSEY
JERSEY

Cherbourg
Bay of the Seine
Le Havre
Dieppe
Abbeville
Somme R.
St. Quentin
Amiens
XXXX
EIGHTEENTH
Noyon
XXXX
Rouen
XXXX
Compiegne
FOURTH
Seine R.
Oise R.

NINTH
XXXX
SIXTH
XXXX
Soissons
Aisne R.
TWELFTH
XXXX
Reims
SECOND
XXXX
Marne R.
Chalons

SIXTEENTH
XXXX
Hirson
Thionville
Verdun
Metz
Meuse R.
Nancy

Pirmasens
Saarbrücken
Bitche

Strasbourg

19 June
18 June
St. Lo
Avranches
Caen   13 June
Verneuil
Mantes
Argentan
HOTH
XXX

Paris

Chartres
Chateaudun
Orleans
Le Mans
Rennes   17 June
Lorient

St. Nazaire   19 June
Nantes

Romilly
St. Dizier
Troyes
Chaumont
Chatillon
Dijon   17 June
Nevers
Autun
Cluny
KLEIST
Vichy

Commercy
Mirecourt
Epinal
Vesoul
Mulhouse
Belfort
Besancon
Colmar
SEVENTH
XXXX

17 June
Berne

SWITZERLAND

Saone R.

F R A N C E

La Rochelle
3 (Remnants)
XXXXX

Approximate limit of
German advances by
25 June.

Bordeaux
Dordogne R.
Garonne R.

4 (Remnants)
XXXXX
Valence
Livron
Montelimar
Rhone R.

KLEIST
(-)
(after 22 June)

Toulouse

SPAIN

BAY OF BISCAY

Lyon
St. Etienne
Vienne
Grenoble
Geneva

Milan
Turin
Biancon
Nice
Cannes

Attack
21 June

ITALY
(32 divs.)
XXXX

ALPS
(6 divs.)
XXXX

Po R.

Genoa
Pisa
Leghorn
Bologna
Florence
Ravenna

Marseilles
Toulon

MEDITERRANEAN SEA

ADRIATIC SEA

AUSTRIA

Venice

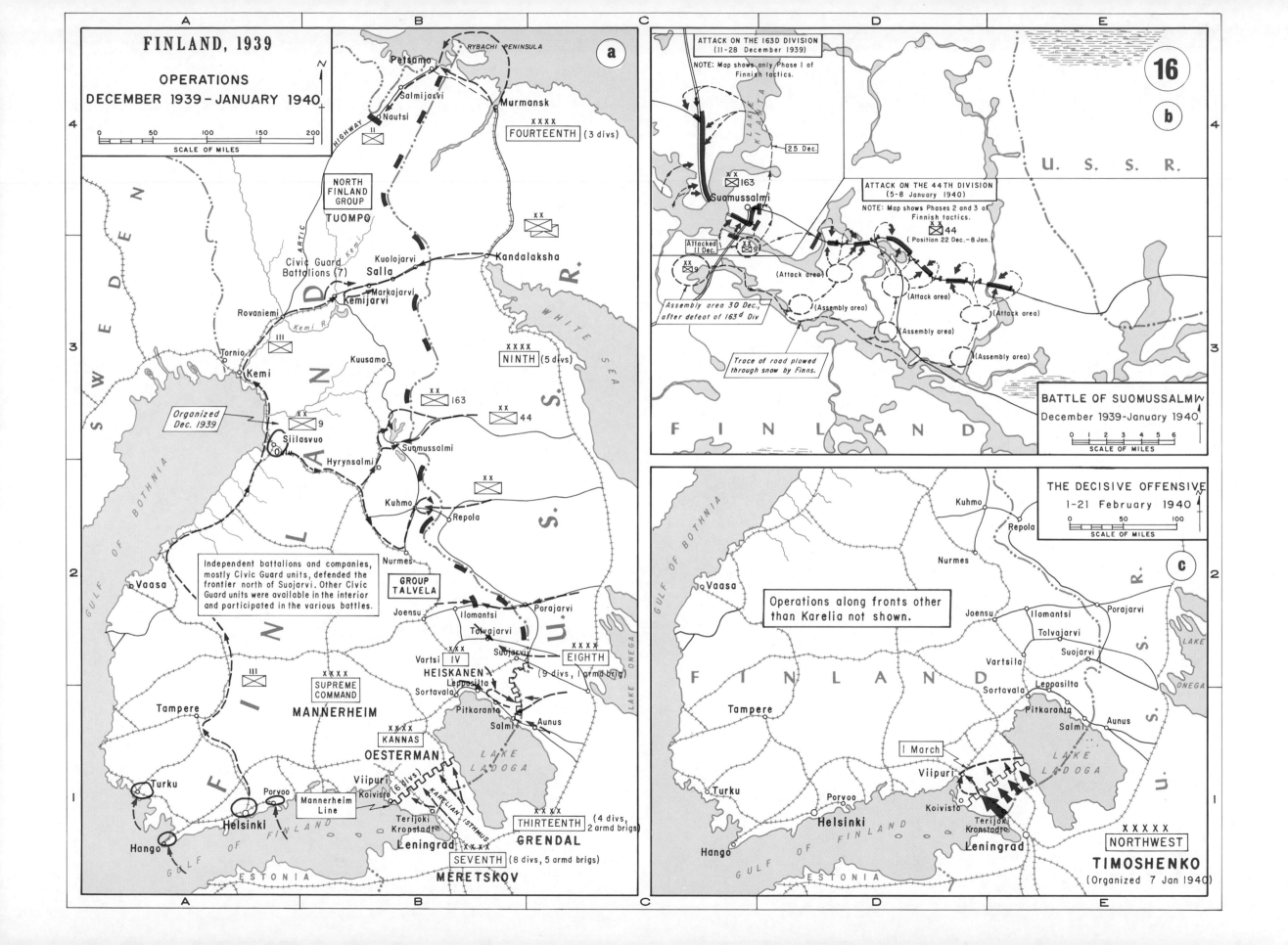

FINLAND, 1939

OPERATIONS
DECEMBER 1939 – JANUARY 1940

SCALE OF MILES
0 50 100 150 200

a

RYBACHI PENINSULA

Petsamo

Salmijarvi
Nautsi

Murmansk

XXXX
FOURTEENTH (3 divs)

NORTH
FINLAND
GROUP

TUOMPO

ARTIC HIGHWAY

Kemi R.

Civic Guard
Battalions (7)

Kuolojarvi
Salla

Kandalaksha

Markajarvi
Kemijarvi

Rovaniemi

Kemi R.

WHITE SEA

III

Tornio

Kemi

Kuusamo

XXXX
NINTH (5 divs)

XX 163

XX 44

XX 9

Organized Dec. 1939

Siilasvuo
Oulu

Hyrynsalmi

Suomussalmi

U. S. S. R.

Kuhmo

XX

Repola

Nurmes

GROUP
TALVELA

Independent battalions and companies,
mostly Civic Guard units, defended the
frontier north of Suojarvi. Other Civic
Guard units were available in the interior
and participated in the various battles.

Joensu

Ilomantsi

Porajarvi

Tolvajarvi

Vartsi

XXX
IV

Suojarvi

XXXX
EIGHTH

HEISKANEN

(9 divs, 1 armd brig)

Leppasilta

Sortavala

Pitkaranta

Salmi

Aunus

LAKE ONEGA

SUPREME
COMMAND

MANNERHEIM

III

XXXX

Tampere

KANNAS

OESTERMAN

LAKE
LADOGA

Viipuri

XXXX (6 divs)

Koivisto

Mannerheim
Line

Turku

Porvoo

KARELIAN ISTHMUS

Terijoki
Kronstadt

XXXX
THIRTEENTH (4 divs, 2 armd brigs)

Helsinki

Hango

Leningrad

GRENDAL

XXXXX

GULF OF
FINLAND

SWEDEN   FINLAND

GULF OF BOTHNIA

XXXX
SEVENTH (8 divs, 5 armd brigs)

ESTONIA

MERETSKOV

16

b

ATTACK ON THE 163D DIVISION
(11-28 December 1939)

NOTE: Map shows only Phase I of Finnish tactics.

25 Dec.

XX 163

LAKE KIANTA

U. S. S. R.

Suomussalmi

ATTACK ON THE 44TH DIVISION
(5-8 January 1940)

NOTE: Map shows Phases 2 and 3 of Finnish tactics.

XX 44
(Position 22 Dec.-8 Jan.)

Attacked 11 Dec.

XX 9

(Attack area)

XX 9

(Attack area)

(Attack area)

*Assembly area 30 Dec.,
after defeat of 163d Div*

(Assembly area)

(Assembly area)

(Attack area)

(Assembly area)

*Trace of road plowed
through snow by Finns.*

BATTLE OF SUOMUSSALMI
December 1939 – January 1940

SCALE OF MILES
0 1 2 3 4 5 6

F I N L A N D

c

THE DECISIVE OFFENSIVE
1-21 February 1940

SCALE OF MILES
0 50 100

Kuhmo

Repola

U. S. S. R.

Nurmes

Operations along fronts other
than Karelia not shown.

GULF OF BOTHNIA

Vaasa

Joensu

Ilomantsi

Porajarvi

Tolvajarvi

Suojarvi

LAKE ONEGA

Vartsila

Leppasilta

Sortavala

Pitkaranta

Salmi

Aunus

LAKE
LADOGA

F I N L A N D

Tampere

1 March

Viipuri

Koivisto

Turku

Porvoo

Terijoki
Kronstadt

Helsinki

Leningrad

NORTHWEST

Hango

GULF OF FINLAND

ESTONIA

TIMOSHENKO
(Organized 7 Jan 1940)

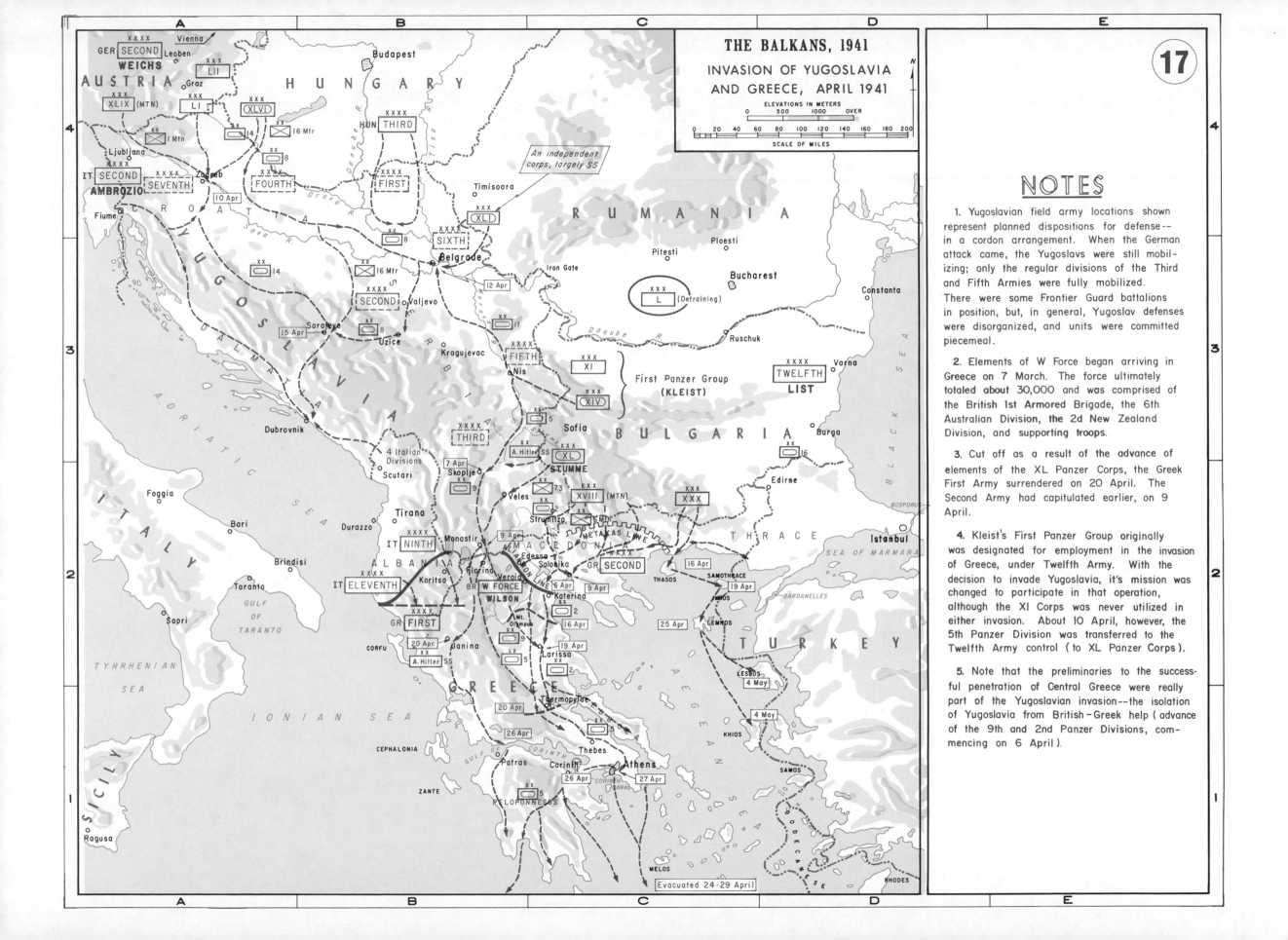

THE BALKANS, 1941
INVASION OF YUGOSLAVIA AND GREECE, APRIL 1941

ELEVATIONS IN METERS

0   500   1000   OVER

0 20 40 60 80 100 120 140 160 180 200

SCALE OF MILES

NOTES

1. Yugoslavian field army locations shown represent planned dispositions for defense—in a cordon arrangement. When the German attack came, the Yugoslavs were still mobilizing; only the regular divisions of the Third and Fifth Armies were fully mobilized. There were some Frontier Guard battalions in position, but, in general, Yugoslav defenses were disorganized, and units were committed piecemeal.

2. Elements of W Force began arriving in Greece on 7 March. The force ultimately totaled about 30,000 and was comprised of the British 1st Armored Brigade, the 6th Australian Division, the 2d New Zealand Division, and supporting troops.

3. Cut off as a result of the advance of elements of the XL Panzer Corps, the Greek First Army surrendered on 20 April. The Second Army had capitulated earlier, on 9 April.

4. Kleist's First Panzer Group originally was designated for employment in the invasion of Greece, under Twelfth Army. With the decision to invade Yugoslavia, it's mission was changed to participate in that operation, although the XI Corps was never utilized in either invasion. About 10 April, however, the 5th Panzer Division was transferred to the Twelfth Army control (to XL Panzer Corps).

5. Note that the preliminaries to the successful penetration of Central Greece were really part of the Yugoslavian invasion—the isolation of Yugoslavia from British-Greek help (advance of the 9th and 2nd Panzer Divisions, commencing on 6 April).

An independent corps, largely SS

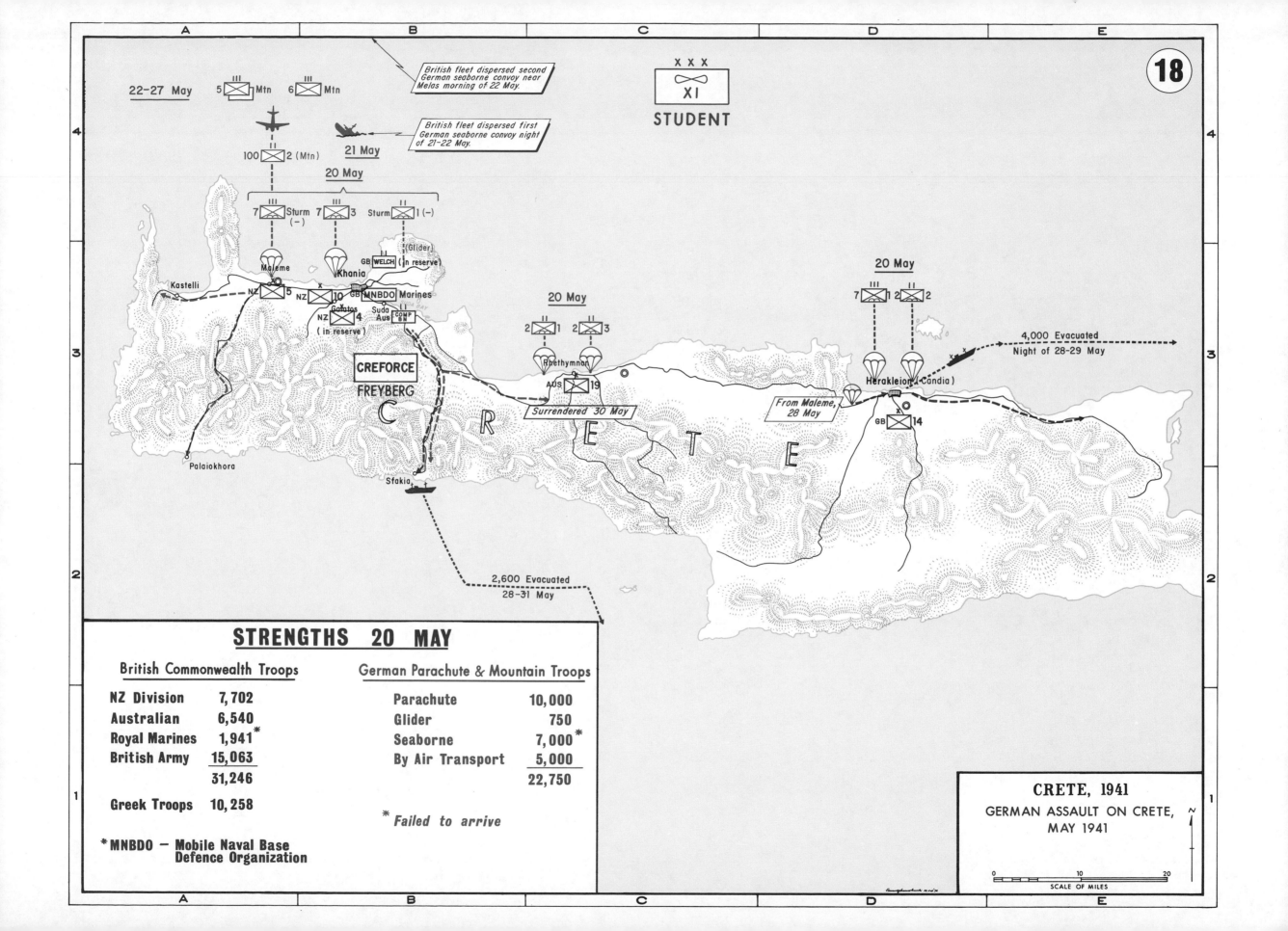

22-27 May 5 ☒☒☒ Mtn   6 ☒☒☒ Mtn

British fleet dispersed second German seaborne convoy near Melas morning of 22 May.

X X X
☒
XI
STUDENT

100 ☒☒☒ 2 (Mtn)

21 May

British fleet dispersed first German seaborne convoy night of 21-22 May.

20 May

7 ☒☒☒ Sturm (-)   7 ☒☒☒ 3   Sturm ☒☒ 1 (-)

(Glider)
GB WELCH (-) (in reserve)

Maleme   Khania
Kastelli

NZ ☒☒ 5   NZ ☒☒ 10   GB MNBDO Marines

NZ ☒☒ 4   Galatos   Suda   Aus COMP BN
(in reserve)

Palaiokhora

CREFORCE
FREYBERG

C R E T E

20 May
2 ☒☒☒ 1   2 ☒☒ 3

Rhethymnon

AUS ☒☒ 19

Surrendered 30 May

20 May
7 ☒☒☒ 1   2 ☒☒ 2

Herakleion (Candia)

From Maleme, 28 May

GB ☒☒ 14

4,000 Evacuated
Night of 28-29 May

Sfakia

2,600 Evacuated
28-31 May

STRENGTHS 20 MAY

British Commonwealth Troops		German Parachute & Mountain Troops	
NZ Division	7,702	Parachute	10,000
Australian	6,540	Glider	750
Royal Marines	1,941*	Seaborne	7,000*
British Army	15,063	By Air Transport	5,000
	31,246		22,750
Greek Troops	10,258		

*Failed to arrive

*MNBDO — Mobile Naval Base Defence Organization

CRETE, 1941
GERMAN ASSAULT ON CRETE, MAY 1941

0   10   20
SCALE OF MILES

18

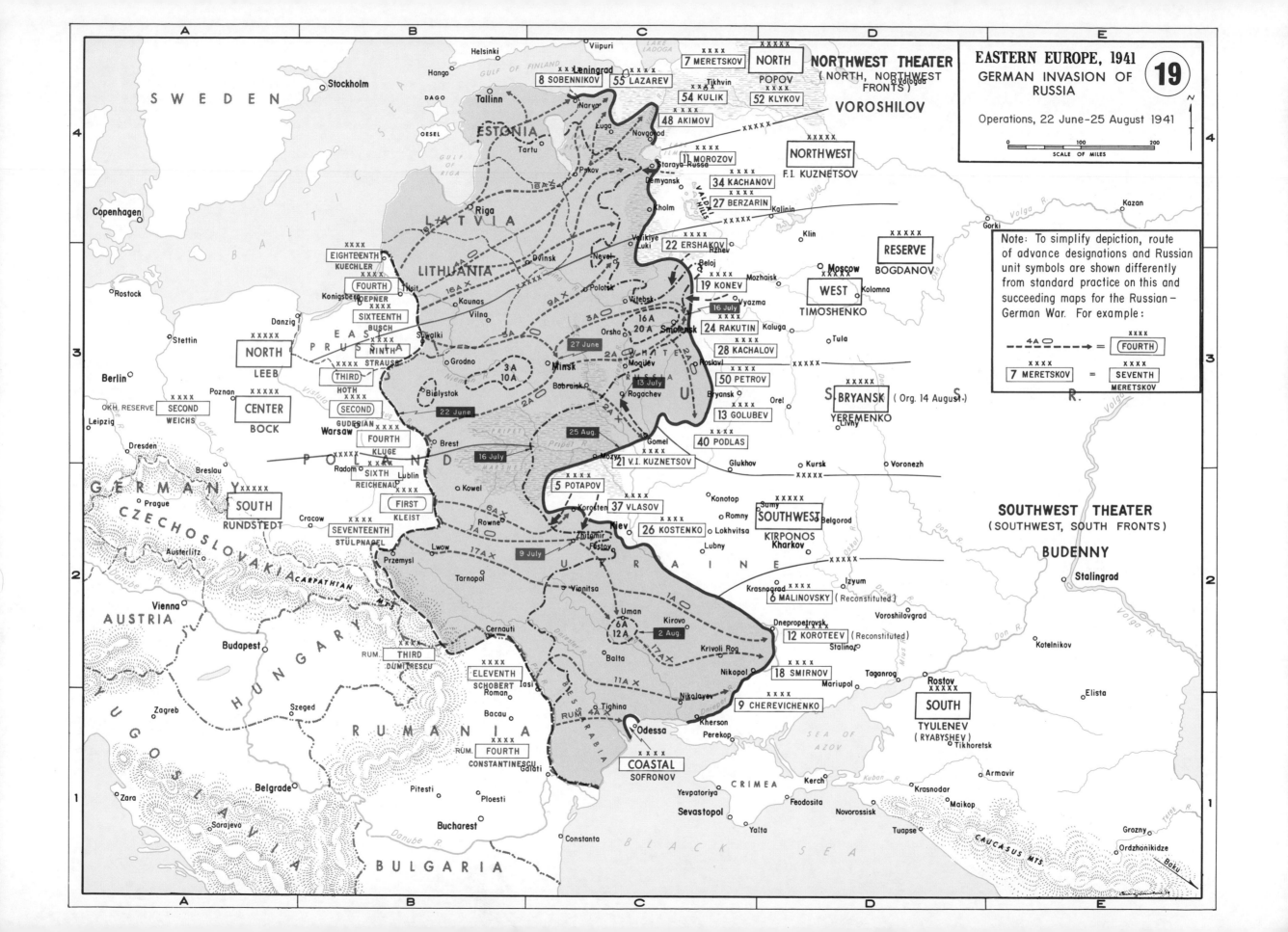

EASTERN EUROPE, 1941
GERMAN INVASION OF RUSSIA

19

Operations, 22 June–25 August 1941

SCALE OF MILES
0   100   200

NORTHWEST THEATER
(NORTH, NORTHWEST FRONTS)

VOROSHILOV

NORTH — POPOV

7 MERETSKOV
8 SOBENNIKOV
55 LAZAREV
54 KULIK
52 KLYKOV
48 AKIMOV

NORTHWEST — F.I. KUZNETSOV

11 MOROZOV
34 KACHANOV
27 BERZARIN
22 ERSHAKOV

RESERVE — BOGDANOV

WEST — TIMOSHENKO

19 KONEV
24 RAKUTIN
28 KACHALOV
50 PETROV
13 GOLUBEV
40 PODLAS
21 V.I. KUZNETSOV

BRYANSK (Org. 14 August) — YEREMENKO

SOUTHWEST THEATER
(SOUTHWEST, SOUTH FRONTS)

BUDENNY

SOUTHWEST — KIRPONOS

5 POTAPOV
37 VLASOV
26 KOSTENKO
6 MALINOVSKY (Reconstituted)
12 KOROTEEV (Reconstituted)
18 SMIRNOV
9 CHEREVICHENKO

SOUTH — TYULENEV (RYABYSHEV)

COASTAL — SOFRONOV

Note: To simplify depiction, route of advance designations and Russian unit symbols are shown differently from standard practice on this and succeeding maps for the Russian–German War. For example:

4A = FOURTH

7 MERETSKOV = SEVENTH MERETSKOV

German forces

NORTH — LEEB
EIGHTEENTH — KUECHLER
FOURTH — HOEPNER
SIXTEENTH — BUSCH

CENTER — BOCK
NINTH — STRAUSS
THIRD — HOTH
SECOND — WEICHS
SECOND
FOURTH — KLUGE
SIXTH — REICHENAU

SOUTH — RUNDSTEDT
SEVENTEENTH — STÜLPNAGEL
FIRST — KLEIST

RUM. THIRD — DUMITRESCU
ELEVENTH — SCHOBERT
RUM. FOURTH — CONSTANTINESCU

OKH RESERVE — SECOND

Dates of advance: 22 June, 27 June, 9 July, 13 July, 16 July, 16 July, 2 Aug., 25 Aug.

U.S.S.R.

Place names:
Stockholm, Copenhagen, Berlin, Stettin, Danzig, Königsberg, Tilsit, Leipzig, Dresden, Breslau, Prague, Vienna, Budapest, Belgrade, Zagreb, Sarajevo, Zara, Bucharest, Ploesti, Constanta, Sofia, Helsinki, Viipuri, Hango, Tallinn, Tartu, Riga, Pskov, Novgorod, Leningrad, Tikhvin, Staraya Russa, Demyansk, Kholm, Kalinin, Klin, Moscow, Kolomna, Gorki, Kazan, Rzhev, Vyazma, Mozhaisk, Kaluga, Tula, Orel, Kursk, Voronezh, Smolensk, Orsha, Mogilev, Roslavl, Bryansk, Minsk, Bobruisk, Rogachev, Gomel, Glukhov, Konotop, Romny, Lokhvitsa, Lubny, Sumy, Belgorod, Kharkov, Izyum, Krasnograd, Dnepropetrovsk, Stalino, Voroshilovgrad, Stalingrad, Krivoi Rog, Nikopol, Nikolayev, Kherson, Odessa, Perekop, Mariupol, Taganrog, Rostov, Elista, Kotelnikov, Tikhoretsk, Armavir, Krasnodar, Maikop, Novorossisk, Tuapse, Sevastopol, Yalta, Feodosita, Kerch, Yevpatoriya, Grozny, Ordzhonikidze, Baku, Austerlitz, Cracow, Przemysl, Lwow, Tarnopol, Vinnitsa, Uman, Kirovo, Balta, Cernauti, Iasi, Roman, Bacau, Galati, Tighina, Pitesti, Ploesti

Regions/Geography:
SWEDEN, DAGO, OESEL, ESTONIA, LATVIA, LITHUANIA, EAST PRUSSIA, POLAND, GERMANY, CZECHOSLOVAKIA, AUSTRIA, HUNGARY, YUGOSLAVIA, RUMANIA, BULGARIA, UKRAINE, WHITE RUSSIA, GULF OF FINLAND, LAKE LADOGA, BALTIC SEA, GULF OF RIGA, BLACK SEA, SEA OF AZOV, CRIMEA, CAUCASUS MTS, CARPATHIAN MTS, VALDAI HILLS, PRIPET MARSHES, Volga R., Don R., Danube R., Dnieper R., Dniester R., Niemen R., Oder R., Vistula R., Pripet R., Kuban R.

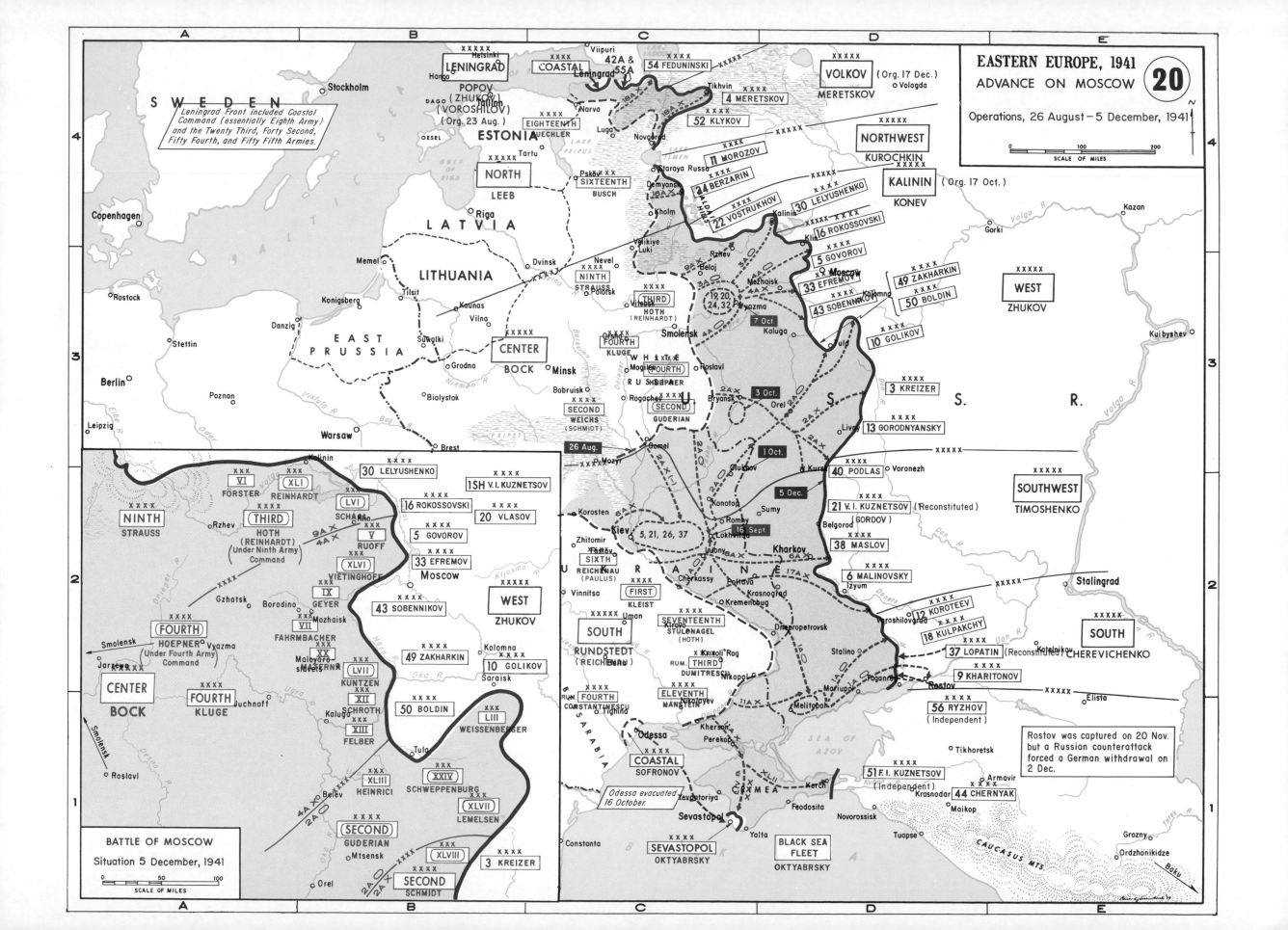

EASTERN EUROPE, 1941
ADVANCE ON MOSCOW
20
Operations, 26 August – 5 December, 1941

SWEDEN

Leningrad Front included Coastal Command (essentially Eighth Army) and the Twenty Third, Forty Second, Fifty Fourth, and Fifty Fifth Armies.

LENINGRAD
POPOV (ZHUKOV)
(VOROSHILOV)
(Org. 23 Aug.)
COASTAL
42A & 55A
54 FEDUNINSKI
VOLKOV (Org. 17 Dec.)
MERETSKOV
4 MERETSKOV
52 KLYKOV
NORTHWEST
KUROCHKIN

ESTONIA
EIGHTEENTH
KUECHLER
11 MOROZOV
34 BERZARIN
22 VOSTRUKHOV

NORTH
LEEB
SIXTEENTH
BUSCH
KALININ (Org. 17 Oct.)
KONEV

LATVIA

LITHUANIA
NINTH
STRAUSS
THIRD
HOTH (REINHARDT)
30 LELYUSHENKO
16 ROKOSSOVSKI
5 GOVOROV
33 EFREMOV
43 SOBENNIKOV
49 ZAKHARKIN
50 BOLDIN
WEST
ZHUKOV

EAST PRUSSIA

CENTER
BOCK
FOURTH
KLUGE
SECOND
WEICHS (SCHMIDT)
SECOND
GUDERIAN
10 GOLIKOV
3 KREIZER
13 GORODNYANSKY

U. S. S. R.

40 PODLAS
SOUTHWEST
TIMOSHENKO

21 V.I. KUZNETSOV (Reconstituted)
(GORDOV)
38 MASLOV
6 MALINOVSKY

SOUTH
RUNDSTEDT (REICHENAU)
SIXTH
REICHENAU (PAULUS)
FIRST
KLEIST
SEVENTEENTH
STULPNAGEL (HOTH)
12 KOROTEEV
18 KULPAKCHY
37 LOPATIN (Reconstituted)
9 KHARITONOV
SOUTH
CHEREVICHENKO

RUM. THIRD
DUMITRESCU
ELEVENTH
MANSTEIN
56 RYZHOV (Independent)

RUM. FOURTH
CONSTANTINESCU
COASTAL
SOFRONOV
Odessa evacuated 16 October.
51 F.I. KUZNETSOV (Independent)
44 CHERNYAK

Rostov was captured on 20 Nov. but a Russian counterattack forced a German withdrawal on 2 Dec.

SEVASTOPOL
OKTYABRSKY
BLACK SEA FLEET
OKTYABRSKY

BATTLE OF MOSCOW
Situation 5 December, 1941

NINTH
STRAUSS
VI FÖRSTER
XLI REINHARDT
THIRD
HOTH (REINHARDT) (Under Ninth Army Command)
LVI
SCHAAL
V RUOFF
XLVI VIETINGHOFF
IX GEYER
VII FAHRMBACHER
XX
LVII KUNTZEN
XII SCHROTH
XIII FELBER
XLIII HEINRICI
XLVII LEMELSEN
SECOND
GUDERIAN
FOURTH
HOEPNER (Under Fourth Army Command)
CENTER
BOCK
FOURTH
KLUGE
XXIV SCHWEPPENBURG
LIII WEISSENBERGER
XLVIII

30 LELYUSHENKO
1SH V.I. KUZNETSOV
16 ROKOSSOVSKI
20 VLASOV
5 GOVOROV
33 EFREMOV
43 SOBENNIKOV
49 ZAKHARKIN
50 BOLDIN
10 GOLIKOV
3 KREIZER
WEST
ZHUKOV

7 Oct.
3 Oct.
1 Oct.
5 Dec.
16 Sept
26 Aug.

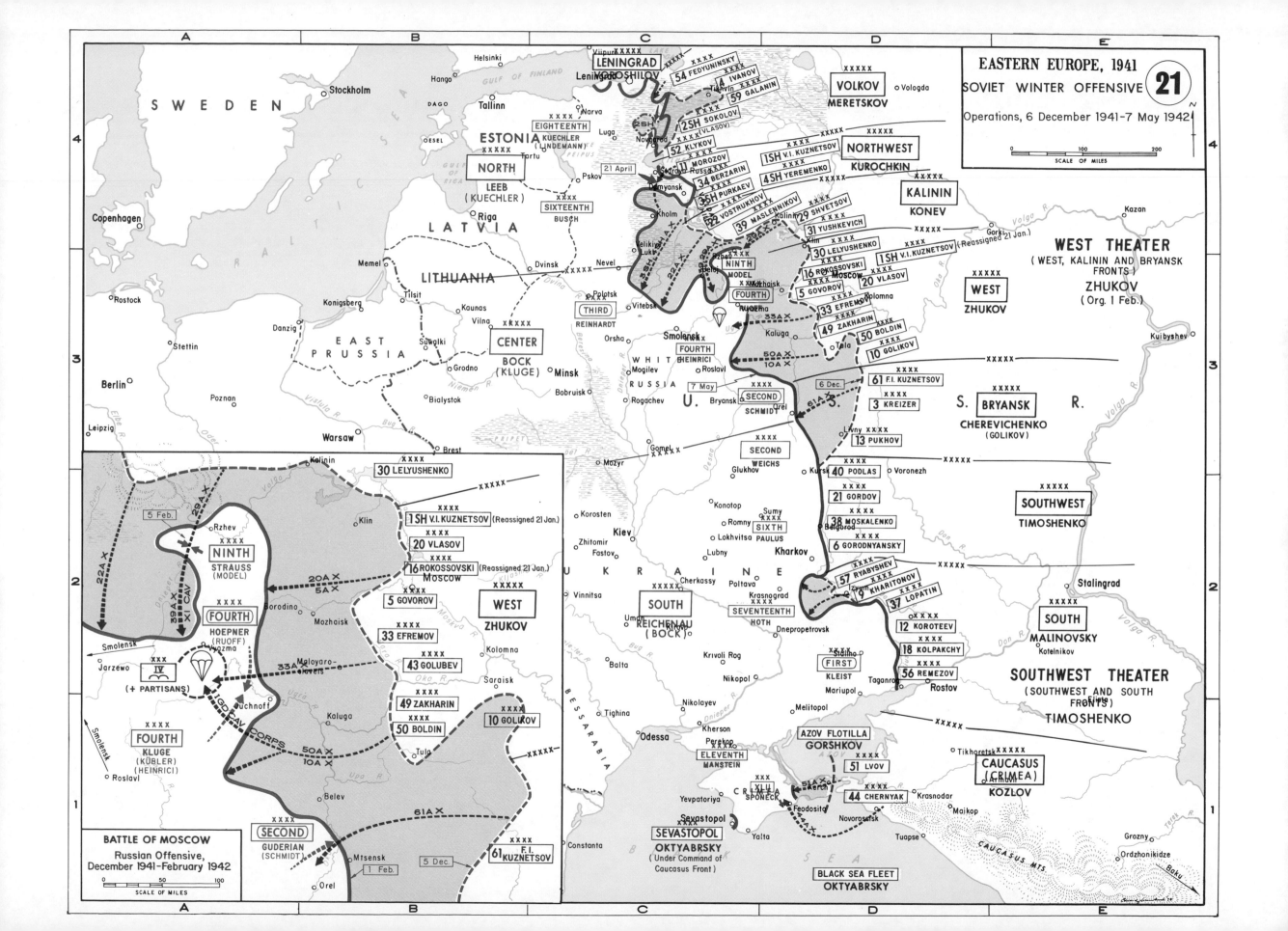

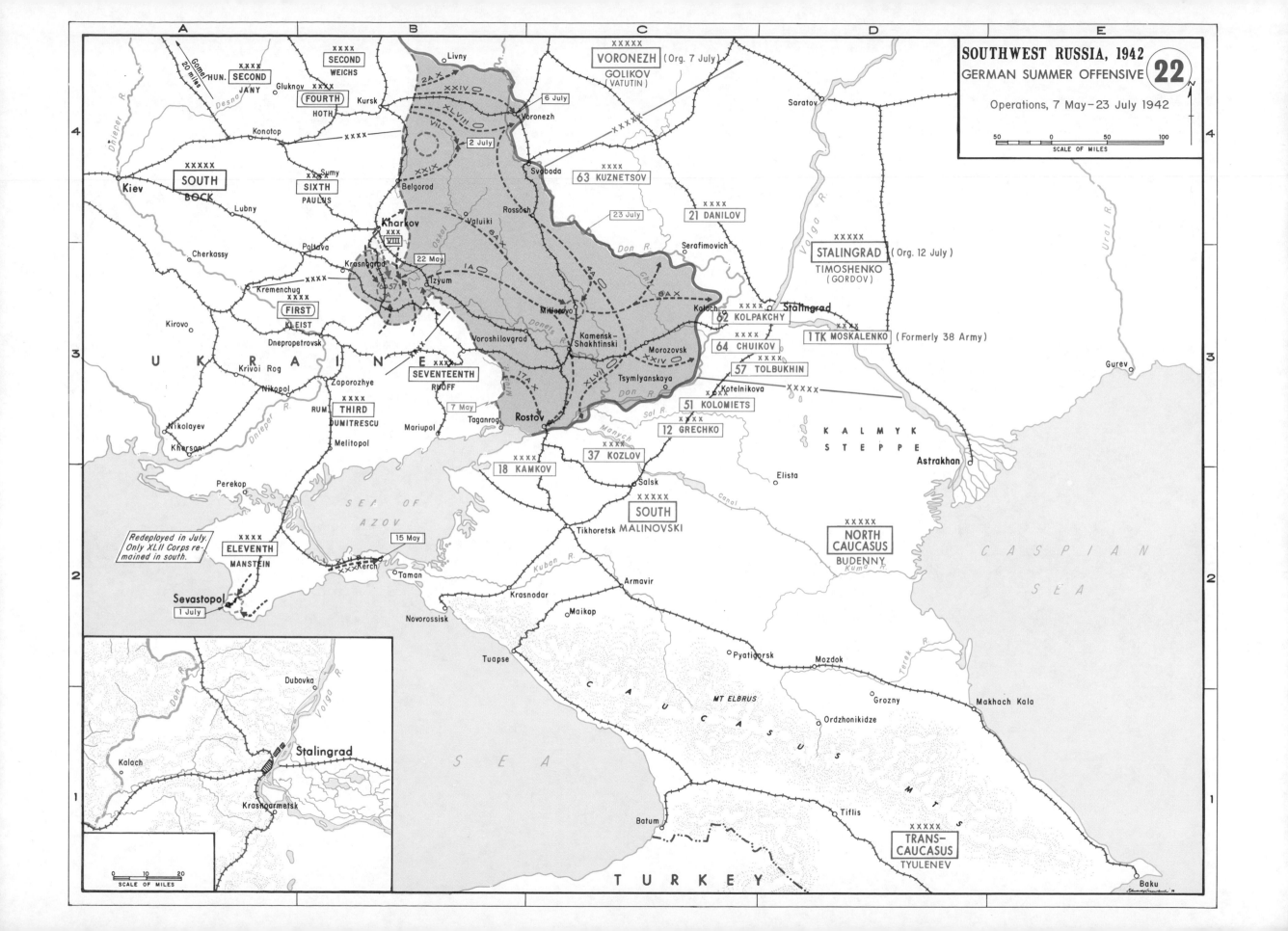

SOUTHWEST RUSSIA, 1942
GERMAN SUMMER OFFENSIVE
22

Operations, 7 May–23 July 1942

SCALE OF MILES
50 0 50 100

Gomel
20 miles

Dnieper R.
Desna R.

XXXX HUN. SECOND
JANY
XXXX SECOND
WEICHS
XXXXX VORONEZH (Org. 7 July)
GOLIKOV
(VATUTIN)

Gluknov
Glukhov
Konotop
Kursk
Livny
Voronezh
6 July
2 July
Saratov

XXXX FOURTH
HOTH

2 AX
XXIV
XLVIII
VII

Kiev
SOUTH
BOCK
Sumy
XXXX SIXTH
PAULUS
Belgorod
XXIX
Svoboda

XXXX 63 KUZNETSOV

Lubny
Kharkov
XXX VIII
Valuiki
Rossosh
23 July

Cherkassy
Poltava
Oskol R.

XXXX 21 DANILOV

Don R.
Serafimovich

Krasnograd
22 May
6 AX
Izyum
1 AX

Volga R.
Ural R.

XXXXX STALINGRAD (Org. 12 July)
TIMOSHENKO
(GORDOV)

Kremenchug
XXXX FIRST
KLEIST
57 A

4 AX
Gurev

Kirovo
Dnepropetrovsk
Krivoi Rog
Millerovo
Kalach
Stalingrad

XXXX 62 KOLPAKCHY

Nikopol
Zaporozhye
Voroshilovgrad
Kamensk-Shakhtinski
Donets R.
6 AX
Morozovsk

1 TK MOSKALENKO (Formerly 38 Army)

XXXX 64 CHUIKOV

U K R A I N E

XXXX SEVENTEENTH
RUOFF

17 AX
XLVII
Tsymlyanskaya
XXIV

XXXX 57 TOLBUKHIN

XXXX THIRD
DUMITRESCU
RUM.
7 May
Taganrog
Rostov
Don R.
Kotelnikova

XXXX 51 KOLOMIETS

Nikolayev
Kherson
Mariupol
Melitopol
Manych R.
Sal R.

XXXX 12 GRECHKO

K A L M Y K
S T E P P E

Perekop
SEA OF AZOV
XXXX 37 KOZLOV
Elista
Astrakhan

XXXX 18 KAMKOV
Salsk

Redeployed in July.
Only XLII Corps re-
mained in south.

XXXX ELEVENTH
MANSTEIN
15 May
Kerch
Taman

XXXXX SOUTH
MALINOVSKI
Tikhoretsk

XXXXX NORTH
CAUCASUS
BUDENNY

C A S P I A N
S E A

Sevastopol
1 July

Kuban R.
Armavir
Krasnodar

Kuma R.

Novorossisk
Maikop
Pyatigorsk
Mozdok

C A U C A S U S
MT ELBRUS
Grozny
Makhach Kala

Tuapse
Terek R.

S E A
Ordzhonikidze

Tiflis
M T S

Batum
Baku

XXXXX TRANS-
CAUCASUS
TYULENEV

T U R K E Y

Inset
Dubovka
Volga R.
Don R.
Kalach
Stalingrad
Krasnoarmetsk

SCALE OF MILES
0 10 20

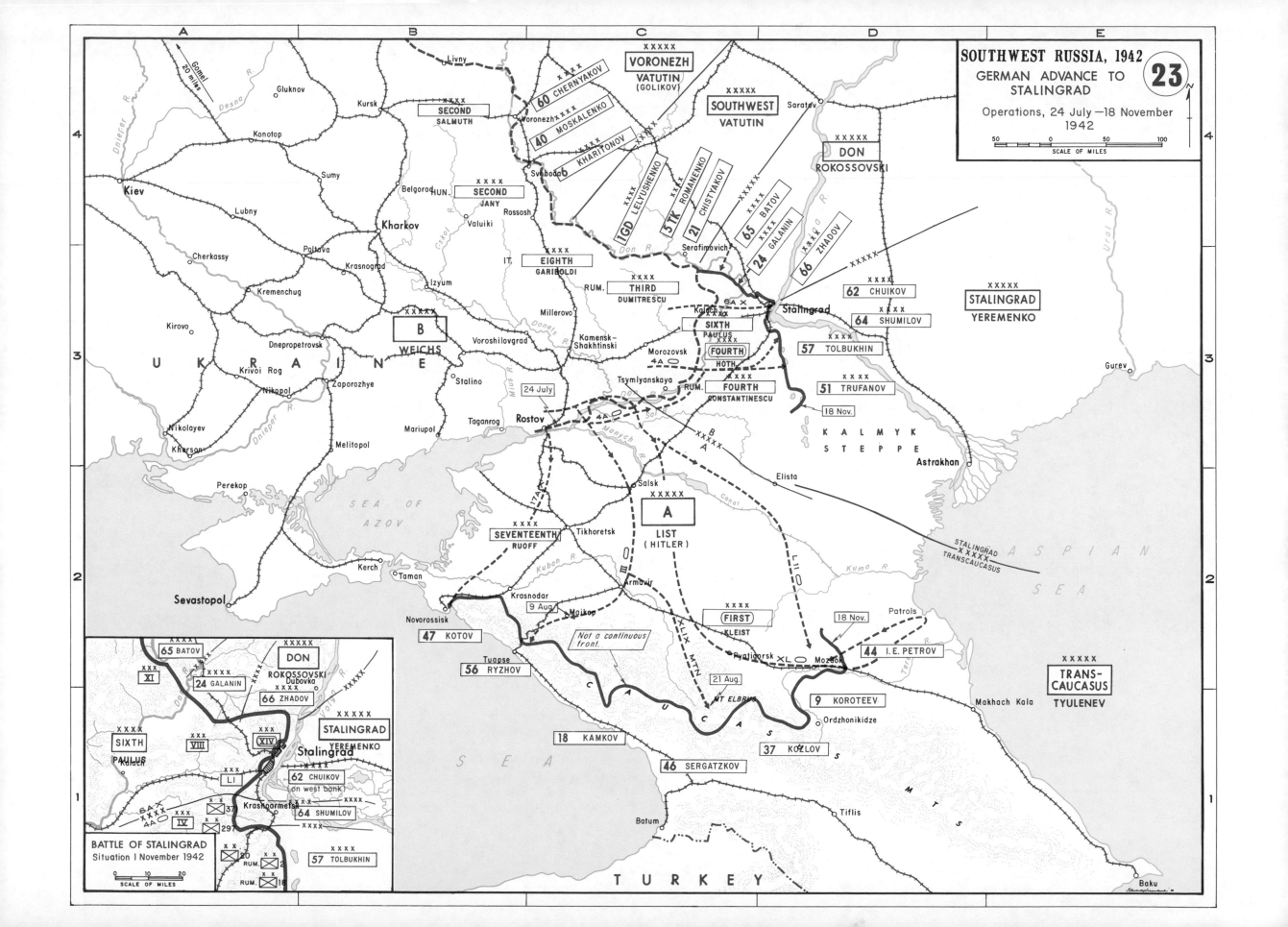

SOUTHWEST RUSSIA, 1942

23

GERMAN ADVANCE TO STALINGRAD

Operations, 24 July – 18 November 1942

SCALE OF MILES
50   0   50   100

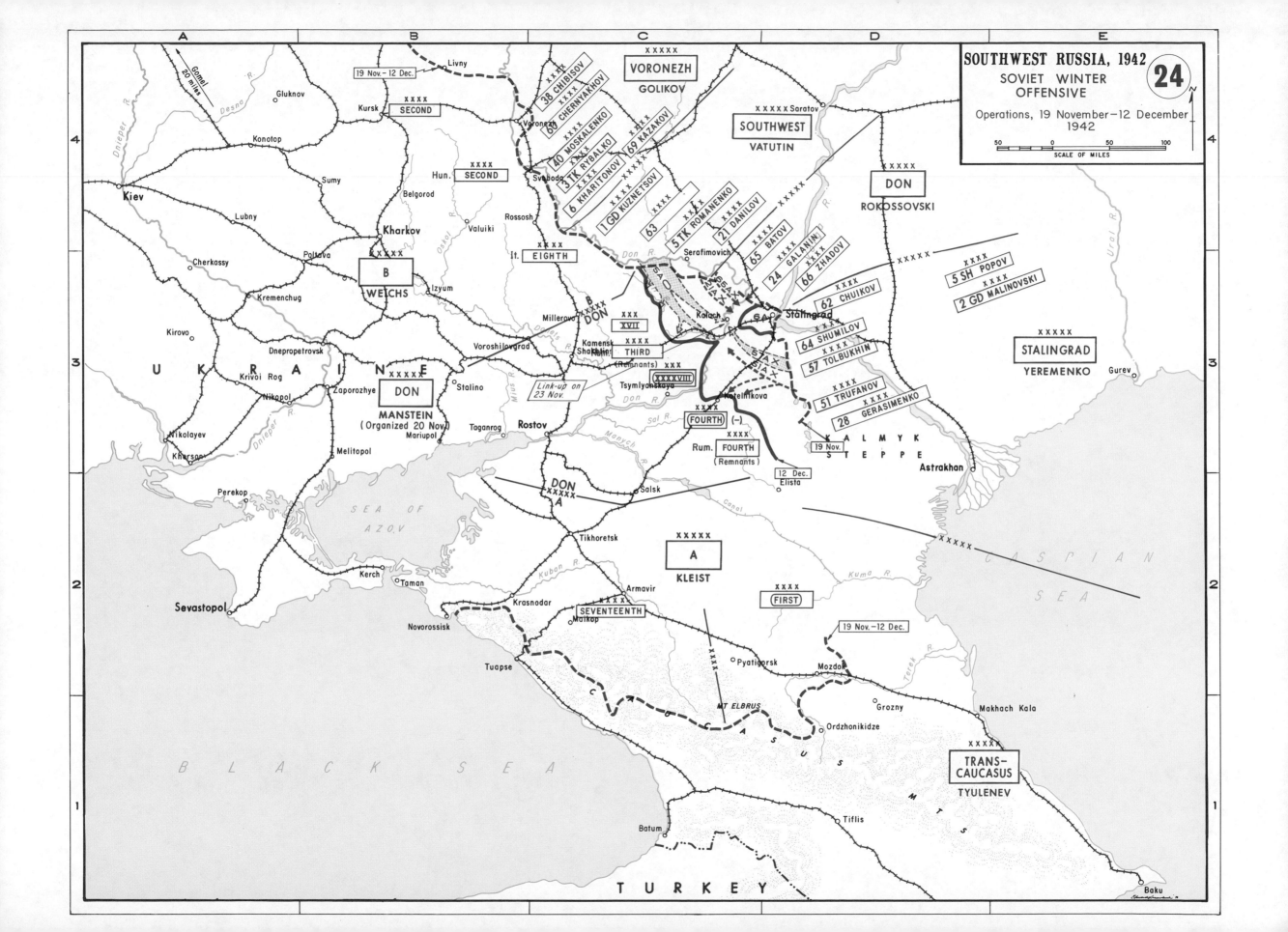

SOUTHWEST RUSSIA, 1942

24

SOVIET WINTER OFFENSIVE

Operations, 19 November–12 December 1942

SCALE OF MILES
50   0   50   100

VORONEZH
GOLIKOV

SOUTHWEST
VATUTIN

DON
ROKOSSOVSKI

STALINGRAD
YEREMENKO

B
WEICHS

DON
MANSTEIN
(Organized 20 Nov)

A
KLEIST

TRANS-
CAUCASUS
TYULENEV

19 Nov. – 12 Dec.

38 CHIBISOV
60 CHERNYAKHOV
40 MOSKALENKO
3 TK RYBALKO
69 KAZAKOV
6 KHARITONOV
1 GD KUZNETSOV
63
5 TK ROMANENKO
21 DANILOV
65 BATOV
24 GALANIN
66 ZHADOV
62 CHUIKOV
64 SHUMILOV
57 TOLBUKHIN
51 TRUFANOV
28 GERASIMENKO
5 SH POPOV
2 GD MALINOVSKI

SECOND
Hun. SECOND
It. EIGHTH
B DON
XVII
THIRD (Remnants)
XXXXVIII
FOURTH (—)
Rum. FOURTH (Remnants)
DON A
SEVENTEENTH
FIRST

Link-up on 23 Nov.

19 Nov.

12 Dec. Elista

KALMYK STEPPE

19 Nov. – 12 Dec.

UKRAINE

TURKEY

BLACK SEA

SEA OF AZOV

CASPIAN SEA

CAUCASUS MTS

Place names

Gomel, Desna R., Livny, Gluknov, Konotop, Kursk, Voronezh, Sumy, Belgorod, Kiev, Kharkov, Lubny, Valuiki, Rossosh, Svoboda, Cherkassy, Poltava, Izyum, Kremenchug, Kirovo, Dnepropetrovsk, Krivoi Rog, Stalino, Voroshilovgrad, Nikopol, Zaporozhye, Nikolayev, Kherson, Melitopol, Perekop, Kerch, Taman, Sevastopol, Taganrog, Rostov, Salsk, Tikhoretsk, Krasnodar, Maikop, Novorossisk, Tuapse, Batum, Pyatigorsk, Mozdok, Grozny, Ordzhonikidze, Makhach Kala, Tiflis, Baku, Astrakhan, Gurev, Saratov, Serafimovich, Kalach, Stalingrad, Millerovo, Kamensk, Shakhtin, Tsymlyanskaya, Kotelnikova, Elista

Don R., Oskol R., Donets R., Mius R., Manych R., Sal R., Kuban R., Kuma R., Terek R., Dnieper R., Ural R., Canal

MT ELBRUS

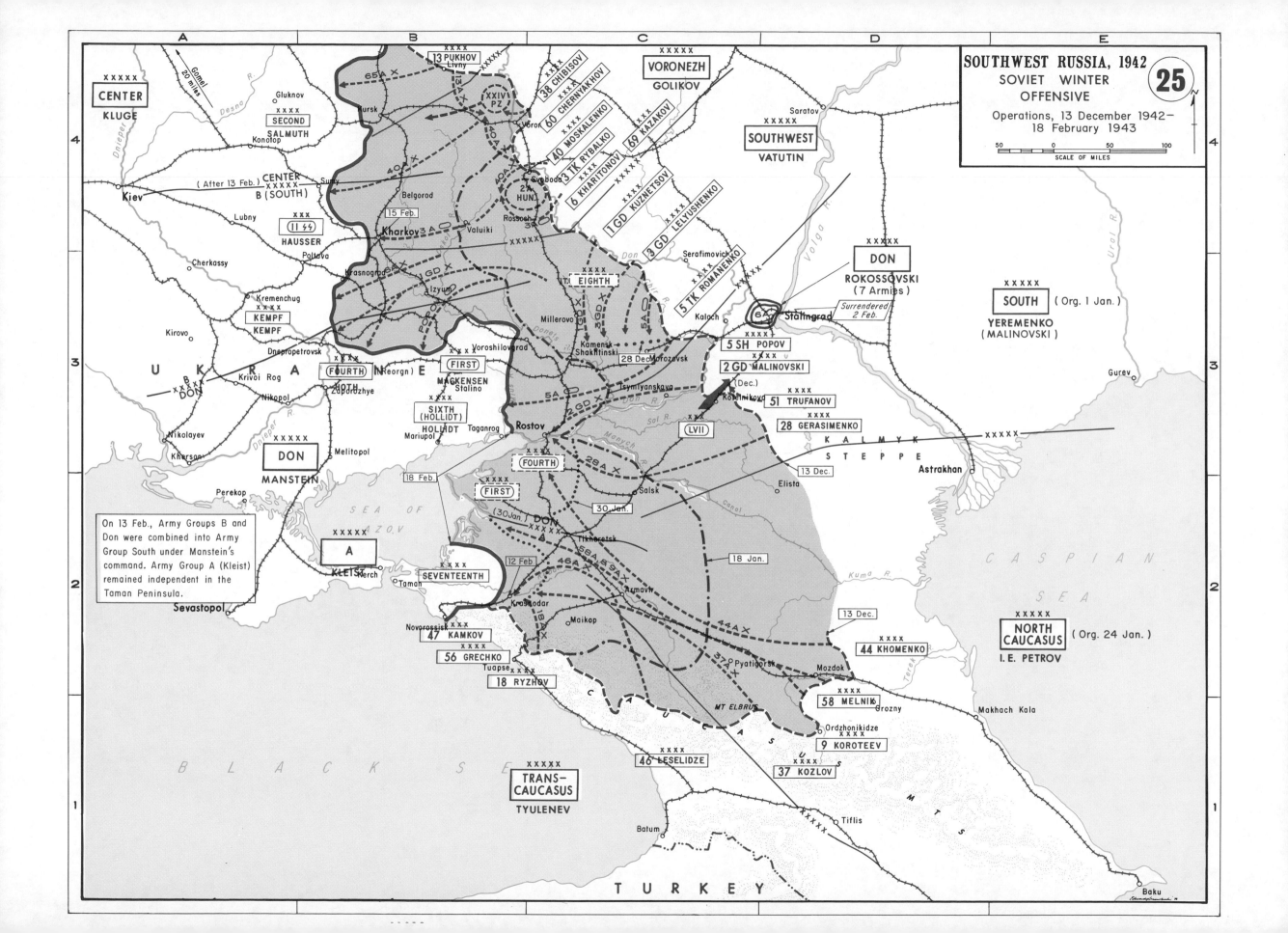

SOUTHWEST RUSSIA, 1942
SOVIET WINTER
OFFENSIVE
25

Operations, 13 December 1942–
18 February 1943

SCALE OF MILES
50   0   50   100

On 13 Feb., Army Groups B and
Don were combined into Army
Group South under Manstein's
command. Army Group A (Kleist)
remained independent in the
Taman Peninsula.

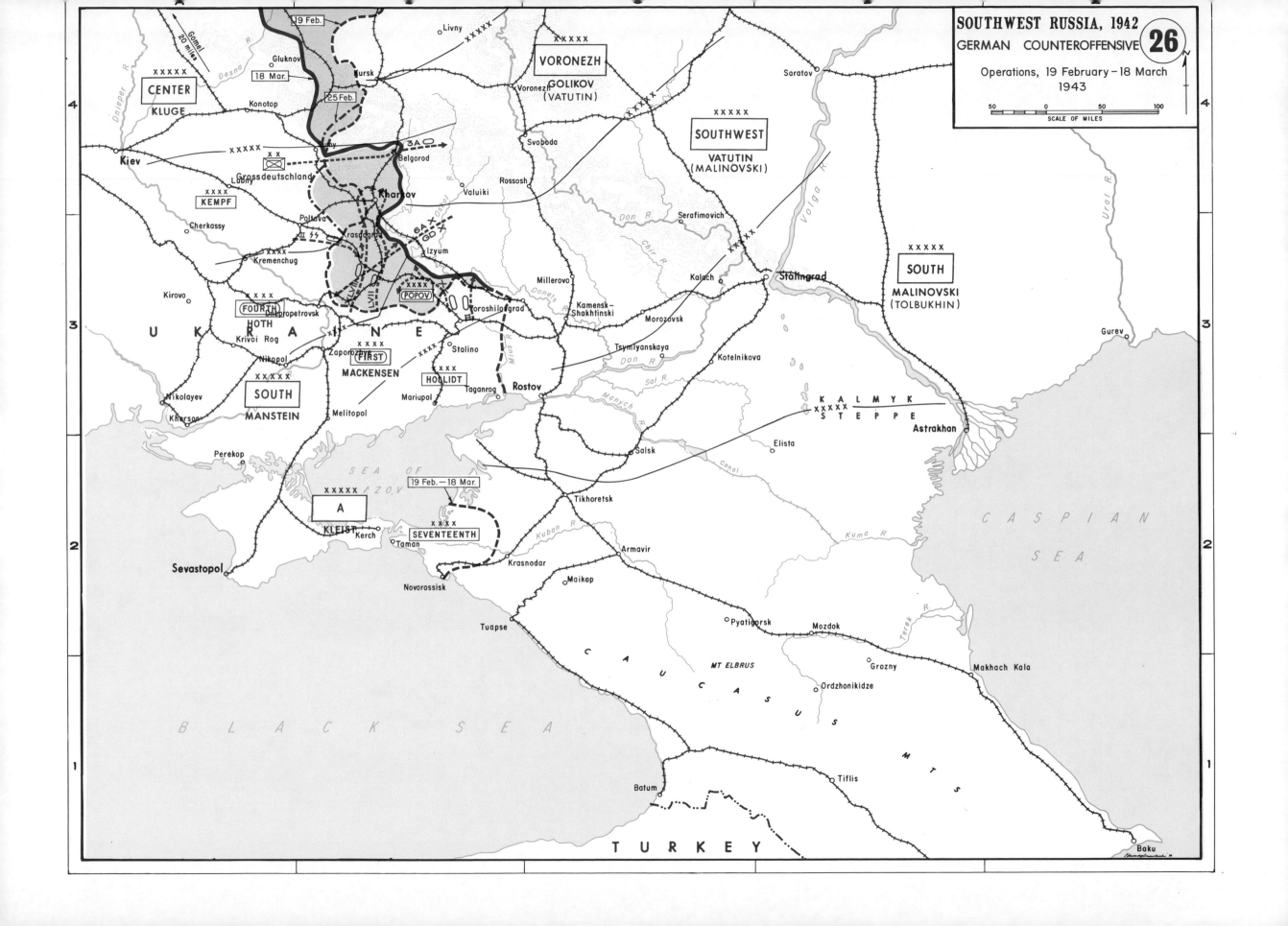

SOUTHWEST RUSSIA, 1942
GERMAN COUNTEROFFENSIVE
26
Operations, 19 February – 18 March
1943

SCALE OF MILES
50   0   50   100

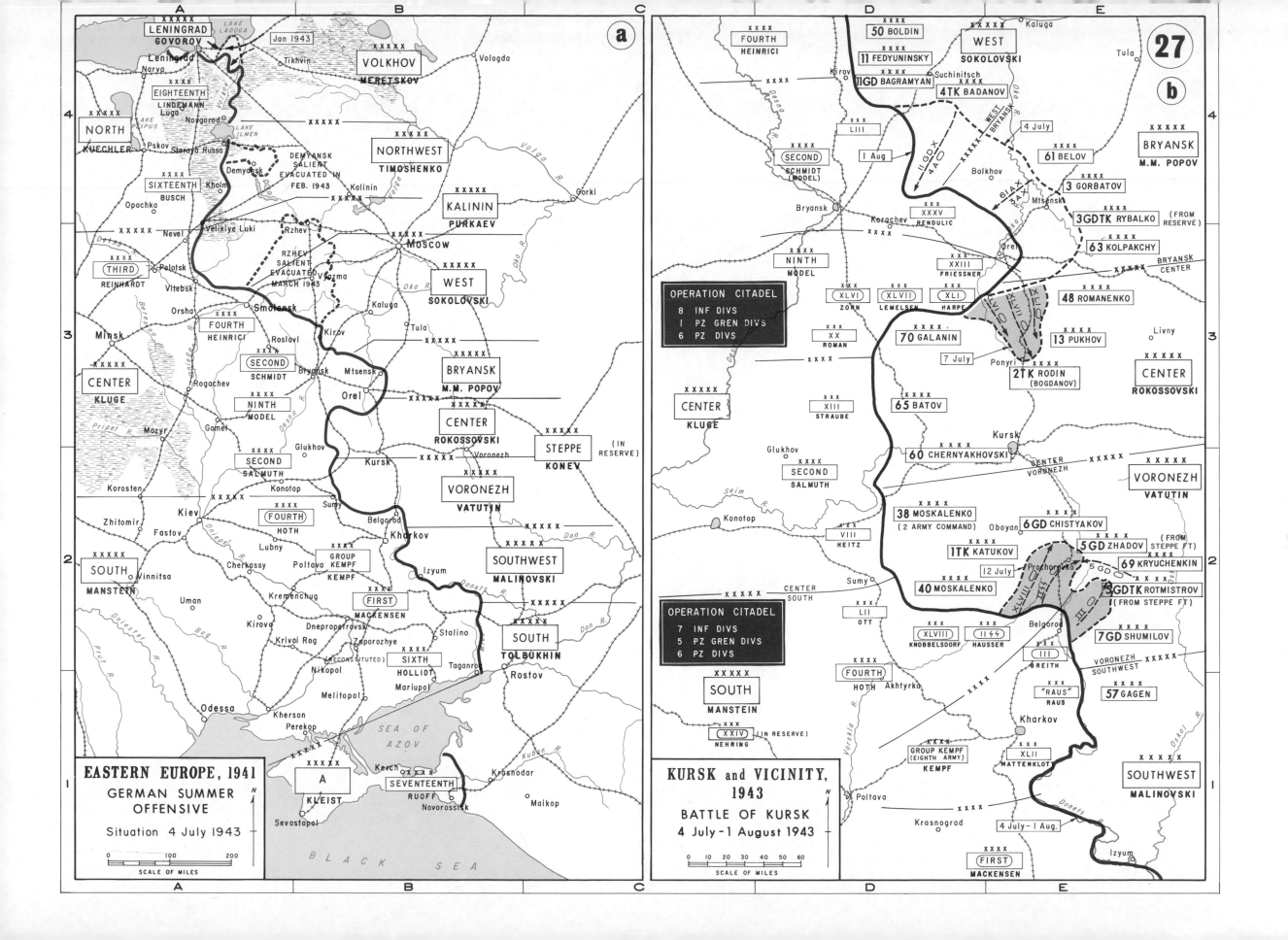

a

LENINGRAD
GOVOROV

Leningrad

Narva

Jan 1943

Tikhvin

VOLKHOV
MERETSKOV

Vologda

EIGHTEENTH
LINDEMANN
Luga

Novgorod

NORTH
KUECHLER

Pskov

Staraya Russa

LAKE ILMEN

NORTHWEST
TIMOSHENKO

Gorki

Opochka

Kholm

DEMYANSK SALIENT EVACUATED IN FEB. 1943

Demyansk

Kalinin

KALININ
PURKAEV

SIXTEENTH
BUSCH

Nevel

Velikiye Luki

Rzhev

Moscow

THIRD
REINHARDT

Polotsk

Vitebsk

RZHEV SALIENT EVACUATED MARCH 1943

Vyazma

Oka R.

WEST
SOKOLOVSKY

Minsk

Orsha

Smolensk

Kirov

Tula

CENTER
KLUGE

FOURTH
HEINRICI

Roslavl

SECOND
SCHMIDT

Bryansk

Mtsensk

BRYANSK
M.M. POPOV

Rogachev

NINTH
MODEL

Orel

Gomel

Glukhov

CENTER
ROKOSSOVSKI

SECOND
SALMUTH

Kursk

Voronezh

STEPPE
KONEV

(IN RESERVE)

Korosten

Konotop

Sumy

VORONEZH
VATUTIN

Kiev

FOURTH
HOTH

Belgorod

Zhitomir

Fastov

Lubny

Kharkov

Izyum

SOUTHWEST
MALINOVSKI

SOUTH
MANSTEIN

Vinnitsa

Cherkassy

Poltava

GROUP KEMPF
KEMPF

Don R.

Uman

Kirovo

Kremenchug

FIRST
MACKENSEN

Krivoi Rog

Dnepropetrovsk

Stalino

SOUTH
TOLBUKHIN

Nikopol

Zaporozhye

(RECONSTITUTED)
SIXTH
HOLLIDT

Taganrog

Rostov

Odessa

Melitopol

Mariupol

Kherson

Perekop

SEA OF AZOV

Kerch

Krasnodar

A
KLEIST

Sevastopol

SEVENTEENTH
RUOFF

Novorossisk

Maikop

Kuban R.

BLACK SEA

EASTERN EUROPE, 1941

GERMAN SUMMER OFFENSIVE

Situation 4 July 1943

0   100   200

SCALE OF MILES

27

b

FOURTH
HEINRICI

50 BOLDIN

11 FEDYUNINSKY

WEST
SOKOLOVSKI

Kaluga

Tula

11GD BAGRAMYAN

4TK BADANOV

SECOND
SCHMIDT (MODEL)

LIII

1 Aug

II GD X
4 A O

WEST
BRYANSK

4 July

61 AX
4A X

61 BELOV

BRYANSK
M.M. POPOV

Bryansk

Karachev

Bolkhov

3 GORBATOV

Mtsensk

3GDTK RYBALKO

(FROM RESERVE)

NINTH
MODEL

XXXV
RENDULIC

Orel

63 KOLPAKCHY

BRYANSK CENTER

XXIII
FRIESSNER

OPERATION CITADEL
8 INF DIVS
1 PZ GREN DIVS
6 PZ DIVS

XLVI
ZORN

XLVII
LEMELSEN

XLI
HARPE

48 ROMANENKO

XX
ROMAN

70 GALANIN

13 PUKHOV

Livny

CENTER
KLUGE

7 July

Ponyri

2TK RODIN
(BOGDANOV)

CENTER
ROKOSSOVSKI

XIII
STRAUBE

65 BATOV

Kursk

Glukhov

SECOND
SALMUTH

60 CHERNYAKHOVSKI

CENTER
VORONEZH

VORONEZH
VATUTIN

Seim R.

38 MOSKALENKO
(2 ARMY COMMAND)

Oboyan

6GD CHISTYAKOV

Konotop

VIII
HEITZ

1TK KATUKOV

5GD ZHADOV

(FROM STEPPE FT)

Sumy

12 July

Prochorovka

69 KRYUCHENKIN

5 GD O

CENTER SOUTH

40 MOSKALENKO

XLVIII

5GDTK ROTMISTROV

(FROM STEPPE FT)

LII
OTT

XLVIII
KNOBBELSDORF

II SS
HAUSSER

Belgorod

7GD SHUMILOV

III
BREITH

VORONEZH SOUTHWEST

OPERATION CITADEL
7 INF DIVS
5 PZ GREN DIVS
6 PZ DIVS

FOURTH
HOTH

Akhtyrka

"RAUS"
RAUS

57 GAGEN

SOUTH
MANSTEIN

XXIV
NEHRING

(IN RESERVE)

Kharkov

GROUP KEMPF
(EIGHTH ARMY)
KEMPF

XLII
MATTENKLOTT

SOUTHWEST
MALINOVSKI

Poltava

Krasnograd

4 July–1 Aug.

Izyum

FIRST
MACKENSEN

KURSK and VICINITY, 1943

BATTLE OF KURSK
4 July–1 August 1943

0 10 20 30 40 50 60

SCALE OF MILES

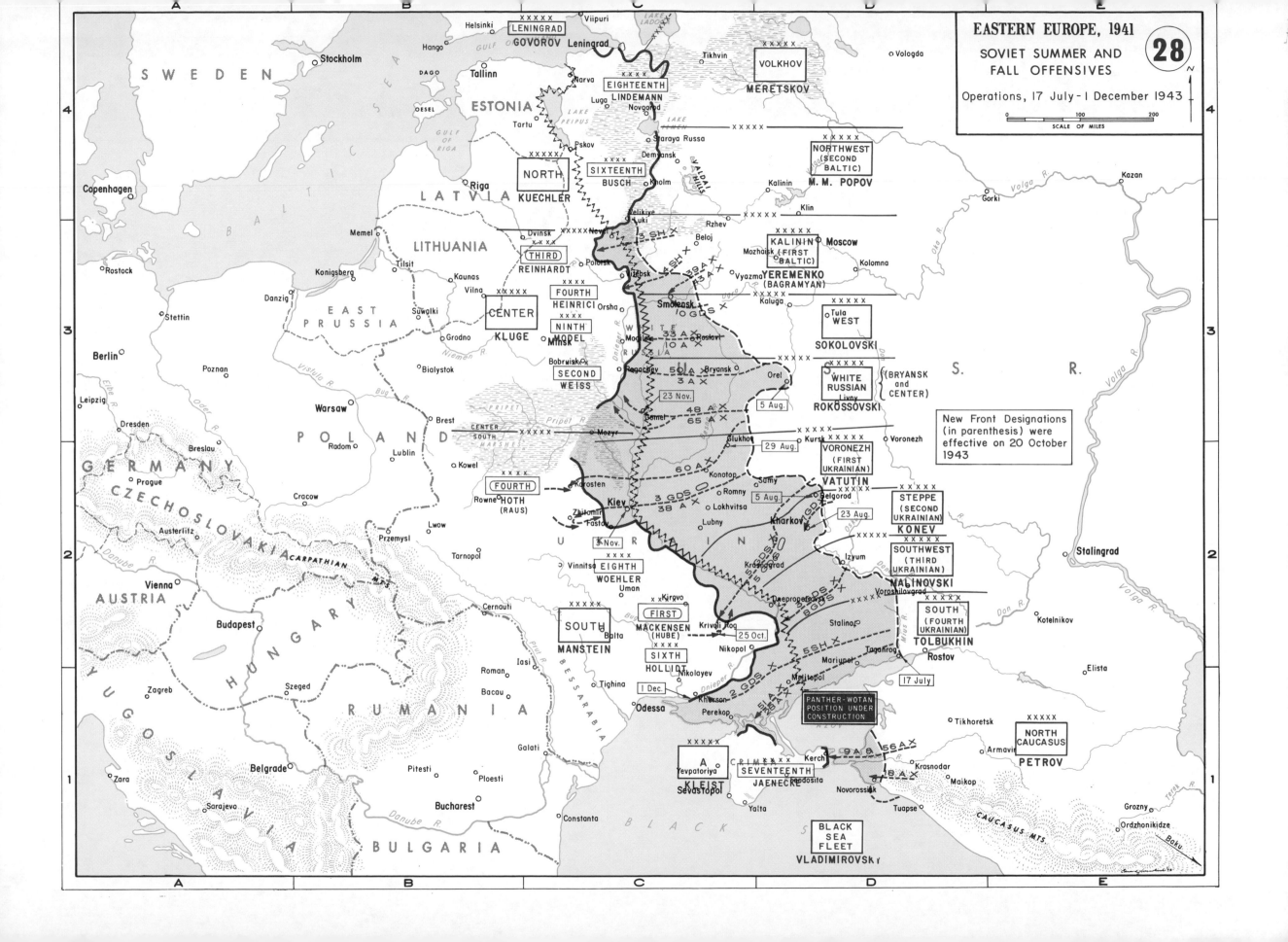

EASTERN EUROPE, 1941

SOVIET SUMMER AND FALL OFFENSIVES

Operations, 17 July – 1 December 1943

28

0   100   200
SCALE OF MILES

New Front Designations
(in parenthesis) were
effective on 20 October
1943

PANTHER-WOTAN
POSITION UNDER
CONSTRUCTION

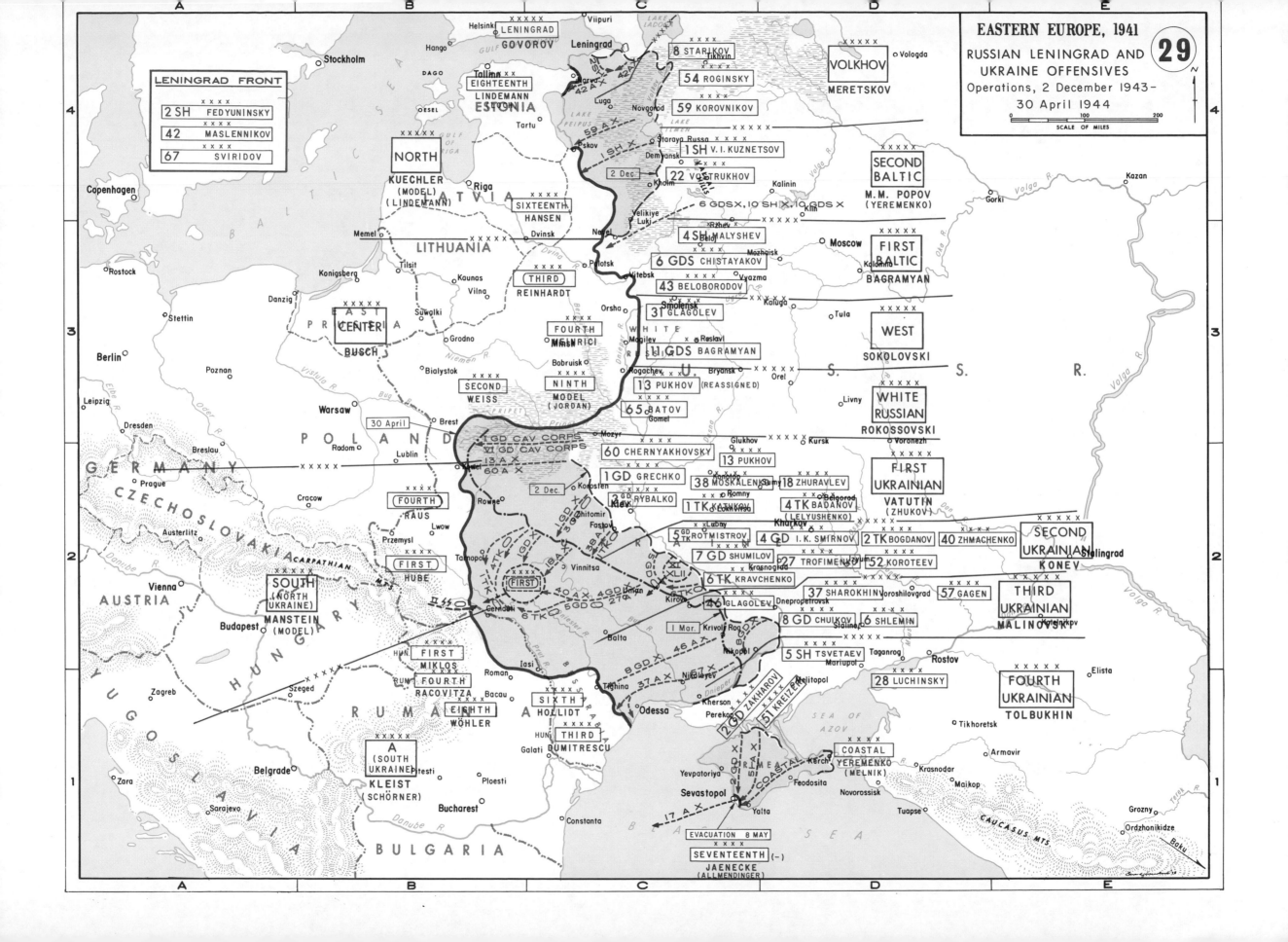

EASTERN EUROPE, 1941
RUSSIAN LENINGRAD AND
UKRAINE OFFENSIVES
Operations, 2 December 1943 –
30 April 1944

29

SCALE OF MILES
0   100   200

LENINGRAD FRONT

2 SH	FEDYUNINSKY
42	MASLENNIKOV
67	SVIRIDOV

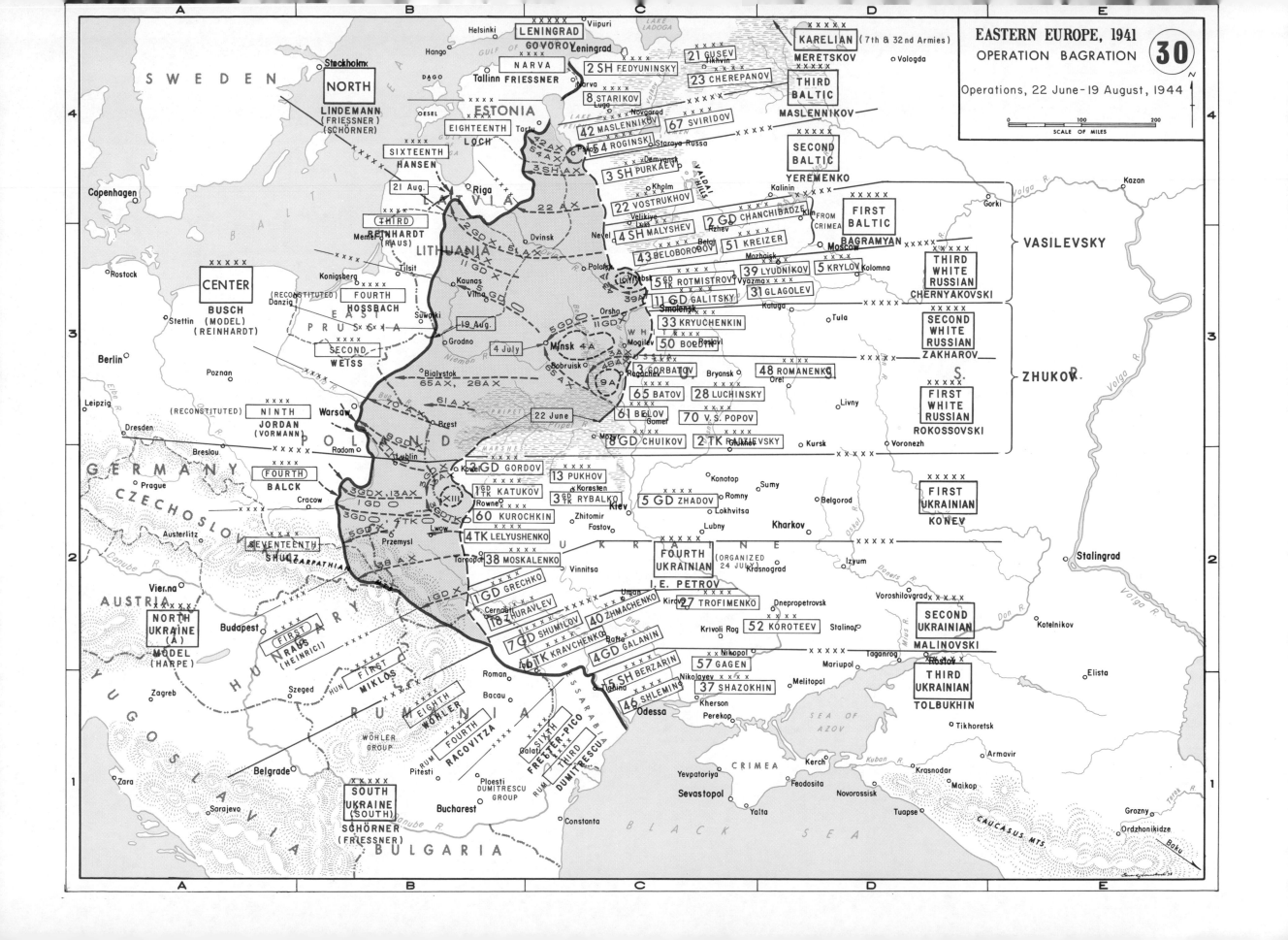

EASTERN EUROPE, 1941
OPERATION BAGRATION
30

Operations, 22 June–19 August, 1944

0   100   200
SCALE OF MILES

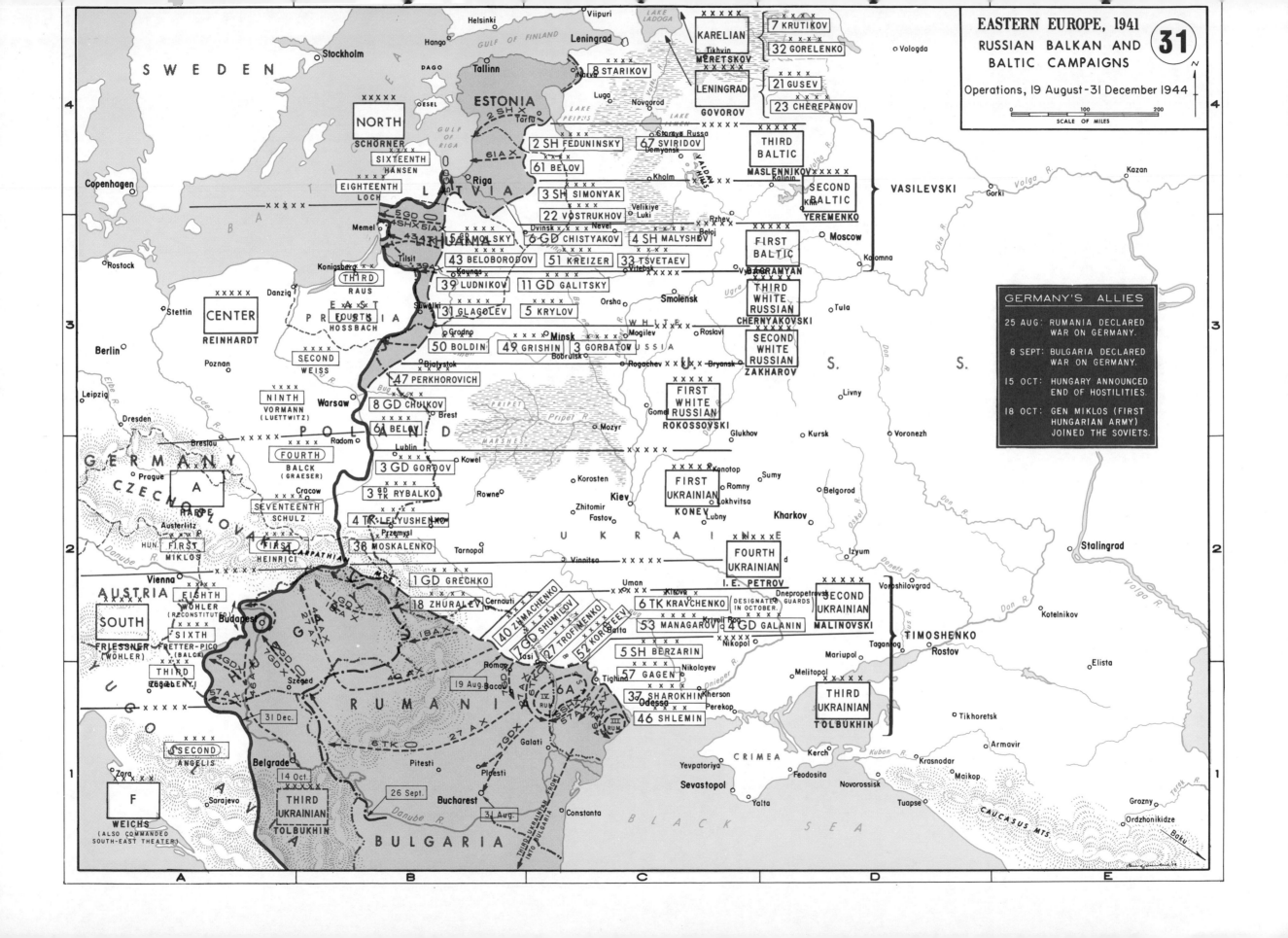

SCALE OF MILES
0   100   200

GERMANY'S ALLIES

25 AUG: RUMANIA DECLARED
WAR ON GERMANY.

8 SEPT: BULGARIA DECLARED
WAR ON GERMANY.

15 OCT: HUNGARY ANNOUNCED
END OF HOSTILITIES.

18 OCT: GEN MIKLOS (FIRST
HUNGARIAN ARMY)
JOINED THE SOVIETS.

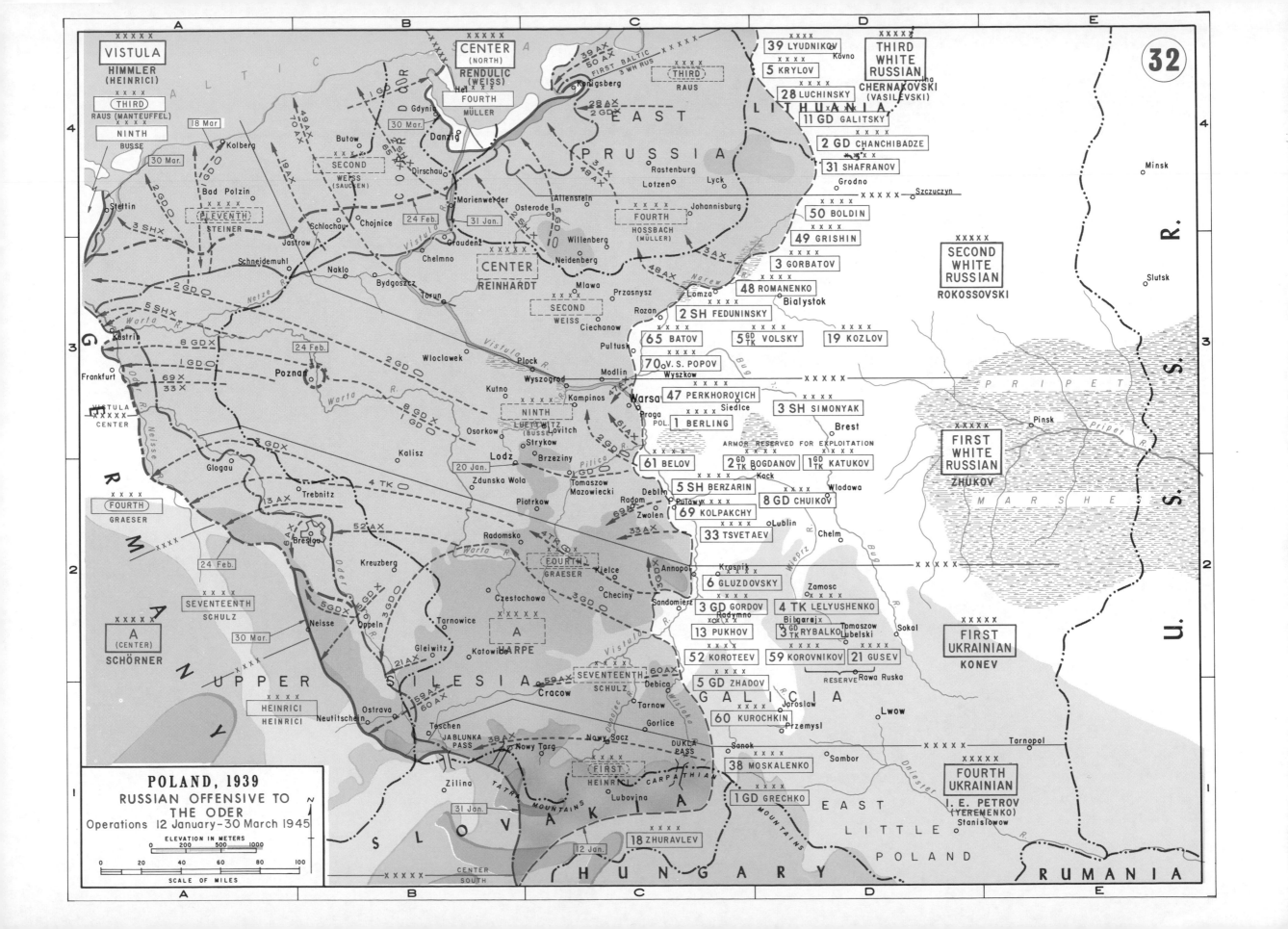

POLAND, 1939
RUSSIAN OFFENSIVE TO
THE ODER
Operations 12 January-30 March 1945

ELEVATION IN METERS
200   500   1000

0   20   40   60   80   100
SCALE OF MILES

32

VISTULA
HIMMLER (HEINRICI)

THIRD
RAUS (MANTEUFFEL)

NINTH
BUSSE

CENTER
(NORTH)
RENDULIC (WEISS)

FOURTH
MÜLLER

THIRD
RAUS

39 LYUDNIKOV
5 KRYLOV
28 LUCHINSKY
11 GD GALITSKY
2 GD CHANCHIBADZE
31 SHAFRANOV

THIRD
WHITE
RUSSIAN
CHERNAKOVSKI
(VASILEVSKI)

SECOND
WEISS (SAUCKEN)

ELEVENTH
STEINER

CENTER
REINHARDT

SECOND
WEISS

50 BOLDIN
49 GRISHIN
3 GORBATOV
48 ROMANENKO

FOURTH
HOSSBACH
(MÜLLER)

SECOND
WHITE
RUSSIAN
ROKOSSOVSKI

2 SH FEDUNINSKY
65 BATOV
5 GD TK VOLSKY
19 KOZLOV
70 V. S. POPOV

47 PERKHOROVICH
3 SH SIMONYAK
1 BERLING

NINTH
LUETTWITZ
(BUSSE)

ARMOR RESERVED FOR EXPLOITATION

FIRST
WHITE
RUSSIAN
ZHUKOV

61 BELOV
2 GD TK BOGDANOV
1 GD TK KATUKOV

5 SH BERZARIN
8 GD CHUIKOV
69 KOLPAKCHY
33 TSVETAEV

FOURTH
GRAESER

VISTULA
CENTER

FOURTH
GRAESER

6 GLUZDOVSKY
3 GD GORDOV
4 TK LELYUSHENKO
13 PUKHOV
3 GD TK RYBALKO
52 KOROTEEV
59 KOROVNIKOV
21 GUSEV
5 GD ZHADOV
60 KUROCHKIN
38 MOSKALENKO
1 GD GRECHKO

FIRST
UKRAINIAN
KONEV

SEVENTEENTH
SCHULZ

A (CENTER)
SCHÖRNER

HEINRICI
HEINRICI

A
HARPE

SEVENTEENTH
SCHULZ

FIRST
HEINRICI

RESERVE

FIRST
UKRAINIAN
KONEV

FOURTH
UKRAINIAN
I. E. PETROV
(YEREMENKO)

18 ZHURAVLEV

CENTER
SOUTH

BALTIC   SEA

EAST   PRUSSIA

LITHUANIA

GERMANY

UPPER   SILESIA

SLOVAKIA

HUNGARY

GALICIA

EAST
LITTLE
POLAND

RUMANIA

U.   S.   S.   R.

PRIPET   MARSHES

CARPATHIAN   MOUNTAINS

TATRA MOUNTAINS

Minsk
Slutsk
Szczuczyn
Grodno
Kovno
Königsberg
Hel
Danzig
Gdynia
Butow
Kolberg
Stettin
Bad Polzin
Schlochau
Jastrow
Chojnice
Schneidemuhl
Naklo
Bydgoszcz
Torun
Marienwerder
Graudenz
Chelmno
Dirschau
Osterode
Allenstein
Rastenburg
Lotzen
Lyck
Johannisburg
Willenberg
Neidenberg
Mlawa
Przasnysz
Lomza
Bialystok
Rozan
Ciechanow
Pultusk
Wyszkow
Wyszogrod
Modlin
Plock
Wloclawek
Frankfurt
Kustrin
Poznan
Kutno
Kampinos
Warsaw
Praga
Pol.
Siedlce
Brest
Wlodawa
Kock
Osorkow
Lowicovitch
Strykow
Lodz
Brzeziny
Zdunska Wola
Tomaszow Mazowiecki
Piotrkow
Deblin
Pulawy
Radom
Zwolen
Lublin
Chelm
Kalisz
Glogau
Trebnitz
Breslau
Kreuzberg
Radomsko
Warta
Kielce
Checiny
Annopol
Sandomierz
Krasnik
Zamosc
Czestochowa
Tarnowice
Oppeln
Neisse
Gleiwitz
Katowice
Radymno
Bilgaraj
Tomaszow Lubelski
Sokal
Rawa Ruska
Cracow
Debica
Tarnow
Jaroslaw
Przemysl
Lwow
Tarnopol
Sanok
Sambor
Neutitschein
Ostrava
Teschen
Jablunka Pass
Nowy Targ
Nowy Sacz
Gorlice
Dukla Pass
Zilina
Lubovina
Stanislowow
Dniester R.

18 Mar
30 Mar
24 Feb
31 Jan
24 Feb
24 Feb
20 Jan
30 Mar
30 Mar
12 Jan
31 Jan

N

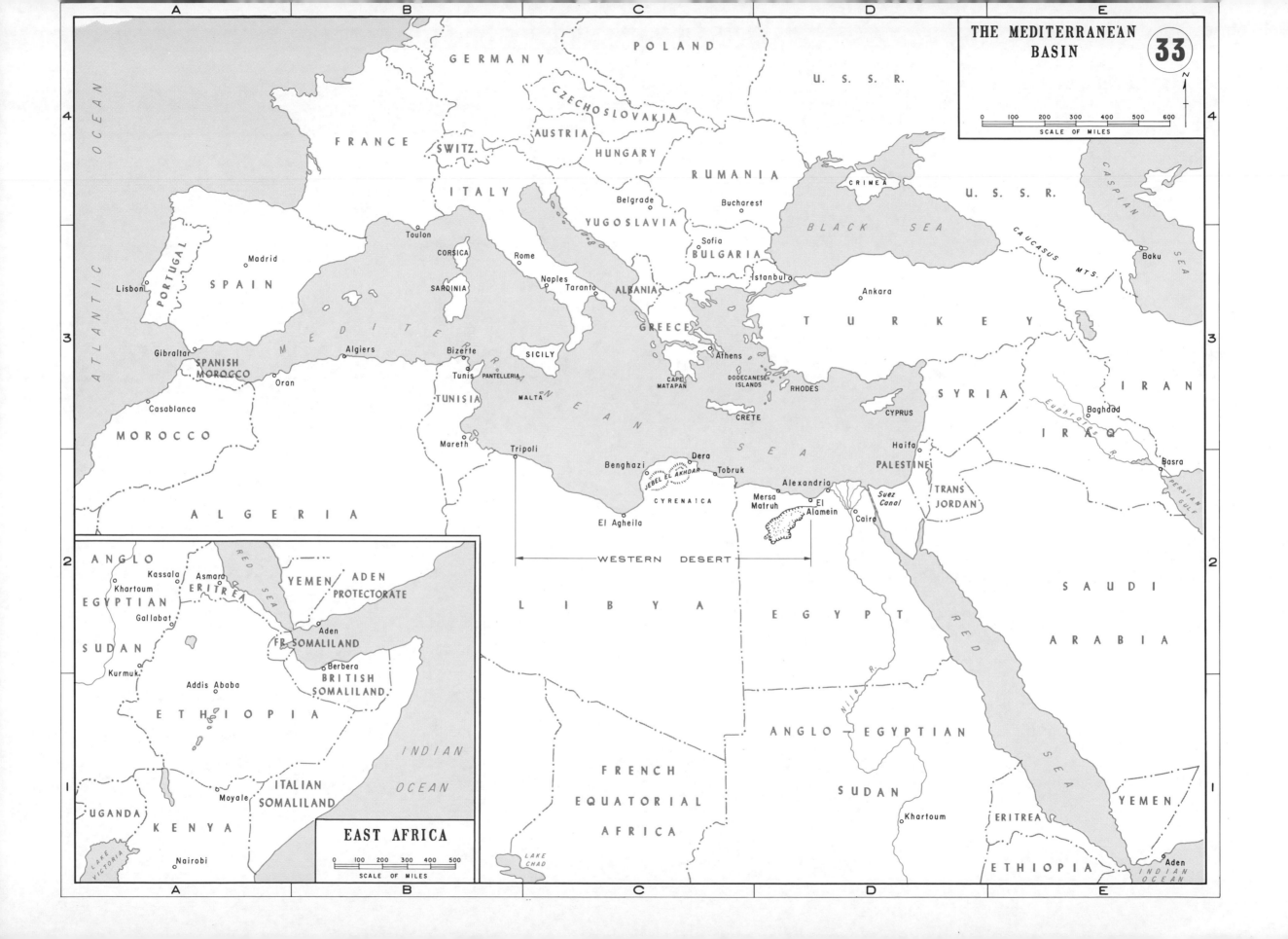

THE MEDITERRANEAN
BASIN

33

SCALE OF MILES
0 100 200 300 400 500 600

POLAND

GERMANY

CZECHOSLOVAKIA

AUSTRIA

HUNGARY

FRANCE

SWITZ.

ITALY

RUMANIA

U. S. S. R.

CRIMEA

U. S. S. R.

Belgrade

Bucharest

BLACK   SEA

CAUCASUS   MTS.

YUGOSLAVIA

Toulon

CORSICA

Rome

Sofia

BULGARIA

Baku

CASPIAN SEA

PORTUGAL

Madrid

SPAIN

SARDINIA

Naples

Taranto

ALBANIA

GREECE

Istanbul

Ankara

TURKEY

IRAN

Lisbon

ATLANTIC   OCEAN

Gibraltar

Algiers

Bizerte

SICILY

Athens

DODECANESE
ISLANDS

RHODES

SYRIA

Baghdad

SPANISH
MOROCCO

MEDITE

CAPE
MATAPAN

Oran

Tunis

PANTELLERIA

CRETE

CYPRUS

IRAQ

Basra

Casablanca

TUNISIA

MALTA

RRANEAN
SEA

Haifa

MOROCCO

Mareth

Tripoli

Benghazi

Dera

Tobruk

PALESTINE

PERSIAN GULF

Alexandria

TRANS
JORDAN

ALGERIA

JEBEL EL AKHDAR

Mersa
Matruh

Suez
Canal

El Agheila

CYRENAICA

El
Alamein

Cairo

WESTERN   DESERT

L I B Y A

E G Y P T

SAUDI

ARABIA

RED   SEA

FRENCH

EQUATORIAL

AFRICA

SUDAN

ANGLO - EGYPTIAN

Khartoum

ERITREA

YEMEN

LAKE
CHAD

ETHIOPIA

Aden

INDIAN
OCEAN

East Africa inset:

ANGLO

EGYPTIAN

SUDAN

Kassala

Khartoum

Gallabat

Kurmuk

RED SEA

Asmara

ERITREA

YEMEN

ADEN
PROTECTORATE

Aden

FR. SOMALILAND

Berbera

BRITISH
SOMALILAND

Addis Ababa

ETHIOPIA

INDIAN
OCEAN

UGANDA

KENYA

Moyale

ITALIAN
SOMALILAND

LAKE
VICTORIA

Nairobi

EAST AFRICA

SCALE OF MILES
0 100 200 300 400 500

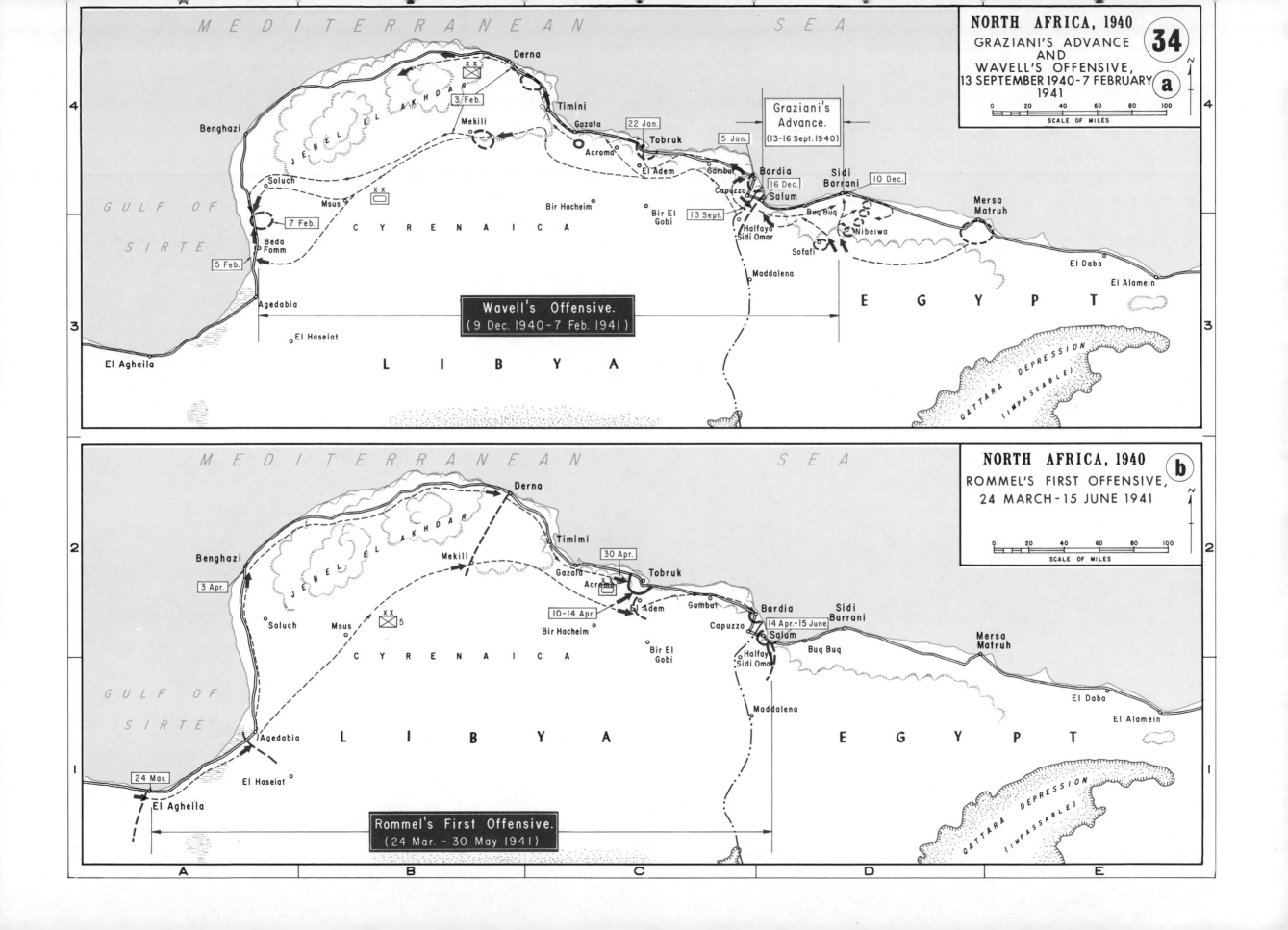

Map a (top):

MEDITERRANEAN SEA

NORTH AFRICA, 1940
GRAZIANI'S ADVANCE
AND
WAVELL'S OFFENSIVE,
13 SEPTEMBER 1940-7 FEBRUARY 1941

34 **a**

SCALE OF MILES
0 20 40 60 80 100

Derna
Timini
Benghazi
Gazala
3 Feb.
22 Jan.
Mekili
Tobruk
Acroma
Graziani's Advance.
(13-16 Sept. 1940)
5 Jan.
JEBEL EL AKHDAR
El Adem
Gambut
Bardia
Sidi Barrani
10 Dec.
Soluch
Msus
Capuzzo
Salum
16 Dec.
Mersa Matruh
Bir Hacheim
Bir El Gobi
13 Sept.
Buq Buq
CYRENAICA
7 Feb.
Halfaya
Sidi Omar
Nibeiwa
El Daba
Beda Fomm
Sofafi
El Alamein
5 Feb.
Maddalena
EGYPT
Agedabia
Wavell's Offensive.
(9 Dec. 1940-7 Feb. 1941)
El Haseiat
GULF OF SIRTE
LIBYA
El Agheila
QATTARA DEPRESSION
(IMPASSABLE)

Map b (bottom):

MEDITERRANEAN SEA

NORTH AFRICA, 1940
ROMMEL'S FIRST OFFENSIVE,
24 MARCH-15 JUNE 1941

b

SCALE OF MILES
0 20 40 60 80 100

Derna
Timimi
Benghazi
Mekili
30 Apr.
Gazala
Acroma
Tobruk
3 Apr.
JEBEL EL AKHDAR
10-14 Apr.
El Adem
Gambut
Bardia
Sidi Barrani
Soluch
Msus
5
Bir Hacheim
Capuzzo
14 Apr.-15 June
Salum
Mersa Matruh
CYRENAICA
Bir El Gobi
Halfaya
Sidi Omar
Buq Buq
El Daba
Maddalena
El Alamein
Agedabia
LIBYA
EGYPT
24 Mar.
El Haseiat
GULF OF SIRTE
Rommel's First Offensive.
(24 Mar. - 30 May 1941)
El Agheila
QATTARA DEPRESSION
(IMPASSABLE)

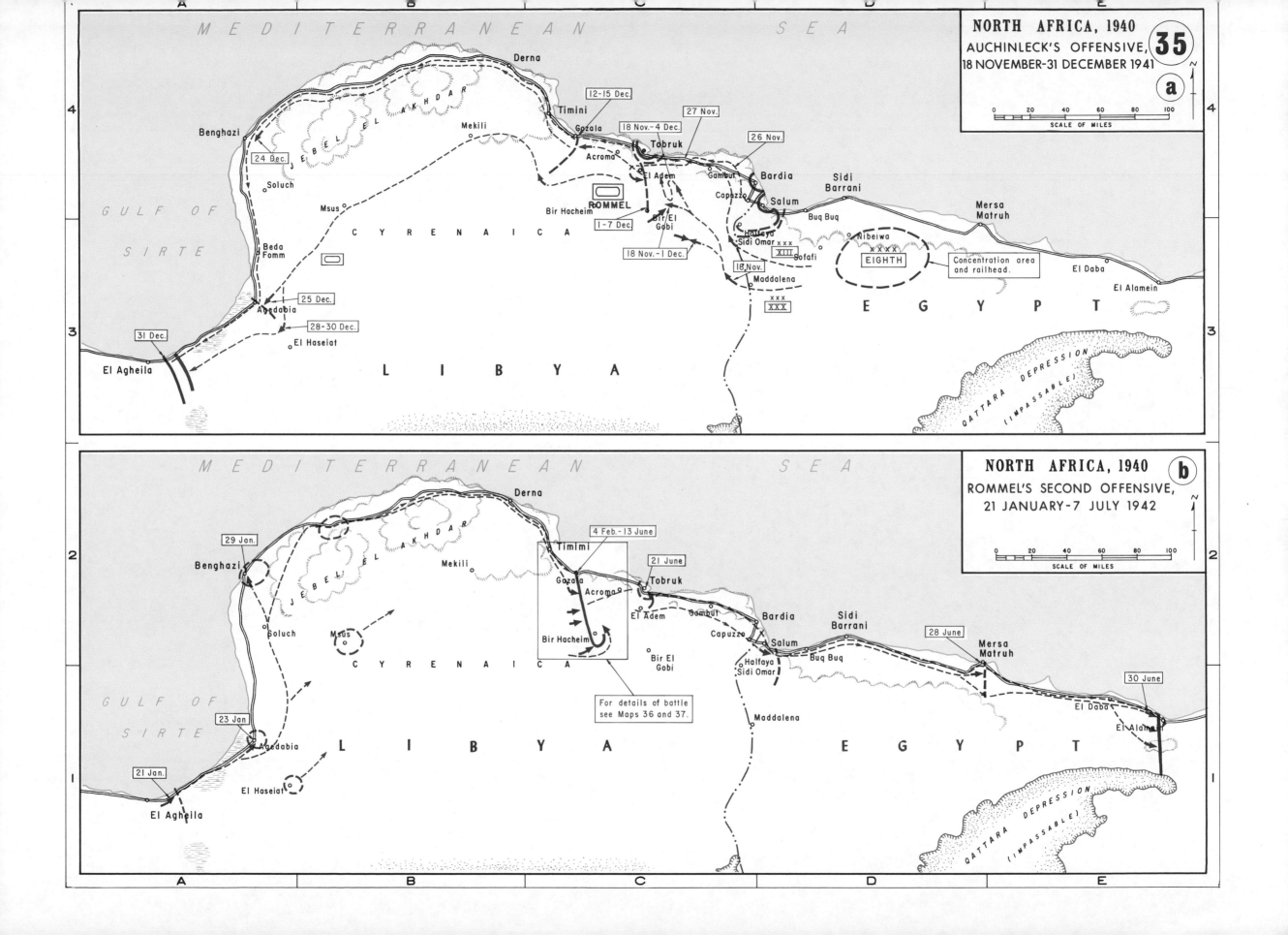

MEDITERRANEAN SEA

SCALE OF MILES
0 20 40 60 80 100

Derna

12–15 Dec.

27 Nov.

Timini

Benghazi

Gazala

18 Nov.–4 Dec.

26 Nov.

Mekili

Tobruk

24 Dec.

Acroma

El Adem

Gambut

Bardia

Sidi Barrani

Soluch

Bir Hacheim

ROMMEL

Capuzzo

Salum

Mersa Matruh

Msus

Bir El Gobi

1–7 Dec.

Halfaya
Sidi Omar xxx

Buq Buq

CYRENAICA

GULF OF SIRTE

Beda Fomm

18 Nov.–1 Dec.

XIII

Sofafi

Nibeiwa

El Daba

18 Nov.

EIGHTH

Concentration area and railhead.

Maddalena

El Alamein

Agedabia

25 Dec.

xxx
XXX

E G Y P T

31 Dec.

28–30 Dec.

El Haseiat

L I B Y A

El Agheila

QATTARA DEPRESSION
(IMPASSABLE)

SCALE OF MILES
0 20 40 60 80 100

MEDITERRANEAN SEA

Derna

29 Jan.

4 Feb.–13 June

Benghazi

Timimi

21 June

Mekili

Gazala

Tobruk

Acroma

El Adem

Gambut

Soluch

Bardia

Sidi Barrani

Msus

Bir Hacheim

Capuzzo

Salum

28 June

Mersa Matruh

Bir El Gobi

Halfaya
Sidi Omar

Buq Buq

CYRENAICA

GULF OF SIRTE

For details of battle
see Maps 36 and 37.

23 Jan.

Maddalena

30 June

El Daba

Agedabia

L I B Y A

E G Y P T

El Alamein

21 Jan.

El Haseiat

El Agheila

QATTARA DEPRESSION
(IMPASSABLE)

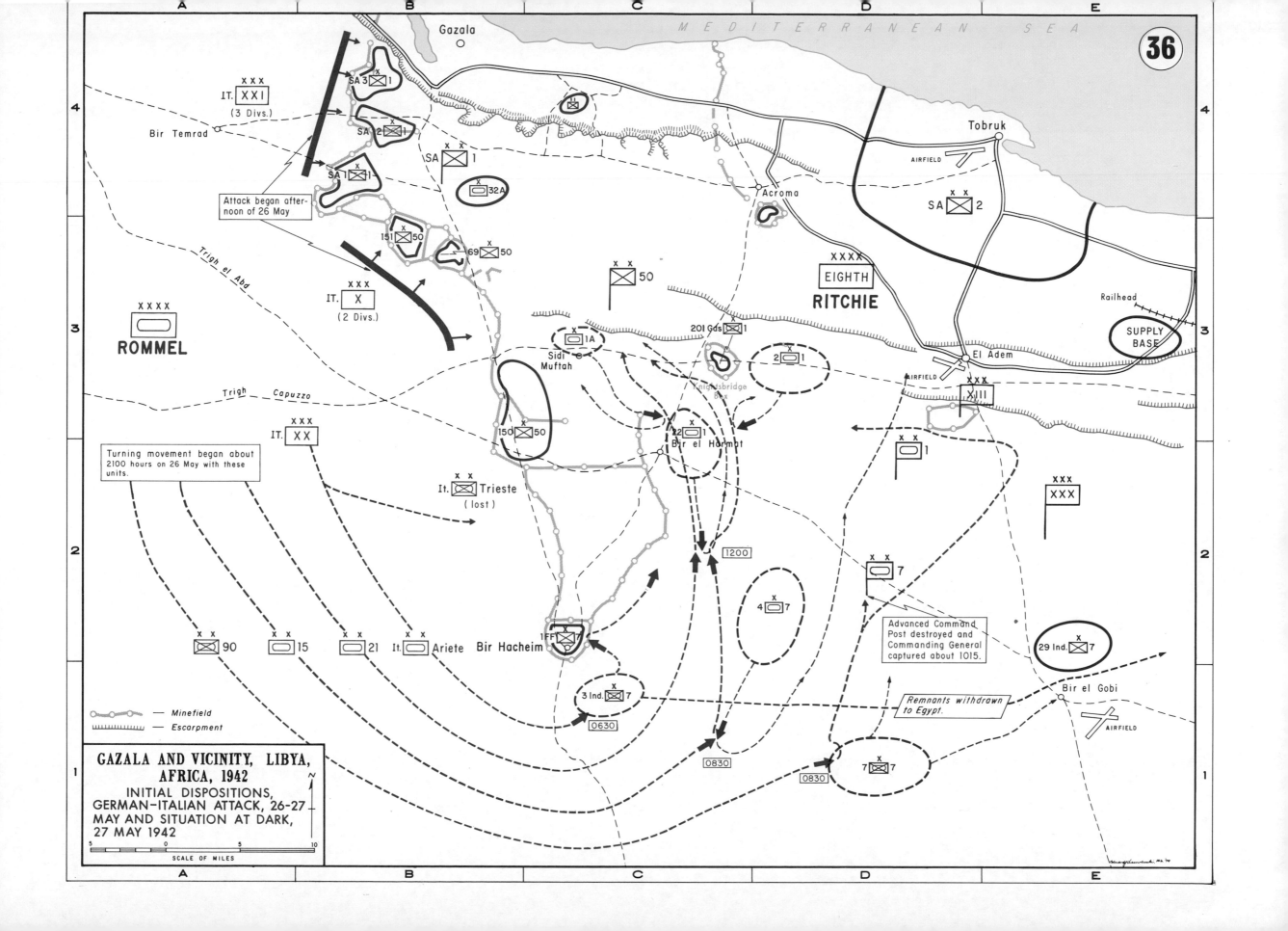

MEDITERRANEAN SEA

36

Gazala

Tobruk

AIRFIELD

Bir Temrad

XXX
IT. XXI
(3 Divs.)

SA 3 ☒ 1

SA 2 ☒ 1

SA ☒ 1

SA ☒ 1

32A

Acroma

SA ☒ 2

Trigh el Abd

151 ☒ 50

69 ☒ 50

XXX
IT. X
(2 Divs.)

☒ 50

XXXX
EIGHTH
RITCHIE

Railhead

ROMMEL

Trigh   Capuzzo

201 Gds ☒ 1

El Adem

SUPPLY
BASE

Attack began after-
noon of 26 May

Sidi
Muftah

☒ 1A

Knightsbridge
Box

☒ 2 ☐ 1

AIRFIELD

XXX
XIII

150 ☒ 50

22 ☒ 1

Bir el Harmat

☒ 1

IT. XX

Turning movement began about
2100 hours on 26 May with these
units.

It. ☒ Trieste
(lost)

1200

XXX
XXX

☐ 7

4 ☐ 7

Advanced Command
Post destroyed and
Commanding General
captured about 1015.

☒ 90   ☒ 15   21   It. ☐ Ariete   Bir Hacheim

1 FF ☒ 7

29 Ind. ☒ 7

Bir el Gobi

3 Ind. ☒ 7

Remnants withdrawn
to Egypt.

AIRFIELD

0630

0830

7 ☒ 7

0830

⊸⊸⊸ —— Minefield
⊤⊤⊤⊤ —— Escarpment

**GAZALA AND VICINITY, LIBYA,
AFRICA, 1942**
INITIAL DISPOSITIONS,
GERMAN-ITALIAN ATTACK, 26-27
MAY AND SITUATION AT DARK,
27 MAY 1942

N

5   5   10

SCALE OF MILES

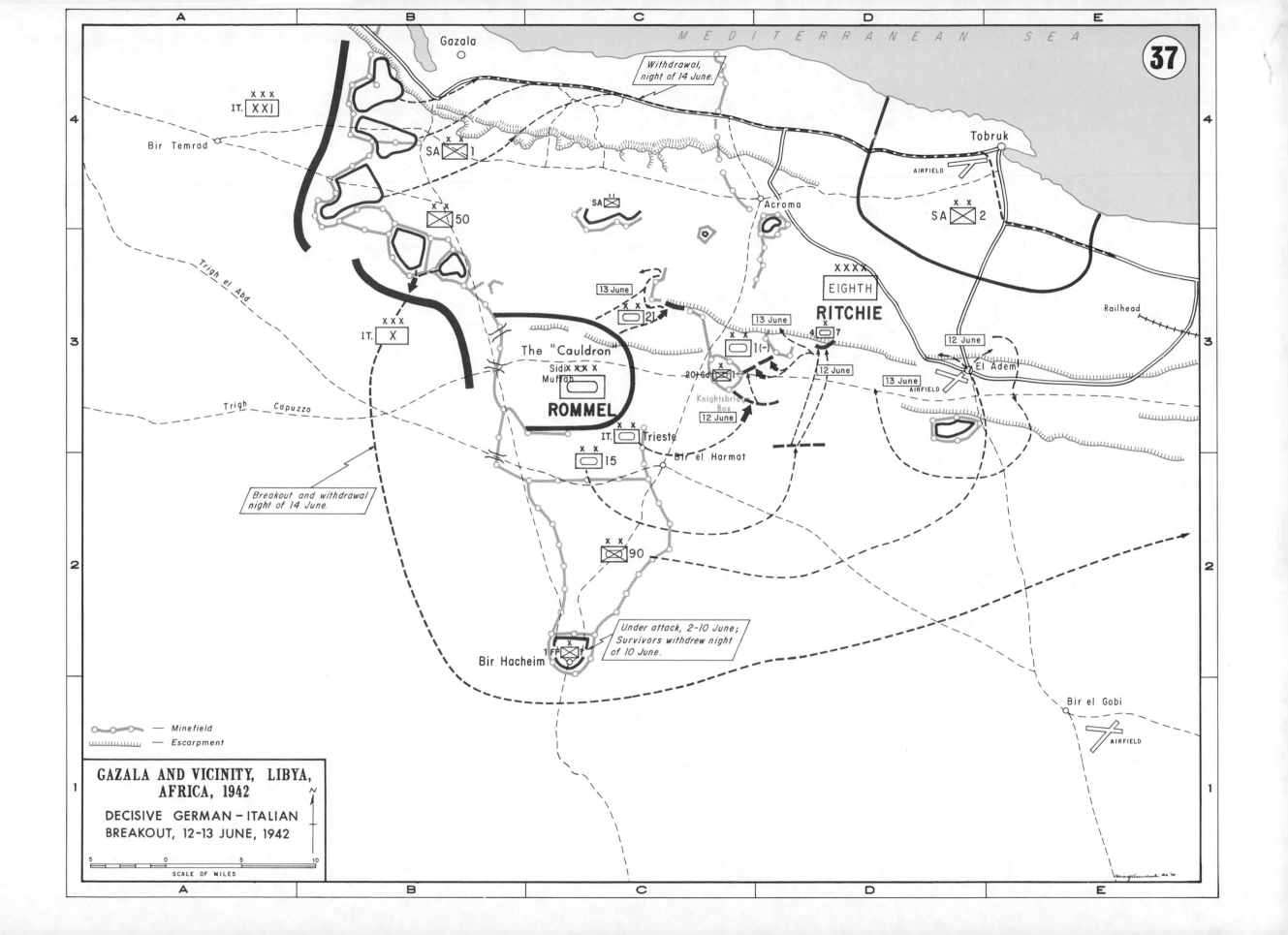

MEDITERRANEAN SEA

37

Gazala

Withdrawal,
night of 14 June.

XXX
IT. XXI

Bir Temrad

Tobruk

AIRFIELD

SA ☒ 1

SA ☒ 2

XX
☒ 50

SA ☒

XXXX

EIGHTH

RITCHIE

13 June

IT. X

XXX

The "Cauldron"

XX
☐ 21

13 June

XX
☐ 1(-)

12 June

Acroma

Railhead

XX
☐ 7

13 June

12 June

El Adem

AIRFIELD

SidiX XX X
Muftah

20/6d ☐ 1

ROMMEL

Knightsbridge
Box

12 June

Trigh Capuzzo

IT. ☐ Trieste

XX
☐ 15

Bir el Harmat

Breakout and withdrawal
night of 14 June.

XX
☒ 90

Under attack, 2-10 June;
Survivors withdrew night
of 10 June.

1 FF ☒ 1

Bir Hacheim

Bir el Gobi

AIRFIELD

Minefield

Escarpment

GAZALA AND VICINITY, LIBYA,
AFRICA, 1942

DECISIVE GERMAN–ITALIAN
BREAKOUT, 12–13 JUNE, 1942

SCALE OF MILES
5 0 5 10

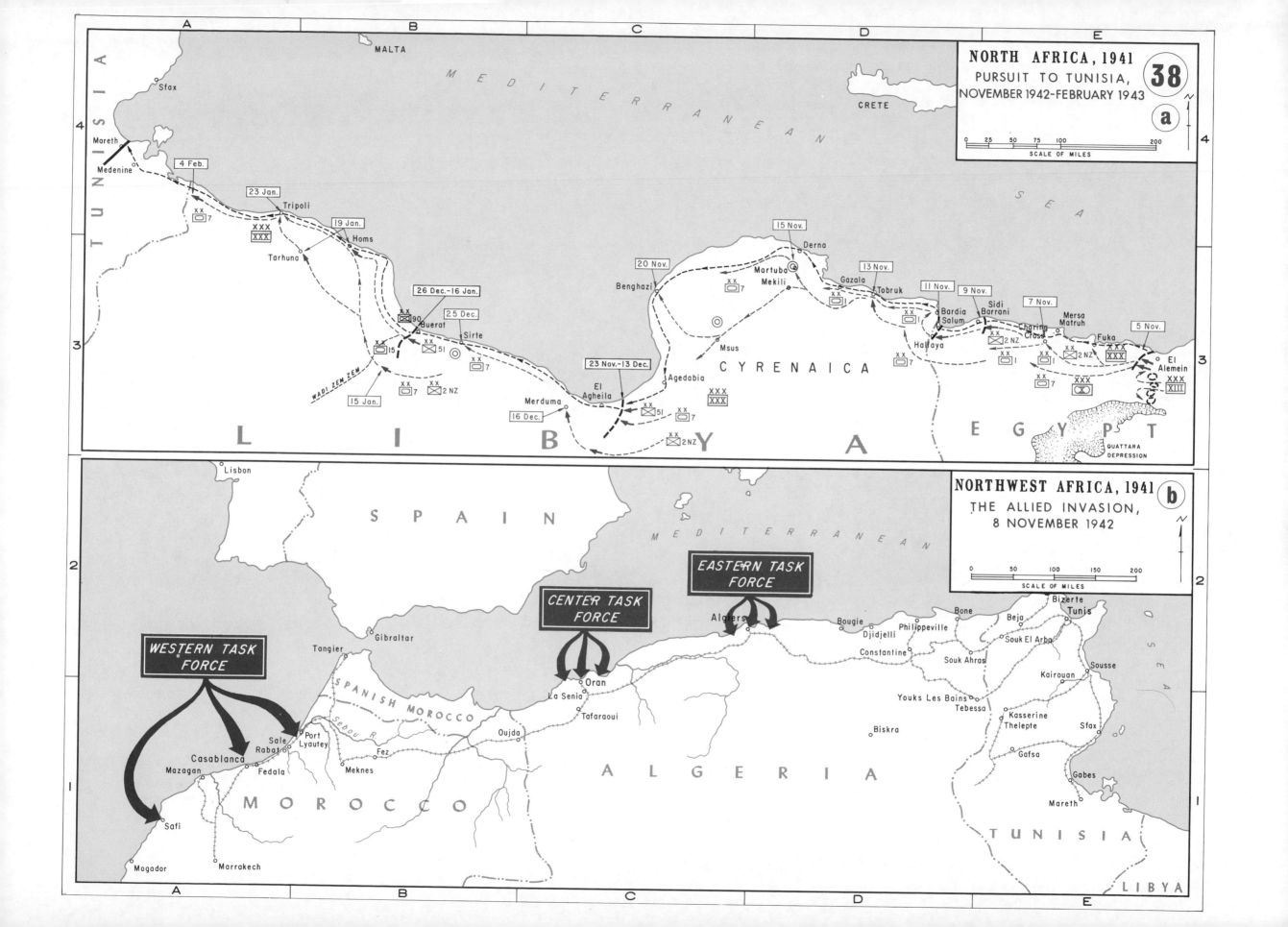

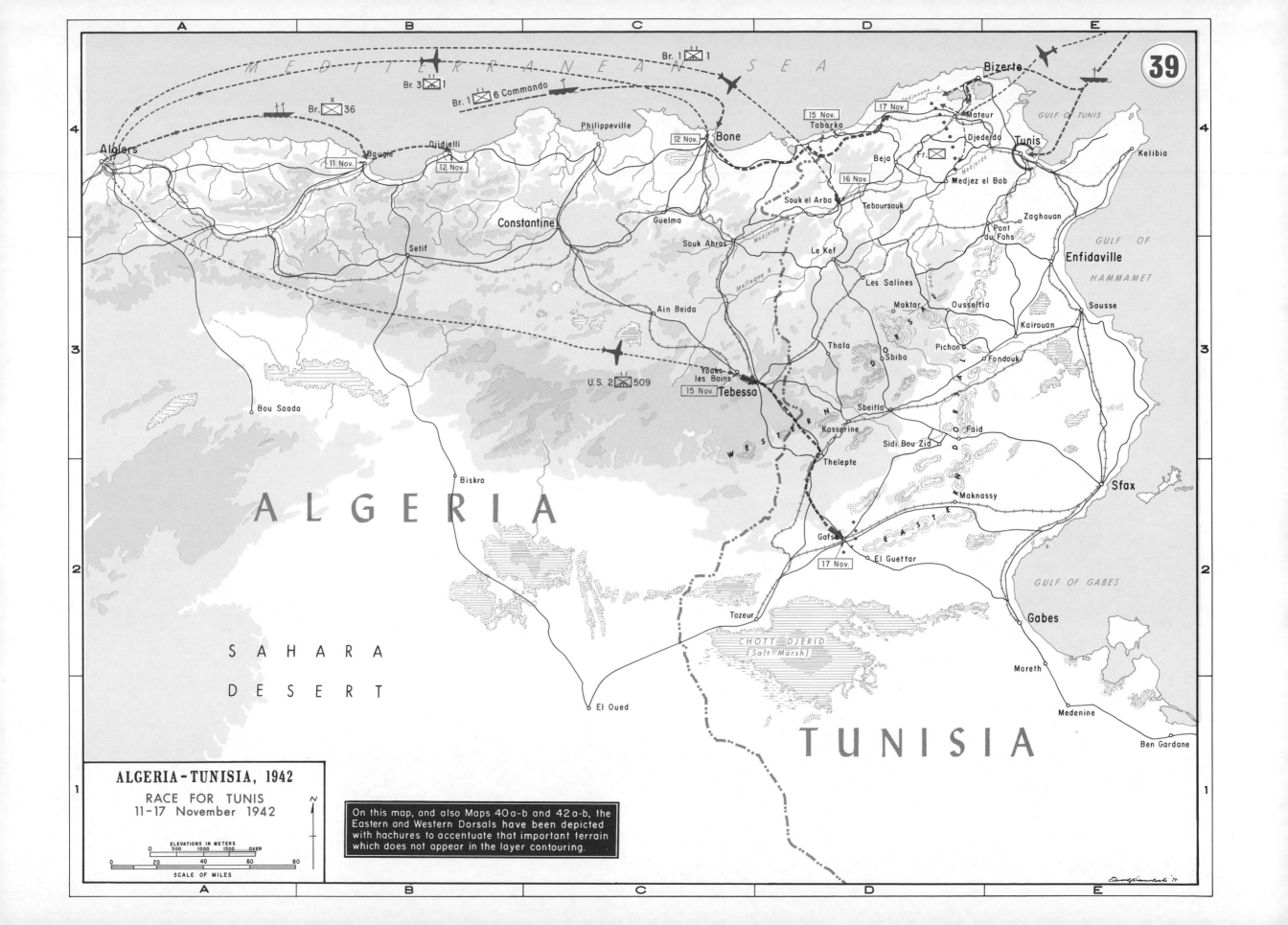

ALGERIA-TUNISIA, 1942

RACE FOR TUNIS
11-17 November 1942

On this map, and also Maps 40a-b and 42a-b, the
Eastern and Western Dorsals have been depicted
with hachures to accentuate that important terrain
which does not appear in the layer contouring.

ELEVATIONS IN METERS
500 1000 1500 OVER

SCALE OF MILES
0   20   40   60   80

39

MEDITERRANEAN SEA

Br. 1 ☒ 1

Br. 3 ☒ 1

Br. 1 ☒ 6 Commando

Br. ☒ 36

Algiers

Bougie

11 Nov.

Djidjelli

12 Nov.

Philippeville

12 Nov.

Bone

Bizerte

15 Nov.
Tabarka

17 Nov.

Mateur

Djederda

Tunis

Kelibia

GULF OF TUNIS

16 Nov.

Beja

Fr. ☒

Constantine

Guelma

Souk el Arba

Teboursouk

Medjez el Bab

Setif

Souk Ahras

Le Kef

Zaghouan

Pont
du Fahs

GULF OF
HAMMAMET

Enfidaville

Les Salines

Ain Beida

Maktar

Ousseltia

Kairouan

Sousse

Thala

Sbiba

Pichon

Fondouk

Bou Saada

Biskra

Yooks-
les Bains

U.S. 2 ☒ 509

15 Nov. Tebessa

Sbeitla

Kasserine

Faid

Sidi Bou Zid

ALGERIA

Thelepte

Maknassy

Sfax

Gafsa

17 Nov.

El Guettar

GULF OF GABES

Tozeur

CHOTT DJERID
(Salt Marsh)

Gabes

SAHARA

DESERT

El Oued

Mareth

Medenine

TUNISIA

Ben Gardane

WESTERN DORSAL

EASTERN DORSAL

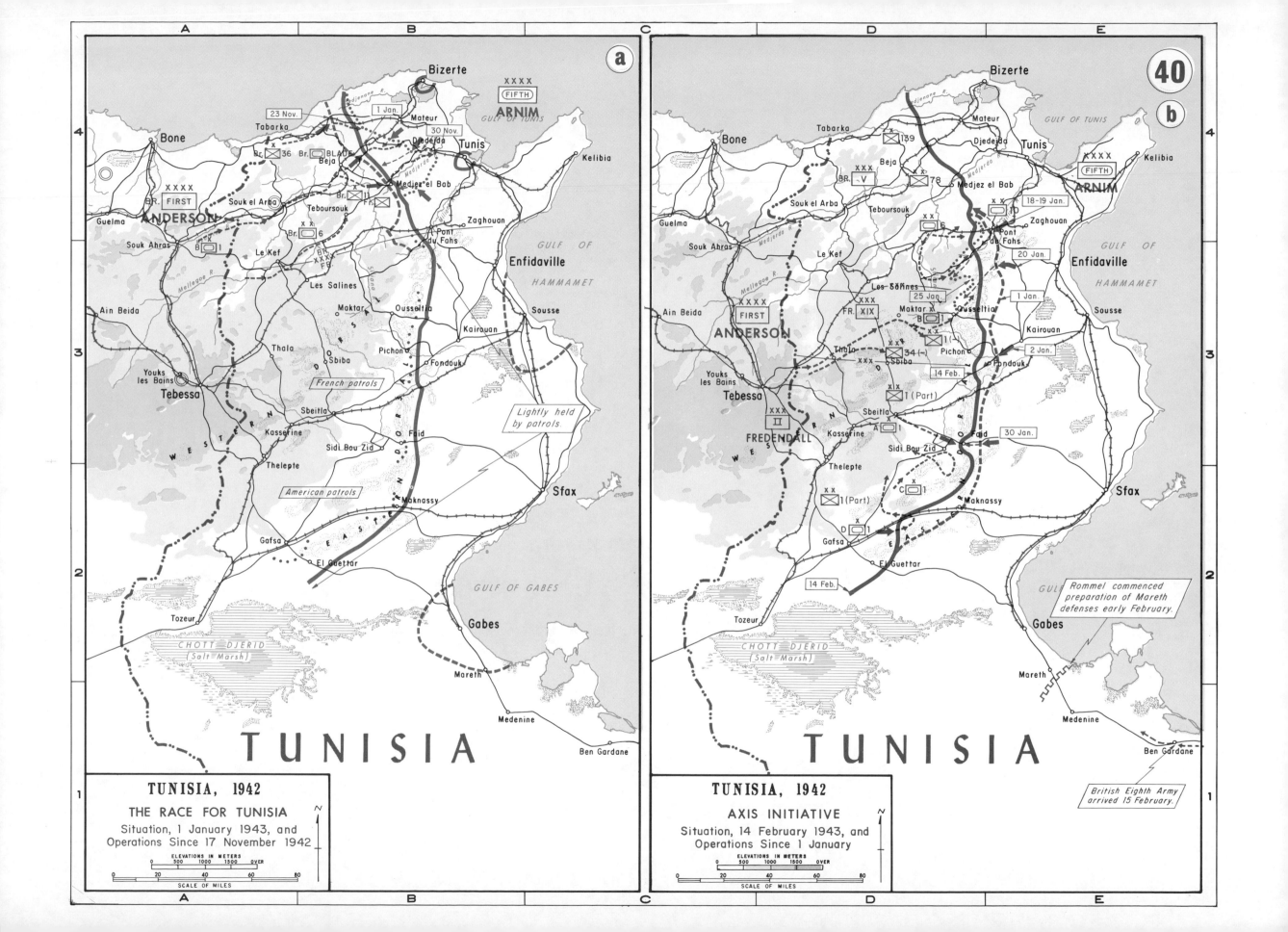

TUNISIA, 1942

THE RACE FOR TUNISIA

Situation, 1 January 1943, and
Operations Since 17 November 1942

ELEVATIONS IN METERS
500 1000 1500 OVER

0   20   40   60   80
SCALE OF MILES

TUNISIA, 1942

AXIS INITIATIVE

Situation, 14 February 1943, and
Operations Since 1 January

ELEVATIONS IN METERS
500 1000 1500 OVER

0   20   40   60   80
SCALE OF MILES

Lightly held by patrols.

Rommel commenced preparation of Mareth defenses early February.

British Eighth Army arrived 15 February.

French patrols

American patrols

40

a

b

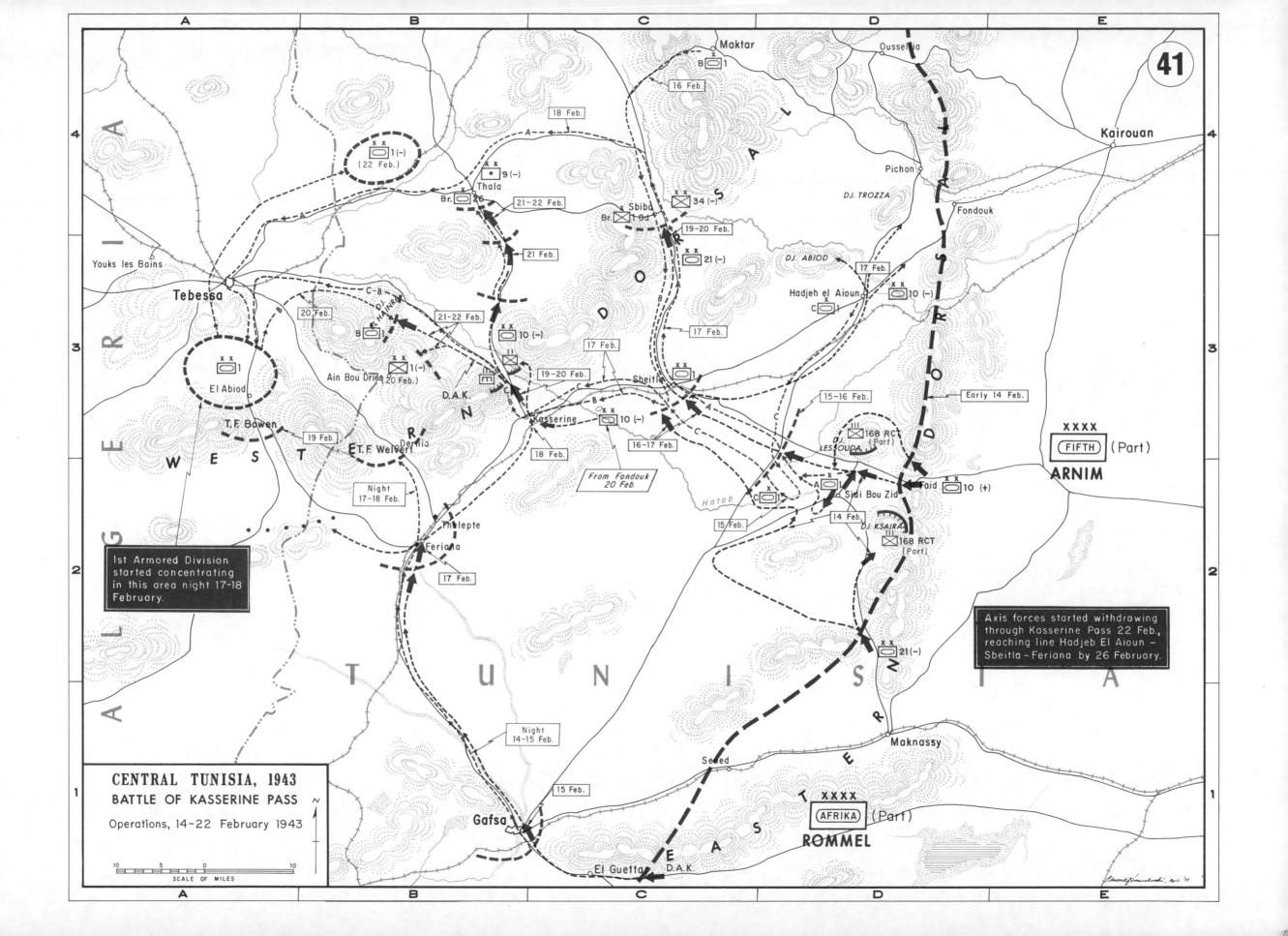

41

Maktar
B ☐ 1
16 Feb.
18 Feb.
Oussellia
Kairouan
Pichon
DJ. TROZZA
Fondouk

xx 1(–)
(22 Feb.)

xx 9(–)
Thala
Br. ☐ 26
21-22 Feb.

xx Sbiba
Br. ☐ 1 Gd
21 Feb.

xx 34(–)
19-20 Feb.

xx 21(–)

DJ. ABIOD
17 Feb.

Hadjeb el Aioun
xx 10(–)
C ☐ 1

Youks les Bains

Tebessa
C-B
DJ.
EL HAMRA
B ☐ 1
20 Feb.
21-22 Feb.

☐ 10 (–)
17 Feb.

xx

19-20 Feb.

Sbeitla
xx 1

17 Feb.

15-16 Feb.
Early 14 Feb.

XXXX
FIFTH (Part)
ARNIM

El Abiod
xx 1

Ain Bou Dries
xx 1(–)
20 Feb.

D.A.K.

Kasserine
xx 10 (–)

16-17 Feb.

DJ.
LESSOUDA
168 RCT
(Part)

Faid
xx 10 (+)

T.F. Bowen
Dernia
T.F. Welvert
19 Feb.

18 Feb.

From Fondouk
20 Feb.

Hatab
xx
C ☐ 1

xx 1
A
Sidi Bou Zid
15 Feb.

14 Feb.
DJ. KSAIRA
168 RCT
(Part)

Night
17-18 Feb.

Thelepte
Feriana
17 Feb.

1st Armored Division
started concentrating
in this area night 17-18
February.

Axis forces started withdrawing
through Kasserine Pass 22 Feb.,
reaching line Hadjeb El Aioun –
Sbeitla – Feriana by 26 February.

xx 21(–)

Maknassy

Night
14-15 Feb.

Sened

15 Feb.

XXXX
AFRIKA (Part)
ROMMEL

CENTRAL TUNISIA, 1943
BATTLE OF KASSERINE PASS
Operations, 14-22 February 1943

Gafsa

El Guettar
D.A.K.

10   5   0   10
SCALE OF MILES

ALGERIA

TUNISIA

WESTERN DORSAL

EASTERN DORSAL

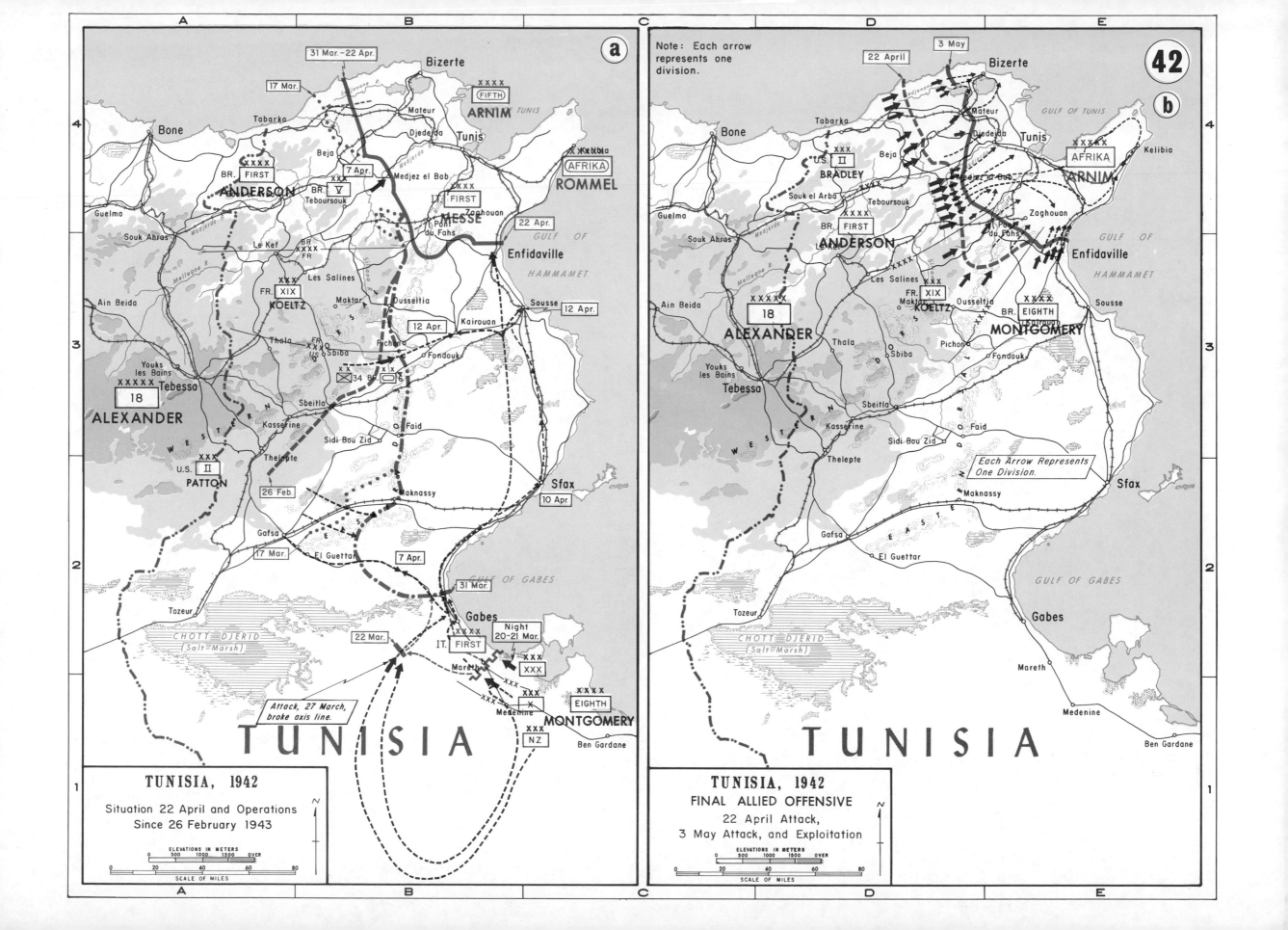

a

31 Mar.–22 Apr.

17 Mar.

Bizerte

XXXX
FIFTH
ARNIM

Mateur

Djedeida

Tunis

7 Apr.

Tabarka

Beja

Medjez el Bab

Xxxx
(AFRIKA)
ROMMEL

XXXX
BR. FIRST
ANDERSON

BR.
V
Teboursouk

IT.
FIRST
MESSE

Zaghouan

Bone

Guelma

Souk Ahras

Le Kef

BR.
XXXX
FR

Pont
du Fahs

22 Apr.

Enfidaville

Maktar

Ousseltia

HAMMAMET

FR. XIX
KOELTZ

Les Salines

12 Apr.

GULF OF

Ain Beida

Thala

FR
XXXX
US
Sbiba

Pichon

Kairouan

Sousse

12 Apr.

Youks
les Bains

XXXXX Tebessa
18
ALEXANDER

34 BR.
6

Fondouk

Sbeitla

Kasserine

Faid

U.S. XXX
II
PATTON

Sidi Bou Zid

Thelepte

26 Feb.

Maknassy

Sfax

10 Apr.

Gafsa

17 Mar.

El Guettar

7 Apr.

GULF OF GABES

22 Mar.

31 Mar.

Tozeur

Gabes

CHOTT DJERID
(Salt Marsh)

Night
20-21 Mar.

IT.
FIRST

XXX

Mareth

XXX

XXX

XXXX
EIGHTH

Attack, 27 March,
broke axis line.

Medenine

MONTGOMERY

XXX
NZ

Ben Gardane

TUNISIA

TUNISIA, 1942

Situation 22 April and Operations
Since 26 February 1943

ELEVATIONS IN METERS
500 1000 1500 OVER

SCALE OF MILES
20 40 60 80

b

Note: Each arrow
represents one
division.

22 April

3 May

Bizerte

Mateur

Djedeida

Tunis

GULF OF TUNIS

Tabarka

Beja

XXX
U.S. II
BRADLEY

Souk el Arba

Teboursouk

Medjez el Bab

XXXX
AFRIKA
ARNIM

Kelibia

Bone

BR.
FIRST
ANDERSON

Zaghouan

Guelma

Souk Ahras

Les Salines

Maktar

Pont
du Fahs

Enfidaville

FR. XIX
KOELTZ

Ousseltia

HAMMAMET

Ain Beida

XXXXX
18
ALEXANDER

Youks
les Bains

Tebessa

Thala

Sbiba

Pichon

Fondouk

BR. EIGHTH
MONTGOMERY

Sousse

Each Arrow Represents
One Division.

Sbeitla

Kasserine

Faid

Sidi Bou Zid

Thelepte

Maknassy

Sfax

Gafsa

El Guettar

GULF OF GABES

Tozeur

CHOTT DJERID
(Salt Marsh)

Gabes

Mareth

Medenine

Ben Gardane

TUNISIA

TUNISIA, 1942
FINAL ALLIED OFFENSIVE

22 April Attack,
3 May Attack, and Exploitation

ELEVATIONS IN METERS
500 1000 1500 OVER

SCALE OF MILES
20 40 60 80

42

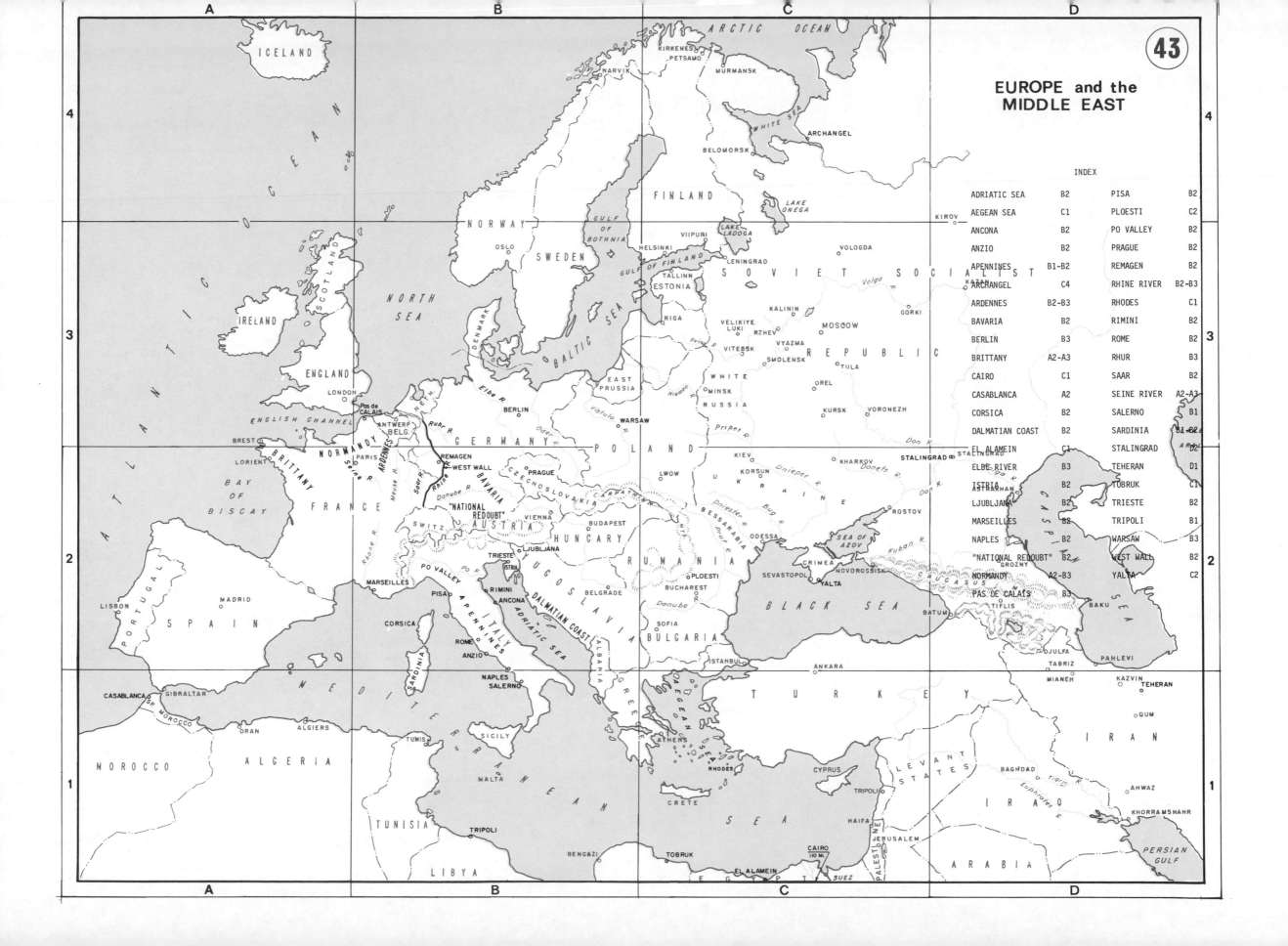

EUROPE and the MIDDLE EAST

43

INDEX

ADRIATIC SEA	B2	PISA	B2
AEGEAN SEA	C1	PLOESTI	C2
ANCONA	B2	PO VALLEY	B2
ANZIO	B2	PRAGUE	B2
APENNINES	B1-B2	REMAGEN	B2
ARCHANGEL	C4	RHINE RIVER	B2-B3
ARDENNES	B2-B3	RHODES	C1
BAVARIA	B2	RIMINI	B2
BERLIN	B3	ROME	B2
BRITTANY	A2-A3	RHUR	B3
CAIRO	C1	SAAR	B2
CASABLANCA	A2	SEINE RIVER	A2-A3
CORSICA	B2	SALERNO	B1
DALMATIAN COAST	B2	SARDINIA	B1-B2
EL ALAMEIN	C1	STALINGRAD	D2
ELBE RIVER	B3	TEHERAN	D1
ISTRIA	B2	TOBRUK	C1
LJUBLJANA	B2	TRIESTE	B2
MARSEILLES	B2	TRIPOLI	B1
NAPLES	B2	WARSAW	B3
"NATIONAL REDOUBT"	B2	WEST WALL	B2
		YALTA	C2

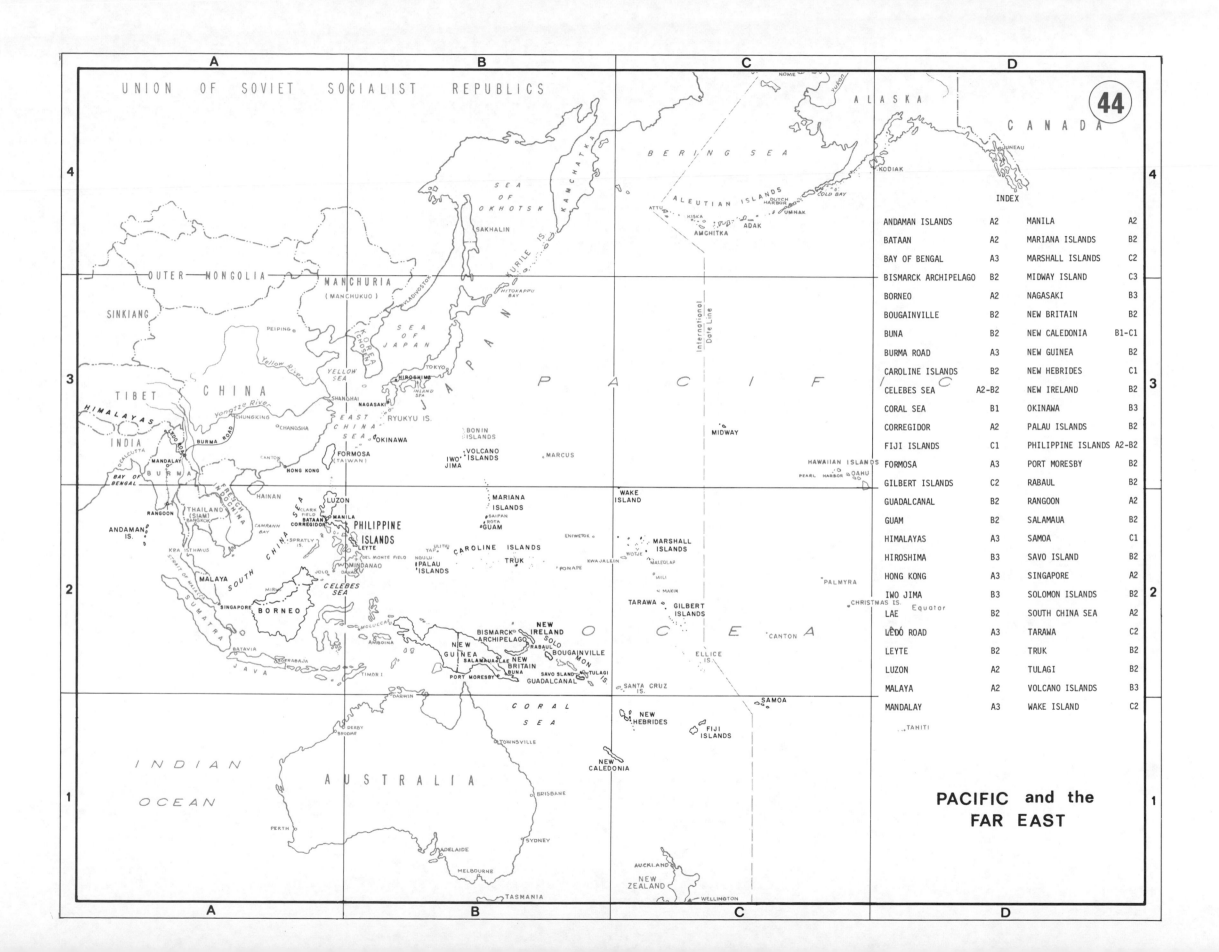

PACIFIC and the
FAR EAST

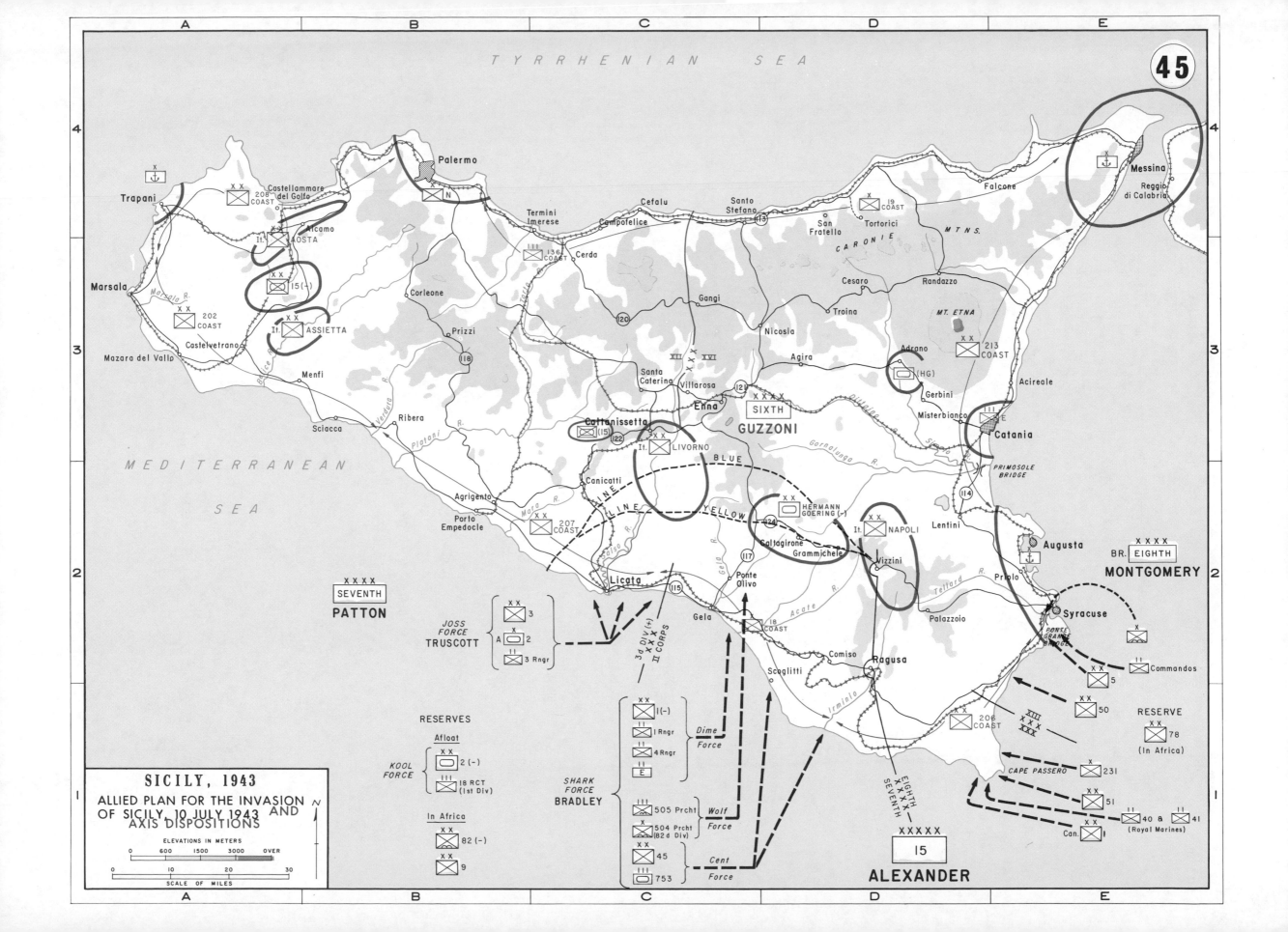

TYRRHENIAN SEA

45

Messina
Reggio di Calabria

Trapani
Castellammare del Golfo
208 COAST
It. AOSTA
Alcamo
Palermo
N
Cefalu
Campofelice
Termini Imerese
Santo Stefano
Falcone
19 COAST
San Fratello
Tortorici
CARONIE MTNS.

Marsala
15(-)
Corleone
Cesaro
Randazzo
MT. ETNA
213 COAST
Adrano

202 COAST
It. ASSIETTA
Prizzi
Gangi
Nicosia
Troina
(HG)
Gerbini

Mazara del Vallo
Castelvetrano
Menfi
118
120
Agira
Misterbianco
Acireale

Santa Caterina
Villarosa
XII XXX XVI
Catania
It. E

Ribera
Enna
SIXTH
GUZZONI
PRIMOSOLE BRIDGE

Sciacca
Caltanissetta
(15)
It. LIVORNO
BLUE
114

MEDITERRANEAN
122
LINE

Agrigento
Canicatti
LINE
YELLOW
Hermann Goering (-)
It. NAPOLI
Lentini

SEA
Porto Empedocle
207 COAST
124
Caltagirone
Grammichele
Vizzini
Augusta

SEVENTH
Licata
115
Ponte Olivo
BR. EIGHTH
MONTGOMERY

PATTON
Gela
18 COAST
Acate R.
Palazzolo
Priolo

JOSS FORCE
TRUSCOTT
3
A 2
3 Rngr
Comiso
Ragusa
Syracuse
PONTE GRANDE BRIDGE
Commandos

Scoglitti
5
50
206 COAST
XIII XXX XXX
RESERVE
78
(In Africa)

RESERVES
Afloat
I(-)
1 Rngr
4 Rngr
E
Dime Force
CAPE PASSERO
231

KOOL FORCE
2(-)
18 RCT
(1st Div)
SHARK FORCE
BRADLEY
505 Prcht
Wolf Force
EIGHTH XXXXX SEVENTH
51

In Africa
82(-)
9
504 Prcht
(82d Div)
45
753
Cent Force
Can. 1
40 & 41
(Royal Marines)

SICILY, 1943
ALLIED PLAN FOR THE INVASION
OF SICILY 10 JULY 1943 AND
AXIS DISPOSITIONS
ELEVATIONS IN METERS
0 600 1500 3000 OVER
0 10 20 30
SCALE OF MILES
XXXXX
15
ALEXANDER

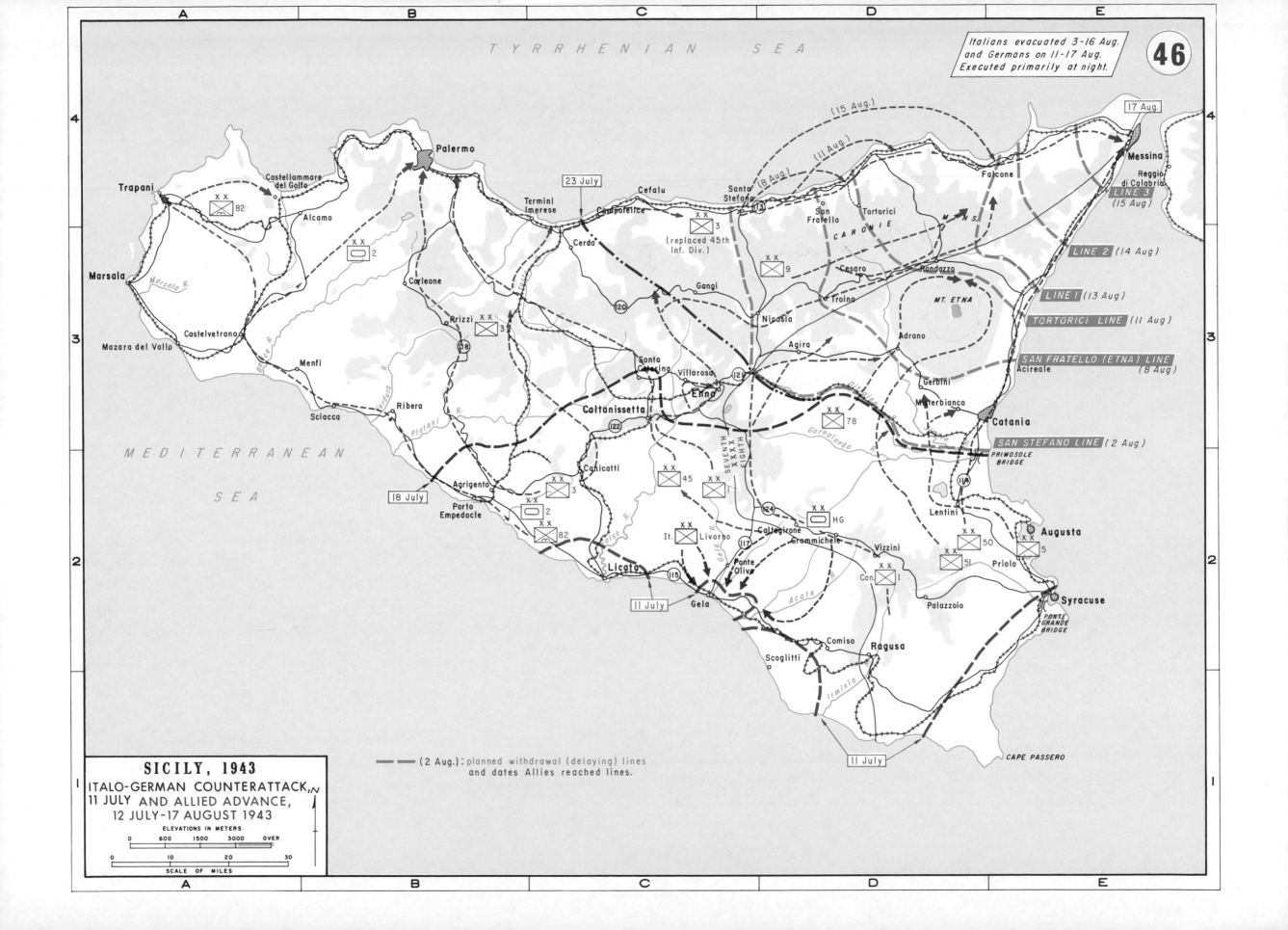

TYRRHENIAN SEA

Italians evacuated 3-16 Aug.
and Germans on 11-17 Aug.
Executed primarily at night.

46

Trapani

Castellammare del Golfo

Palermo

Alcamo

Cefalu

23 July

Santo Stefano

(8 Aug.)

Falcone

Messina

Reggio di Calabria

Marsala

Termini Imerese

Campofelice

X X 3

(replaced 45th Inf. Div.)

San Fratello

Tortorici

CARONIE

LINE 3 (15 Aug.)

Mazara del Vallo

Corleone

Cerda

XX 2

XX 9

Cesaro

Randazzo

LINE 2 (14 Aug.)

Castelvetrano

Marsala R.

Belice R.

Gangi

MT. ETNA

LINE 1 (13 Aug.)

Rizzi

XX 3

120

Troina

TORTORICI LINE (11 Aug.)

Menfi

Verdura R.

Nicosia

Adrano

SAN FRATELLO (ETNA) LINE (8 Aug.)

Ribera

18

Santa Caterina

Agira

Gerbini

Acireale

Sciacca

Platani R.

Villarosa

121

Enna

MEDITERRANEAN

Caltanissetta

122

78

Misterbianco

Catania

SEVENTH XXXX EIGHTH

Gornalunga R.

SAN STEFANO LINE (2 Aug.)

SEA

Agrigento

Canicatti

XX 45

XX

Dittaino R.

PRIMOSOLE BRIDGE

18 July

XX 3

Falso R.

124

Gela R.

Caltagirone

XX HG

Lentini

114

Porto Empedocle

XX 2

XX 82

It. XX Livorno

117

Grammichele

Vizzini

XX 50

Augusta

XX 51

Priolo

XX 5

11 July

Licata

115

Pante Oliva

Can. XX 1

Palazzoio

Syracuse

Gela

Acate R.

PONTE GRANDE BRIDGE

Comiso

Ragusa

Scoglitti

Irminio R.

11 July

CAPE PASSERO

SICILY, 1943
ITALO-GERMAN COUNTERATTACK, IN
11 JULY AND ALLIED ADVANCE,
12 JULY-17 AUGUST 1943

ELEVATIONS IN METERS

0   600   1500   3000   OVER

0   10   20   30

SCALE OF MILES

—— (2 Aug.): planned withdrawal (delaying) lines
and dates Allies reached lines.

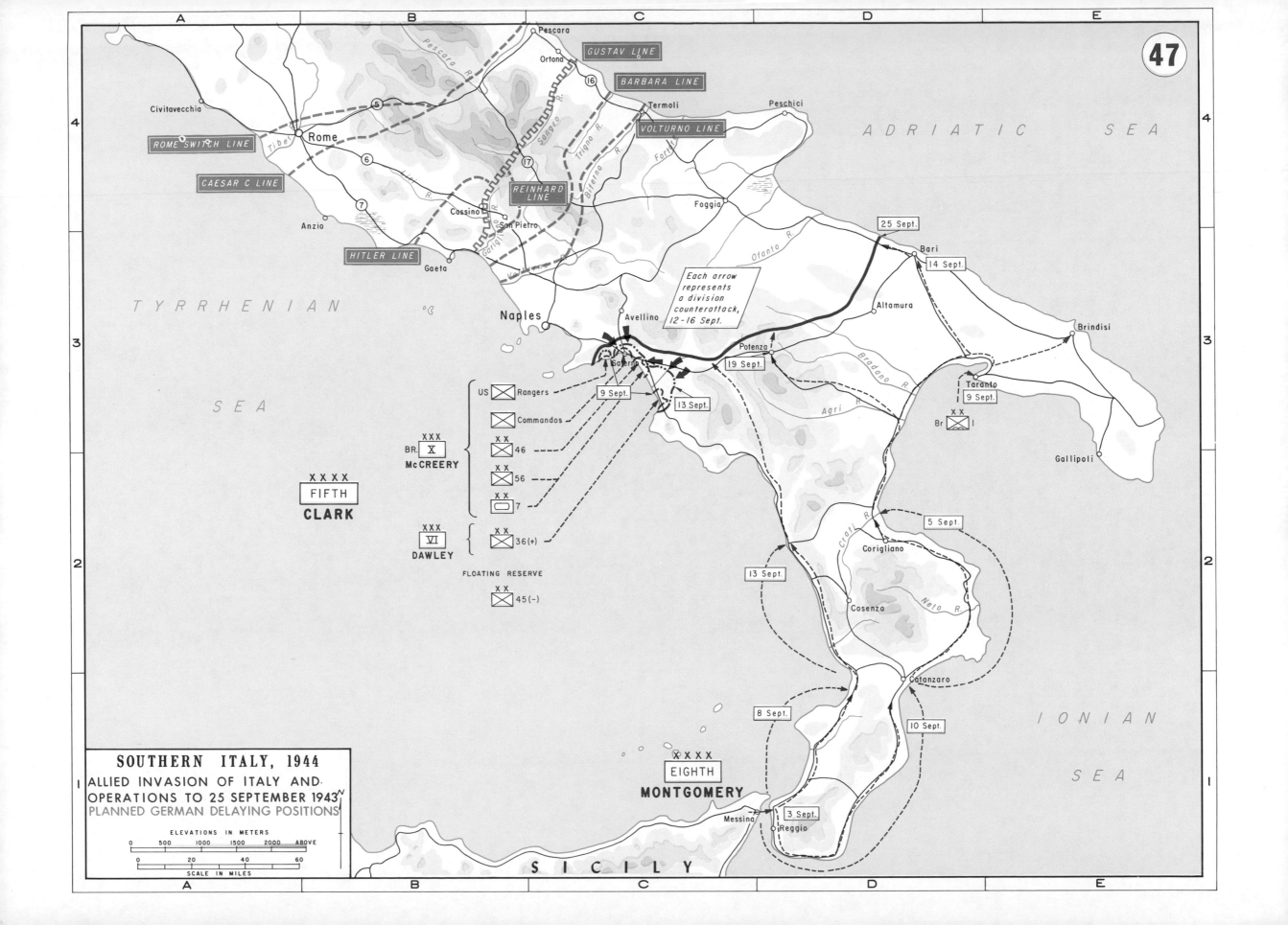

47

GUSTAV LINE

BARBARA LINE

VOLTURNO LINE

ROME SWITCH LINE

CAESAR C LINE

REINHARD LINE

HITLER LINE

Pescara

Ortona

Termoli

Peschici

Civitavecchia

Rome

Anzio

Cassino

San Pietro

Gaeta

Foggia

Naples

Avellino

Bari

Altamura

Brindisi

Taranto

Gallipoli

Potenza

Salerno

Each arrow represents a division counterattack, 12-16 Sept.

25 Sept.

14 Sept.

9 Sept.

19 Sept.

9 Sept.

Br XX I

13 Sept.

5 Sept.

Corigliano

13 Sept.

Cosenza

Catanzaro

8 Sept.

10 Sept.

3 Sept.

Messina

Reggio

ADRIATIC SEA

TYRRHENIAN SEA

IONIAN SEA

SICILY

Pescara R.

Sangro R.

Trigno R.

Biferno R.

Ofanto R.

Bradano R.

Agri R.

Crati R.

Neto R.

Tiber R.

Garigliano R.

Volturno R.

US ☒ Rangers

☒ Commandos

BR. XXX X
McCREERY

XX 46

XX 56

XX 7

XXX VI
DAWLEY

XX 36(+)

XXXX
FIFTH
CLARK

FLOATING RESERVE

XX 45(-)

XXXX
EIGHTH
MONTGOMERY

SOUTHERN ITALY, 1944
ALLIED INVASION OF ITALY AND
OPERATIONS TO 25 SEPTEMBER 1943
PLANNED GERMAN DELAYING POSITIONS

ELEVATIONS IN METERS

0   500   1000   1500   2000   ABOVE

0   20   40   60

SCALE IN MILES

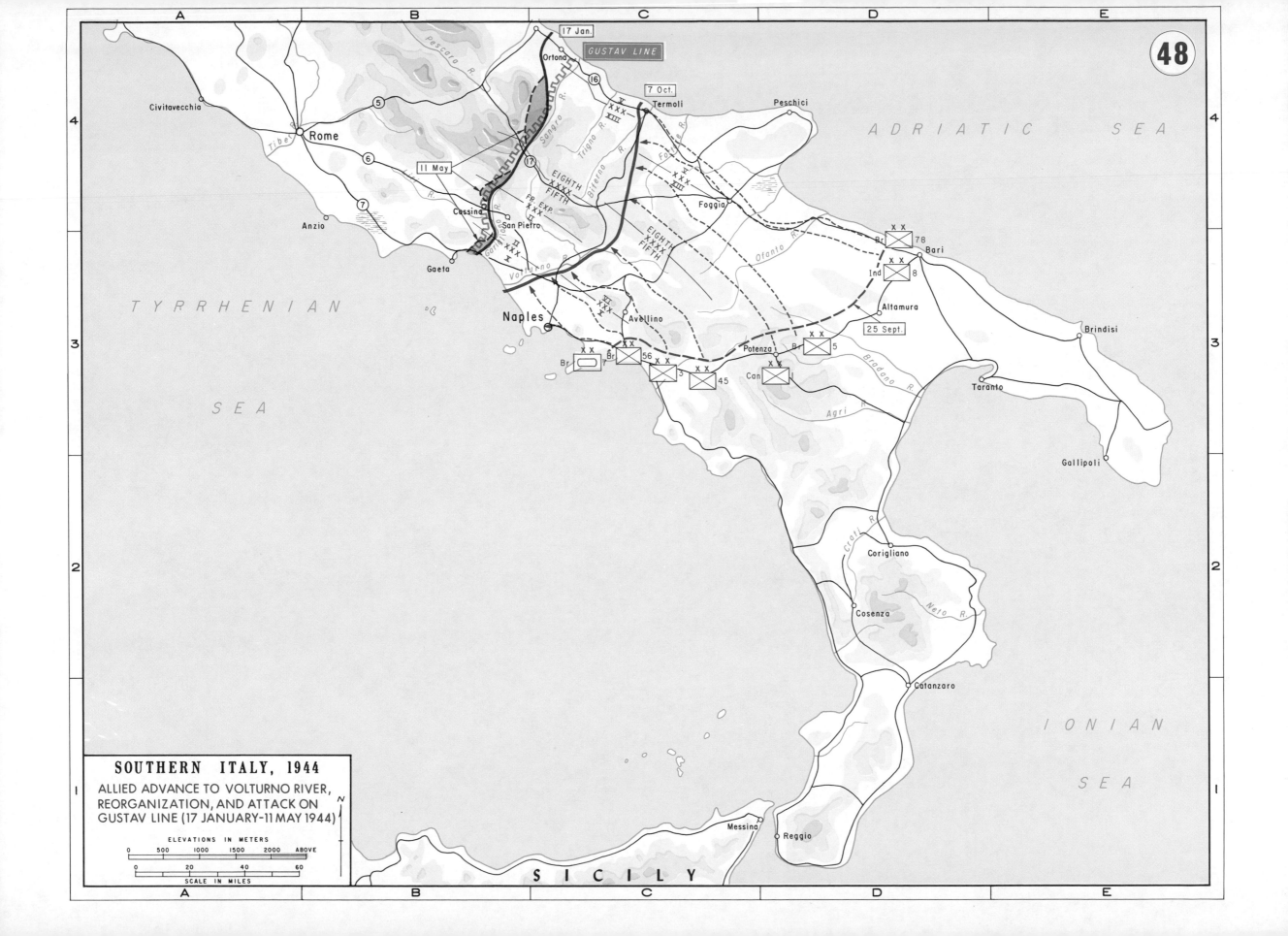

48

17 Jan.

GUSTAV LINE

7 Oct.

ADRIATIC SEA

Civitavecchia

5

Ortona

16

Termoli

Peschici

Rome

Tiber

6

17

EIGHTH
XXXX
FIFTH

Foggia

X X
78

Br

Bari

11 May

Anzio

7

Cassino

FR. EXP.
XXX

San Pietro
XXX

EIGHTH
XXXX
FIFTH

V
XXX
XIII

X X
8

Ind

Gaeta

TYRRHENIAN

Ofanto R.

Altamura

25 Sept.

Brindisi

SEA

VI
XXX

Naples

Avellino

Potenza

B

X X
5

Br

X X
Br
7

X X
56

X X

X X
3

X X
45

Can

X X
I

Taranto

Gallipoli

Agri R.

Bradano R.

IONIAN

Crati R.

Corigliano

Neto R.

SEA

Cosenza

Catanzaro

Messina

Reggio

SICILY

SOUTHERN ITALY, 1944

ALLIED ADVANCE TO VOLTURNO RIVER,
REORGANIZATION, AND ATTACK ON
GUSTAV LINE (17 JANUARY-11 MAY 1944)

N

ELEVATIONS IN METERS

0   500   1000   1500   2000 ABOVE

0   20   40   60

SCALE IN MILES

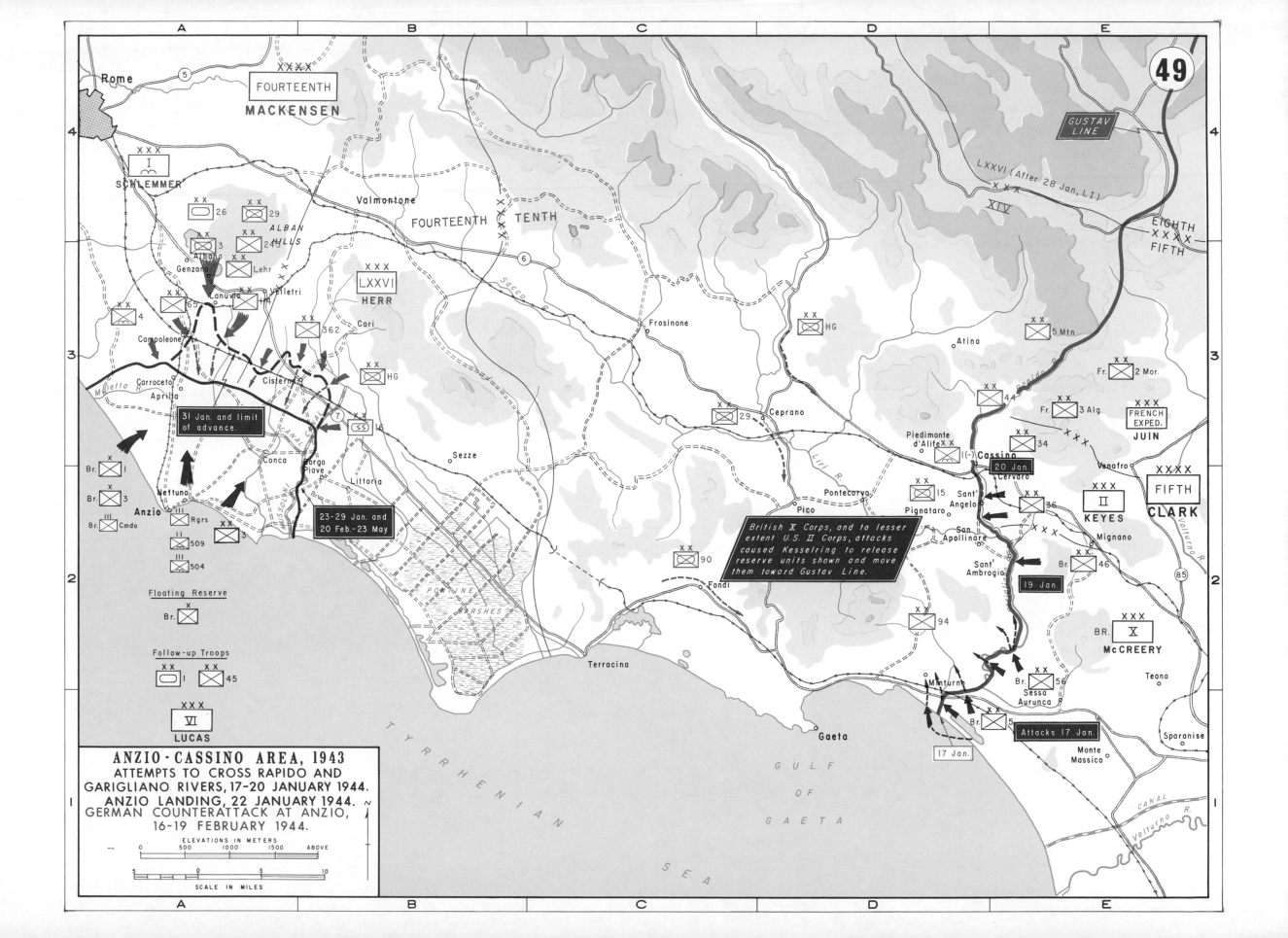

49

ROME
5

FOURTEENTH

MACKENSEN

I
SCHLEMMER

26   29
ALBAN HILLS
3   24
Albano
Genzano   Lehr
Lanuvio   Velletri
65   4

Campoleone
4
Carroceto
Aprilia

31 Jan. and limit
of advance.

Valmontone

FOURTEENTH   **TENTH**

6

LXXVI
HERR

362   Cori

Cisterna

HG

Sacco R.

Frosinone

Atina

Ceprano
29

Piedimonte
d'Alife

Sant'
Angelo
15
Pico

San
Apollinare

Sant'
Ambrogia

94
Fondi

GUSTAV
LINE

LXXVI (After 28 Jan., LI)
XIV

EIGHTH
FIFTH

5 Mtn.

Fr.   2 Mor.

44   Fr.   3 Alg.   FRENCH
EXPED.
JUIN

34

Cassino   20 Jan.
Cervaro
Venafro

36   II
KEYES   FIFTH
CLARK

Mignano
85
46   19 Jan.

90

British X Corps, and to lesser
extent U.S. II Corps, attacks
caused Kesselring to release
reserve units shown and move
them toward Gustav Line.

Conca
Borgo
Piave   7   SS   LG
Littoria

23-29 Jan. and
20 Feb.-23 May

Sezze

PONTINE
MARSHES

Br.   1
Br.   3
Br.   Cmdo
Anzio   Rgrs
509
504

Floating Reserve
Br.

Follow-up Troops
1   45

VI
LUCAS

Nettuno

Terracina

Gaeta

TYRRHENIAN

SEA

GULF

OF

GAETA

Minturno
17 Jan.

Sessa
Aurunca
Br.   5
Attacks 17 Jan.

56
Br.

BR.   X
McCREERY

Teano

Sparanise

Monte
Massico

CANAL
Volturno R.

ANZIO - CASSINO AREA, 1943
ATTEMPTS TO CROSS RAPIDO AND
GARIGLIANO RIVERS, 17-20 JANUARY 1944.
ANZIO LANDING, 22 JANUARY 1944.
GERMAN COUNTERATTACK AT ANZIO,
16-19 FEBRUARY 1944.

ELEVATIONS IN METERS
0   500   1000   1500   ABOVE

SCALE IN MILES
5   0   5   10

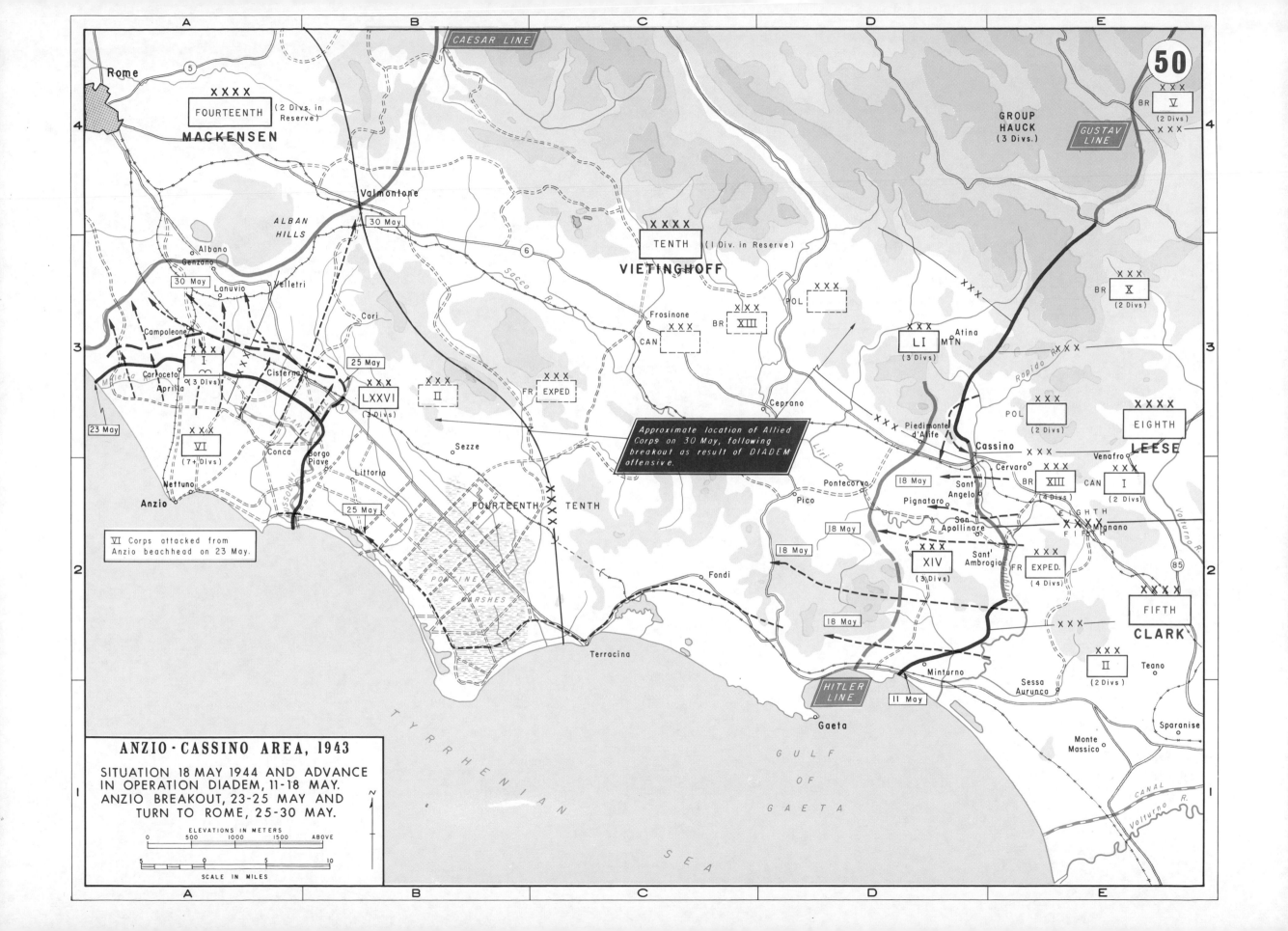

CAESAR LINE

50

Rome

XXXX
FOURTEENTH (2 Divs. in Reserve)
MACKENSEN

GROUP HAUCK (3 Divs.)

BR V (2 Divs)

GUSTAV LINE

Valmontone
30 May

ALBAN HILLS

XXXX
TENTH (1 Div. in Reserve)
VIETINGHOFF

Albano
Genzano
30 May
Lanuvio
Velletri

Campoleone
25 May

XXX
I (3 Divs)
Carroceto
Cisterna
Aprilia

XXX
LXXVI (3 Divs)
25 May

Cori

XXX
II

Frosinone

BR XIII

POL

CAN

FR EXPED

BR X (2 Divs)

XXX
LI (3 Divs)
Atina
MTN

Ceprano

POL (2 Divs)

XXXX
EIGHTH
LEESE

Conca
Borgo Piave

XXX
VI (7+ Divs)

Nettuno

Anzio

Sezze

Approximate location of Allied Corps on 30 May, following breakout as result of DIADEM offensive.

Piedimonte d'Alife

Cassino

Cervaro

Venafro

BR XIII (4 Divs)

CAN I (2 Divs)

Littoria

Pontecorva

Pico

18 May

Sant' Angelo

Pignataro

San Apollinare

Mignano

FR EXPED (4 Divs)

23 May

VI Corps attacked from Anzio beachhead on 23 May.

FOURTEENTH TENTH

18 May

Fondi

18 May

18 May

XIV (3 Divs)

Sant' Ambrogio

XXXX
FIFTH
CLARK

II (2 Divs)
Teano

Terracina

HITLER LINE

11 May

Minturno

Gaeta

Sessa Aurunca

Monte Massico

Sparanise

TYRRHENIAN

GULF OF GAETA

SEA

ANZIO · CASSINO AREA, 1943

SITUATION 18 MAY 1944 AND ADVANCE IN OPERATION DIADEM, 11-18 MAY. ANZIO BREAKOUT, 23-25 MAY AND TURN TO ROME, 25-30 MAY.

ELEVATIONS IN METERS
0   500   1000   1500   ABOVE

SCALE IN MILES
5   0   5   10

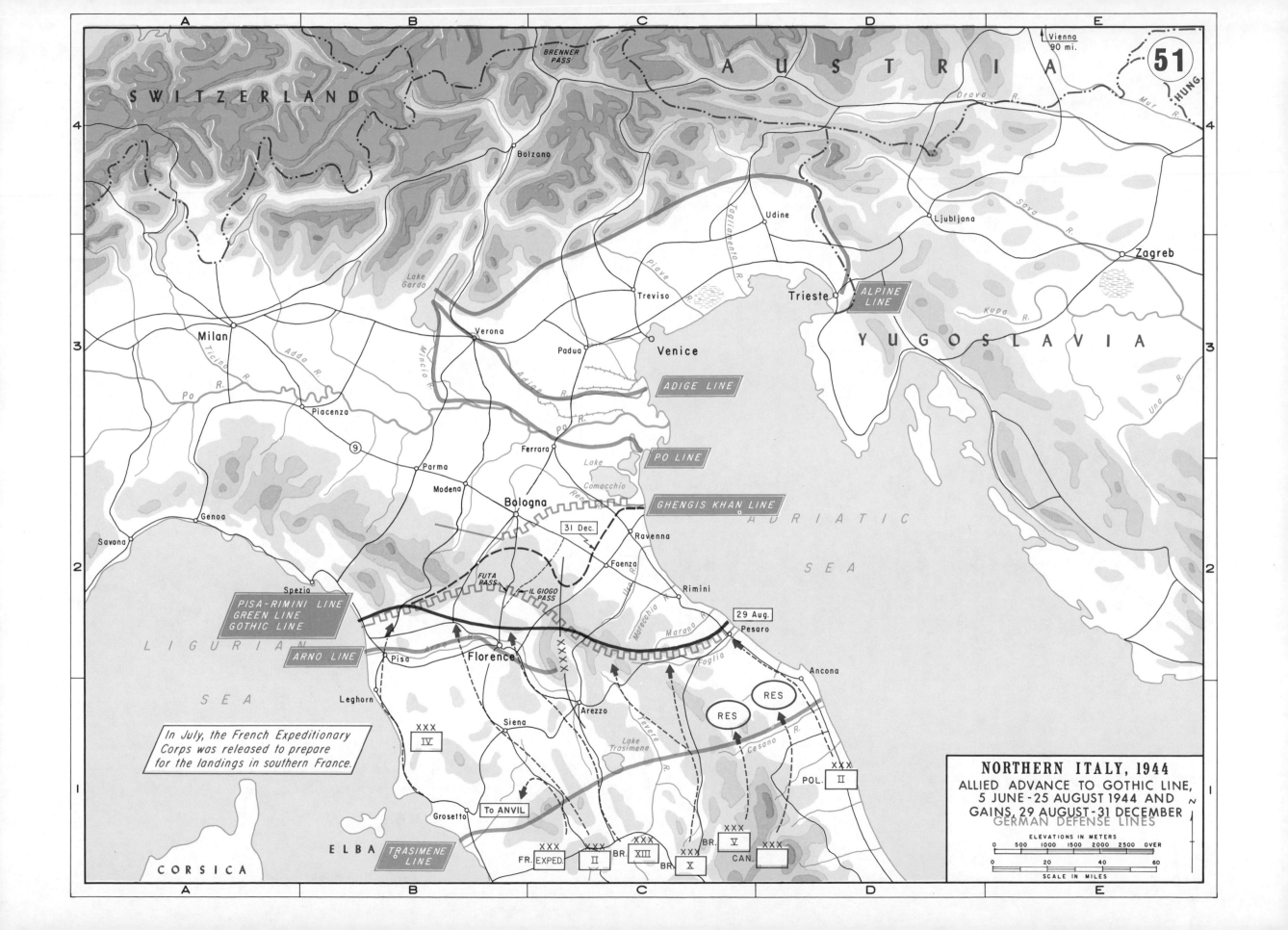

SWITZERLAND

AUSTRIA

Vienna 90 mi.

51

HUNG.

YUGOSLAVIA

Zagreb

Ljubljana

Udine

Trieste

ALPINE LINE

Bolzano

BRENNER PASS

Lake Garda

Treviso

Venice

ADIGE LINE

Milan

Verona

Padua

Piacenza

Parma

Ferrara

PO LINE

Lake Comacchio

ADRIATIC

Modena

Bologna

GHENGIS KHAN LINE

Ravenna

Genoa

31 Dec.

Faenza

SEA

Savona

Rimini

FUTA PASS

IL GIOGO PASS

Spezia

PISA-RIMINI LINE
GREEN LINE
GOTHIC LINE

29 Aug.

Pesaro

ARNO LINE

Pisa

Florence

XXXX

Ancona

LIGURIAN

Leghorn

SEA

Arezzo

RES

RES

Siena

Lake Trasimene

XXX
IV

In July, the French Expeditionary Corps was released to prepare for the landings in southern France.

POL.
XXX
II

To ANVIL

Grosetto

ELBA

TRASIMENE LINE

XXX
FR. EXPED.

XXX
II

XXX
BR. XIII

XXX
BR. X

XXX
BR. V
CAN.

XXX

CORSICA

NORTHERN ITALY, 1944
ALLIED ADVANCE TO GOTHIC LINE,
5 JUNE-25 AUGUST 1944 AND
GAINS, 29 AUGUST-31 DECEMBER
GERMAN DEFENSE LINES

ELEVATIONS IN METERS
0 500 1000 1500 2000 2500 OVER

0   20   40   60
SCALE IN MILES

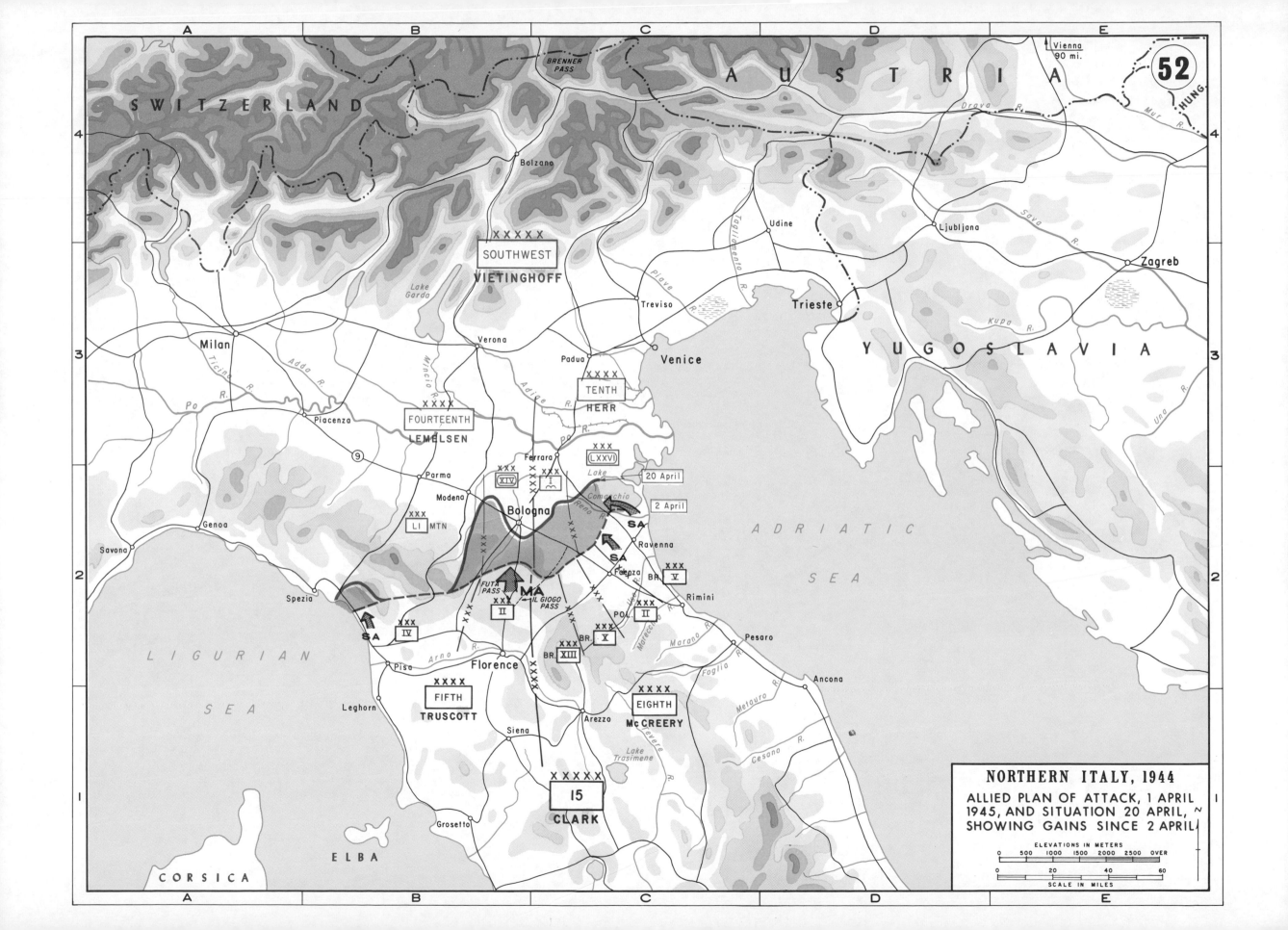

NORTHERN ITALY, 1944

ALLIED PLAN OF ATTACK, 1 APRIL
1945, AND SITUATION 20 APRIL, ~
SHOWING GAINS SINCE 2 APRIL

ELEVATIONS IN METERS

0 500 1000 1500 2000 2500 OVER

0   20   40   60

SCALE IN MILES

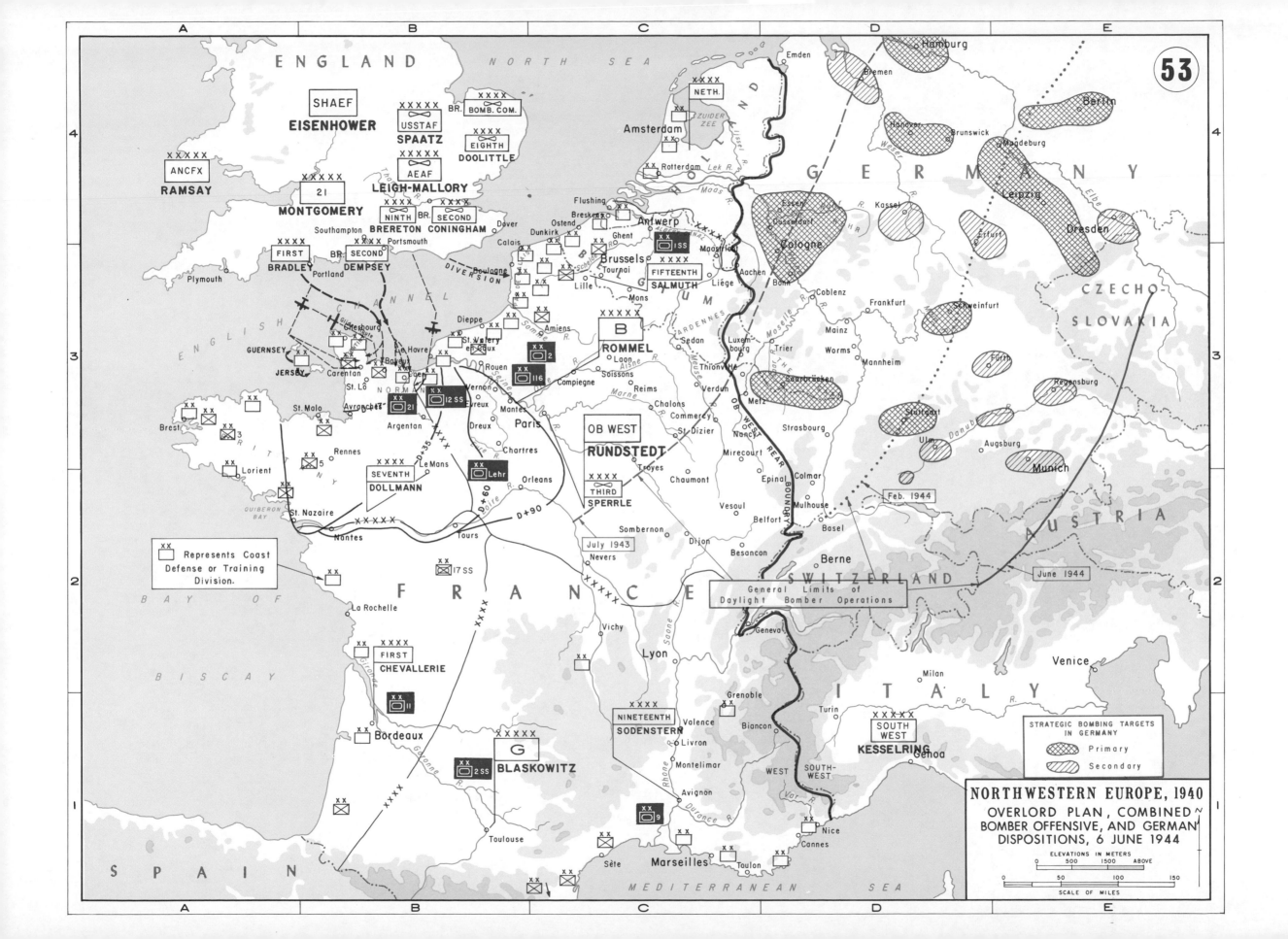

ENGLAND

NORTH SEA

GERMANY

CZECHO-SLOVAKIA

AUSTRIA

ITALY

SWITZERLAND

FRANCE

SPAIN

BAY OF BISCAY

ENGLISH CHANNEL

MEDITERRANEAN SEA

53

SHAEF
EISENHOWER

XXXXX USSTAF
SPAATZ

BR. BOMB. COM.

XXXX EIGHTH
DOOLITTLE

XXXXX AEAF
LEIGH-MALLORY

XXXXX ANCFX
RAMSAY

XXXXX 21
MONTGOMERY

NINTH   BR. SECOND
BRERETON CONINGHAM

XXXX FIRST
BRADLEY

BR. SECOND
DEMPSEY

NETH.

B
ROMMEL

FIFTEENTH
SALMUTH

OB WEST
RUNDSTEDT

SEVENTH
DOLLMANN

THIRD
SPERRLE

FIRST
CHEVALLERIE

NINETEENTH
SODENSTERN

G
BLASKOWITZ

SOUTH WEST
KESSELRING

Represents Coast Defense or Training Division.

General Limits of Daylight Bomber Operations

July 1943

Feb. 1944

June 1944

DIVERSION

D+35
D+60
D+90

NORTHWESTERN EUROPE, 1940
OVERLORD PLAN, COMBINED
BOMBER OFFENSIVE, AND GERMAN
DISPOSITIONS, 6 JUNE 1944

ELEVATIONS IN METERS
500   1500   ABOVE

0   50   100   150
SCALE OF MILES

STRATEGIC BOMBING TARGETS
IN GERMANY
Primary
Secondary

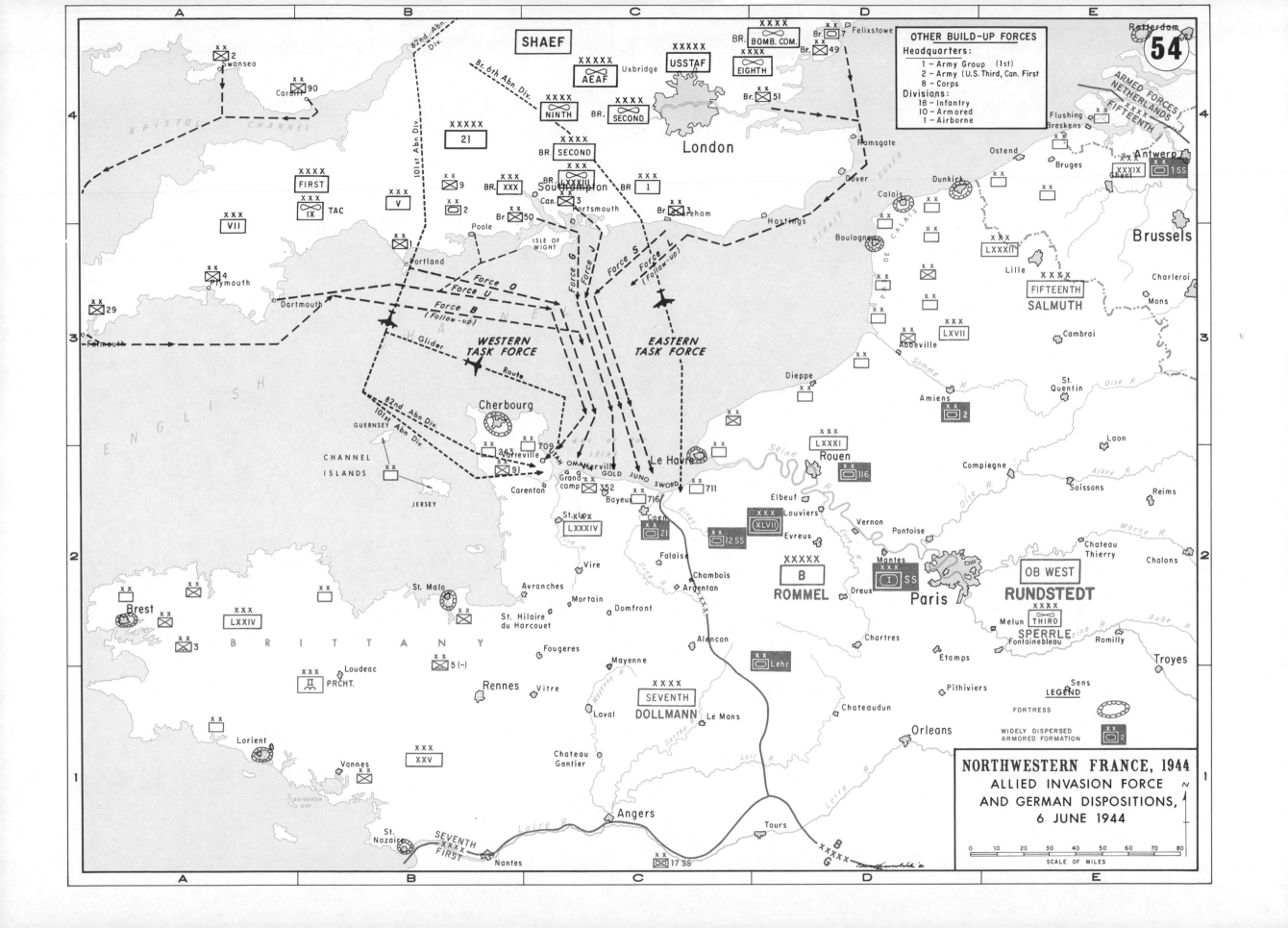

NORTHWESTERN FRANCE, 1944
ALLIED INVASION FORCE
AND GERMAN DISPOSITIONS,
6 JUNE 1944

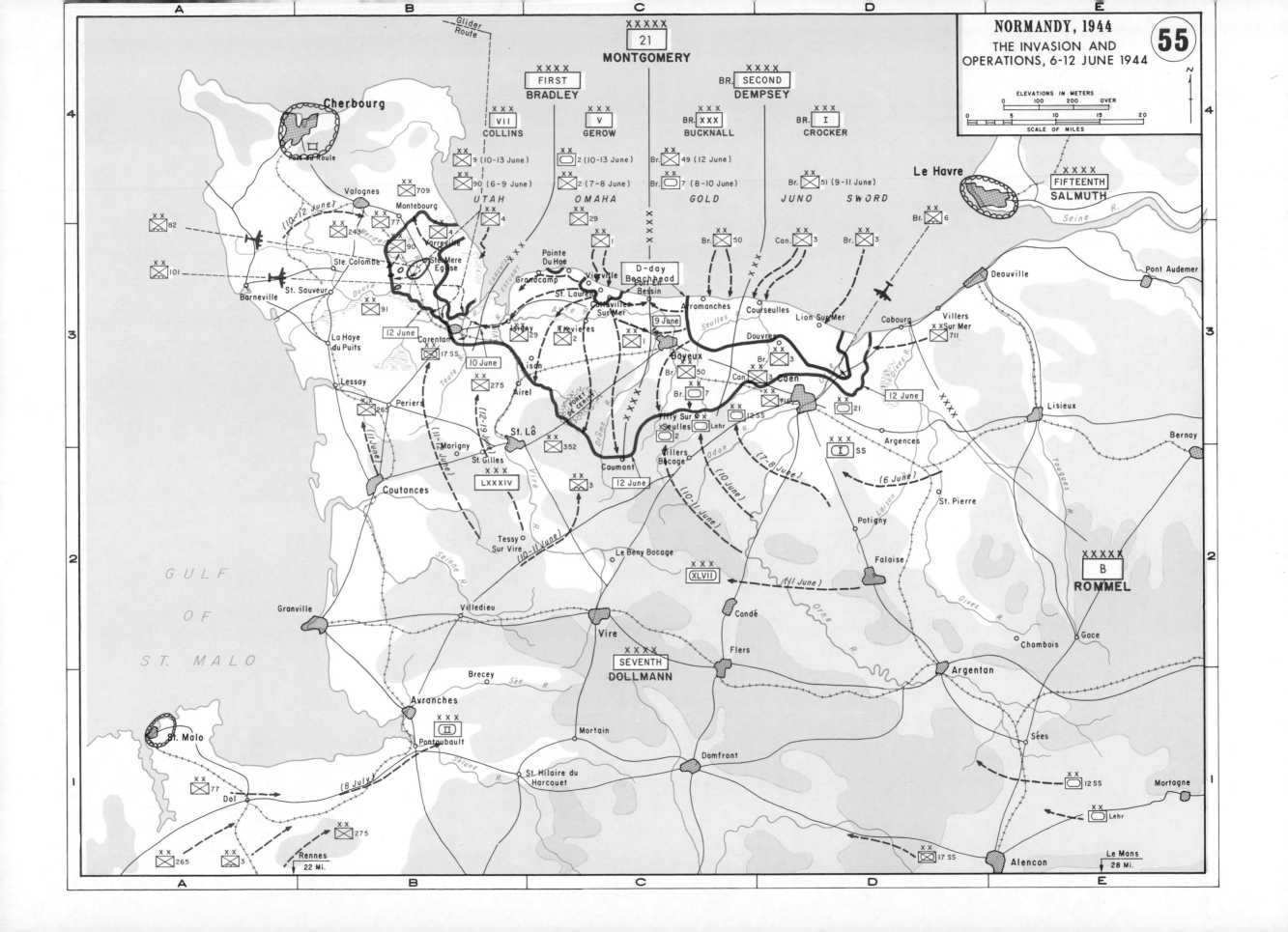

NORMANDY, 1944
THE INVASION AND OPERATIONS, 6-12 JUNE 1944

55

ELEVATIONS IN METERS

0   100   200   OVER

SCALE OF MILES
0   5   10   15   20

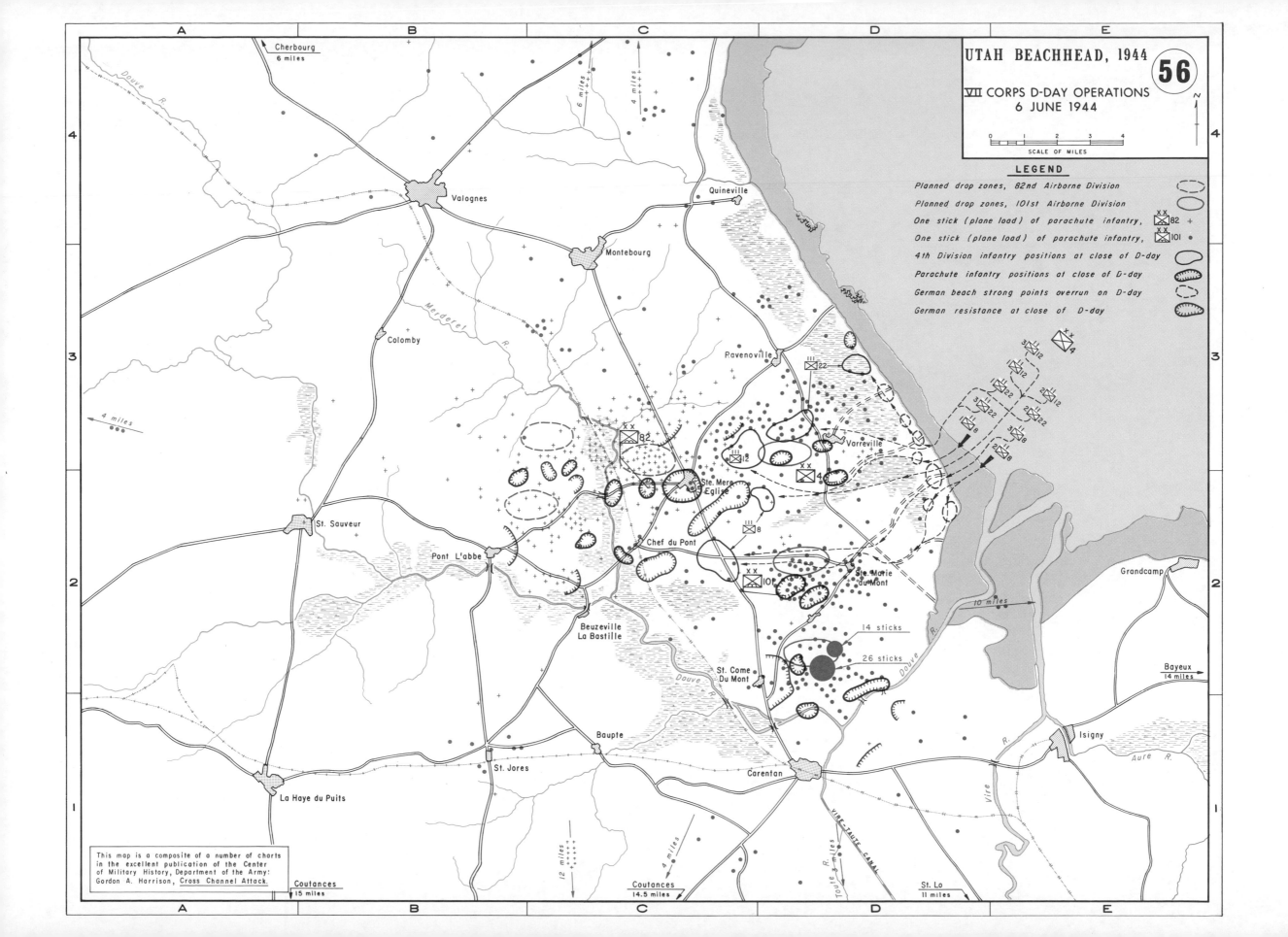

UTAH BEACHHEAD, 1944

56

VII CORPS D-DAY OPERATIONS
6 JUNE 1944

N

0 1 2 3 4
SCALE OF MILES

LEGEND

Planned drop zones, 82nd Airborne Division
Planned drop zones, 101st Airborne Division
One stick (plane load) of parachute infantry,   ⊠ 82 +
One stick (plane load) of parachute infantry,   ⊠ 101 •
4th Division infantry positions at close of D-day
Parachute infantry positions at close of D-day
German beach strong points overrun on D-day
German resistance at close of D-day

Cherbourg
6 miles

Douve R.

6 miles   4 miles

Valognes

Quineville

Montebourg

Merderet R.

Colomby

Ravenoville

4 miles

Varreville

Ste. Mere Eglise

St. Sauveur

Chef du Pont

Pont L'abbe

Ste. Marie du Mont

Beuzeville La Bastille

Grandcamp

10 miles

Douve R.

14 sticks

26 sticks

Bayeux
14 miles

St. Come Du Mont

Baupte

Isigny

St. Jores

Aure R.

Carentan

Vire R.

La Haye du Puits

This map is a composite of a number of charts
in the excellent publication of the Center
of Military History, Department of the Army:
Gordon A. Harrison, Cross Channel Attack.

Coutances
15 miles

12 miles

Coutances
14.5 miles

VIRE-TAUTE CANAL

Taute R.

4 miles

St. Lo
11 miles

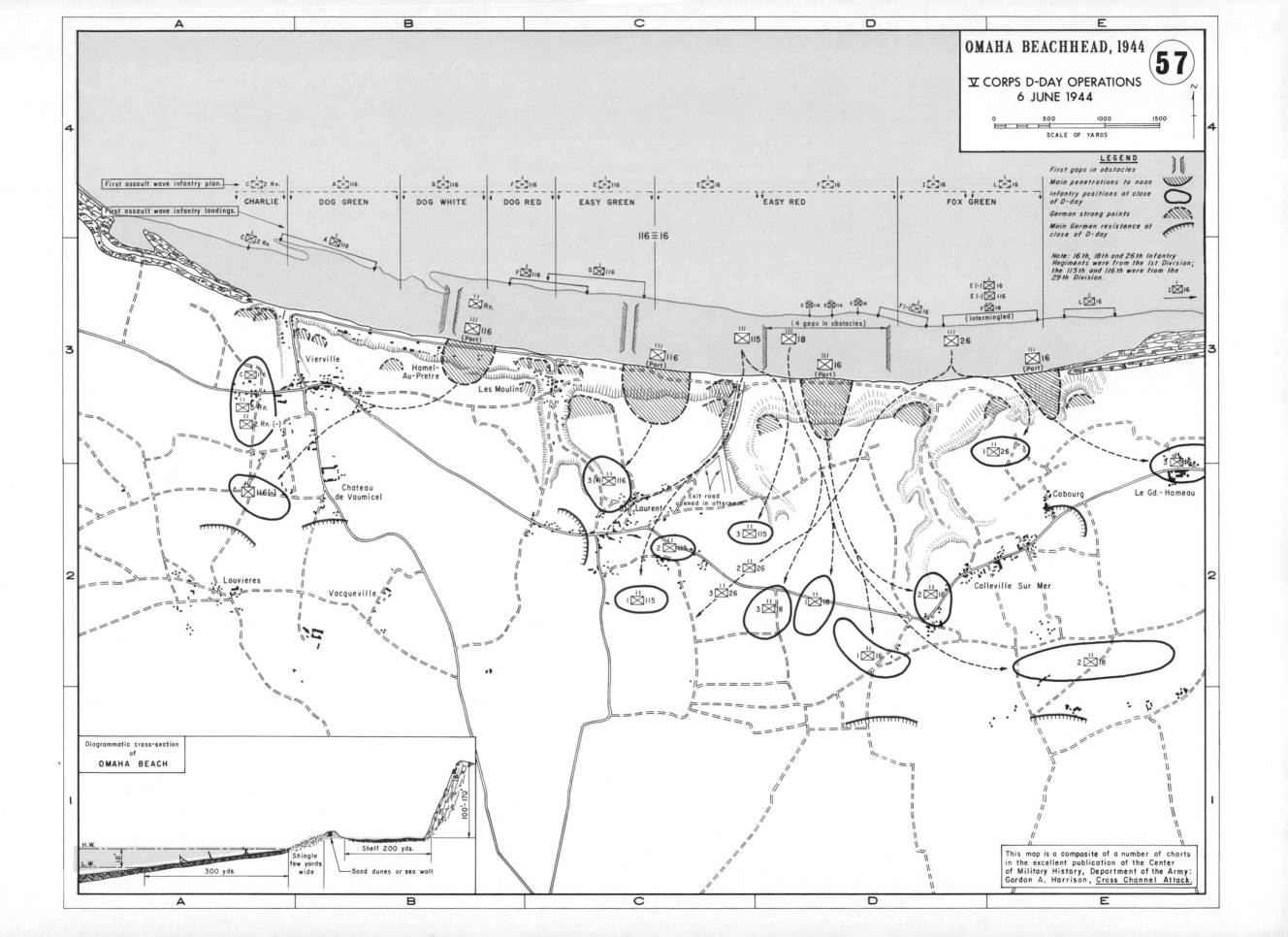

OMAHA BEACHHEAD, 1944

57

V CORPS D-DAY OPERATIONS
6 JUNE 1944

0   500   1000   1500
SCALE OF YARDS

LEGEND

First gaps in obstacles

Main penetrations to noon

*Infantry positions at close
of D-day*

German strong points

*Main German resistance at
close of D-day*

Note: 16th, 18th and 26th Infantry
Regiments were from the 1st Division;
the 115th and 116th were from the
29th Division.

First assault wave infantry plan.

First assault wave infantry landings.

CHARLIE   DOG GREEN   DOG WHITE   DOG RED   EASY GREEN   EASY RED   FOX GREEN

116 ≡ 16

(4 gaps in obstacles)   (Intermingled)

Vierville

Hamel-
Au-Pretre

Les Moulins

Chateau
de Vaumicel

St. Laurent

Exit road
opened in afternoon.

Cabourg

Le Gd.- Hameau

Louvieres

Vacqueville

Colleville Sur Mer

Diagrammatic cross-section
of
OMAHA BEACH

H.W.

L.W.

8'

300 yds.

Shingle
few yards
wide

Shelf 200 yds.

Sand dunes or sea wall

100-170'

This map is a composite of a number of charts
in the excellent publication of the Center
of Military History, Department of the Army:
Gordon A. Harrison, *Cross Channel Attack.*

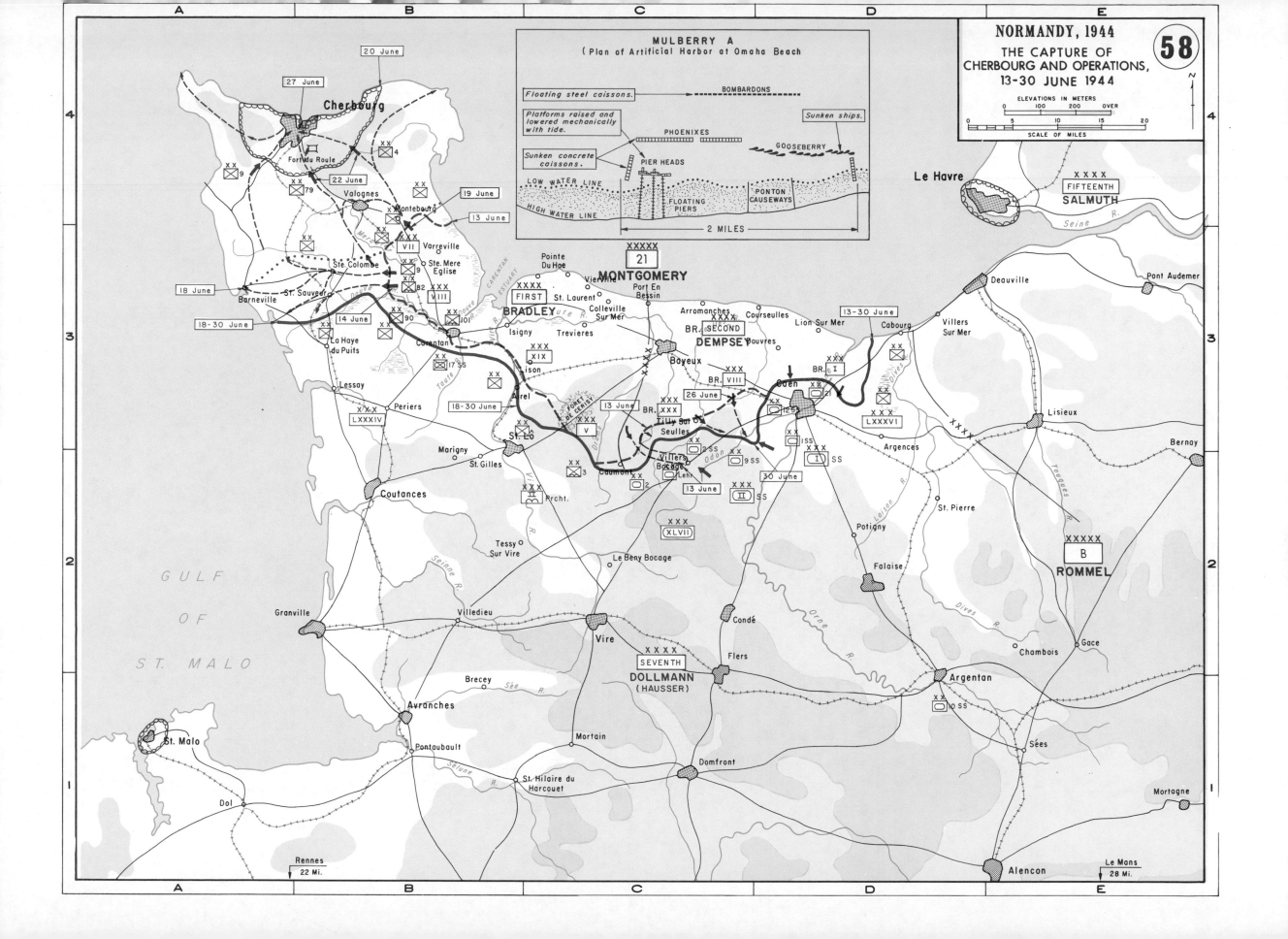

NORMANDY, 1944
THE CAPTURE OF CHERBOURG AND OPERATIONS, 13-30 JUNE 1944

58

N

ELEVATIONS IN METERS

0   100   200   OVER

0   5   10   15   20

SCALE OF MILES

MULBERRY A
(Plan of Artificial Harbor at Omaha Beach)

Floating steel caissons. ————————— BOMBARDONS

Platforms raised and lowered mechanically with tide.

PHOENIXES

Sunken ships.

Sunken concrete caissons.

PIER HEADS

GOOSEBERRY

LOW WATER LINE

HIGH WATER LINE

FLOATING PIERS

PONTON CAUSEWAYS

2 MILES

20 June

27 June

Cherbourg

Fort du Roule

XX 9

22 June

XX 79

XX 4

19 June

13 June

Valognes

Montebourg

VII

Varreville

Ste. Colombe

Ste. Mere Eglise

XX 9

18 June

St. Sauveur

XX 82

XXX

VIII

Barneville

18-30 June

14 June

XX 90

XX 101

La Haye du Puits

Lessay

Periers

Carentan

XX 17 SS

Pointe Du Hoe

Vierville

Port En Bessin

Isigny

Treviers

Colleville Sur Mer

St. Laurent

MONTGOMERY 21

FIRST **BRADLEY**

XXXX

Arromanches

Courseulles

Lion Sur Mer

BR. **SECOND** **DEMPSEY**

Douvres

Cabourg

13-30 June

Deauville

Pont Audemer

Le Havre

XXXX **FIFTEENTH** **SALMUTH**

Seine R.

Villers Sur Mer

XXX XIX

Lison

XX

Arel

FORET DE CERISY

18-30 June

13 June

St. Lo

LXXXIV

Marigny

St. Gilles

XX 3

II Prcht.

XXX

XXX

BR. VIII

26 June

BR. XXX

Tilly Sur Seulles

Villers Bocage

Lehr

XX 2

XX

13 June

II SS

XXX XLVII

Tessy Sur Vire

Le Beny Bocage

Bayeux

Caen

BR. I

XX 21

XX 12 SS

2 SS

9 SS

XXX I SS

30 June

I SS

LXXXVI

Argences

St. Pierre

Potigny

Lisieux

Bernay

Gace

ROMMEL B

Coutances

VII II

Condé

Falaise

Granville

Villedieu

Vire

XXXX **SEVENTH** **DOLLMANN** (HAUSSER)

Mortain

Flers

Orne R.

Argentan

XX 10 SS

Chambois

Brecey

See R.

Domfront

Sees

Avranches

Pontaubault

St. Hilaire du Harcouet

Selune R.

GULF OF ST. MALO

St. Malo

Dol

Rennes 22 Mi.

Le Mans 28 Mi.

Alencon

Mortagne

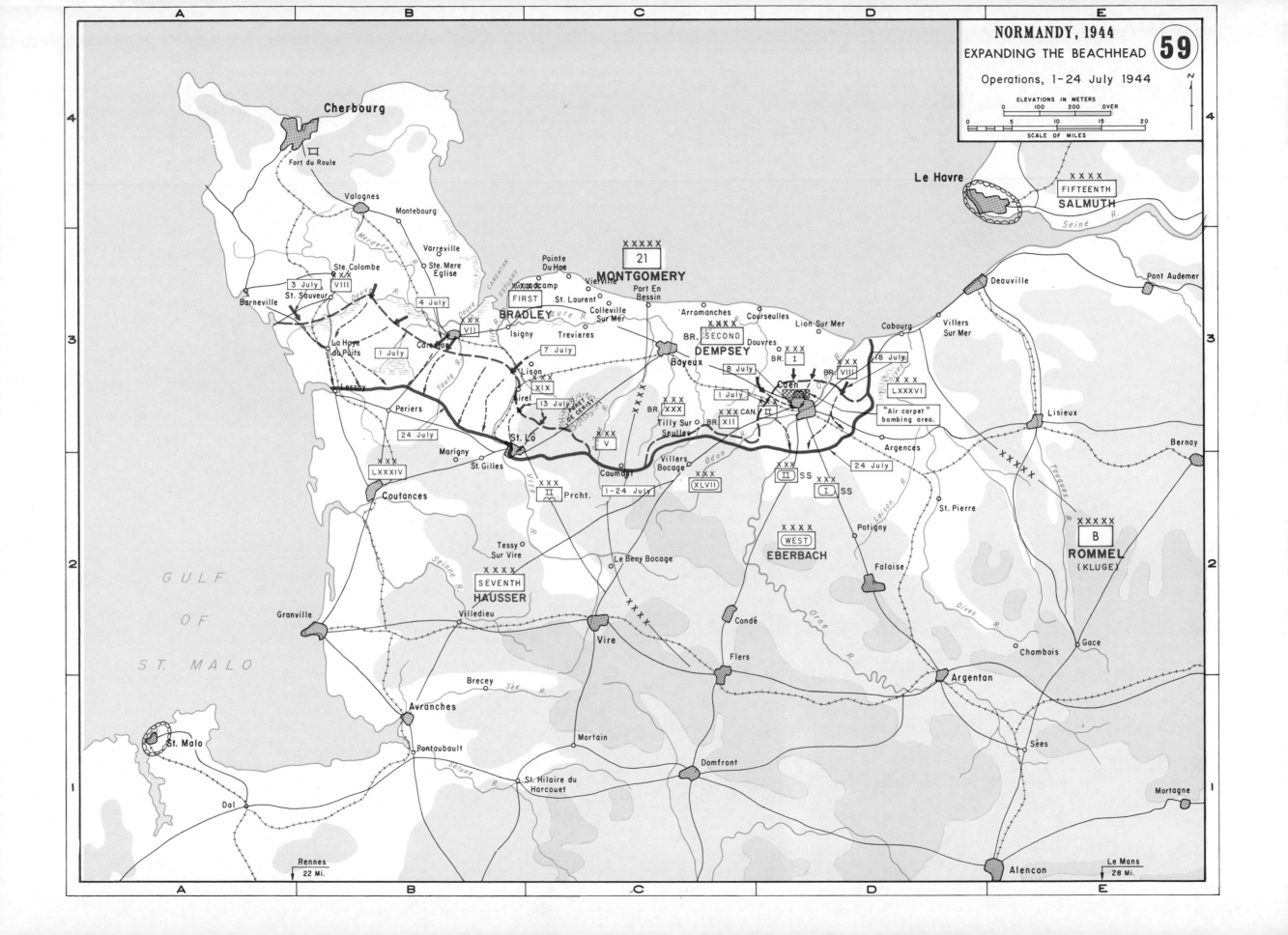

NORMANDY, 1944
EXPANDING THE BEACHHEAD
59
Operations, 1-24 July 1944

ELEVATIONS IN METERS
0   100   200   OVER
0   5   10   15   20
SCALE OF MILES

Cherbourg

Fort du Roule

Le Havre

XXXX
FIFTEENTH
SALMUTH

Seine R.

Valognes

Montebourg

Varreville

Ste. Colombe
X/X
3 July   VIII
St. Sauveur

Barneville

La Haye
du Puits

1 July

4 July

Ste. Mere
Eglise

Pointe
Du Hoe

XXXXX
21
MONTGOMERY

FIRST
BRADLEY

Vierville
St. Laurent

Port En
Bessin

Arromanches

Courseulles   Lion Sur Mer

BR.   SECOND
DEMPSEY

Deauville

Pont Audemer

XXXX

Colleville
Sur Mer

XXX
VII

Carentan

Lessay

Periers

Isigny

Trevieres

Lison

Airel

13 July

7 July

XXX
XIX

Bayeux

BR.   XXX

Caen

XXX
BR.   I

Cabourg

XXX
BR.   VIII

Villers
Sur Mer

18 July

XXX
LXXXVI

Lisieux

Bernay

24 July

XXXX

"Air carpet"
bombing area.

FORET
DE CERISY

XXX
CAN.   II

1 July

Tilly Sur
Seulles

BR.   XII

St. Lo

Marigny

St. Gilles

XXX
LXXXIV

Coutances

XXX
II   Prcht.

1-24 July

XXX
V

Caumont

Villers
Bocage

XXX
XLVII

Odon R.

II   SS

XXX
I   SS

Argences

24 July

St. Pierre

Potigny

Tessy
Sur Vire

Le Beny Bocage

XXXX
WEST
EBERBACH

Falaise

XXXXX
B
ROMMEL
(KLUGE)

Gace

Granville

Villedieu

Vire

Condé

XXXX
SEVENTH
HAUSSER

Flers

Chambois

GULF
OF
ST. MALO

Brecey

Sée R.

Argentan

Avranches

Pontaubault

Mortain

Sées

St. Malo

Dol

St. Hilaire du
Harcouet

Domfront

Mortagne

Rennes
22 Mi.

Alencon

Le Mans
28 Mi.

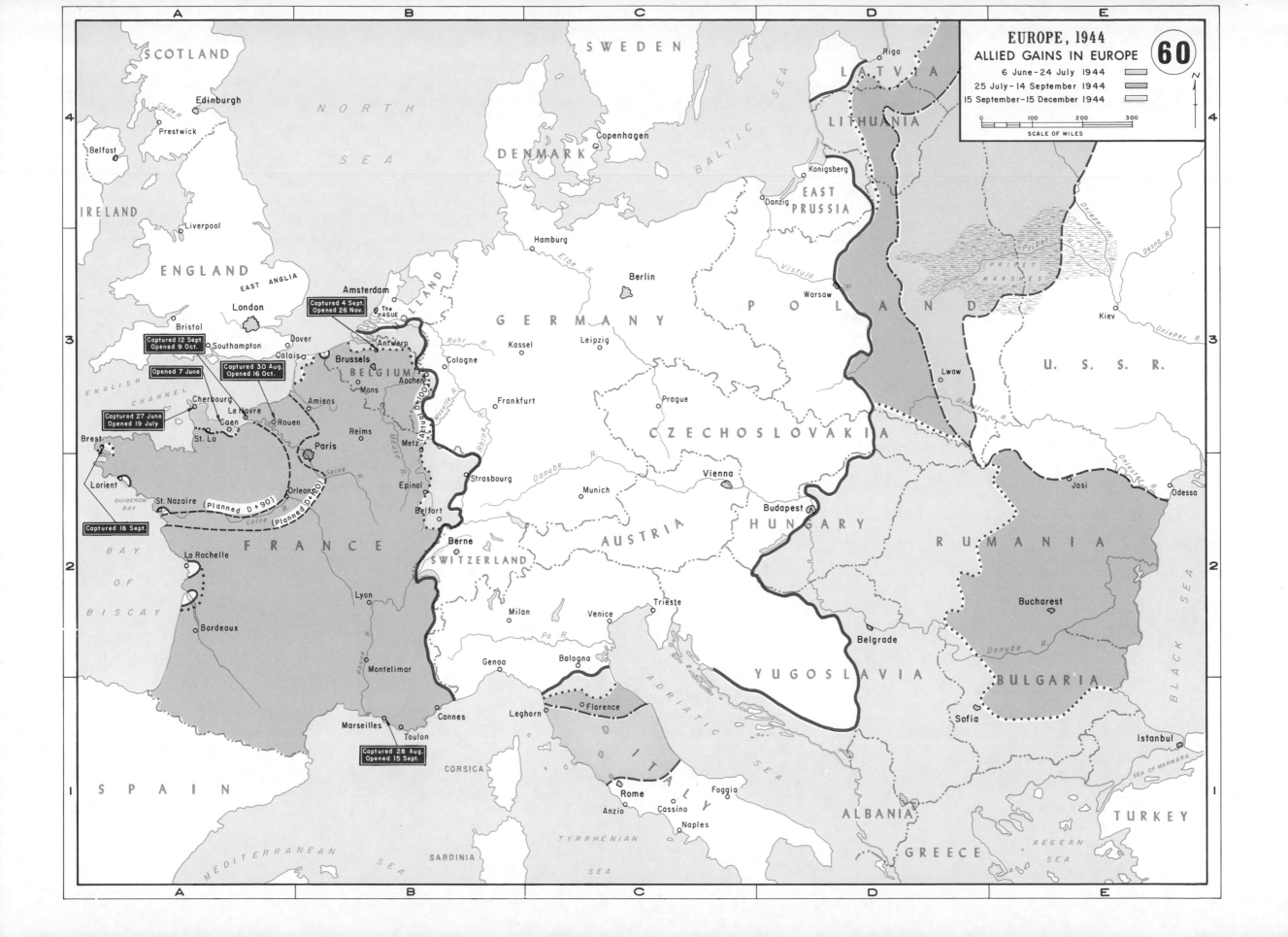

EUROPE, 1944
ALLIED GAINS IN EUROPE
60

6 June–24 July 1944
25 July–14 September 1944
15 September–15 December 1944

SCALE OF MILES
0   100   200   300

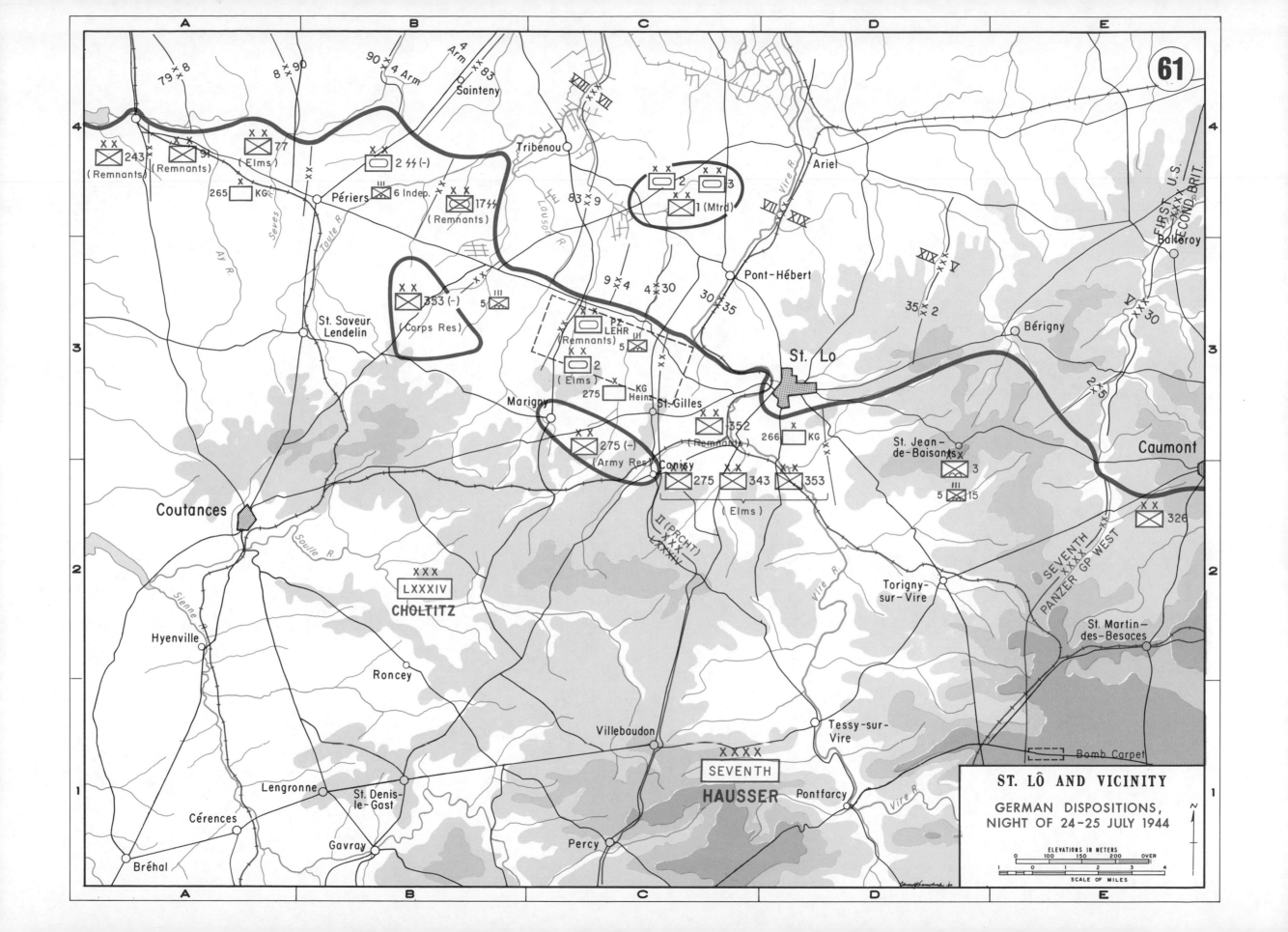

61

ST. LÔ AND VICINITY

GERMAN DISPOSITIONS,
NIGHT OF 24–25 JULY 1944

ELEVATIONS IN METERS
100 150 200 OVER

SCALE OF MILES

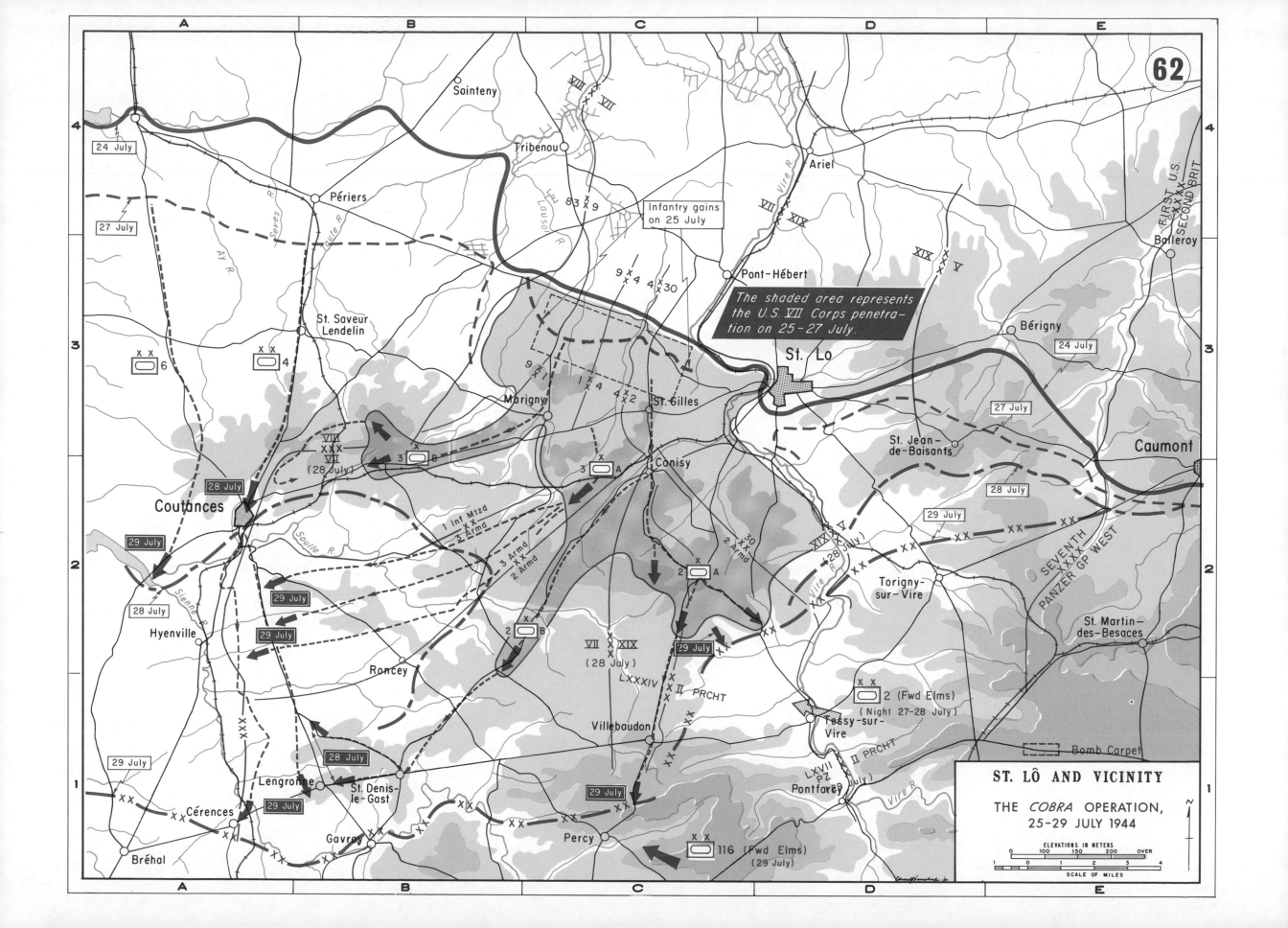

ST. LÔ AND VICINITY

THE *COBRA* OPERATION,
25-29 JULY 1944

62

The shaded area represents the U.S. VII Corps penetration on 25-27 July.

Infantry gains on 25 July

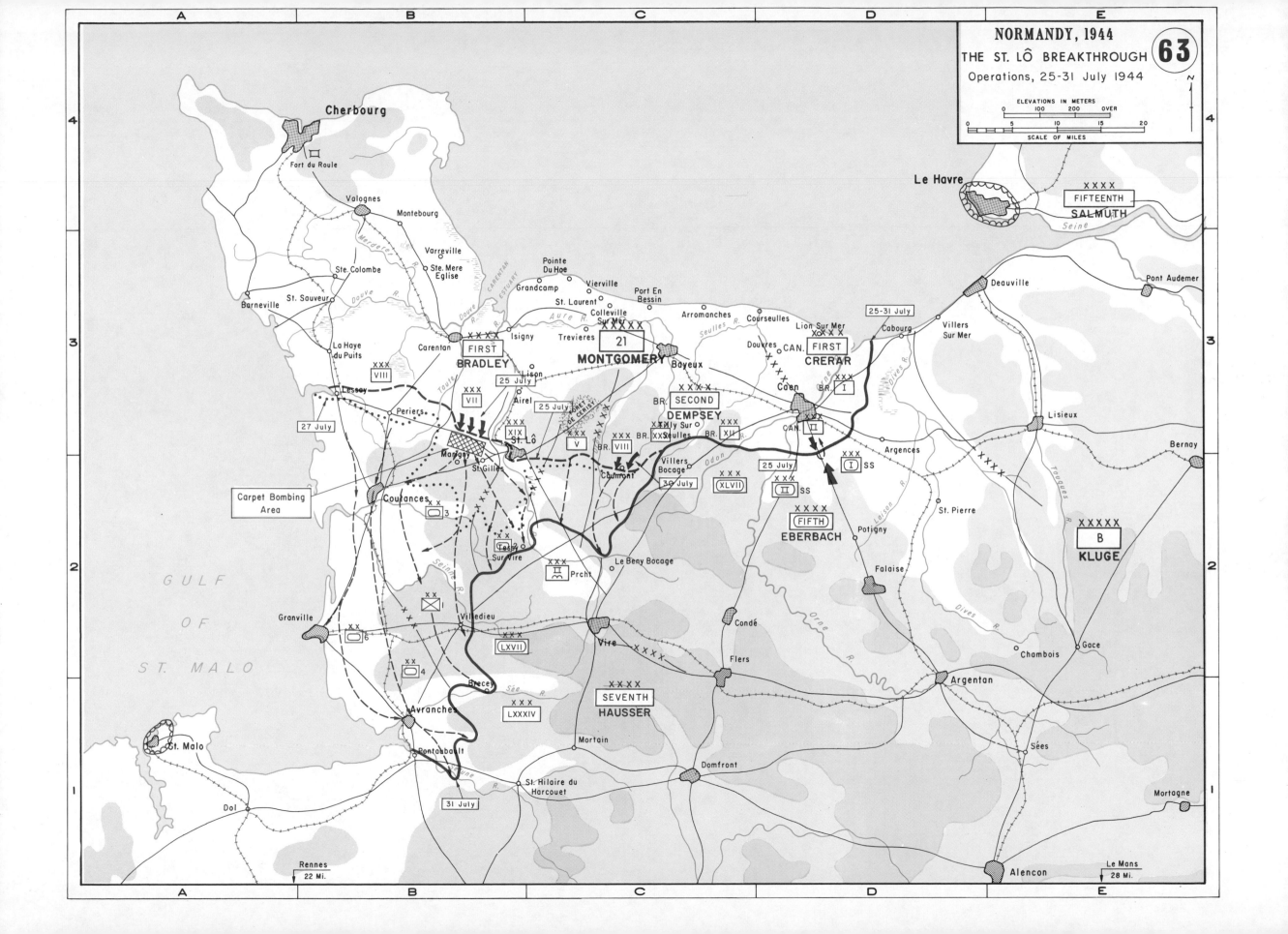

NORMANDY, 1944
THE ST. LÔ BREAKTHROUGH
Operations, 25-31 July 1944

63

ELEVATIONS IN METERS
0   100   200   OVER

0   5   10   15   20
SCALE OF MILES

Cherbourg

Fort du Roule

Valognes

Montebourg

Varreville

Ste. Colombe

Ste. Mere Eglise

Barneville

St. Sauveur

La Haye du Puits

Carentan

Lison

Isigny

Trevieres

Pointe Du Hoe

Grandcamp

Vierville

St. Laurent

Colleville Sur Mer

Port En Bessin

Arromanches

Courseulles

Lion Sur Mer

Douvres

Bayeux

Caen

Le Havre

XXXX
FIFTEENTH
SALMUTH

Deauville

Pont Audemer

Villers Sur Mer

Cabourg

25-31 July

Lisieux

Bernay

XXXX
FIRST
BRADLEY

XXXXX
21
MONTGOMERY

CAN. XXXX
FIRST
CRERAR

BR. XXX
I

Lessay

XXX
VIII

25 July

XXX
VII

Periers

Airel

27 July

St. Lô

XXX
XIX

25 July

FORET DE CERISY

XXX
V

Marigny

St. Gilles

BR. XXX
VIII

BR. XXXX
SECOND
DEMPSEY

Ly Sur Seulles

BR. XXX

BR. XXX
XII

CAN. XXX
II

Argences

XXXX

Carpet Bombing Area

Caumont

Villers Bocage

30 July

XXX
XLVII

25 July

XXX
I SS

XXX
II SS

St. Pierre

Coutances

XX
3

Tessy Sur Vire

XXX
II Prcht

Le Beny Bocage

XXXX
FIFTH
EBERBACH

Potigny

Falaise

XXXXX
B
KLUGE

XX
I

Villedieu

Odon

Condé

Orne R.

Dives R.

Gace

Granville

XX
6

XXX
LXVII

Vire

XXXX

Flers

Chambois

GULF OF ST. MALO

XX
4

Brecey

See R.

XXX
LXXXIV

XXXX
SEVENTH
HAUSSER

Mortain

Argentan

Sées

St. Malo

Avranches

Pontaubault

St. Hilaire du Harcouet

Domfront

Mortagne

31 July

Dol

Alencon

Rennes
22 Mi.

Le Mans
28 Mi.

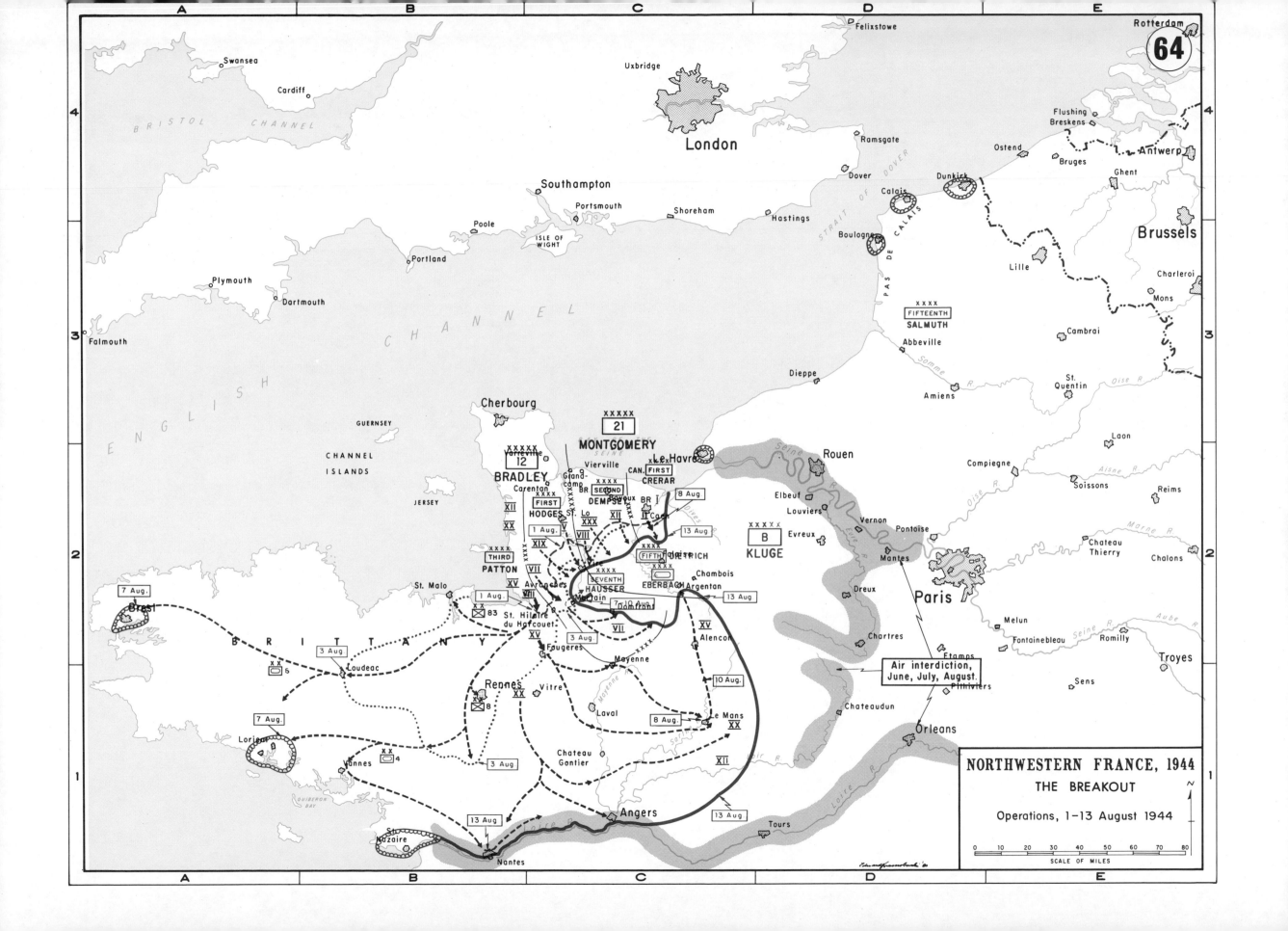

NORTHWESTERN FRANCE, 1944

THE BREAKOUT

Operations, 1–13 August 1944

SCALE OF MILES

0 10 20 30 40 50 60 70 80

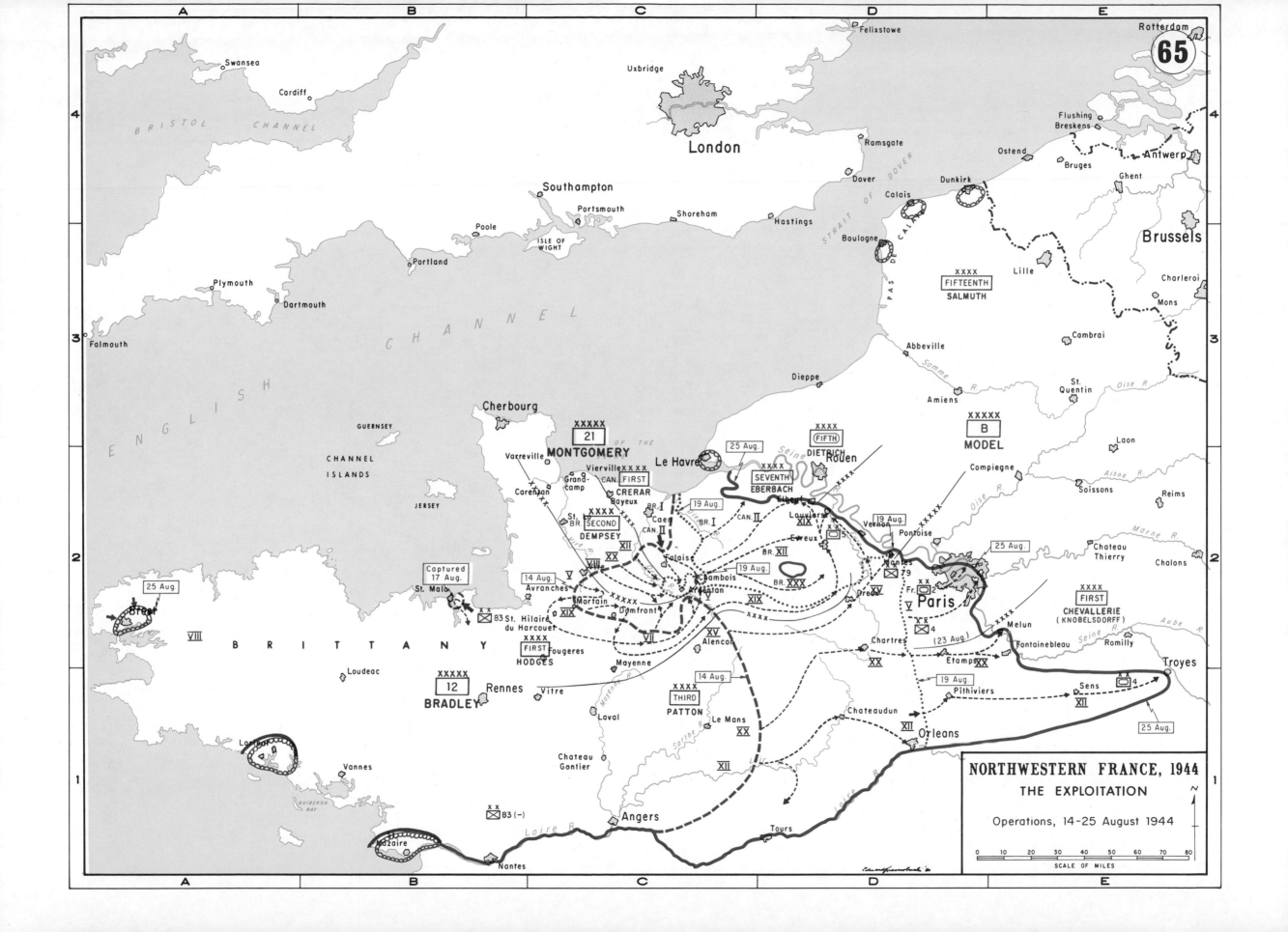

NORTHWESTERN FRANCE, 1944

THE EXPLOITATION

Operations, 14-25 August 1944

SCALE OF MILES

0 10 20 30 40 50 60 70 80

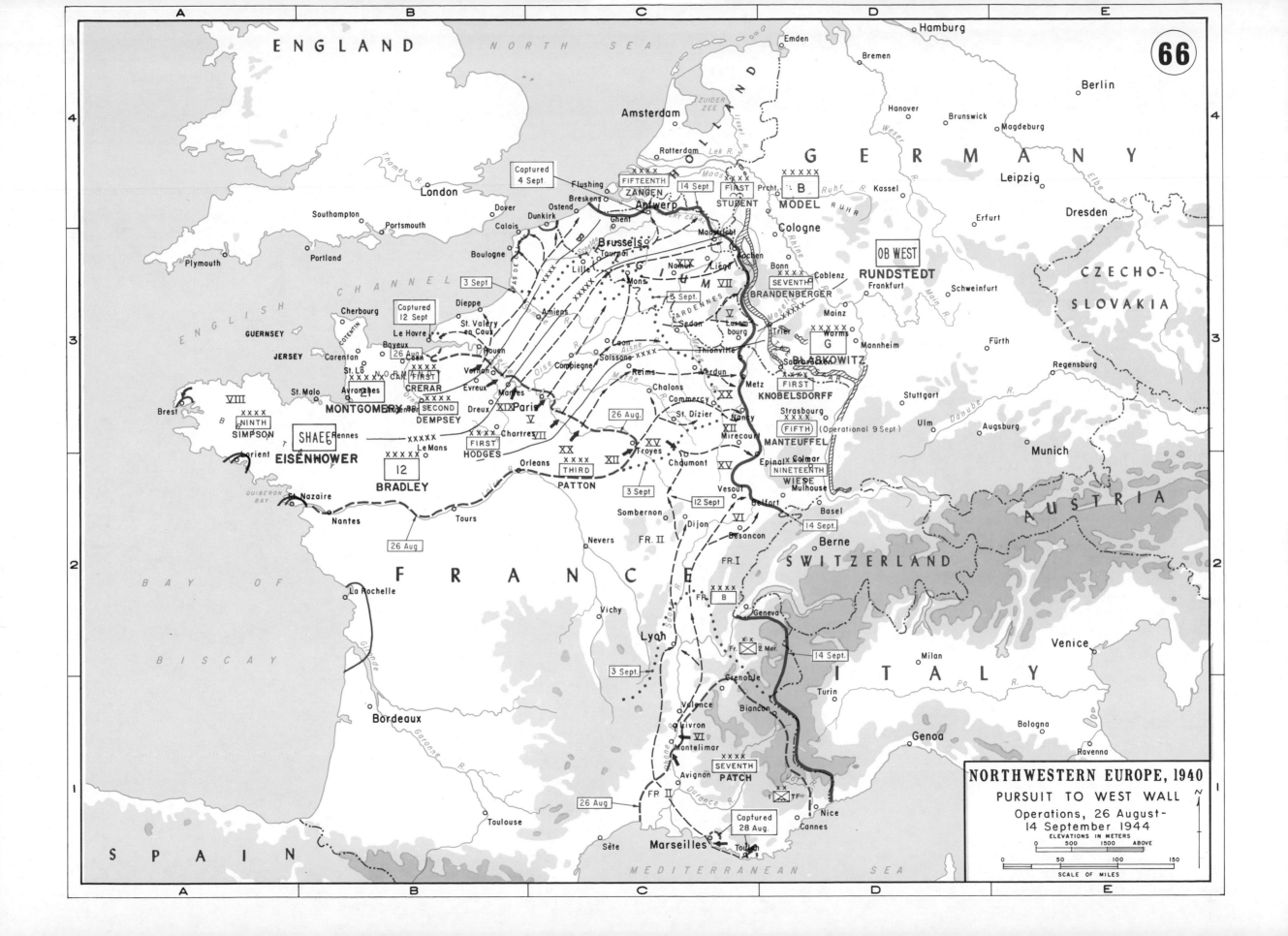

NORTHWESTERN EUROPE, 1940
PURSUIT TO WEST WALL
Operations, 26 August–
14 September 1944

ELEVATIONS IN METERS
500   1500   ABOVE

0   50   100   150
SCALE OF MILES

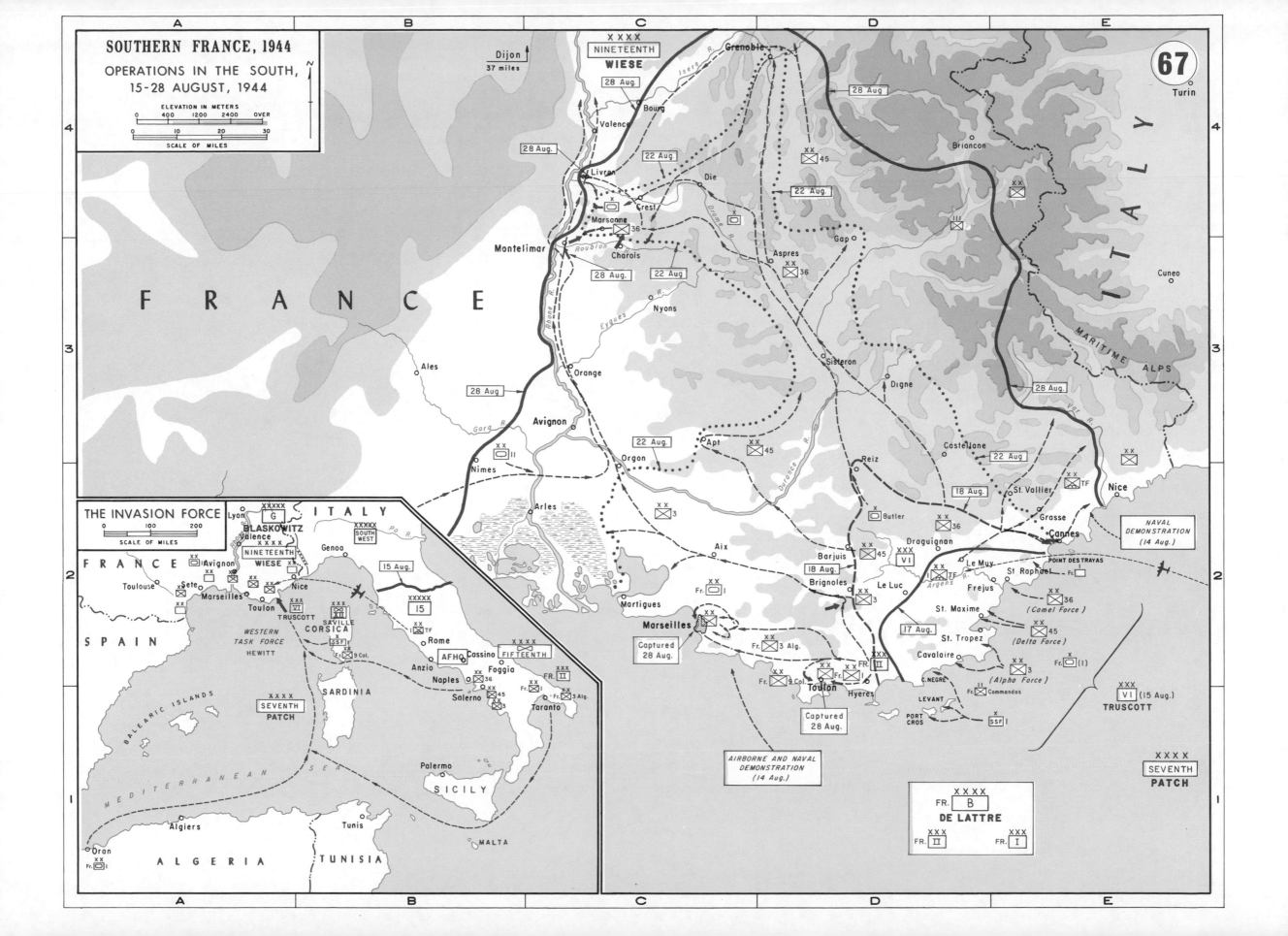

SOUTHERN FRANCE, 1944

OPERATIONS IN THE SOUTH,
15-28 AUGUST, 1944

ELEVATION IN METERS
400 1200 2400 OVER
0   10   20   30
SCALE OF MILES

67

THE INVASION FORCE
0   100   200
SCALE OF MILES

FRANCE

SPAIN

ALGERIA   TUNISIA

MEDITERRANEAN   SEA

BALEARIC ISLANDS

SARDINIA

CORSICA

SICILY

ITALY

FRANCE   ITALY

Lyon
Valence
Genoa
Po R.
Toulouse
Avignon
Sete
Marseilles
Toulon
Nice
Rome
Anzio
Naples
Cassino
Foggia
Salerno
Taranto
Palermo
Algiers
Tunis
Oran
MALTA

G
BLASKOWITZ
SOUTH WEST
NINETEENTH
WIESE
TRUSCOTT
SAVILLE
SSF
9 Col.
AFHQ
FIFTEENTH
WESTERN TASK FORCE
HEWITT
SEVENTH
PATCH
15 Aug.
15
36
45
3
VI

FRANCE

Dijon
37 miles

NINETEENTH
WIESE

Grenoble   Turin

Isere R.

28 Aug.
Bourg
Valence
28 Aug.
Livron
22 Aug.
Die
28 Aug.
Crest
Marsanne   36
Montelimar
28 Aug.
Charois
22 Aug.
Roubion
Rhone R.
Drome R.
Aspres   36
22 Aug.
Gap
45
III
Briancon
22 Aug.
ITALY   Cuneo

MARITIME ALPS

Nyons
Eygues R.

Ales

Orange
28 Aug
Avignon
Garg R.
II
Nimes
Arles
Orgon
22 Aug.
Apt
45
3
Sisteron
Digne
Duranco R.
Reiz
28 Aug.
Var R.
Castellane
22 Aug
St. Vallier   TF
Grasse
Cannes
NAVAL DEMONSTRATION
(14 Aug.)

Butler
36
18 Aug.
Draguignan
VI
Barjuis   45
Le Muy
Le Luc   TF
St Raphael   Ft.
POINT DESTRAYAS

Aix
Brignoles
3
Fr.   I
II
St. Maxime
Frejus
36
(Camel Force)
45
(Delta Force)
17 Aug.
St. Tropez
Cavalaire
3
Fr.   (1)
(Alpha Force)

Martigues

Marseilles
Captured 28 Aug.
Fr.   3 Alg.
Fr.   9 Col.
Toulon
Hyeres
Captured 28 Aug.
C. NEGRE
LEVANT
Fr.   II   Commandos
PORT CROS
SSF
VI   (15 Aug.)
TRUSCOTT

AIRBORNE AND NAVAL DEMONSTRATION
(14 Aug.)

SEVENTH
PATCH

FR.   B
DE LATTRE
FR.   II   FR.   I

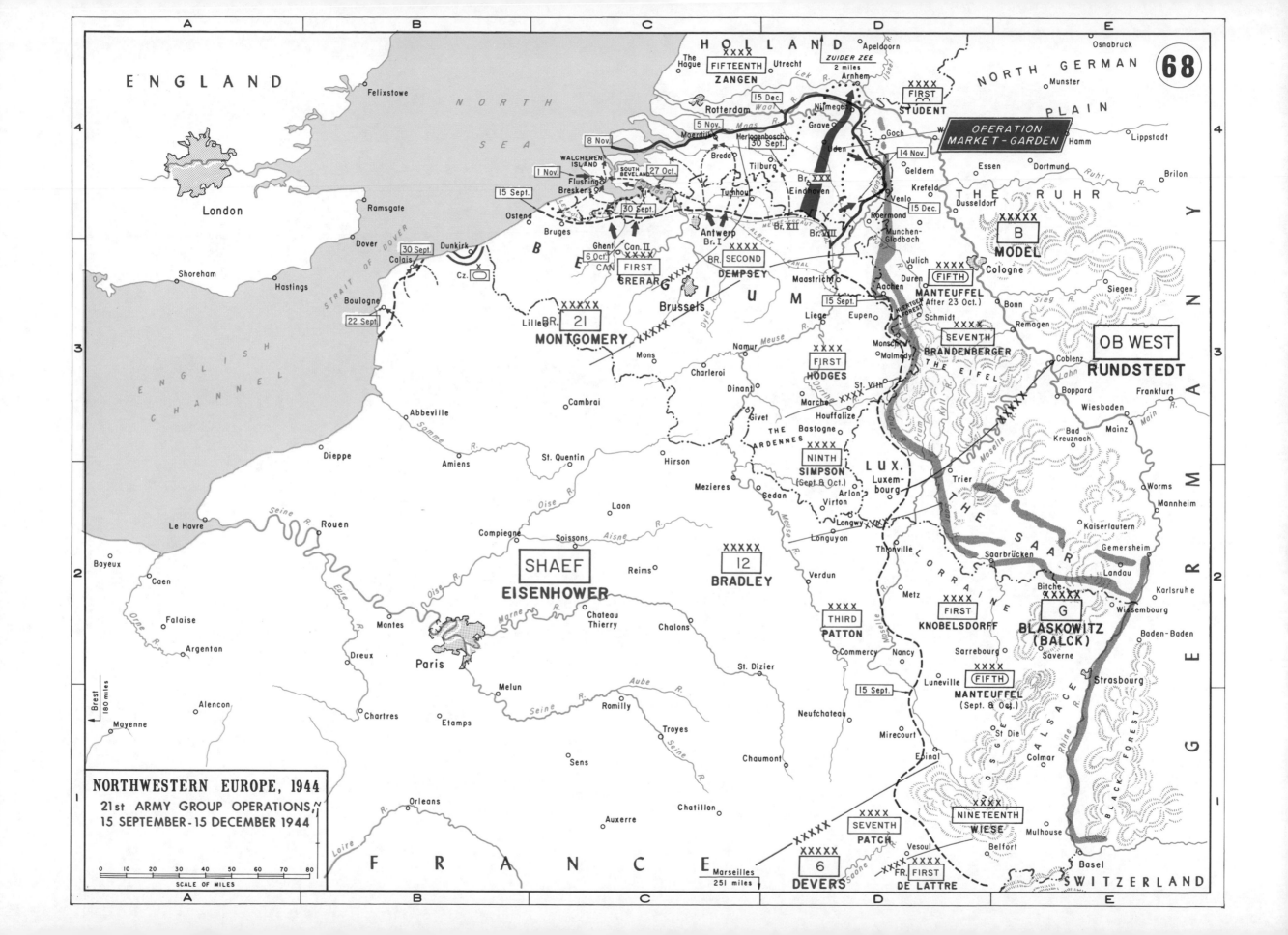

NORTHWESTERN EUROPE, 1944
21st ARMY GROUP OPERATIONS
15 SEPTEMBER-15 DECEMBER 1944

SCALE OF MILES
0 10 20 30 40 50 60 70 80

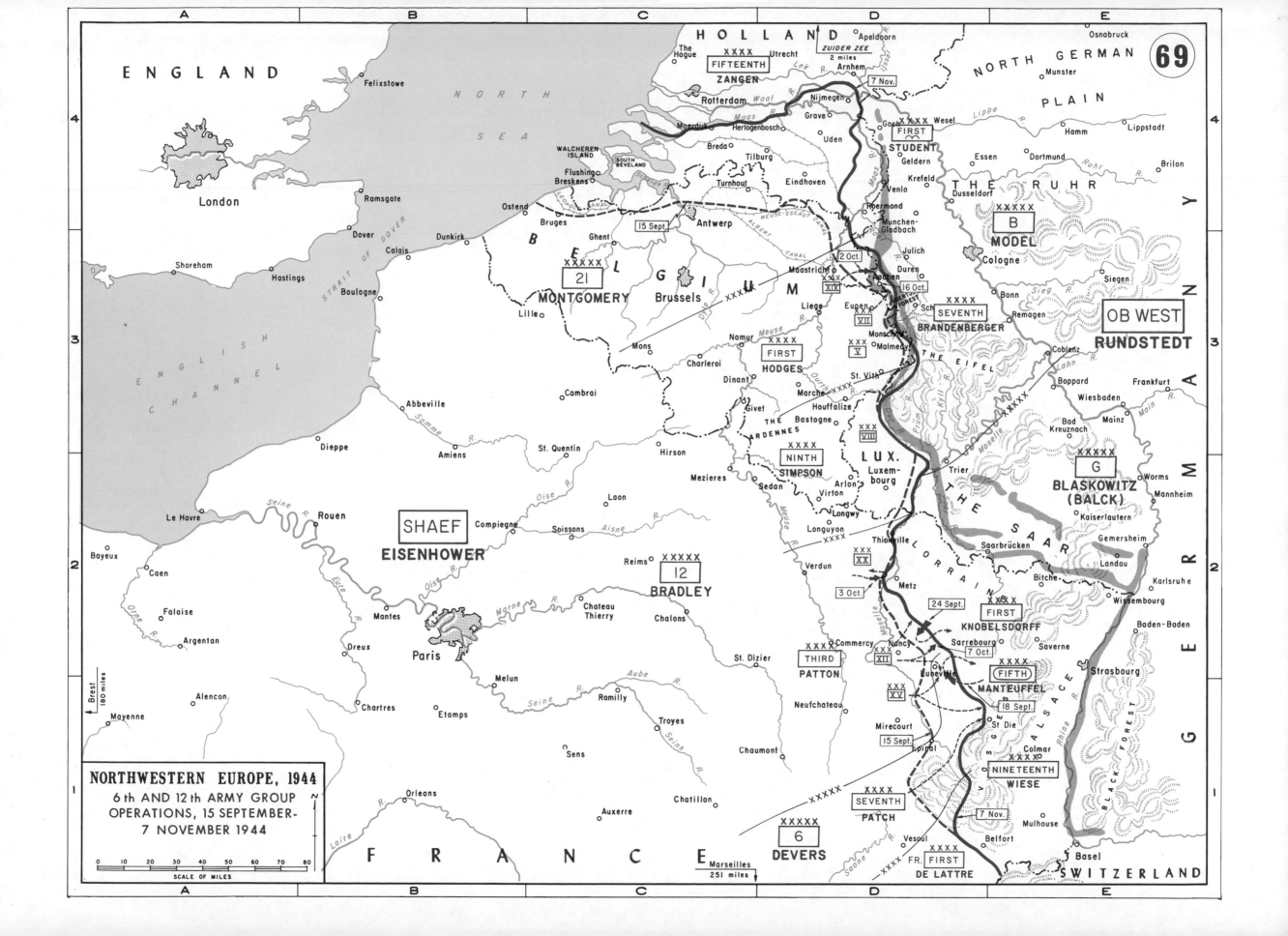

NORTHWESTERN EUROPE, 1944
6th AND 12th ARMY GROUP
OPERATIONS, 15 SEPTEMBER-
7 NOVEMBER 1944

SCALE OF MILES
0 10 20 30 40 50 60 70 80

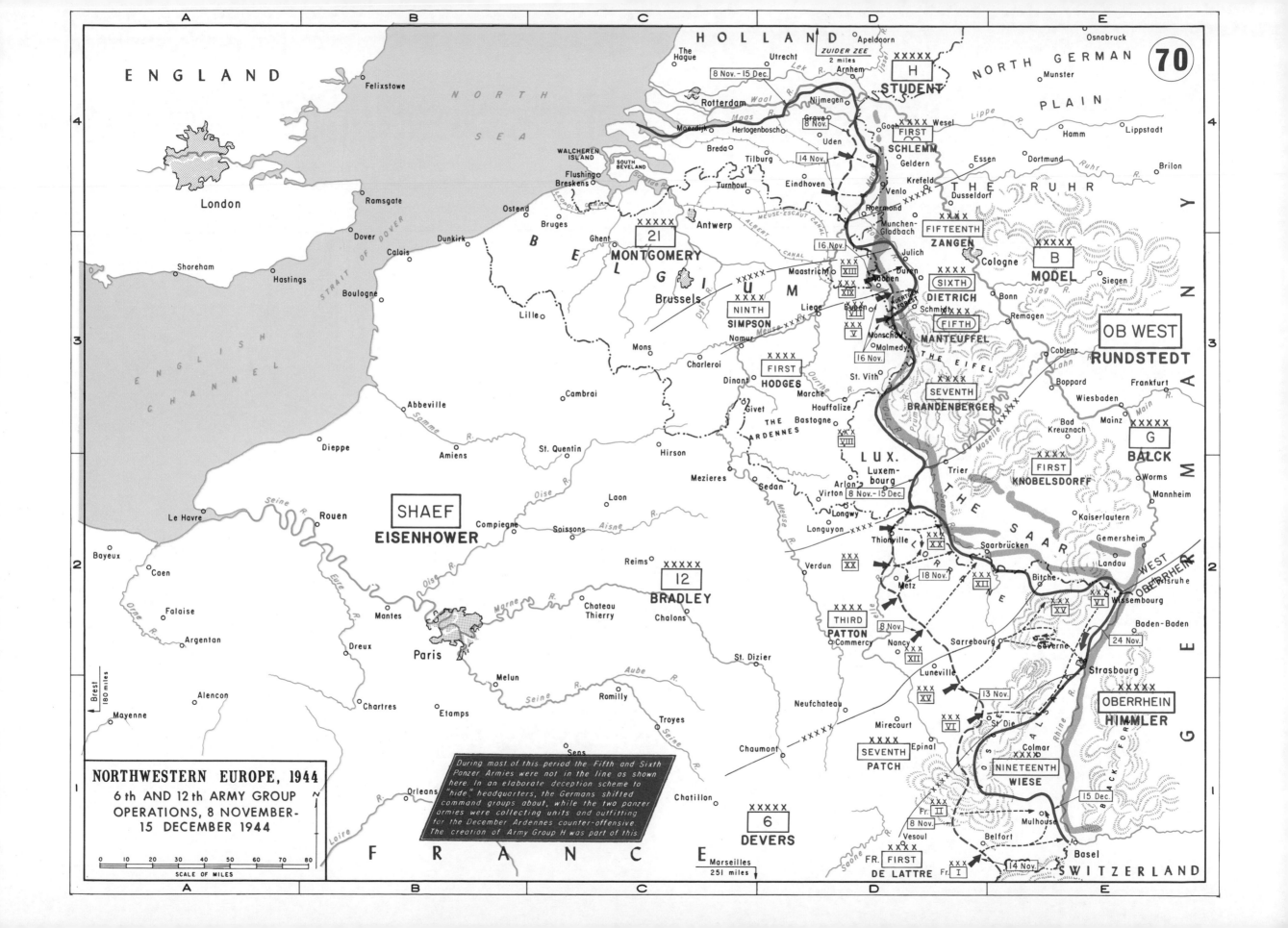

ENGLAND

NORTH SEA

HOLLAND

NORTH GERMAN PLAIN

(70)

NORTHWESTERN EUROPE, 1944
6th AND 12th ARMY GROUP OPERATIONS, 8 NOVEMBER- 15 DECEMBER 1944

SHAEF
EISENHOWER

12
BRADLEY

21
MONTGOMERY

NINTH
SIMPSON

FIRST
HODGES

THIRD
PATTON

SEVENTH
PATCH

6
DEVERS

FR. FIRST
DE LATTRE

H
STUDENT

FIRST
SCHLEMM

FIFTEENTH
ZANGEN

SIXTH
DIETRICH

FIFTH
MANTEUFFEL

SEVENTH
BRANDENBERGER

FIRST
KNOBELSDORFF

G
BALCK

NINETEENTH
WIESE

OBERRHEIN
HIMMLER

OB WEST
RUNDSTEDT

B
MODEL

THE RUHR

THE EIFEL

THE SAAR

THE ARDENNES

LUX.
Luxembourg

BELGIUM

FRANCE

SWITZERLAND

During most of this period the Fifth and Sixth Panzer Armies were not in the line as shown here. In an elaborate deception scheme to "hide" headquarters, the Germans shifted command groups about, while the two panzer armies were collecting units and outfitting for the December Ardennes counter-offensive. The creation of Army Group H was part of this.

SCALE OF MILES
0 10 20 30 40 50 60 70 80

Brest 180 miles

Marseilles 251 miles

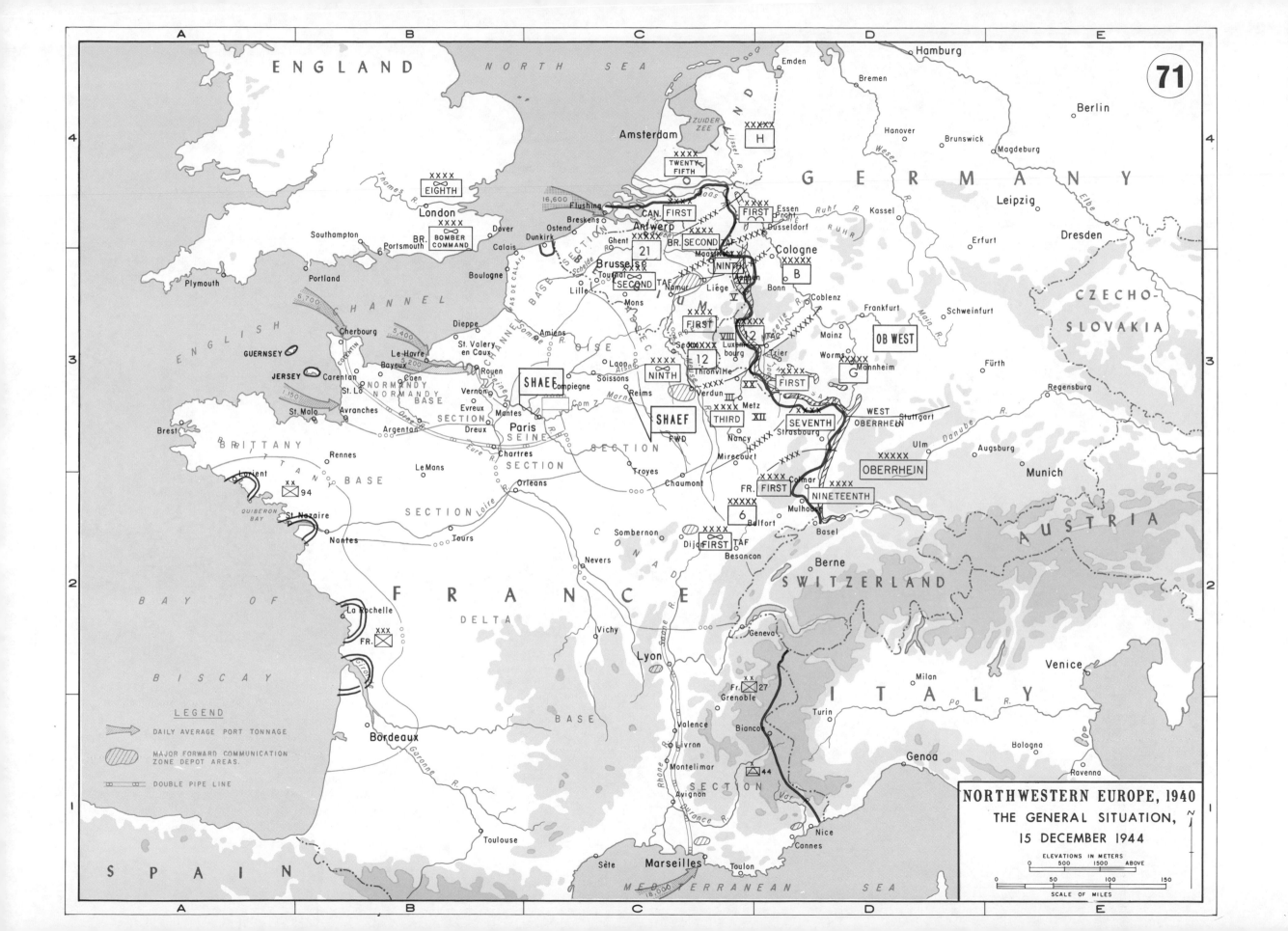

NORTHWESTERN EUROPE, 1940
THE GENERAL SITUATION,
15 DECEMBER 1944

ELEVATIONS IN METERS
500   1500   ABOVE

0   50   100   150
SCALE OF MILES

LEGEND

DAILY AVERAGE PORT TONNAGE

MAJOR FORWARD COMMUNICATION
ZONE DEPOT AREAS.

DOUBLE PIPE LINE

71

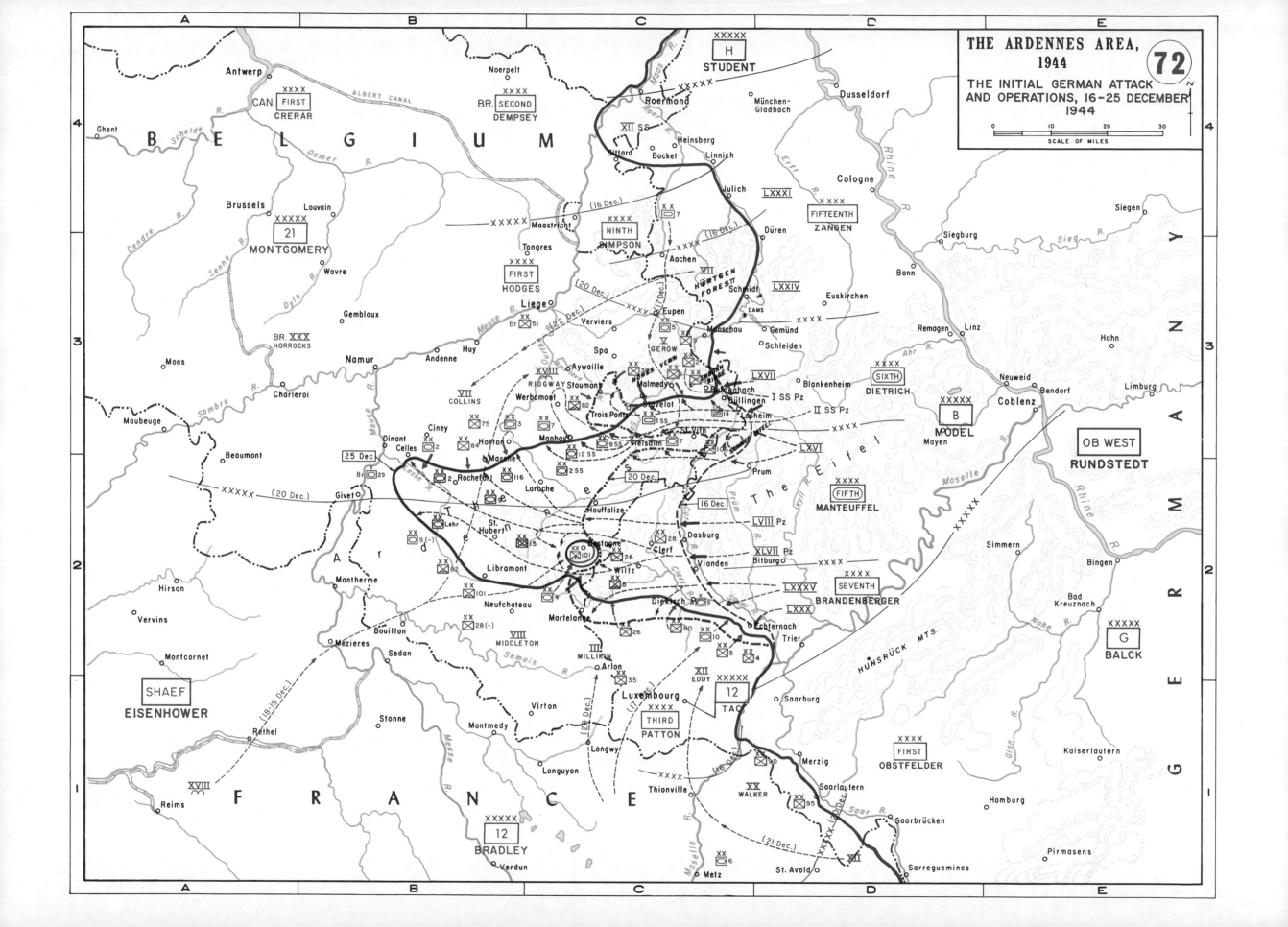

THE ARDENNES AREA,
1944

72

THE INITIAL GERMAN ATTACK
AND OPERATIONS, 16-25 DECEMBER
1944

SCALE OF MILES
0   10   20   30

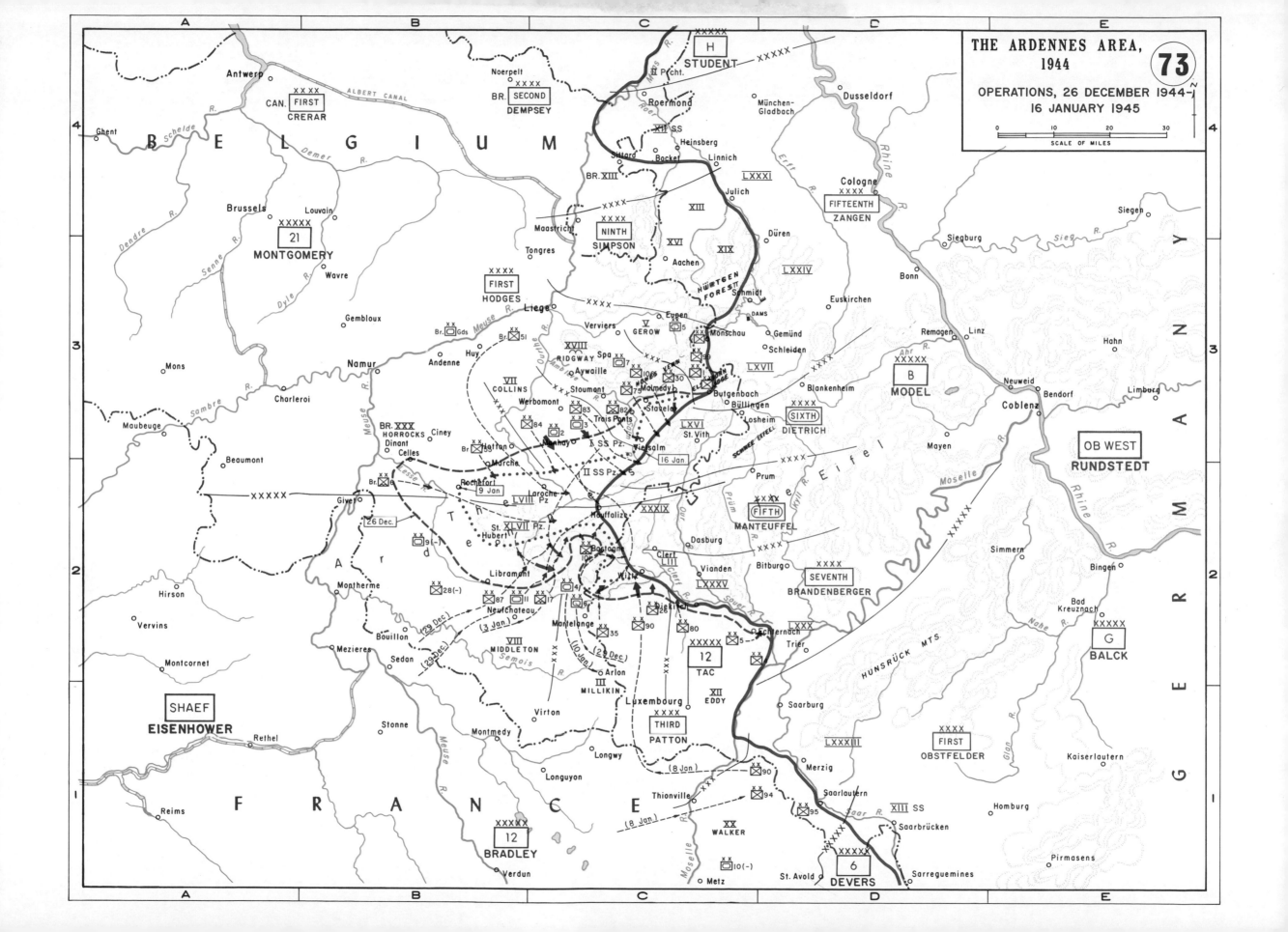

THE ARDENNES AREA, 1944

73

OPERATIONS, 26 DECEMBER 1944–
16 JANUARY 1945

SCALE OF MILES
0   10   20   30

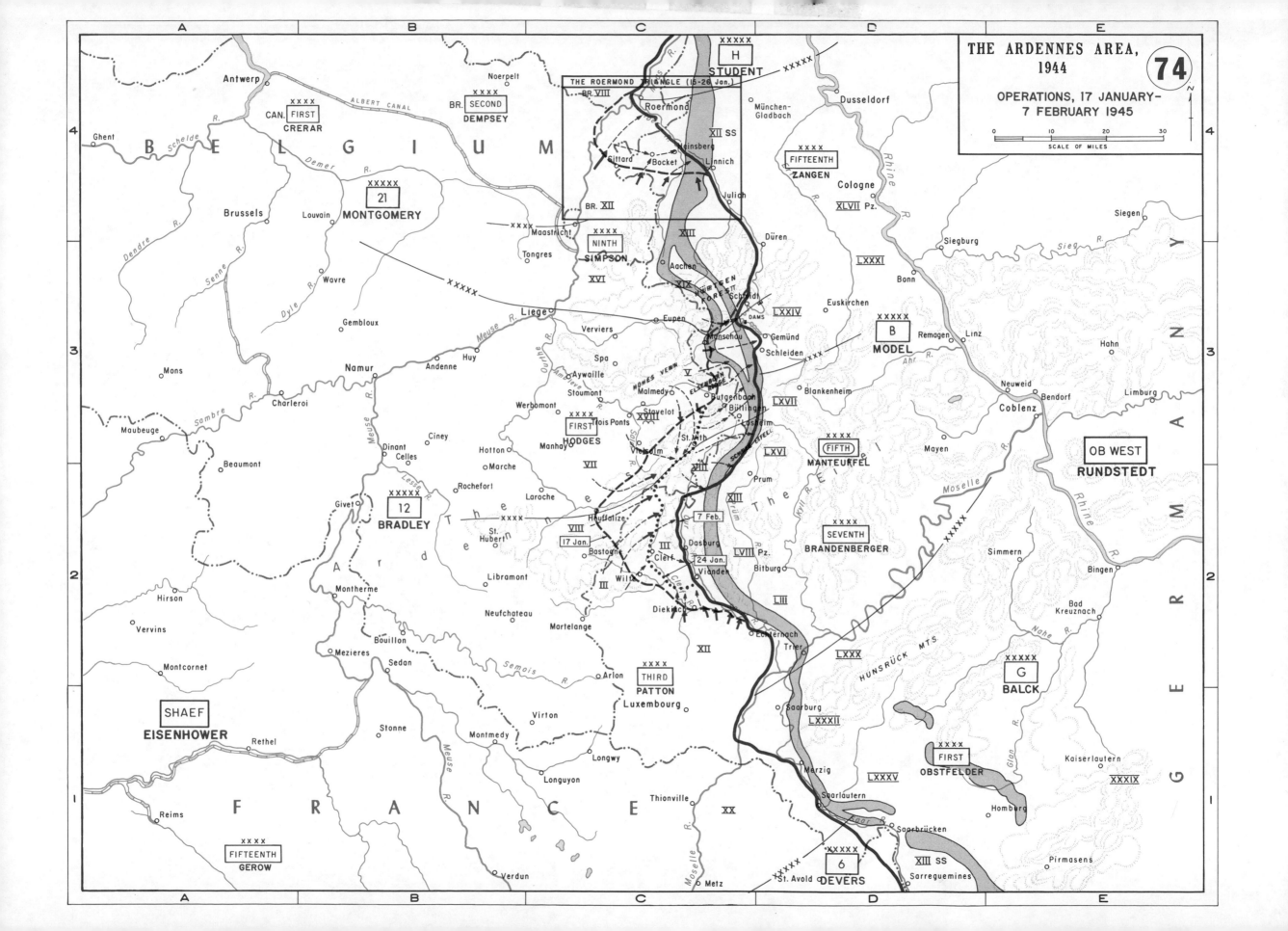

THE ARDENNES AREA, 1944

74

OPERATIONS, 17 JANUARY–
7 FEBRUARY 1945

SCALE OF MILES
0   10   20   30

GERMANY

BELGIUM

FRANCE

Antwerp
Noerpelt
Ghent
ALBERT CANAL
CAN. FIRST
CRERAR
BR. SECOND
DEMPSEY
STUDENT
H
THE ROERMOND TRIANGLE (15–26 Jan.)
BR. VIII
Roermond
Dusseldorf
München-Gladbach
Brussels
Louvain
XXXXX
21
MONTGOMERY
Gittard
Bocket
Heinsberg
Linnich
XII SS
FIFTEENTH
ZANGEN
Cologne
Rhine R.
Siegen
Maastricht
Julich
XII
XLVII Pz.
Tongres
NINTH
SIMPSON
XVI
Aachen
Düren
LXXXI
Bonn
Siegburg
Sieg R.
Wavre
Gembloux
Demer R.
Schelde R.
Dendre R.
Senne R.
Dyle R.
Mons
Andenne
Huy
Verviers
Eupen
Monschau
HÜRTGEN FOREST
Schmidt
DAMS
LXXIV
Euskirchen
MODEL
B
Remagen
Linz
Hahn
Namur
Spa
Malmedy
HOHES VENN
ELSENBORN RIDGE
Butgenbach
Billingen
Gemünd
Schleiden
Blankenheim
Coblenz
Neuweid
Bendorf
Limburg
Meuse R.
Charleroi
Sambre R.
Ourthe R.
Amblève R.
Stoumont
Werbomont
Stavelot
Trois Ponts
FIRST
HODGES
XVIII
St. Vith
Vielsalm
Losheim
LXVII
Ahr R.
Maubeuge
Beaumont
Dinant
Celles
Ciney
Hotton
Marche
Manhay
VII
Laroche
Prum
LXVI
FIFTH
MANTEUFEL
Mayen
OB WEST
RUNDSTEDT
Lesse R.
Givet
Rochefort
Houffalize
7 Feb.
SCHNEE EIFEL
XIII
The EIFEL
Moselle R.
12
BRADLEY
St. Hubert
VIII
17 Jan.
Bastogne
Dasburg
Clerf
24 Jan.
Vianden
LVIII Pz.
Bitburg
SEVENTH
BRANDENBERGER
Simmern
Bingen
Libramont
III
Wiltz
Clerf R.
LIII
Bad Kreuznach
Montherme
Neufchateau
Martelange
Diekirch
Echternach
XII
Trier
LXXX
HUNSRÜCK MTS.
Nahe R.
Hirson
Vervins
Bouillon
Sedan
Arlon
THIRD
PATTON
Luxembourg
Saarburg
Moselle R.
G
BALCK
Montcornet
Meuse R.
SHAEF
EISENHOWER
Rethel
Stonne
Virton
Montmedy
Longwy
LXXXII
Merzig
LXXXV
FIRST
OBSTFELDER
Kaiserlautern
Homburg
Glan R.
Pirmasens
Reims
FIFTEENTH
GEROW
Verdun
Longuyon
Thionville
XX
Saarlautern
Saarbrücken
XIII SS
Sarreguemines
XXXIX
St. Avold
6
DEVERS
Metz
Saar R.

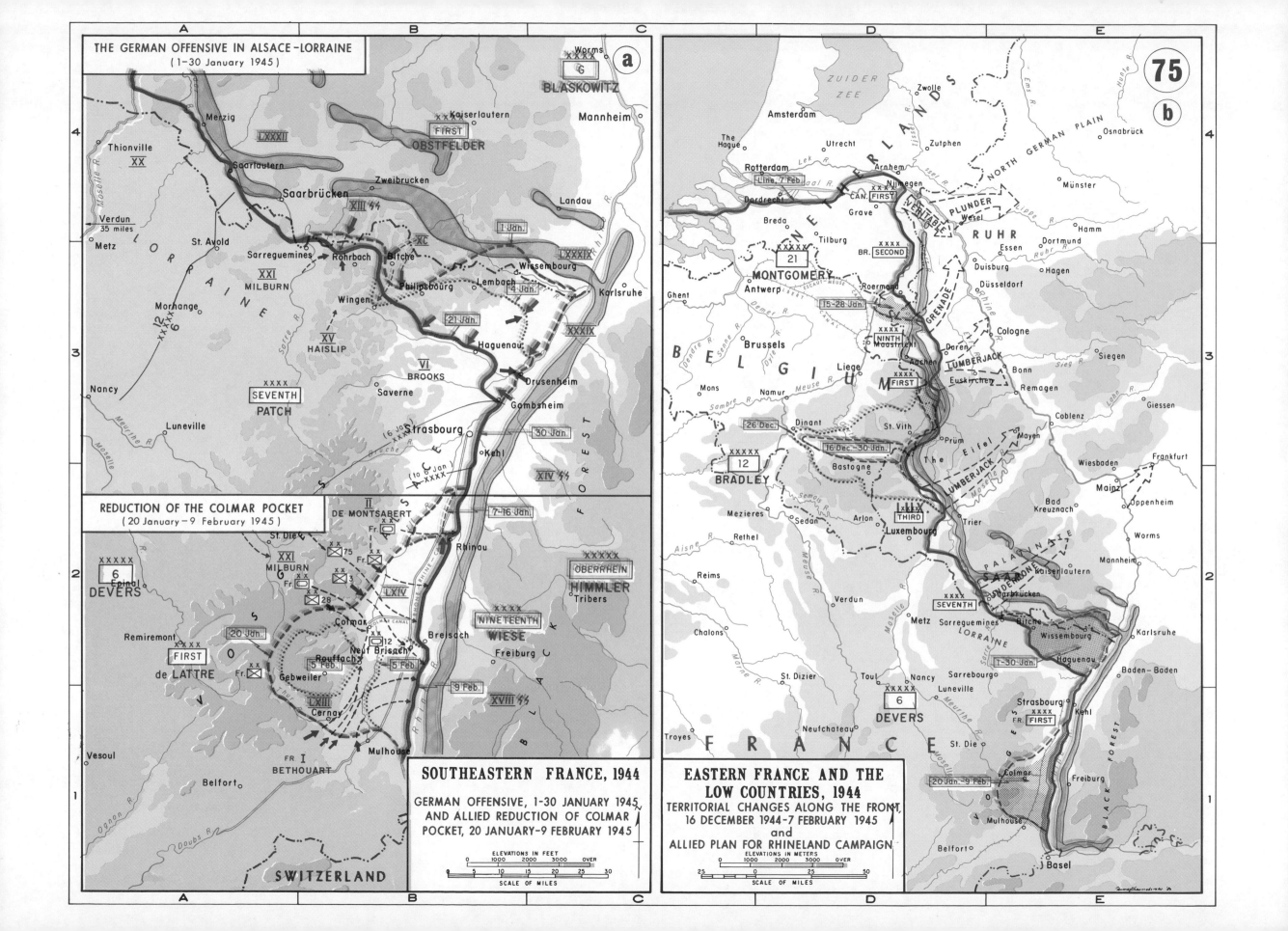

THE GERMAN OFFENSIVE IN ALSACE-LORRAINE
(1-30 JANUARY 1945)

REDUCTION OF THE COLMAR POCKET
(20 JANUARY - 9 FEBRUARY 1945)

SOUTHEASTERN FRANCE, 1944

GERMAN OFFENSIVE, 1-30 JANUARY 1945
AND ALLIED REDUCTION OF COLMAR
POCKET, 20 JANUARY-9 FEBRUARY 1945

ELEVATIONS IN FEET
1000 2000 3000 OVER

0   5   10   15   20   25   30
SCALE OF MILES

EASTERN FRANCE AND THE
LOW COUNTRIES, 1944

TERRITORIAL CHANGES ALONG THE FRONT,
16 DECEMBER 1944-7 FEBRUARY 1945
and
ALLIED PLAN FOR RHINELAND CAMPAIGN

ELEVATIONS IN METERS
1000 2000 3000 OVER

25   0   25   50
SCALE OF MILES

75
a
b

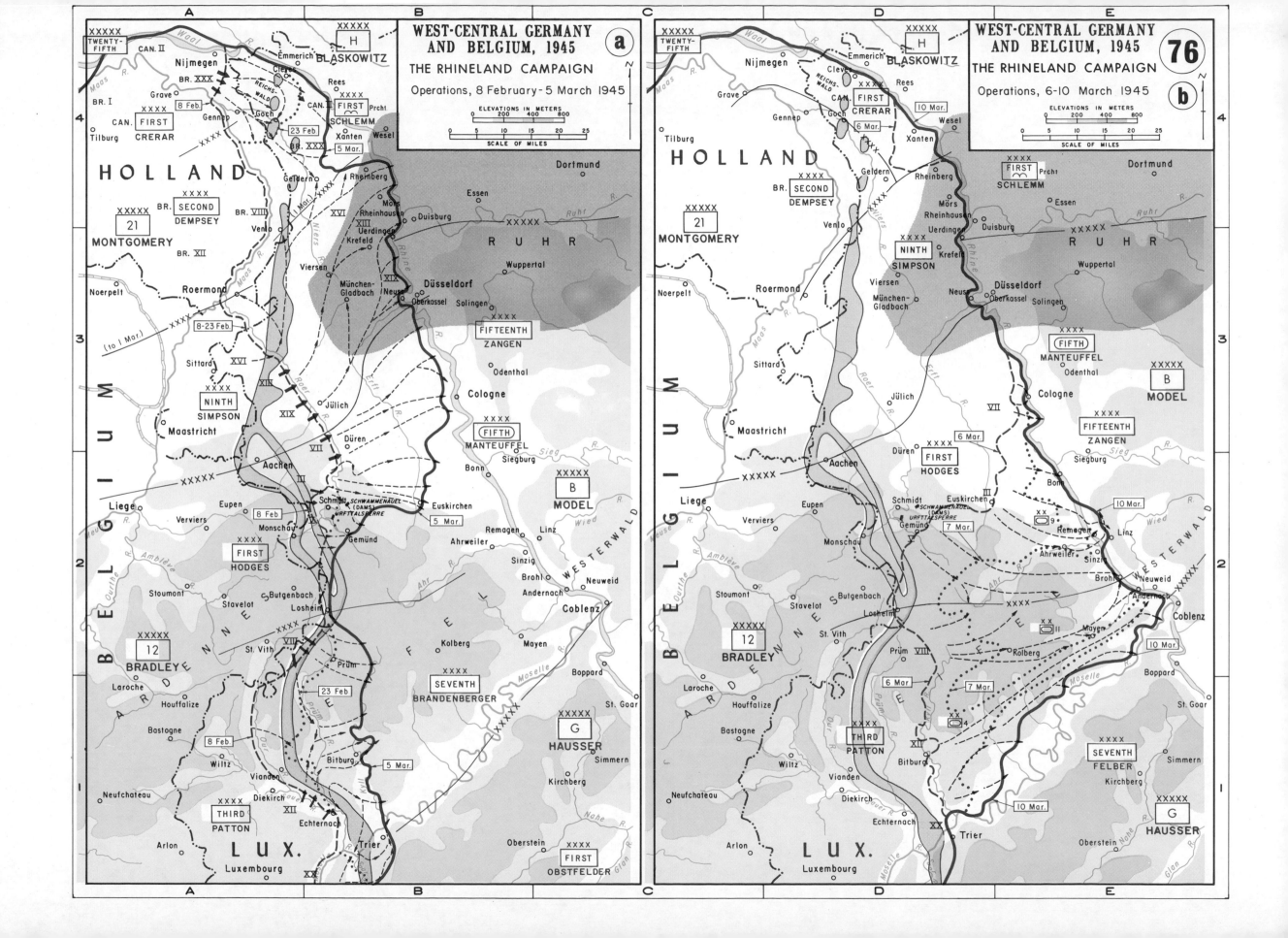

WEST-CENTRAL GERMANY AND BELGIUM, 1945

THE RHINELAND CAMPAIGN

Operations, 8 February–5 March 1945

(a)

ELEVATIONS IN METERS
200   400   800

SCALE OF MILES
0   5   10   15   20   25

WEST-CENTRAL GERMANY AND BELGIUM, 1945

THE RHINELAND CAMPAIGN

Operations, 6–10 March 1945

76

(b)

ELEVATIONS IN METERS
200   400   800

SCALE OF MILES
0   5   10   15   20   25

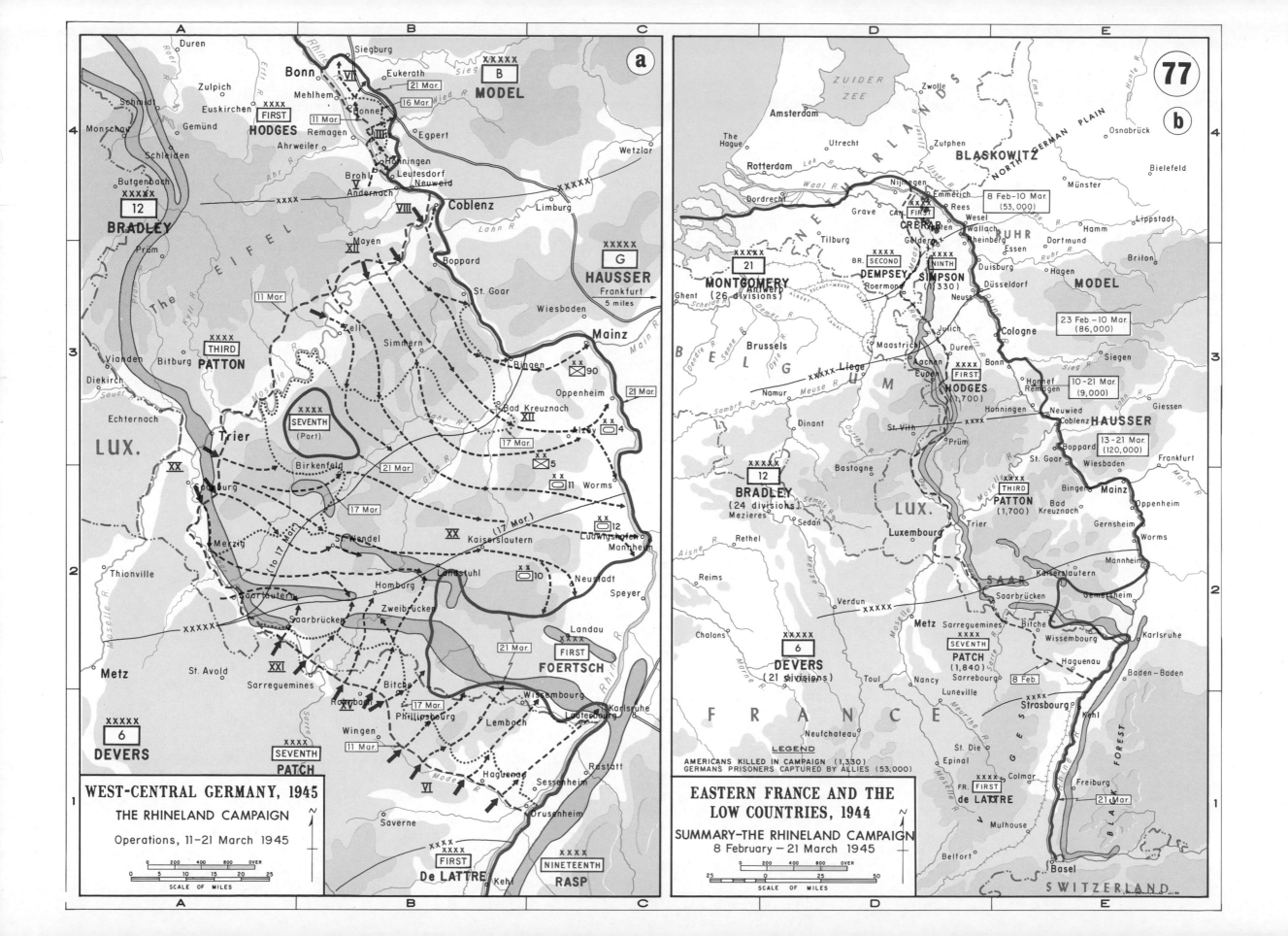

a

Duren
Zulpich
Schmidt
Euskirchen
Gemünd
Monschau
Schleiden
Butgenbach

XXXXX
12
BRADLEY

Prüm

The EIFEL

Vianden
Bitburg
Diekirch

LUX.
Echternach

Trier

Metz

XXXXX
6
DEVERS

Bonn
Siegburg
Eukerath
Mehlhem
Bonnef
Ahrweiler

XXXX
FIRST
HODGES
11 Mar.
Remagen
16 Mar.
21 Mar.

XXXXX
B
MODEL

Wetzlar

Honningen
Leutesdorf
Neuweid
Brohl
Andernach

Coblenz
Egpert
Limburg

XXXX

XXXX
THIRD
PATTON
Mayen
Boppard
St. Goar

XXXXX
G
HAUSSER
Frankfurt
5 miles

Simmern
Zell

Wiesbaden
Bingen
Mainz

XXXX
SEVENTH
(Part)
Birkenfeld
11 Mar.
21 Mar.
17 Mar.

Bad Kreuznach
Oppenheim
21 Mar.

XII
Alzey
4
5
Worms
11

St. Wendel
Kaiserslautern
(17 Mar.)
Ludwigshofen
Mannheim
12

Merzig
Saarburg
17 Mar.
10 to 17 Mar.

Landstuhl
Homburg
Neustadt
10
Speyer

Thionville
Saarbrücken
Zweibrücken

XXI
Sarreguemines
Rohrbach
Bitche
17 Mar.
Phillipsbourg
Wissembourg
Lembach

Landau

XXXX
FIRST
FOERTSCH

Metz
St. Avold
Wingen
11 Mar.
Hagenau
Karlsruhe
Lauterbourg
Drusenheim
Sessenheim
Rastatt

VI

XXXX
SEVENTH
PATCH

Saverne

XXXX
FIRST
De Lattre
Kehl

XXXX
NINETEENTH
RASP

WEST-CENTRAL GERMANY, 1945
THE RHINELAND CAMPAIGN
Operations, 11–21 March 1945

SCALE OF MILES
0 200 400 800 OVER
0 5 10 15 20 25

b

77

ZUIDER ZEE
Amsterdam
The Hague
Utrecht
Rotterdam
Dordrecht

Zwolle
Zutphen
NORTH GERMAN PLAIN
Osnabrück

BLASKOWITZ

Bielefeld

NETHERLANDS
Nijmegen
Emmerich
Grave
Rees
Wesel
Wallach
Rheinberg
Geldern
Münster
Hamm
Lippstadt

8 Feb–10 Mar.
(53,000)

XXXX
CAN. FIRST
CRERAR

RUHR
Essen
Dortmund
Briton
Hagen

XXXXX
21
MONTGOMERY
(26 divisions)
Antwerp
Ghent
Tilburg

BR. SECOND
DEMPSEY
Roermond
Maastricht

XXXX
NINTH
SIMPSON
(1,330)
Jülich
Duisburg
Düsseldorf
Neuss

MODEL

23 Feb–10 Mar.
(86,000)

Brussels
Liege
Namur
Aachen
Eupen
Cologne
Duren
Bonn
Siegen

XXXX
FIRST
HODGES
(1,700)

10–21 Mar.
(9,000)

BELGIUM
Dinant
St. Vith
Prüm
Honnef
Remagen
Honningen
Neuwied
Coblenz
Giessen

HAUSSER

XXXXX
12
BRADLEY
(24 divisions)
Mezieres
Bastogne
Sedan

LUX.
Luxembourg

13–21 Mar.
(120,000)
Boppard
St. Goar
Wiesbaden
Frankfurt

XXXX
THIRD
PATTON
(1,700)
Trier
Bad
Kreuznach
Bingen
Mainz
Oppenheim

Reims
Rethel

Verdun

SAAR
Kaiserslautern
Worms
Gernsheim
Mannheim

Chalons
Metz
Sarreguemines
Saarbrücken
Bitche
Gemersheim
Wissembourg
Karlsruhe

XXXX
SEVENTH
PATCH
(1,840)
Sarrebourg
Haguenau

8 Feb.
Nancy
Strasbourg
Kehl

F R A N C E
Toul
Neufchateau
Luneville
Baden-Baden

St. Die
Epinal

FR. FIRST
de Lattre
Colmar
Freiburg
21 Mar.

Mulhouse

BLACK FOREST

Belfort

Basel
SWITZERLAND

LEGEND
AMERICANS KILLED IN CAMPAIGN (1,330)
GERMANS PRISONERS CAPTURED BY ALLIES (53,000)

EASTERN FRANCE AND THE
LOW COUNTRIES, 1944
SUMMARY—THE RHINELAND CAMPAIGN
8 February – 21 March 1945

SCALE OF MILES
25 0 200 400 800 OVER
25 0 25 50

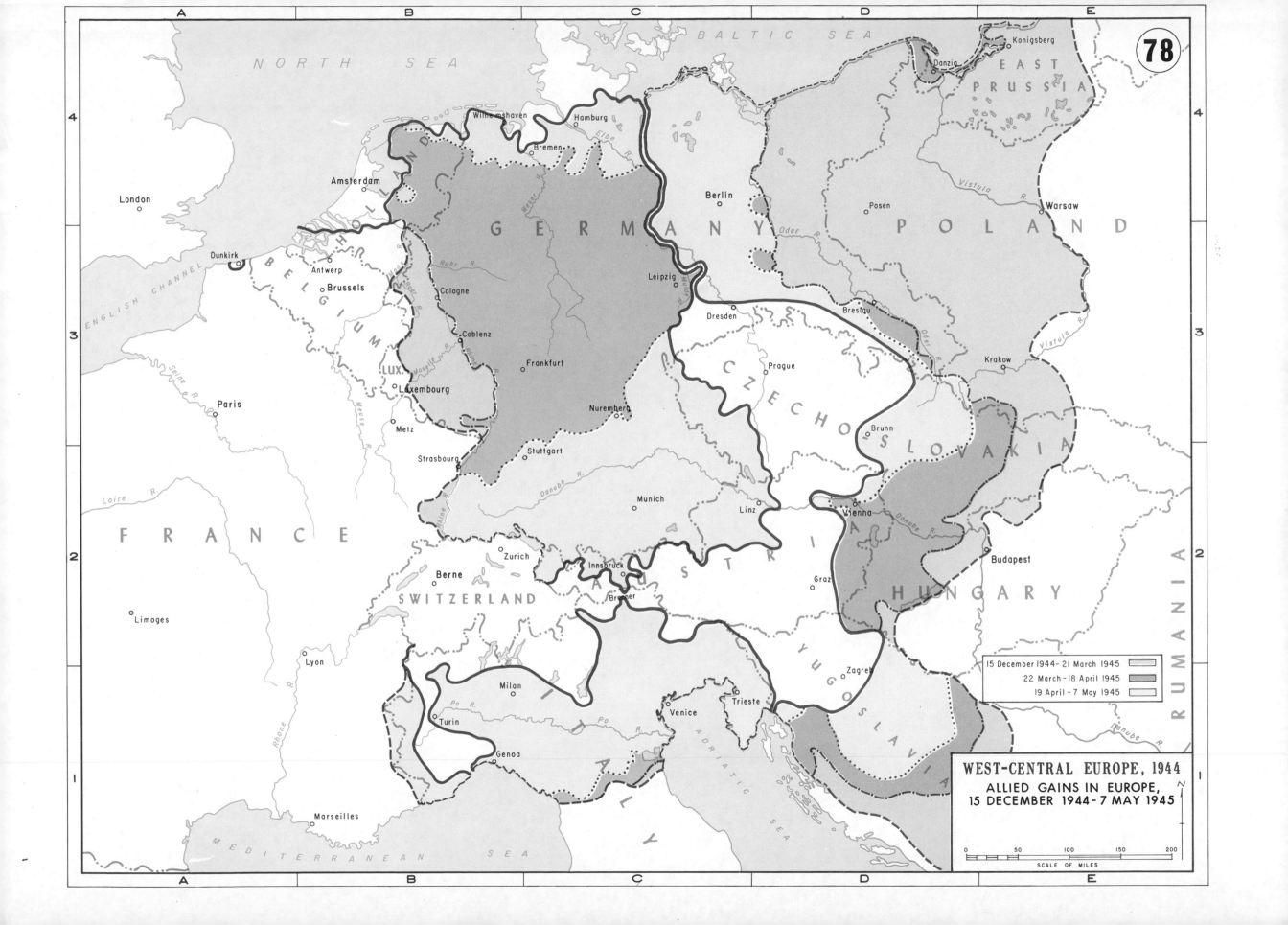

WEST-CENTRAL EUROPE, 1944
ALLIED GAINS IN EUROPE,
15 DECEMBER 1944-7 MAY 1945

15 December 1944- 21 March 1945	
22 March -18 April 1945	
19 April - 7 May 1945	

SCALE OF MILES
0   50   100   150   200

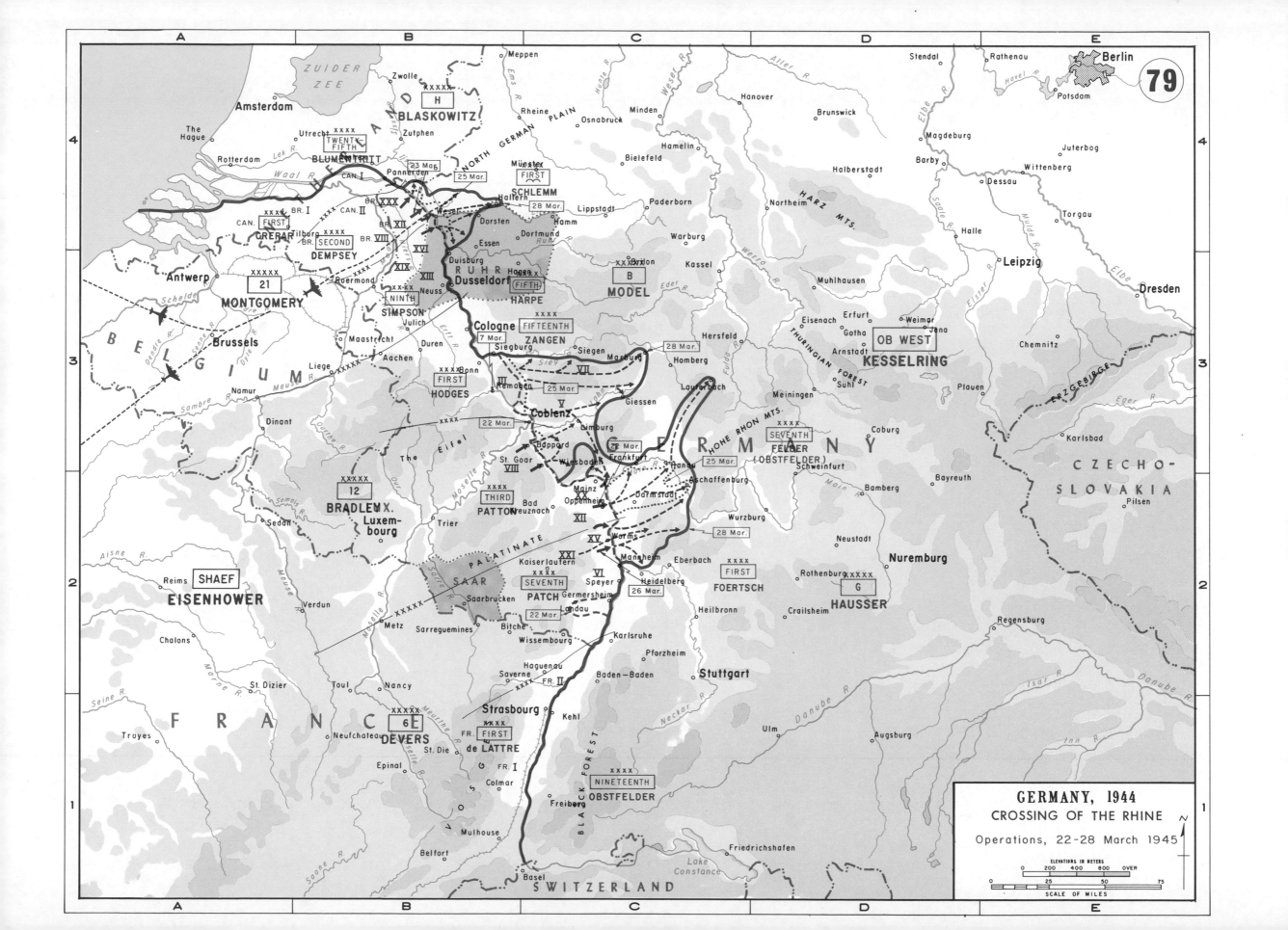

GERMANY, 1944
CROSSING OF THE RHINE
Operations, 22-28 March 1945

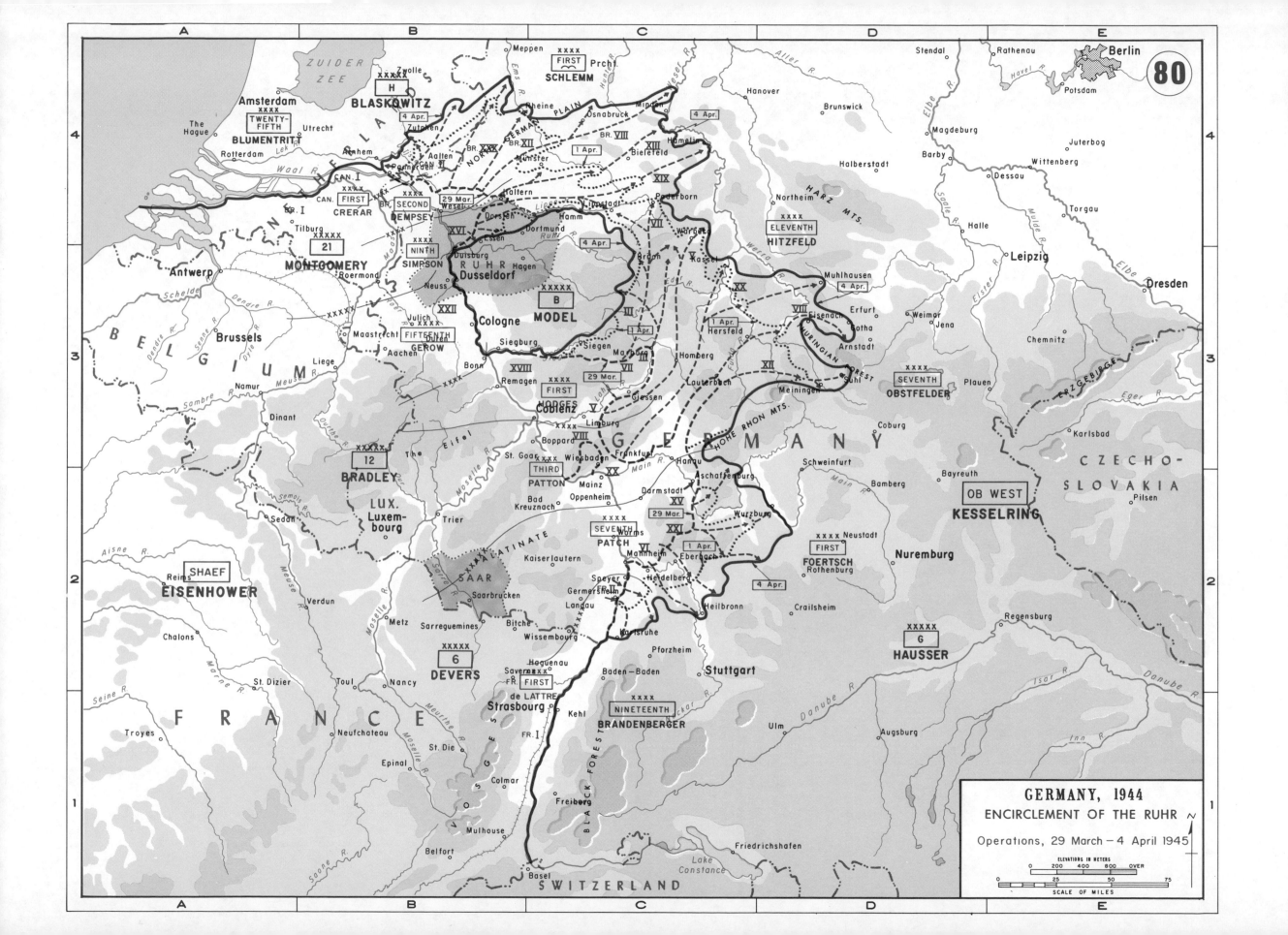

GERMANY, 1944
ENCIRCLEMENT OF THE RUHR
Operations, 29 March – 4 April 1945

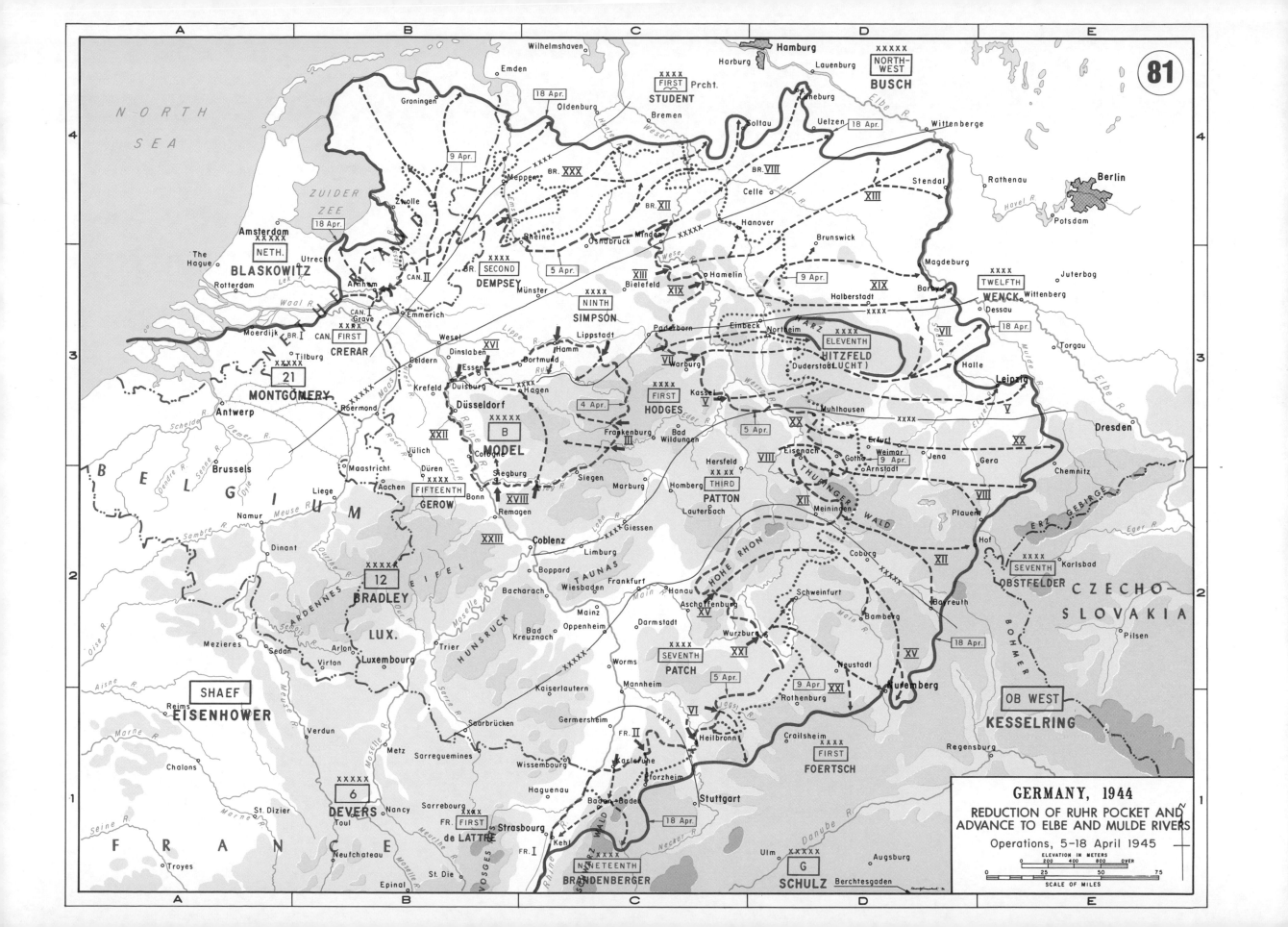

GERMANY, 1944

REDUCTION OF RUHR POCKET AND
ADVANCE TO ELBE AND MULDE RIVERS

Operations, 5-18 April 1945

ELEVATION IN METERS

200   400   800   OVER

0   25   50   75

SCALE OF MILES

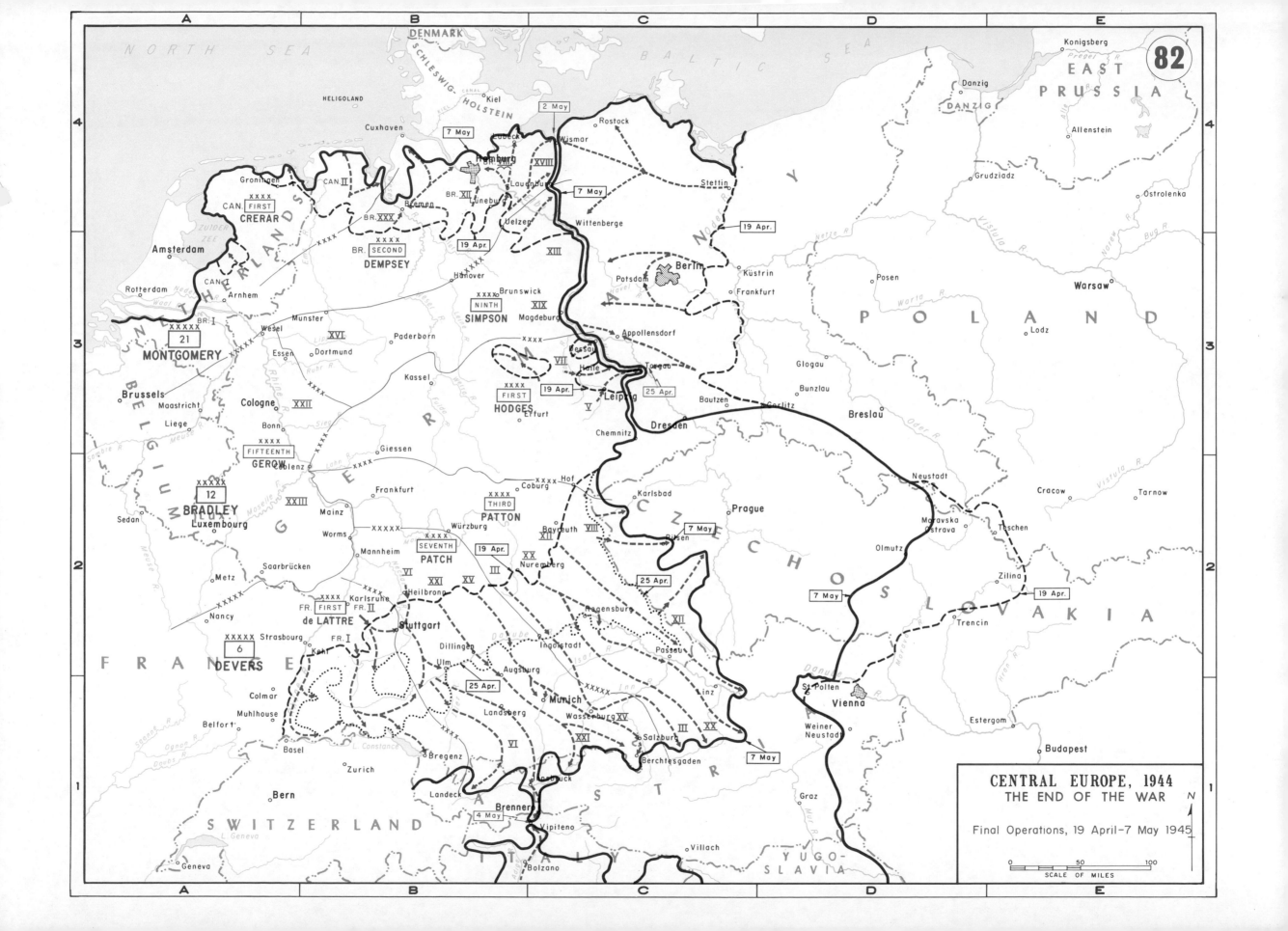

CENTRAL EUROPE, 1944
THE END OF THE WAR

Final Operations, 19 April–7 May 1945

SCALE OF MILES
0   50   100

CENTRAL EUROPE, 1944

ALLIED OCCUPATION ZONES

83

NORTH SEA

BALTIC SEA

DENMARK

SCHLESWIG-HOLSTEIN

EAST PRUSSIA

HELIGOLAND

Konigsberg
Pregel R.
Allenstein
Danzig
DANZIG

Kiel
CANAL
KIEL

Cuxhaven
Rostock
Wismar
Lubeck

Grudziadz
Ostrolenka

Groningen
Bremen
U.S. ENCLAVE
Hamburg
Lauenburg
Lüneburg
Stettin

Vistula R.
Narew R.
Bug R.

Amsterdam
ZUIDER ZEE

NETHERLANDS
Arnhem
Rotterdam
Nederr R.
Waal R.
Maas R.

BRITISH ZONE
Wesel
Munster
Ems R.
Aller R.
Weser R.
Leine R.
Hanover
Uelzen
Brunswick
Wittenberge
Elbe R.
Magdeburg

RUSSIAN ZONE
Oder R.
ALLIED
Berlin
Potsdam
Havel R.
Küstrin
Frankfurt
Neisse R.

Posen
Warta R.

POLAND
Lodz
Warsaw

Antwerp
Brussels
Maastricht
Liege
Meuse R.
Sombre R.
BELGIUM

Essen
Dortmund
Lippe R.
Ruhr R.
Rhine R.
Paderborn
Cologne
Bonn
Sieg R.
Kassel
Fulda R.
Werra R.

Erfurt
Dessau
Mulde R.
Halle
Leipzig
Torgau
Chemnitz
Dresden
Bautzen
Gorlitz
Oder R.

Glogau
Bunzlau
Breslau

Giessen
Coblenz
Lahn R.
Moselle R.

Frankfurt
Main R.
Coburg
Hof
Karlsbad
Prague
Neustadt

Cracow
Tarnow
Vistula R.

Sedan
LUX
Luxembourg
Metz
Moselle R.

Mainz
Worms
Mannheim
Saarbrücken

UNITED
Würzburg
Bamberg
Bayreuth
Nuremberg
Neckar R.

CZECHOSLOVAKIA
Pilsen
Olmutz
Moravska Ostrava
Teschen
Zilina
Trencin

Nancy
Strasbourg
Kehl
Karlsruhe
Heilbronn

STATES
Stuttgart
Dillingen
Ulm
Danube R.
Regensburg
Ingolstadt
Isar R.
Passau

RUSSIAN
ALLIED
Danube R.
St. Polten
Vienna
Weiner Neustadt

Hran R.
Morava R.
Estergom

FRENCH
GERMANY
FRANCE

Colmar
Muhlhouse
Belfort
Basel

ZONE
Rhine R.
Augsburg
Landsberg
Munich
Wasserburg
Inn R.
Salzburg
Berchtesgaden
Linz

ZONE
Weiner Neustadt

Budapest

Saone R.
Ognon R.
Doubs R.

Zurich
Bern
L. Constance
Bregenz
Landeck
AUSTRIA
Innsbruck
Brenner
Vipiteno

BRITISH ZONE
Graz
Mur R.
Villach

Geneva
L. Geneva

SWITZERLAND
ITALY
Bolzano
Adige R.

YUGO-SLAVIA

SCALE OF MILES
0   50   100

N